"Brown shows why she
remains in the top rank of her field."
—PUBLISHERS WEEKLY, STARRED REVIEW

"Sandra Brown proves
herself top-notch."
—ASSOCIATED
PRESS

"There are
shoot-outs and
reformed prostitutes
and a no-good hillbilly family,
but none of it feels like an empty
stereotype.... Combined with Brown's
knack for romantic tension and page-turning
suspense, [*Blind Tiger*] is a winner."
—BOOKLIST, STARRED REVIEW

"BROWN HAS FEW TO ENVY
AMONG LIVING AUTHORS."
—KIRKUS

"A MASTERFUL STORYTELLER." —USA TODAY

PRAISE FOR *BLIND TIGER* AND #1 *NEW YORK TIMES* BESTSELLING AUTHOR SANDRA BROWN

"Set in 1920, this superior thriller from bestseller Brown firmly anchors all the action in the plot.... Laurel and Thatcher are strong and inventive characters, and their surprising decisions and evolving relationship will keep readers engaged. Brown shows why she remains in the top rank of her field." —*Publishers Weekly*, starred review

"Brown doesn't often delve into historical fiction territory, but she does here with gusto, and readers will practically taste the dusty streets of Foley and feel every rickety bump of the moonshiners' trucks. There are shoot-outs and reformed prostitutes and a no-good hillbilly family, but none of it feels like an empty stereotype—it's just all a lot of fun. Combined with Brown's knack for romantic tension and page-turning suspense, [*Blind Tiger*] is a winner." —*Booklist*, starred review

"A thrill ride... The historical nature of [*Blind Tiger*] regarding the West Texas setting, the Texas Rangers, and how Prohibition made criminals out of those just wanting a beer is intriguing." —BookReporter.com

"*Blind Tiger* is a winner." —AARP

"[Brown] is a masterful storyteller, carefully crafting tales that keep readers on the edge of their seats." —*USA Today*

"Suspense that has teeth." —Stephen King

"Sandra Brown proves herself top-notch." —Associated Press

"Brown deserves her own genre." —*Dallas Morning News*

BLIND TIGER

BLIND TIGER

SANDRA BROWN

GRAND CENTRAL
PUBLISHING

NEW YORK   BOSTON

Grand Central Publishing
Hachette Book Group
1290 Avenue of the Americas, New York, NY 10104
grandcentralpublishing.com
twitter.com/grandcentralpub

Originally published in hardcover and ebook by Grand Central Publishing in August 2021
First trade paperback edition: March 2022

Grand Central Publishing is a division of Hachette Book Group, Inc. The Grand Central Publishing name and logo is a trademark of Hachette Book Group, Inc.

The publisher is not responsible for websites (or their content) that are not owned by the publisher.

The Hachette Speakers Bureau provides a wide range of authors for speaking events. To find out more, go to www.hachettespeakersbureau.com or call (866) 376-6591.

Library of Congress Control Number: 2021939235

ISBNs: 978-1-5387-5197-8 (trade paperback), 978-1-5387-5198-5 (ebook)

Printed in the United States of America

LSC-C

Printing 1, 2022

*To my family—Michael, Rachel, Ryan, Pete, Raff,
Luke, Lawson, and Cash. Thank you for your
unwavering forbearance, encouragement, and love.
You are the heroes and heroine of my heart.*

BLIND TIGER

ONE

———◆———

March 1920

Won't be much longer."

Derby had been telling her that for the past two hours. He said the same four words at intervals that had become so regular she could now predict, to within a minute, the next repetition. His tone was terse and emphatic, as though he were trying to convince himself.

Laurel had stopped responding because whatever she said, he took as an affront. He sat hunched over the steering wheel, his shoulders stacked with so much tension they were nearly touching his earlobes.

They had gotten a late start, not leaving Sherman until past noon. Since the day had been half gone, and daylight with it, she had suggested they wait until tomorrow to set out, but Derby had stubbornly stuck to his plan.

"My old man's expecting us. I didn't spend good money on a telegram telling him when we were coming, only to be no-shows."

It wasn't a trip to be making with an infant just barely a month old. She certainly hadn't expected to be uprooted with only a few hours' notice. But here they were, Derby, her, and baby Pearl, driving through the night. The farther they traveled, the more concerned she became about their welfare.

Derby had told her that his father lived roughly a hundred and fifty miles southwest of Sherman. He had showed her on a map the route they would take. Until today, she had never been on a road trip in an automobile, but she hadn't counted on it taking the six-plus hours they'd been traveling to cover a hundred and fifty miles.

She was huddled inside her coat, the lower half of her face wrapped in a muffler, a cap hugging her head. But even bundled up as she was, she had kept careful track of the highway signs. Freezing precipitation made them difficult to spot unless the T-model's one working headlight caught them at a good angle. They were still on the right highway, but how much farther could it possibly be?

Or maybe, in order to avoid a quarrel, Derby had fudged on the distance.

To be fair, though, neither of them had counted on the abrupt change in the weather. North Texas had enjoyed a reasonably mild winter through Christmas and New Year, but the *Farmer's Almanac* had predicted a spring that would be colder than usual, with hard freezes expected well into mid-March. This was day two of the month, and it had come in like a lion.

They'd just reached the western outskirts of Dallas when the norther had caught up to them. The leading gust of frigid air had broadsided the Tin Lizzy like a runaway freight train.

She wouldn't be surprised to learn that that first buffet had left a dent in the car door. Not that another dent would be noticed. It was already banged up.

──◈──

The day Derby had driven the car home, she had been flabbergasted by his impulsiveness. When she'd asked where he'd gotten it, he'd told her about a former war buddy who lived in a town nearby.

"He hadn't been in France a month when the poor bastard lost his left leg clean up to here." He'd made a slice across his groin. "Can't work the pedals to drive. He let me have this beauty for a song."

They didn't have a *song*, but she hadn't pointed that out, because, in that boastful moment, some of Derby's rakish charm, which had attracted her to him in the first place, had resurfaced.

He'd swung open the passenger door and made a sweeping gesture with his arm as he bowed. "Your chariot awaits, Miz Plummer." He'd winked and grinned, and she'd seen a flash of the dashing young man who had marched off to fight the Great War, rather than the quarrelsome stranger who had returned from it.

She'd seized on his sudden lightheartedness and had giggled helplessly as he'd driven them through town going faster than he should and needlessly honking at everything and everybody, making her laugh harder. He'd seemed mindless of the jostling, until one pothole sent her bouncing so hard in her seat, she placed her hands protectively over her belly.

"Careful of those chuckholes or the baby might pop out of me like a cork from a bottle."

She had gone into labor that very night. By three o'clock the following afternoon, she was a mother and Derby a father. That had been four weeks ago.

At first Derby had been prideful and happy and solicitous to her and their baby girl. But the newness of fatherhood had soon worn off, and the grinning man who'd taken her on the joy ride retreated once more behind a perpetual scowl she couldn't allay.

In the thirty or so days since Pearl's entrance into the world, Derby had lost another job. He'd spent a lot of time away from the house and snapped at her whenever she'd inquired where he'd been. In a heartbeat, he would become testy and short-tempered. She never knew what to expect.

During supper last evening, out of the clear blue, he'd announced, "We're moving to Foley." He'd avoided looking at her by keeping his head bent over his meal.

Afraid to overreact, she'd blotted her mouth with her napkin. "I think I've heard of it. Isn't it near—"

"It's not *near* anything. But my old man's found me work out there."

She had actually felt a spark of hopefulness. "Really? That's wonderful. Doing what?"

"Does it matter? He's expecting us tomorrow."

The floor, none too level already, had seemed to undulate beneath her chair. "Tomorrow?"

Pearl was a fussy baby who demanded to be nursed several times a night. For a month, Laurel hadn't slept for more than a couple of hours at a time. She was exhausted, worried about Derby's state of mind, worried about their shortage of money, and now...this.

Leaving half his supper uneaten, he'd shoved back his chair, left the table, and lifted his jacket off the peg near the back door. "Pack tonight. I want to get away early."

"Wait, Derby. We can't just..." Words had failed her. "Sit back down. Please. We need to talk about this."

"What's to talk about?"

She gaped at him with bafflement. "Everything. Do we have a place to live?"

"I wouldn't up and move you and the baby without having a plan, would I?"

"It just seems awfully sudden."

"Well, it's not. I've been thinking on it for a time."

"You should have talked it over with me."

"I'm talking it over with you now."

His raised voice had caused Pearl to flinch where she lay asleep in Laurel's lap. Laurel had lifted her to her shoulder and patted her back. Derby's expression had turned impatient, but whether at her, the baby, or himself, she'd been unable to tell.

"I've got some things to see to before we clear town. Rent's due on this place the day after tomorrow. I'll leave notice of our departure in the landlord's mailbox." He'd reached for the doorknob.

"Derby, hold on." She'd gone over to him. "I welcome the idea of us making a fresh start. I just want it to be a good fresh start. Thought through, not so rushed."

"I told you, I have been thinking on it."

"But making a move to another town seems drastic. When you talked to Mr. Davis, he told you that he might have an opening at his store soon."

"Scooping chicken feed into tow sacks?" He'd made a sour face. "No thanks."

"Something else could—"

"There's nothing for me here, Laurel. Anyway, it's decided. We're leaving." He'd pulled open the door and said over his shoulder as he went out, "You'd better get started packing."

He hadn't returned home until after two o'clock in the morning, disheveled and red-eyed, reeking of bootleg whiskey, too drunk to stand without support. When he'd stumbled into the bedroom, he'd propped himself against the doorjamb and blearily focused on her where she'd sat in the rocking chair next to the bed, nursing Pearl.

"Things ready?" he'd asked in a mumble.

Their duplex had rented furnished, so there hadn't been much to pack except for their clothing and her personal possessions, which were few in number and didn't amount to anything.

In answer to his question, she'd motioned to the two suitcases lying open on the floor. She'd carefully folded his army uniform and laid it on top.

Laurel had eased Pearl away from her breast and tucked it back inside her nightgown. "Couldn't we give this decision a week, talk it over some more?"

"I'm sick of talking." He'd staggered to the bed, crawled onto it, and passed out.

He'd slept late, and had been irritable and hungover when he woke up. Laurel had wished he'd forgotten about their departure, about the whole harebrained idea. But he'd fortified himself with several cups of strong coffee and a dozen hand-rolled cigarettes, and by the time she'd packed them a lunch with what food was left in the icebox, Derby was impatient to be off.

While he was loading their suitcases, putting one in the trunk and strapping down the other on top of it, she'd walked through the duplex one final time, checking to see that nothing belonging to them had been overlooked.

Derby had hung his army uniform back in the closet.

The top on the Ford was up, which kept some of the frozen precipi-tation off them, but it was open-air. During the whole trip, Laurel had kept Pearl clutched to her chest inside her coat, inside her dress, wanting to be skin-to-skin with her. She was afraid the baby would freeze to death and she wouldn't even know it because she was so numb with cold herself. But Pearl had nursed well her last feeding, and her breath had remained reassuringly humid and warm.

"Won't be much longer."

Laurel held her tongue.

This time, Derby added, "A crossroads is up ahead. He's only a few miles past that."

However, beyond the crossroads, the road narrowed and the pave-ment gave way to gravel. The surrounding darkness was unrelieved except for the faulty headlight that blinked intermittently like a distress signal from a foundering ship.

So when Laurel caught a flicker of light out of the corner of her right eye, she first thought it was the headlight reflecting off pellets of blowing sleet.

But she squinted through the precipitation and then gave a soft cry of desperate hope. "Derby? Could that be his place?"

"Where?"

"Up there. I thought I saw a light."

He slowed down and looked in the direction she indicated. "Gotta be," he muttered.

He put the car in low gear and turned onto a dirt track formed by tire treads. The sleet made it look like it had been salted. The Model T ground its way up the incline.

At the higher elevation, the north wind was vicious. Howling, it lashed against the car as Derby brought it to a stop.

Whatever relief Laurel might have felt evaporated when she saw the dwelling beyond the windshield. It could be described only as a shack. Light seeped through vertical slits in the walls made of weathered lumber. On the south side of the structure, the roof steeply sloped downward and formed an extension that provided cover for stacked firewood.

She didn't say anything, and Derby avoided looking at her. He pushed open the driver's door against the fierce wind and climbed out. A fan of light spread onto the ground in front of him as the door to the shack came open.

Derby's father was silhouetted, so Laurel couldn't make out his features, but she was heartened by the welcoming tone of his voice as he shouted into the wind, "I'd 'bout given up on you." He waved Derby forward.

Less enthusiastically, Derby approached his father and shook hands. They exchanged a few words, which Laurel couldn't hear. Derby's father jerked his head backward, then he leaned to one side in order to see around Derby and peered at the car.

Derby did a quick about-face, came over to the passenger door, opened it, and motioned Laurel out. "Hurry. It's cold."

Her legs almost gave out beneath her when she stepped onto the ground. Derby took her elbow and closed the car door. Together they made their way to the open doorway, where her father-in-law had stepped aside for them.

Derby hustled her inside, then firmly shut the door.

The wind continued to roar. Or, Laurel wondered, was the roaring in her ears actually caused by the sudden silence, or her weariness and gnawing hunger? All that, she assumed. Plus the alarming and humiliating realization that she and Pearl had not been expected.

"Daddy, this is my wife, Laurel. I'll get the suitcases." With no more ceremony than that, Derby left them.

———◆———

There was little resemblance between Derby and his father, who was half a head shorter and didn't have Derby's lanky build. The crescent of his baldness was so precise it could have been traced from a pattern.

The hair around it was wiry and gray and grew straight out from his head like brush bristles. His eyebrows looked like twin caterpillars stuck to his forehead.

They assessed each other. She said, "Mr. Plummer." Clearing her throat of self-conscious scratchiness, she added, "Pleased to meet you."

"Laurel, he said?"

"Yes, sir."

"We're kin now, so I 'spect you ought to drop the sir and call me Irv."

She gave him a faint smile, and some of the tension in her chest eased. Pearl squirmed inside her coat, drawing his notice.

"That the baby? What's its name?"

Laurel unbuttoned her coat, lifted Pearl out, and transferred her to the crook of her elbow. "Her name is Pearl."

He didn't step closer, but tentatively leaned forward and inspected what he could see of Pearl, which wasn't much, swaddled as she was, and considering the meager light provided by a kerosene lantern that hung from a hook in the low ceiling.

He appeared to be pleased enough with his granddaughter, because he smiled. But all he said was, "Well, how 'bout that?"

Then he turned away and went over to a potbellied stove. Laurel noticed that he favored his left leg, making his bowlegged gait even more lopsided. He opened the door to the stove and tossed in two split logs he took from the stack of firewood against the wall.

He came back around, dusting his hands. "Y'all are hungry, I 'spect. I've got a rabbit fried up. Fresh killed and dressed this morning. I've kept a batch of biscuits warm. I was waiting till Derby got here to make the gravy."

Laurel's stomach had been growling for the past several hours, but to be polite, she said, "I hate that you've gone to so much trouble."

"No trouble. Coffee's—"

The door burst open, and Derby came in with their suitcases. He dropped them at his sides and pushed the door closed with his heel.

Irv said to him, "Move over there closer to the stove. I'll pour y'all some coffee."

"Got any hooch? Or are you abiding by the new law of the land, even though it's horseshit?"

Looking displeased by his son's crudity, Irv glanced at Laurel, then walked over to a small chest that had only three legs. In place of the missing one was a stack of catalogues with faded, curled, dusty covers. He grunted as he went down on his right knee. He opened the bottom drawer, reached far back into it, and came out with a mason jar that was two-thirds full of clear liquid.

As he heaved himself up, he said, "Sometimes my hip gets to bothering me so's I can't sleep. A nip of 'shine helps."

Derby reached for the jar without so much as a thank you. He uncapped it and took a swig. The corn liquor must've seared his gullet. When he lowered the jar, his eyes were watering.

Laurel was already furious at him. Weren't their present circumstances dreadful enough without his getting drunk? She didn't conceal the resentment in her voice when she told him she needed the necessary.

Irv said, "Around back, twenty paces or so. You can lay the baby down over there." He nodded toward a mattress on the floor in the corner. "Take a lantern, Derby."

Laurel didn't want to leave Pearl, but not having any choice, she laid her on the mattress. The ticking looked reasonably clean compared to the hard-packed dirt floor. She wrapped the baby tightly in her blankets, hoping that a varmint wouldn't crawl into them before she returned.

Between taking sips of moonshine, Derby had lit a lantern. Bracing herself for the brutal cold, Laurel followed him out. It had started to snow, and it was sticking.

She was glad Derby was with her to help her find her way, but she was too angry to speak to him. She went into the foul-smelling outhouse and relieved herself as quickly as she could.

When she emerged, Derby passed the lantern to her. "Get back inside. I'm gonna have a smoke."

"It's freezing out here."

"I'm gonna have a smoke."

"And finish that?" she said, glaring at the fruit jar.

"I'm sick of you nagging me about every goddamn thing."

"As if things aren't bad enough, you're going to get skunk drunk?"

He smirked. "Thought I would." He raised the jar to his mouth, but she slapped it aside, almost knocking it out of his hand.

"Do as I tell you, Laurel. Go inside."

"Your daddy didn't know about Pearl and me, did he?" When he just stared back at her, she shouted, "Did he?"

"No."

Even though she wasn't surprised, hearing him admit it caused her to see red. "How could you do this to me, Derby? To Pearl? To all of us? Why in the world did you bring us here?"

"I had to do something with you first."

"First?"

"You'll thank me later."

He produced a pistol from the pocket of his coat, put it beneath his chin, and pulled the trigger.

TWO

Laurel's father-in-law waited until daylight and the worst of the storm had blown itself out to notify the authorities. Before leaving for town, he made her swear that she would stay inside the shack while he was gone. Listlessly, she agreed to remain inside, having no desire to subject herself to see in the dreary, gray daylight what she had beheld in darkness.

She hadn't even known that Derby owned a pistol.

In Irv's absence, she sat on the mattress near the potbellied stove, where she had endured the long night, benumbed by what Derby had done. She'd held Pearl to her the entire time, her infant being the only thing that seemed real, the one thing she could cling to in this ongoing nightmare.

She couldn't even take comfort in fond memories of Derby. Those she'd cherished had died with him. They'd been obliterated by what would be her final memory of him.

She resented him for that.

Irv returned, followed by the sheriff and the justice of the peace. They came into the shack and spoke to her briefly, but there was little she could say that would make the circumstances any clearer than the gore they'd seen splashed onto the door of the outhouse.

After Derby's body had been removed and taken to the funeral parlor, Irv dismantled the outhouse and burned it. By the early dusk, he had built another enclosure. He probably wouldn't have been so industrious on the day after his son's suicide if it hadn't been for the privacy Laurel required.

Now, less than twenty-four hours after meeting her father-in-law, they were alone in the shack, except for Pearl. He was at the cookstove, preparing food she didn't think she could eat, but knew she must in order to sustain Pearl.

"Thank you for replacing the outhouse."

"Easier to start over than try to clean the old one. He'd made a goddamn mess."

Softly she said, "He wasn't right in his mind."

He turned away from the stove and looked over at her. "Shell shock?"

"I suppose. A light had gone out inside him, and it never came back on. I thought he would get better as time passed. I tried to help him, but he wouldn't even talk about it."

Irv dragged one hand down his creased face. "He was like that after his mama died. Shut down, like. He ever tell you about that?"

"No."

"TB got her. Derby was seven, eight. Had to watch her decline, then die. That's tough on a kid." He paused, lost in thought, then cleared his throat. "After she passed, I couldn't earn a living and look after him at the same time. I had no choice but to put him in a home. For what it was, it was a nice place. Subsidized by the railroad. I'd go see him whenever I could, but..."

He raised his shoulders. "He never forgave me for leaving him. Soon as he was old enough, he went his own way. I'd hear from him off and on. Mostly off. But it seemed to me like he'd found himself again and was doing all right. Then the war came along. If it was as bad as they say, it's a wonder any one of them who survived it haven't done what he did."

He heaved a sigh that invoked Laurel's pity. The wretched memory of Derby's death would stay with Irv until his own final breath.

"Can I help you there?" she asked.

"No thanks. I'm just making some gravy for that rabbit we didn't eat last night. It's almost ready."

Pearl was sleeping peacefully on the mattress. She probably needed to be changed, but in the process, she would wake up. Right now, it was better for Laurel, as well as for the baby, that she remain asleep. Because Laurel needed time to think.

She was viewing her life as a spool of ribbon that had gotten away from her, rolling out of her reach, unwinding rapidly and haphazardly, and she was powerless to stop it.

She shivered, as much from despair as from the cold air that seeped through the cracks in the walls of the shack. She hadn't removed her coat since she arrived. Shoving her hands deep into its pockets, she said, "Right before he...did it...Derby admitted that he hadn't told you about me and Pearl."

Irv set down the long spoon he was using and turned toward her. "He didn't even tell me he'd survived the war."

Derby and she had still been in a honeymoon haze when he had left for overseas. She would have gone crazy if she hadn't received periodic letters from him. Usually they were filled with cryptic references to his misery, but at least she'd known that he was alive. Learning that Derby hadn't extended his father that courtesy made her heartsick for the old man.

"That was terribly thoughtless of him."

"I got one letter telling me he'd been drafted and was going to Europe to kill Huns. I moved around a lot for work, so he'd been long gone by the time that letter caught up with me.

"Armistice came and went without a word from him. I took that as a bad sign, but the military is supposed to let folks back home know when their loved one has fallen or is missing, right?

"So I went up to Camp Bowie, where he'd been stationed before shipping out. After a lot of rigamarole and sorting through red tape, I was told he'd made it back stateside. His last paycheck from the army had been mailed to a post office box in Sherman. I wrote to him there just to tell him where I'd lit in case he ever wanted to find me."

He took in the rustic interior of the shack, as though seeing it from her perspective for the first time. She followed the track of his eyes. Cobwebs laced the rafters that were blackened from age and smoke. A cowhide that looked like it had mange was nailed to the north wall. She supposed that it wasn't so much for decoration as to keep out the elements. The flue of the potbellied stove was piecemeal, forming a leaky and crooked outlet to the hole in the ceiling.

"Ain't much," he said.

Laurel didn't detect any degree of humility or apology in that statement, and she couldn't help but admire him for that.

He gave the simmering gravy a stir. "I didn't hear anything from Derby until the telegram office sent a boy out here day before yesterday. All it said was that he was coming. Nothing more."

Laurel dug at a crack in the dirt floor with the toe of her shoe. "There was no job, no work waiting for him, was there?"

He shifted his weight, redistributing it unevenly, placing more on the right side of his body. "There's work around."

"Of what kind?"

"Same as me."

"Forgive me, Mr. Plummer, but—"

"Irv."

"Irv. What kind of work do you do?"

"I was a railroad man. Over thirty years at it. Went all over, repairing tracks. That's how I got the bum hip." He patted his left leg joint. "Coupler backed into it. Didn't stop me from working, though. Just made it harder.

"But I got old and tired, so I stopped railroading several years ago and settled into this place. Now I do odd jobs in and around town." He looked over at her with something of a grin. "I guess you could say I'm a fix-it man."

"Are there enough things around here that need fixing to keep you busy?" *And solvent?* She wanted to ask that, but didn't.

"I'm stretched pretty thin, all right." He set tin plates and cutlery on the small table, which was not much larger than a checkerboard.

"How much had Derby told you about me? Not much good, I reckon."

"He hadn't told me anything except that you were still living, as far as he knew. He said the two of you weren't close."

He gave a sad nod. "Well, then at least that didn't come as a shock to you."

"What caused the rift?"

He pursed his lips thoughtfully, then said, "His mama died young." He gave the gravy another stir. "What about you? Is your family up in North Texas?"

"Yes. My daddy and uncle grow cotton. Or did. The last three crops got ruined by the boll weevil."

"You'll want to notify your folks of this."

She took a breath, wishing she could postpone this, but reasoned that he needed to know sooner rather than later. "We don't speak."

He came around and studied her for a moment, then asked, "Was it Derby that split y'all up?" He must've seen the answer in her expression, because he said, "Figured."

"The blame wasn't all his. The split was my daddy's doing. He's a hard man. He disapproved of Derby's sinful ways."

"Drinking and dancing?"

She huffed a laugh. "To my daddy's mind, even a game of dominoes will send you to hell. Derby enjoyed egging him on. One day Daddy had enough and put his foot down. He told me that Derby's sinfulness was rubbing off on me, and that if I married him, no one in my family would be allowed to utter my name again. Not ever. It would be as though I'd never been born."

She gazed down at her sleeping daughter, relieved that her stern, intolerant father would never exercise any influence over her. "Fine, I told him. I didn't want to be a member of a family so wrathful and unloving. Both of us meant what we said. Mama, of course, had to go along with Daddy."

Her mother's plight made Laurel sad. She'd been cowed into letting Laurel go without a quibble. But there was no help for that. Her mother, taking seriously her submissive role, had made her bed, and she would die in it.

Suddenly it occurred to Laurel that she unwittingly had been taking that same path. If she hadn't yielded to Derby's irrational decision, hadn't gone dumbly along for harmony's sake, she wouldn't be in this predicament.

Her father-in-law was saying, "Maybe after what's happened, your folks will take you back. I'm happy to drive you up there—"

"No," she said swiftly and firmly. "Thank you for offering, but I won't go back."

Irv rubbed his bristly chin, looked down at Pearl, then at Laurel. "Well then, looks like you're stayin'."

THREE

May 1920

Thatcher had worn out his welcome.

He knew it, although he tried not to act like he did. He lay on his back, using his duffel bag as a pillow, fingers linked over his stomach, fedora covering his face.

He pretended to be asleep. He was far from it. He was acutely aware of everything going on inside the boxcar, the atmosphere of which had turned ripe to the stinking point with hostility.

Beneath him, the wheels of the train rhythmically clickety-clacked over the rails, but their noisy cadence didn't drown out the snores of the three men sharing the freight car with him. Thatcher didn't trust their snorts and snuffles. They were too irregular and loud. Like him, they were playing possum, waiting for an opportunity to spring.

The door to the car had been left partially open to provide them fresh air. The gap was no wider than a few feet. Three, four at best. Once he made his move, he couldn't hesitate. He would get only one chance, so, within a second or two of moving, he'd have to make a clean jump through that slim gap.

If he didn't make it out, a fight was inevitable. Three against one. Bad odds in any contest. Until fate had put them together on this train, they'd been strangers to him and to one another. But last night, somewhere between coastal Louisiana and wherever they were now, the other three had become unified against him.

The last thing he wanted was a damned fight. He'd fought in one. A bloody one. He'd been on the winning side of it, but victory hadn't felt as glorious as people had let on. To his mind, the loss of so many men and women wasn't a fit reason to hold parades.

No, he wouldn't welcome a fight, but if he had to defend himself, he would, and he wouldn't fight fair. He hadn't cheated death in France to die in this railroad car that reeked of its cargo of yellow onions and unwashed men.

One advantage the other three had over him was that they weren't new to riding freights. He was the amateur. But he'd listened to their idle conversation, had paid attention, had sifted the facts out of the bullshit.

They'd jawed about the stationmasters who were charitable and looked the other way when they spotted a hobo, and others who were die-hard company men, "by-the-rules sons o' bitches" who were well known up and down the line for showing no mercy to men they caught hitching a ride.

Thatcher's plan had been to wait until the train began to slow on the outskirts of the next town and to get off before it reached the depot, in case the stationmaster there happened to be one of the less tenderhearted.

But these men, who were seasoned in the art, were probably expecting him to do just that. No doubt *their* plan was to jump him before he could jump from the train.

They were on a track that cut across the broad breast of Texas where towns were few and far between. But within the last few minutes, Thatcher had decided that no matter how desolate the landscape was where he landed, it would be safer than staying in this boxcar and at the mercy of men who didn't have anything left to lose.

Jumping from a moving train couldn't be much worse than being thrown from a horse, could it? He'd been pitched off too many times to count. But he'd never been thrown when it was full dark, when he didn't know his exact location or where his next drink of water would come from.

How long till daylight? He didn't dare check his wristwatch. The army invention was still a novelty to folks who hadn't been issued one during the war. He didn't want to draw attention by consulting the time, which would be a giveaway that he was awake and planning a departure.

As unobtrusively as possible, he used his index finger to raise his hat just far enough to gauge the degree of darkness beyond the opening. Since the last time he'd sneaked a look, the rectangular gap had turned from solid black to dull gray.

Moving only his gaze, he looked toward the men who were a short distance away, lying at various angles to each other. Two were snoring loudly, feigning sleep. One, Thatcher could tell, was watching him through slitted eyelids. Thatcher lowered his finger from the underside of the brim. His hat resettled over his face.

He forced himself to breathe evenly while he counted to sixty. Then in one motion, he lurched to his feet as he popped his hat onto his head and grabbed his duffel bag by the strap. He made it to the opening and hurled his bag out.

Just as he was about to spring, one of the men grabbed his sleeve from behind.

Shit!

Thatcher came around and swung his fist toward the guy's head, but he saw it coming, ducked, and held on to Thatcher's sleeve like a bulldog. Out the corner of his eye, he saw another approaching in a crouch, making wide swipes with a knife.

The man holding on to him threw a punch that caught Thatcher in the ribs. He retaliated by chopping the guy across the throat with the side of his hand. His attacker let go of his sleeve and staggered backward, holding his throat with both hands and wheezing.

Thatcher spun around to the one with the knife. He had less than a second to throw up his hand to protect his face from being slashed. The sharp blade sliced across his palm. Thatcher yelped.

The hobo grinned and charged. With his good hand, Thatcher

caught hold of the vertical iron handle on the door and kicked the knifer in the balls. Dropping the knife, he screamed in agony, grabbed himself, dropped to his knees, then fell onto his side. Thatcher picked up the knife. The third in the group was poised to attack. Thatcher, winded, his cut hand hurting like bloody hell, said, "Call it quits why don't you?"

But the tramp didn't listen. He came up on his toes, preparing to lunge. Thatcher threw the knife end over end. The point pierced through the man's right shoe, nailing his foot to the floor of the boxcar.

Thatcher turned and made a blind leap through the opening. As he went airborne, howled obscenities trailed him into the predawn light as the train rumbled on.

He landed on his feet, but his knees buckled at the jarring impact. Unable to break his fall, he tumbled down the incline, cussing the pounding he was taking from boulders and stumps.

On one of his revolutions, he recognized the shape of a large agave, dead ahead and coming up fast. As he slid downhill toward it, he dug in his heels. They kicked up loose rocks and grit that struck him in the face, but he was able to stop within inches of being impaled by one of the plant's barbed spines.

As the dust settled around him, he took mental stock of himself and determined that none of his limbs hurt bad enough to have been broken. His breathing was hard and fast, but it didn't hurt to suck in air, so no busted or sprained ribs despite the blow he'd taken on one side. He wasn't dizzy, didn't feel like puking.

Accepting that he was basically all right except for his throbbing palm, adrenaline seemed to leak from his pores like sweat. He stayed as he was, lying there on his back, taking in his expansive and unobstructed view of the sky. It was turning paler by the second, causing the panoply of stars to dim, and he thought what a hell of a thing it was that he was still alive and could admire that sky.

Then, as only one who had slept standing up in a trench while rats scuttled across his blood-soaked boots could do, he dropped into a deep sleep.

He woke up to an early sun, but kept his eyes closed against its brightness, basking in the clean warmth of it on his face. He savored the stillness of the ground beneath him. He'd been unsteadily rocking for two days in that mother-lovin' boxcar. It had been almost as bad as the merchant marine freighter requisitioned and re-outfitted to ship troops home from Europe. If he never saw the Atlantic again, or a wave stronger than a ripple in a stock pond, it would be fine with him.

After several minutes, he sat up. His vision was still clear, and he wasn't dizzy, although he had taken a clout to the head during his downhill plunge. A goose egg had formed on his right temple at his hairline.

He took a handkerchief from his pocket and used it to wipe the blood away from the cut across his palm. It wasn't all that deep, but it made his hand ache. He wrapped the handkerchief around it.

By the position of the sun, he figured out the directions. The landscape was dominated by rugged limestone outcroppings, some bare, some with live oak trees or cedar breaks seeming to grow straight out of the rock. Scrub brush, like that wicked-looking agave, dotted the shallow topsoil.

He figured he was somewhere in the hill country. Still hundreds of miles from home.

He stood up and dusted himself off as best he could, then climbed the incline back to the tracks. The wind was southerly and warm, but strong. It had blown his hat off when he'd made the jump, but miraculously it was still there, lying in the railbed.

He clamped it onto his head and pulled the brim down low over his eyes, then started walking along the tracks in the direction from which the train had come, until he reunited with his duffel bag.

Shouldering it, he reversed his direction and continued in the northwesterly direction the train had been traveling. He saw no indication that a settlement of any kind was anywhere close. He didn't even see a road. The only living things he spotted were a small herd of cattle on a distant hill, and three buzzards, circling their breakfast. Or what soon would be their breakfast.

His stomach was gnawing at its own emptiness, but the only food left in his duffel were a few saltine crackers and the last of a hunk of cheddar. Eating them would make him thirsty, so he decided to hold off until he found water.

He hiked along the tracks for an hour before he reached a crossing. A gravel road ran north and south perpendicular to the tracks, extending for seeming miles in both directions without a turnoff. He took the northern route, hoping that he wouldn't have to hoof it for too long before someone came along who would give him a lift.

The road was easier to walk on than the railbed, but the sky was cloudless, and the sun grew hotter than what you'd expect in mid-May. He shucked off his jacket and draped it over the duffel bag, unbuttoned the cuffs of his shirt and rolled them up.

Sighting a thin trail of smoke rising from behind one of the hills, he was tempted to go in search of the source. A ranch house, or even a campsite, could provide him with a drink of water.

But the smoke was swiftly dispersed by the high wind, so he couldn't be certain how far away it was, and he was reluctant to go exploring off the beaten path. He was no stranger to living without a roof over his head, but he wasn't equipped to do so now.

He estimated he'd walked three or four miles before he spotted a structure on the crest of a rise. At first it was only a dark dot, but the closer he got, it began to take shape. He smelled wood smoke, even though he didn't see any coming from the flue sticking out of the roof at an angle. A Model T was parked in front, along with a truck that looked like a junkyard on wheels.

The place didn't look hospitable, but somebody was at home, and he was damned thirsty.

He started up the dirt lane. As he got closer to the house, he saw that it wasn't a house at all, but a line shack, as ill-kempt a one as he'd ever seen. It must belong to a slipshod outfit that instilled no sense of pride in the cowboys who worked for it.

However, it was no cowboy in the yard, but a young woman who was wrestling with a wet bedsheet. She was trying to get it onto a makeshift clothesline strung between the back corner of the shack and the outhouse. The strong wind was hampering her effort, but she was putting up a fight.

He said, "The sheet is winning."

FOUR

At the sound of his voice, she spun around, looking at him wide-eyed, her hand slapping against her chest where her breath seemed to have become trapped.

"I'm sorry. I didn't mean to scare you." Thatcher took off his hat.

She recovered enough to close her mouth. In the process of hastily gathering up the flapping sheet, a corner of it dragged through the dirt, which made her frown. She dropped the sheet back into a cauldron of water, obviously her wash pot. As she wiped her wet palms on the skirt of her dress, she looked beyond him toward the road.

Coming back to him, she said, "Who are you?"

"My name's Thatcher Hutton."

"How'd you get here?"

"Train."

"There's no depot within miles of here. Why was the train stopped?"

"It wasn't. I jumped off."

Knowing what that implied about him, she raised her hand and shaded her eyes against the sun as she regarded him with even more wariness. "Out in the middle of nowhere?"

"It was the lesser of two evils."

"What was the other one?"

"The men sharing the boxcar with me bore a grudge."

The admission didn't earn him her favor. "So I see." She looked pointedly at the goose egg on his temple and his bandaged hand. She squared her shoulders and motioned him toward the road. "Well, you lived to tell of it. Get on now."

"I've walked several miles, and your place here is the first sign of civilization I've seen. What's the nearest town?"

"Foley."

He'd heard of it, but had never been there. But he hadn't been much of anywhere before the war. "How far is it?"

"Five miles."

Tapping his hat against his leg, he glanced over his shoulder at the road. "Five, huh?"

"At least."

"I don't suppose you'd be going that way any time soon." He glanced toward the vehicles.

"No. Maybe you should've stayed on the train."

"No, I needed to jump off."

"How many of them were there?"

"In the boxcar? Three."

"How did you get crosswise with them?"

"They got sore at me for taking their money."

"You stole their money?"

He shook his head. "Won at cards."

"Did you cheat?"

"No."

She made a scoffing sound, expressing doubt.

"It's true. I have a knack."

Still frowning with skepticism, she raised her arm and pointed toward the road. "Go north about three miles. At the crossroads go east. It's a state highway that leads straight to town and becomes Main Street."

"Thank you."

"You're welcome. Now move along."

"Could you spare me a drink of water first?"

She glanced toward the shack, seemed to debate it, then tilted her head. "Back here."

He set his duffel on the ground and piled his coat and hat on top of it. She led him past a chicken coop that looked relatively new. Two hens were inside it, nesting. A rooster, strutting outside the coop, ruffled his feathers and challenged him and the woman with an aggressive beating of his wings. She told him to shoo or he'd find himself in a stewpot.

On the back side of the shack, a rough wood bench leaned lengthwise against the exterior wall. A bucket of water was sitting on it, a dented metal ladle hanging on a nail above it.

"Help yourself."

"Thanks."

He lifted the ladle off the nail, dipped it into the bucket, and brought it to his mouth. The water was tepid but it was wet. He wanted to gulp but drank slowly in order to study her.

Her dress was baggy, indicating that either it was a hand-me-down from a woman of more substance or that there used to be more to her than there was now. There was nothing wrong with her shape, though. He'd noticed that each time the wind bonded the ill-fitting dress to her slender frame.

Her hair was honey-colored, lighter around her face, and pulled into a bun worn low on the back of her head. The wind had pulled strands loose, which seemed to aggravate her because she kept impatiently trying to tuck them back in.

In fact, her whole aspect was one of agitation. She was strung up a whole lot tighter than her clothesline.

Before he finished drinking, she lost patience. "I've got to get back to my wash."

He drained the ladle and replaced it on the nail. "Much obliged."

"You're welcome." She turned around and started back the way they'd come. He fell into step behind her. They were nearing the corner of the shack when the rooster came flapping around it with an angry squawk and tried to peck her hand.

She recoiled, bumping into Thatcher. Instinctively, he caught her upper arms. "Did he get you?"

"Not this time."

"But he has?"

"More than once."

The bird charged again. She flinched. Thatcher said, "Git!"

The rooster, having established his superiority, strutted away.

She eased herself free of Thatcher's hands, but turned her head to speak over her shoulder. "He's a wretched bird. I ought to wring—"

Then she winced and came full around to face him. At first Thatcher thought the rooster had pecked her after all, but it wasn't her hand she was grimacing over, it was his. When he'd clasped her arms, the handkerchief had come unwound, exposing the cut on his palm.

She reached for his hand and held it supported in hers as she examined the cut, gently pressing the flesh on either side of it. "You should have that looked at. It could get—"

She broke off when she looked up into his face and realized how close they were standing, how still he'd become, and how fixated he was on her face.

She snatched her hand back, then, with a swirl of her skirt, rounded the corner of the building out of sight.

Thatcher blew out a long breath, wadded up the bloodstained handkerchief and stuffed it into his pants pocket, then followed her back to the wash pot where she was jabbing the contents with a stick as though punishing the soaking sheets. She didn't look at him.

"I'll help you wring out that sheet and hang it on the line. It's my fault it got dirty again."

"No, thank you."

"It's the least I can do."

"No, thank you."

Her words were polite enough, but there was no mistaking her tone. She wanted him gone. He bent down, retrieved his hat, and put it on, then picked up his jacket and folded it over his arm. He lifted his duffel by the strap and was about to haul it onto his shoulder when he saw that he'd earned her notice after all.

She'd stopped what she had been doing and was staring at his jacket where it lay across his arm.

He fingered the torn seam that attached his sleeve, the one grabbed and held onto as he'd made his escape. "It was ripped during the altercation."

She gave her head a slight shake. "It's not the tear. I noticed the buttons."

"Oh. They're keepsakes from off my army uniform."

When he'd mustered out, the army had reclaimed his uniform for reasons never explained. Did they expect another war to break out soon? Were they going to pass down his mud- and bloodstained uniform to the next guy they drafted into service?

He never knew. But before he'd relinquished the uniform, he'd ripped off the dull brass buttons bearing insignias. As soon as he'd acquired a suit of civilian clothes, he'd swapped out the buttons.

He ran his fingertip over the one with an embossed pair of crossed rifles and the capital letter *B*. "The 360th Infantry regiment. All us draftees from Texas and Oklahoma."

"Yes, I know." She spoke with a huskiness to her voice that hadn't been there before. "B Company."

"You know someone who served in it?"

"My husband."

Her eyes flicked up to his, then away as she resumed swishing the water in the cauldron.

"He make it back?"

"Yes."

She kept her head down and didn't elaborate, but he'd had his question answered. He hoisted the duffel bag onto his shoulder. "I'll need a place to stay in town. Any suggestions?"

She was about to shake her head, when she hesitated, as though remembering. "In the window of Hancock's store. There's a sign advertising a room."

"Where's the store?"

"You can't miss it."

"Laurel?"

Startled, she looked in the direction of the shack from where the man's voice had come. "I'm here," she called.

"The baby's coughing again."

Just then a baby's wail could be heard coming from inside. The woman propped her stick against the lip of the wash pot and started toward the door of the shack. As she rushed past Thatcher she said, "Be on your way now."

"Thanks for the water." Before she disappeared inside, he said, "Wait, what was that name again?"

She paused in the open doorway and looked back at him. "Hancock's."

"No. Your name."

"Oh. Laurel. Plummer."

FIVE

As Laurel rushed inside, she nearly ran directly into Irv, who was standing just beyond the threshold but far enough back in the shadows that he couldn't be seen from the yard. He held a double-barreled shotgun crosswise against his chest. He raised his index finger to his lips, signaling for her not to make a sound.

She went over to the crib that Irv had made for Pearl out of scrap lumber he'd salvaged from one of his fix-it jobs. Her daughter's face was near purple from crying and coughing. Laurel picked her up and held her against her shoulder as she firmly patted her back, trying to loosen the phlegm that had made her croupy for more than a week.

Irv remained stock-still, watching the stranger until he had reached the road and headed in the direction Laurel had told him would lead to Foley. Only then did Irv relax his stance. He returned the shotgun to its usual spot, resting it between two hooks mounted above the door.

Laurel said, "He hopped off a freight car and wasn't sure of where he was."

"That's what he told you, anyway."

"Why would he lie?"

"Any number of reasons, and none of them good."

"He startled me, but apologized for it." For reasons she couldn't explain, she felt compelled to defend the stranger. "He was mannerly."

"That's the worst sort. They sneak up on you and act like your friend."

"The worst sort of what?"

"Of anything. How many times have I told you to be suspicious of strangers? Out this far? He could've been up to all kinds of mischief."

"He was only asking for directions and a drink of water."

"He must've had the thirst of a damn camel. What took so long?"

"While we were back there, the rooster made a nuisance of himself."

She thought the less said about that incident, the better. The mean rooster had been the least of it. She'd known what to expect from that damn bird.

Her thoughts lingered now on what had come after. She hadn't touched a man, or vice versa, since Derby's death. Not even Irv. Despite the stranger's leanness, he'd felt as solid as a tree trunk when she'd backed into him. When he'd steadied her with his hands on her arms, she'd had a momentary yearning to lean against him. It hadn't lasted any longer than the flit of a butterfly's wings, so it didn't merit dwelling on now. She forced herself to tune into Irv's grumbling.

"He didn't look like any hobo I ever saw."

Not to Laurel, either. "No, but he looked like a man who'd jumped off a train. His clothes were dusty. He had a ripped sleeve and a bruised bump on his forehead. And a cut on his hand."

She didn't want to think at all about that business with his hand. Any woman in the world would have responded the same way to seeing a nasty cut like that. She'd reacted in a typically female way. Instinctually. Maternally. Although, held in her palm, his hand hadn't felt like that of a child.

"What was that hogwash about saving his army buttons?"

Seeing them had been a bleak reminder of Derby's uniform hanging abandoned in the empty closet. She hadn't told Irv about that, and saw no point in telling him now. It would only make him sad.

"The man was just passing by, Irv," she said. "For heaven's sake. Really, you're making too much of it."

"And you're not making enough. I've lived longer. I've learned to be more cautious, less friendly." He indicated the shotgun. "I'll teach you how to shoot in case a vagrant, who ain't so *mannerly*, comes along when I'm not here watching your back."

She would be unable to reach the shotgun without dragging something over to the door and standing on it. By the time she did that, her throat could have been cut. So not to give Irv another reason to fret, she didn't cite that. Instead, she gave a small nod of acquiescence.

He started for the door. "You tend to Pearl. I'll hang that wash."

"The wash can wait. I want to talk to you."

His shoulders slumped as he turned back to her. "If it's about moving into town—"

"It is. Let's have this out. Sit down. Please."

With obvious reluctance, he went over to a lidded barrel on which he'd placed a cushion to form a seat for himself. He often perched there instead of sitting in a chair. Laurel guessed it was easier on his hip.

She sat down at the small table at which they ate their meals. Pearl's horrible, barking cough had subsided since she'd picked her up. Laurel laid her cheek against the top of Pearl's head. "Her hair's damp. I think her fever finally broke."

"That's good. She coughed all night long."

"I'm sorry."

"Hell, Laurel, I ain't cross over losing sleep." Watching Pearl, he furrowed his brow. "Pains me to hear that cough. Poor little thing."

Unwittingly he had given Laurel an opening. "I want to talk to you about a couple of things. Well, three, actually."

He folded his arms over his middle. "What's the first?"

"Thank you."

That took him aback. "What for?"

"That night we showed up here, you could have sent us on our way. You could have put up a real fuss with Derby for springing us on you.

You didn't. I don't think you'll ever know how much I appreciated your kindness that night and these two months since. You haven't complained once about Pearl and me being foisted off on you."

He snorted. "You could've took one look at me and this place and raised more than a fuss, Laurel. You could've raised bloody hell, and Derby deserved it."

They'd buried him in Foley's municipal cemetery. At the grave site were only the two of them, Pearl, and the undertaker whom Irv had paid an extra fifty cents to read a suitable scripture and say a prayer.

In the weeks following, she and Irv grieved Derby privately, silently, neither speaking of him, because they had no shared memory except for the final few minutes of his life. Neither wanted to reminisce on those.

Laurel's bereavement had been, and still was, far from pure and holy. It was corrupted by outrage. Were Derby's last words to her, "You'll thank me later," supposed to atone for his cowardly, selfish desertion of her and Pearl, his defection from all responsibility?

Willfully, she tamped down the resentment that continued to smolder even now, two and a half months into her widowhood. If ever she allowed it to boil, it would consume her.

She lifted Pearl off her shoulder and placed her facedown across her knees, swaying them slowly from side to side. "Irv—"

"Is this the start of the second thing?"

"Yes."

"Well, let's hear it."

She began by saying that it would be better for all of them to live at least within shouting distance of town. "I'm sure we could find a place to rent. Nothing fancy, but with separate rooms for us. Pearl and I wouldn't always be underfoot. You'd have your privacy back."

She looked at the blankets he'd strung up around the mattress. He now slept on a pallet of old quilts which he'd placed crosswise against the door, as far away from her corner as possible. The makeshift curtain served to keep them out of sight of each other during the night, but it was a fragile barrier against the forced intimacy and each other's humanness.

He didn't argue her point, so she pressed on. "You could take twice as many jobs if you didn't have to drive that ten-mile round trip each day. That takes up valuable time.

"And I worry about that truck of yours breaking down and stranding you on some back road. If you went missing, I wouldn't know where to start looking for you."

"My truck runs just fine."

"Then why are you tinkering on it all the time?" When he didn't answer, she continued. "I'll find something to do that will bring in extra money."

He lowered his bushy brows. "Like what?"

She knew that money would be a primary concern. Rightly so. There were jobs to be had working in the oil patches that were sprouting up in northwest Texas, some not far from here. But an older man with a gimp hip and a woman with an infant hardly qualified them to be roughnecks, even if they desired to be.

She would have to come up with something she could do at home. Take in laundry and ironing. Teach illiterate adults how to read. She wasn't without skills. Or resources.

She decided to admit now that the cash Derby had on him the night of their arrival wasn't all that they'd had to their name. "I have some cash tucked away that Derby didn't know about. I've been saving it for a rainy day, and this is it."

Her father-in-law took umbrage, but not from knowing she'd secreted money from Derby. "I'll have you know that I ain't destitute, and the idea of taking money from a woman, a young widow woman at that, makes—"

"Would you rather Pearl learn to crawl on a dirt floor?"

He scowled and muttered something unseemly under his breath.

"Why do you live here, Irv?"

"Because I like it."

"You couldn't possibly like it."

"It suits me just fine."

"Well, it doesn't suit me. I don't want my daughter growing up in a dilapidated shack with cracks in the walls. Out in the middle of nowhere, cut off from everything and everybody. No telephone or electricity or running water. No other children. No other *people* except for the two of us. What kind of upbringing is that?"

She stopped before she got too fired up. It wasn't her intention to insult or shame him into compliance. More gently, she said, "I'll be forever grateful to you for taking us in, but the baby and I can't go on living like this."

"Weren't so much of a hardship on me having y'all here," he said. "I'd miss you something fierce if you was to leave now. But, I get what you're sayin'."

He thought on it for a time, then said, "You're a pretty girl, Laurel. A bit scrawny, but that hobo was appreciatin' you. Don't think I didn't notice how he was eyein' you. If you fix yourself up a bit, fill out a little, you'll find another husband in no time, is my guess."

She gave a bitter laugh. "I don't want another husband, thank you. Not ever."

"You say that now, but—"

"I'm not looking for a man, Irv, so put that thought right out of your head."

"You gals got the vote, you don't need men no longer?"

She leveled a look on him. "It's way past time we 'gals' got the vote. But you're only saying that to rile me, so I'll drop this subject. I'm not falling for it."

He mumbled more swear words, then sat with arms folded, glowering as he considered his next line of attack. Laurel waited him out. Finally, he said, "A well-heeled family in town would probably give you a roof in exchange for housekeeping and cooking. Like that."

"Not with a baby."

"But if they've got little ones—"

"I don't want to live with another family and take care of their children. Besides, we should stay together. Help each other." She knew better than to remind him that he wasn't getting any younger. "*We're* family."

Laurel gazed at her gruff and scruffy father-in-law, who her own father would consider hell-bound for taking an occasional nip of moonshine for medicinal purposes, but who had been so ungrudgingly charitable.

"You're my family now, Irv. But whether or not you come with Pearl and me, I must leave here and somehow build a life for us."

He drew a deep breath and exhaled it slowly.

"At least tell me you understand my reasoning," Laurel said.

"I ain't dense."

"Then is that a yes? We'll start looking in town for a place to live?"

"I'm thinking on it," he said grouchily. "What's the third thing under discussion?"

"No discussion to it. You're going to teach me how to drive." When she saw that he was about to object, she added, "Today."

SIX

On this Saturday afternoon, countryfolk had come to town. Main Street in Foley was heavily trafficked with automobiles, trucks, and horse- or mule-drawn wagons top-heavy with everything from bales of hay to prolific families.

Hancock's General Goods was a three-story brick building. Its imposing facade dominated a block of the thoroughfare. In one of its four display windows were a pyramid of canned peas and carrots, several unfurled bolts of checked gingham in a rainbow of colors, a rack of Winchester rifles, and an open red metal tool box showing off a set of shiny wrenches.

The merchandise obscured the pale blue card stuck in the bottom corner of the window frame. It looked to Thatcher like it had been there for a while. The black ink had faded to brown, but the printed words were still legible. "Room for Let to single. 312 Pecan St."

Thatcher waylaid a man who was about to enter the store. He was jowly and prosperous-looking. His pocket watch dangled from a thick gold chain threaded through a buttonhole on his vest.

"Excuse me." Thatcher drew the man's attention to the sign. "Can you aim me toward that address?"

The man took a backward step and sized him up. "New to town?"

"Just rolled in."

The gentleman glanced again at the sign. "And apparently planning to stay."

"Till I take a notion to move on."

"What's your business here?"

His challenging aspect didn't sit well with Thatcher, but he said mildly, "Minding my own."

The man frowned and harrumphed, but pointed down the sidewalk. "Three blocks. Take a right on Crockett. Two blocks to Pecan. Hook a left."

"Thanks."

Thatcher brushed the brim of his hat with his fingertips and set off. But something about the man's manner compelled him to look back without being too obvious about it. Sure enough, the man was still watching him with a scowl of distrust. Thatcher couldn't account for it, but he didn't let it bother him overmuch.

Pecan Street was appropriately named. Several of the trees shaded the front lawn of number 312. The house was white with black shutters. Gingerbread trim lined the roof. A lattice with red climbing roses was attached to one end of the deep porch that ran the width of the house.

A picket fence enclosed the property like the frame around a picture of ideal domesticity. Where the fence and an inlaid stone walkway met, a sign hung from an iron post. On it, written in swirly black letters: "Dr. Gabriel Driscoll." Dangling from it by two little brass hooks was another sign: "Out on Call."

Right off Thatcher knew that he couldn't afford any room in this house. It was far too fine. He was seeking more humble accommodations. Just as he was about to turn away, the screened front door opened, and a woman came out onto the porch holding a watering can with both hands.

She tipped the spout toward some purple flowers that bloomed from a wicker stand next to the front door. Noticing him, she paused and broke a friendly smile. "Hello."

He removed his hat. "Ma'am."

She looked in both directions of the street as though wondering how he'd come to be there, much as Laurel Plummer had done.

She said, "The doctor is out making house calls."

"I'm not in need of the doctor. I came to see about the room for let."

The smile with which she'd greeted him faltered. "Oh."

She bent down to set the watering can on the floor and wiped her hands on her apron as she straightened up. She was in the family way. Pretty far along if Thatcher were to guess.

"I had forgotten the sign still was there." She pronounced it "da-zine" in an unmistakably German accent. "We're no longer taking a lodger." Self-consciously she smoothed her hand over her belly.

"Oh. Well, it probably would have been too rich for my blood anyway. Thanks all the same." He replaced his hat and made to leave when she blurted, "Wait. I want to bring you something, to thank you for inquiring."

He gave a dry laugh. "Ma'am, you don't owe me anything."

"No, wait. Please?"

Her eager nodding persuaded him. "Okay."

She beamed a smile. "Come up to the porch. I'll be right back." Leaving her watering can, she bustled inside.

Thatcher pushed open the gate and went up the walk. He stopped at the bottom of the steps leading onto the porch and eased the duffel bag off his shoulder, setting it on the ground. Then he stood there threading the brim of his hat through his fingers as he took a look around.

The house across the street was comparable to Dr. Driscoll's in size and architecture, and was obviously occupied by a snoopy neighbor. He noticed movement behind a lace curtain in one of the front windows before it dropped back into place.

After a minute or two, the lady returned, pushing through the screen door, happily bobbing her head and making the blond curls framing her face bounce. "Fresh baked shortbread. Come."

He left his hat on top of his duffel bag and climbed the steps.

She met him halfway across the porch and extended a plate to him. It was china and lined with one of those white lacy things. On it were two large squares of shortbread, the aroma of which made Thatcher's stomach growl. He'd eaten the last of the cheese and crackers during his five-mile hike from the Plummers' place, but they hadn't gone far.

"Are you Mrs. Driscoll?"

"Mila Driscoll, yes."

"Thatcher Hutton."

"Mr. Hutton. Please." She thrust the plate toward him.

"Thank you, ma'am."

He took one of the squares from the plate and bit into it. It was soft, buttery, sweet, and still warm from the oven. He swallowed the bite. "Delicious."

"My husband's favorite."

Her face was round and rosy, and shiny with perspiration, which she fanned with her apron. The cloth had red and yellow apples printed on it, bordered in a red ruffle. When she smiled, her whole face lit up.

He thought about the tense set of Laurel Plummer's features. He couldn't feature her smiling so unguardedly or wearing that cheerful apron. "Your husband's office is here in the house?"

"Front parlor, yes." She nodded toward a tall bay window that was both functional and ornamental.

"Do you help with his practice?"

"No. Better I don't."

Her cheerful blue eyes took on a sad cast as she glanced behind him toward where he'd left his duffel, which was obviously U.S. army issue. It showed the wear and tear of having been to war and back.

Even before the states got into it, people of German descent were subjected to resentment and suspicion because of a foreign war they'd had nothing to do with. Mila Driscoll's accent was a giveaway to her heritage. Thatcher reckoned she'd experienced a taste of unfair ostracism.

She didn't refer to the war or his obvious service. Instead she asked him if he was moving to Foley.

"No, ma'am. Just staying for a spell."

During the last mile of his journey today, he'd decided that hitching a free ride in freight cars came with risks he was unwilling to take again. His best option at this point was to earn enough money to buy a train ticket to whatever stop would get him closest to the Hobson ranch up in the Panhandle.

Before going off to do Uncle Sam's bidding, Mr. Henry Hobson had told him, "Don't get yourself maimed or killed over there. Your job here will be waiting on you when you get back."

Thatcher had promised that he would be back, but the army had kept him in Germany for over a year after the armistice, so his return had taken longer than he'd counted on. Now on his way, he was eager to get back to his former life.

It was likely to take him a couple of weeks to earn enough to cover the cost of the train ticket and keep himself fed and sheltered. Say a month at the outside. But he needed to be getting at it and find a place to bunk for however long he was here.

He finished the shortbread. "It sure was good, Mrs. Driscoll."

"Take the other."

He hesitated but reasoned she would be disappointed if he didn't. Besides, at his hungriest in the trenches, he'd sworn he would never again turn down food. "Okay. Hold on."

He went down the steps to fetch a spare, clean handkerchief from his duffel so he wouldn't have to wrap the extra piece of shortbread in the bloody handkerchief he'd used to bandage his hand.

When the treat was wrapped and tucked into his pants pocket, he said, "Thank you kindly, ma'am."

He hefted the duffel bag up by the strap and slid it onto his shoulder, then put on his hat. "Do you know anybody in town with a spare room? Doesn't have to be fancy."

"Near the railroad tracks. Room and board. Big yellow house."

"I'll find it."

"I must remember to ask Mr. Hancock to remove the sign."

"It's not that conspicuous. I wouldn't have noticed it if someone hadn't told me where to look."

"Oh? Who was dat?"

"Lady named Laurel Plummer. Lives out a ways."

"Young woman with baby?"

"That's right. I passed their place this morning. She gave me a drink of water. You're acquainted?"

"Only one time I see her. Her baby girl had bad croup. She brought her to my husband for medicine."

Little good it had done, Thatcher thought. "How old's the baby?"

"Infant. Tiny." She held her hands apart, about the length of a loaf of bread. "Poor Mrs. Plummer was very anxious."

With reason. Living in such a squalid place couldn't be good for a sick baby. "I didn't meet her husband. What's he do out there?"

"No husband. Father-in-law."

He scratched his chin with his thumbnail. "That so?"

"Her husband..." Shaking her head, Mila Driscoll tsked. "He died."

Huh. So it had been her father-in-law who'd had his shotgun at the ready. Thatcher hadn't let on that he'd seen him, but he'd caught sight of that side-by-side as the woman had disappeared into the shadows inside the shack.

She'd told him her husband had come back from the war, and that must've been the truth if her baby was that young. He couldn't stop himself from asking, "How long since her husband passed?"

"Two months? Three? The story..." She paused as though reluctant to gossip. Thatcher didn't encourage her to continue, but he hoped she would. He was itching to know why the elder Mr. Plummer was so trigger-happy. Maybe he was just overprotective of the recent widow and his sick granddaughter. Fair to say, too, that a stranger who showed up out of nowhere could be cause for concern to people who lived in such a remote spot.

Mrs. Driscoll overcame her reticence. "The story is that her husband took her and the baby to his old papa out dere, then shot himself the same night."

Jesus. No wonder she'd looked gaunt and wound up.

"Such a shame for her," Mrs. Driscoll said.

"Yes, ma'am, it is." They were quiet for a moment, then he said, "I'd best see if they have any vacancies in that boardinghouse. Thanks again for the shortbread."

"You're welcome. Good luck to you, Mr. Hutton."

He doffed his hat to her, and then, when he reached the street, he tipped it to the busybody who was still observing them from behind the lacy curtain.

SEVEN

The large house near the railroad tracks was indeed yellow. In its day, it might have been considered grand, but Thatcher figured the loud color was an attempt to draw attention away from the overall seediness of the place.

If he planned to stay longer, he would have passed on it. But, reminding himself that the quarters would be temporary and probably affordable, he pulled on the bell at the front door.

Through the screen, he saw a woman walking toward him down the length of a long central hallway. He'd seen scarecrows that were more comely. As she neared, she slung a damp cup towel over her shoulder and peered at him through the mesh. "Whatever you're selling, I ain't buyin'."

Friendlier scarecrows, too. "I'm not a salesman." He stated his purpose and asked if she had a vacancy.

She shifted a toothpick from one side of her mouth to the other. "You railroad?"

"No, ma'am."

"Most of my boarders are railroad men. They rotate in and out."

"I don't plan on being here long term, either."

She pushed open the door, and motioned him inside. "Name's Arleta May. May's the last name. I got one vacant room. Rents by the week. No refund if you cut out early. Three meals a day, but supper is cold, and you serve yourself off the sideboard."

She passed him a piece of paper on which was a badly typewritten list of house rules. He was allowed barely ten seconds to scan it before she took it back. "Basically, no women, no liquor, no cussing, no fighting, no smoking in bed. I've got beans about to boil dry. You taking it or not?"

He took it. She went over to a cabinet, sorted through a drawer full of keys, and exchanged one of them for his first week's rent money. "Third floor, number two. You can find your own way." She shuffled off down the hall from which she'd come.

Thatcher climbed two sets of stairs to the third floor. Room number two met his expectations. The mattress on the rusty iron bedstead sagged in the middle. Water stains spotted the ceiling. The single window was cloudy with grime. He raised it to let in some fresh air.

A set of sheets and a folded towel had been left on the bed. He took the towel with him into the bathroom midway down the hall, used the toilet, washed his face and hands, and returned to his room only long enough to hang the towel on the footboard to dry and to retrieve his hat.

He descended the stairs and followed the aroma of cooking beans to the kitchen. "Uh, Miz May?" She turned to him, scowling. "Sorry to bother you. Is there a public stable in town?"

"Old man Barker's. North side of town, across the bridge."

An advertisement for Goodyear tires was painted on one exterior side of Barker and Son Automobile Parts & Repair. In front were two gasoline pumps, and, even as Thatcher crossed the bridge, he could smell motor oil. Several vehicles were parked both inside and out of the open garage. One was being worked on by a young man in dirty overalls, no shirt.

"Mr. Barker?"

"He's out back." Without even glancing at Thatcher, he hitched his thumb over his shoulder.

Thatcher walked around the building and found an older man lying on his back beneath a milk delivery truck. He was banging metal against metal and cussing a blue streak.

"Mr. Barker?"

The man slid from beneath the truck and shaded his eyes against the sun. "Yeah?"

"Thatcher Hutton." He walked over, bent down, and extended his right hand.

"Never mind that. My hands are greasy." As Barker came to his feet, he pulled a red shop rag from the pocket of his overalls and wiped his hands. "What can I do for you?"

"You stable horses?"

Barker tipped his head toward a large barn about thirty yards distant. "Stable, shoe, groom. Whatever you need."

"I need a job."

The older man scoffed and looked him over. "Doing what?"

"Whatever needs doing."

"You ever seen the inside of a stable, young man?"

"Spent most of my life in one. Before being drafted, cowboying was all I ever did. I mustered out of the army a month ago in Norfolk, Virginia. I've been working my way back up to the Panhandle. The Hobson ranch?"

He posed it as a question to which Barker shook his head. "Don't know it."

"South of Amarillo, along the Palo Duro. I started working for Mr. Hobson when I was eleven years old. I'm handy with horses."

"That may be," Barker said, still looking unconvinced. "But I ain't hiring."

Thatcher glanced over his shoulder in the direction of the garage before coming back around. "Looks to me like you've got more than you can handle on the automotive side of your business. For the next few weeks, I could relieve you of stable chores, free up you and your son to do the other work."

"That nitwit ain't my son. *I'm* the son. My daddy had a smithy and stables at this location for forty years. Henry Ford changed that. I had to adapt or starve."

Thatcher had figured such was the case. "How many horses are you stabling?"

"Currently six. Plus four of my own that I rent out. And one ill-tempered sumbitch that a fellow left here for me to break."

"Yeah? How's that coming?"

Barker shifted his chaw and spat into the dirt.

Thatcher smiled. "That ill-tempered, huh?"

"High-steppin' stallion. Owner won't hear of gelding him yet."

"Let me take a look at him."

"What for?"

"Why not?"

Barker thought it over, then said, "What the hell? I's tired of working on that clutch, anyway." He kicked the front tire of the milk truck as he walked around the hood. "Come on."

Thatcher followed him around the far side of the large stable to a corral of respectable size, but confining to the bay stallion who was running along the encircling fence, making abrupt directional changes, bucking occasionally, demonstrating his anger and frustration over being penned. When he sensed them coming toward the corral, he pinned back his ears, and his nostrils flared.

"I had to put him out here. He kept the other horses stirred up. Especially the mares."

Thatcher chuckled. "I don't doubt it. He's a handsome devil, and he knows it."

He was a large horse, sixteen hands, perfectly formed. He had the classic black points and a deep red coat that would gleam if he were groomed. Thatcher propped his arms on the top fence rail and watched the stallion strut, tail high.

"Does the owner want him trained to race?"

"To ride," Baker said, adding dryly, "for longer than three seconds at a time."

Thatcher smiled at the quip. "Does he have a name?"

"Ulysses."

"I'd be throwing my owner, too." Thatcher shrugged out of his coat and draped it over the fence rail. "How does a dollar and a half a day sound, Mr. Barker?

"Hold it. What are you doing?"

The stallion was snorting and eyeballing Thatcher as he unlatched the gate, slipped through it, and closed it behind himself. The horse didn't like any of it. He became even more agitated, picking up speed on his next go-around of the corral and coming dangerously close to Thatcher who stood stock-still.

Barker said, "Get out of there. You ain't even dressed for this."

"I had to leave my gear behind when I went into the army. But he doesn't know city shoes from boots."

"At least take this rope." Barker lifted a coiled lariat off the top of a fence post.

"Not for our first meeting."

"That bastard'll kick you into next week."

"I'm mindful that he'd like to. But he also wants to know what I'm up to."

"*I* want to know what you're up to."

"Earning my buck fifty." Thatcher calmly walked to the center of the corral.

"I haven't agreed—"

Thatcher said, "Mr. Barker, I don't want him to see me as a threat, but I do want his undivided attention, and, no offense, you're a distraction. If you could back up a little, please."

Thatcher heard Barker spit another wad of tobacco into the ground before muttering, "Your funeral."

There was a lot to be learned about the horse just from watching how he maneuvered. Thatcher faked indifference, but, without appearing to, he studied the stallion's movements as he cantered along the fence, tossing his head, whinnying, stamping, making sudden shifts in direction, asserting himself.

After several minutes, Thatcher spoke softly, "Won't do you any good to keep that up. You'll wear yourself out before I leave this corral."

He partially turned his back to the animal, remaining very aware of where he was, but intentionally keeping his head turned away from him as though uninterested in his arrogant posturing.

"See, I'm not scared of you. And you don't have to be scared of me."

It didn't take long. The horse slowed his gait and eventually came to a standstill. He stomped a couple of times, then turned toward the center of the corral to face Thatcher. "Well, are we going to be friends?" Thatcher made a nicking sound. Not yet ready to concede, the stallion shook his head.

"All right. Stay there and think it over. I can wait. Sooner or later, your curiosity is going to get the better of you." Thatcher stayed as he was, acting nonchalant. "Those mares you've got stirred up. Are they pretty?" The stallion's ears flicked forward. Thatcher made the nicking sound again.

Slowly the stallion walked toward him and came to a stop, head down. "Good boy. We're making strides. Ulysses, huh? Guess you're stuck with it."

The stallion snuffled and jerked his head when Thatcher reached up to stroke his forehead, but after one more rejected attempt, the horse allowed his touch. "Thata boy." Moving slowly, speaking softly, he praised the stallion's cooperation. As Thatcher rubbed the horse's neck, he looked over at Barker. "A dollar and a half a day?"

Barker spat. Thatcher took that as a yes.

After spending another few minutes smoothing his hands over the stallion, building trust, he left the corral and reclaimed his coat. Barker led him into the stable, introduced him to the horses in the stalls, and showed him where tack and supplies were kept.

"I'll have to borrow one of your saddles," Thatcher told him. "Mine's at the ranch."

"Help yourself. What they're there for."

As Thatcher was leaving, Barker told him there was a second-hand clothing store in town. "You might find yourself a pair of boots, at least."

Thatcher got directions to the shop, but it was closed for the day. He had planned on sending Mr. Hobson a letter tomorrow telling him that he could start looking for him in about a month. In the letter, maybe he'd ask Mr. Hobson if he would send him his gear by train and take the expense out of his salary once he was back.

He made it to the boardinghouse before the cold supper was cleared off the sideboard. After finishing his meal, he wandered out onto the porch where several other boarders were chewing the fat.

Laconically, they all introduced themselves and shook hands, but he didn't get the impression that fast friendships were formed among them, probably because of their transiency.

One thumbed through a magazine. One was quietly playing a harmonica. Some puffed smokes. Thatcher noticed that one of the younger among them slid a flask out of his pants pocket, uncapped it, and took a sip.

Another, an older man who had laid claim to a rocking chair, said, "That's against house rules and against the law."

"Now that's a fact," the young man said. "It is." Then, leaning toward the man in the rocker, he whispered, "And teetotaling is against the laws of nature." He took another drink then taunted the older man by smacking his lips and saying a long, drawn-out *ahhhh*.

Sensing the growing tension, the man with the harmonica stopped playing.

The older man didn't let it drop. He said to the young man, "I doubt you respect any rules."

"That's not so," the young man retorted. "I set rules for myself."

"Such as?"

He seemed to ponder it, then snapped his fingers and said, "I only get half as drunk on Sundays."

The others on the porch were equally divided as to who thought that was funny and who didn't. The one in the rocking chair took umbrage. He excused himself, left the rocker, and stamped into the house, letting the screen door slap closed behind him.

The younger man chortled, "He's a barrel of laughs."

Another man, who Thatcher had noticed earlier because of his sporty attire, left the corner of the porch where he'd been smoking in solitude and sidled up to the younger man. "What's your name?"

"Randy Wells. Who's asking?"

"Chester Landry." He motioned to the flask. "Where'd you get the booze?"

Randy cast a wary look around. When his gaze lighted on Thatcher, he squinted suspiciously. "I feel like a stroll." He indicated for Landry to follow him. They went down the porch steps and set off across the yard, talking softly together.

No one said anything for a moment, then the harmonica player picked up his tune where he'd left off, and another commenced to talk about baseball. Thatcher stayed only a few minutes longer before going inside.

He took a turn in the third floor bathroom, then went into his room, undressed, and took the piece of shortbread to bed with him. As he stretched out on the lumpy mattress, he released a sigh of relative contentment.

It had been a damned long day, but he'd accomplished a lot, too. For a start, he'd survived the fight in the freight car and the jump from it without serious injury.

The miles he'd walked had fatigued him, but hadn't completely exhausted him like the long marches he'd made through the French countryside, fully armed, cold, hungry, and hoping an enemy bullet didn't have his name on it.

His landlady, Arleta May, was scary, but he had a roof. The mattress was bad, but still better than wet ground or the floor of the boxcar.

He had a headstrong horse to train, and if he did that successfully, word would get around, and more work could come from it until he'd earned enough to get him the last few hundred miles to home.

All things considered, he had it pretty good.

He polished off the shortbread and licked the crumbs from his fingers before reaching up for the string attached to the bare-bulb light fixture mounted to the wall above the headboard.

When he closed his eyes, an image of Laurel Plummer came to mind. He fell asleep thinking about her in profile, the wind toying with her hair and holding her shapeless dress tight against her front.

EIGHT

—◆◆◆—

Sheriff William Amos was awakened by the shrill ringing of his telephone. He squinted the clock into focus and cursed under his breath. Nobody called at three o'clock in the morning to impart good news.

As he threw back the sheet and got up, his wife murmured sleepily. He patted her on the rump, then went to the downstairs hall, where the telephone sat on a small table. He picked it up by the stand and lifted the earpiece from the fork, saying into the mouthpiece, "Bill Amos."

One of his younger, greener deputies identified himself. "Hated to wake you, sir."

"I hated you did, too. What's happened?"

He hoped for nothing more major than rowdy boys being caught painting naughty words on a public building. But he mentally ran through the list of better likelihoods: A still had caught a cedar break on fire. Rival moonshiners had gotten into a skirmish with fists, firearms, or both. Lawmen in a neighboring county, tired of chasing a notable bootlegger, were officially dumping him into Bill's jurisdiction.

Even before Prohibition had become federal law several months back, evangelicals had for generations voted in local laws that had kept many Texas counties dry. Thus the illegal making and selling of corn liquor was the second oldest profession in the state.

All the Volstead Act had accomplished so far was to turn the trade into an even more profitable enterprise. Demand was at an all-time high. Production was up. Competition was stiff. And the moonshiners in Bill Amos's county were among the most industrious in Texas.

"We've got a situation, sir," the deputy said.

"Something y'all can't handle?"

"Thought so when we started out. But things has gone down-hill fast."

Bill heaved a sigh. "Somebody must've wound up dead."

"Well, truth is, we don't know yet."

"What's that mean? He's either breathing or he isn't. Is he a Johnson?"

"No, sir. It's Mrs. Driscoll."

With a start, Bill angled his head back and looked at the phone as though the deputy had started speaking in tongues. "Dr. Driscoll's wife? Mila Driscoll?"

"Yes, sir. She's gone missing."

⁎

Ten minutes later, Bill entered the sheriff's office, where Dr. Gabriel Driscoll was carrying on like a crazy person. Usually of an austere nature, the physician was clearly unhinged. His hair was standing on end, as though he'd been trying to tear it out. He was pacing in circles and aggressively warding off anyone who attempted to restrain or calm him down.

When he saw Bill, he lunged toward him. "Sheriff, do something! You've got to find her."

Bill hung his hat on a wall rack. "Get us some coffee," he said, addressing one of his deputies who looked relieved to be charged with something besides the physician.

"I don't want any coffee!" Gabe made an arrow of his right arm, pointing to the door through which Bill had just entered. "Get out there and find my wife!"

"Gabe, I can't help you if you don't help me. First off, you've gotta get hold of yourself." He pulled up a chair. "Sit down and tell me what's happened."

"I've told them." The doctor indicated the several deputies watching him with a mix of pity and wariness, much like they would regard a wounded wild animal that hadn't yet died.

"I need to hear everything for myself," Bill said. "So take a breath and brief me on the situation."

"He came and took her," he shouted. "In brief, that's the situation." Then, as though feeling the impact of his own declaration, he collapsed into the chair, planted his elbows on his knees, cupped his bowed head with all ten fingers, and began to sob. "What if it was your wife, Bill? God knows what's he doing to her."

"Who's he talking about?" Bill asked, addressing one of his most trusted men, Scotty Graves.

"I talked to the old lady who lives across the street from the Driscolls."

"Ol' Miss Wise?"

"Yes, sir. She said a man came to their house today, talked to Mrs. Driscoll up on the porch."

"Miss Wise recognize him?"

"No, sir, and she said she knew a stranger when she saw one."

The illogic of that statement caused Bill to run his hand over the top of his head. "Maybe this stranger was sick and looking for the doc."

"The sign was out, saying the doctor was on a call, but Miss Wise said this man stayed for several minutes. He didn't appear to be ailing, either."

"He go inside the house?"

"No, sir. Didn't go no farther than the porch. Mrs. Driscoll gave him something, but Miss Wise couldn't tell what it was."

"Something like what?"

"Something small enough to fit in his pocket."

"A bottle of medicine, maybe? A jar of pills?"

"We thought of that, but the doctor checked his medicine cabinet.

Everything's accounted for. Besides, he keeps the cabinet locked when he's away. Even Mrs. Driscoll doesn't have a key."

"Did Miss Wise describe this stranger? Was he young, old, what?"

"Young. No more'n thirty, she said. Tall, on the slender side, dressed in a dark suit. He had dark hair. He was wearing a fedora, but he took it off while talking to Mrs. Driscoll. He was carrying a bag that looked heavy."

"Salesman's wares?"

"Miss Wise didn't think so. She said it looked like the kind of bag a soldier would have."

"Soldier?"

"That's what she said."

"Yeah, but she's more than half batty," Bill muttered. "Anything else?"

"She said he was cocky."

"How'd she get that? Did she talk to him?"

"No, but he tipped his hat to her."

Bill hooked his thumb in his gun belt. "Maybe he was just being polite."

"She was watching from behind the curtain in her side parlor."

"Out of sight?"

"She thought so, but apparently not."

So, aware of being watched by a nosy neighbor, the young man had mockingly tipped his hat, making himself certain to be remembered. If he'd brought harm to Mrs. Driscoll, he was either incredibly stupid, or he was cocky just like the old maid had said. Bill had rather him be stupid. Someone that cocky usually didn't give a damn, and that was dangerous.

"You boys have scouted the neighborhood?" he asked his men at large.

Scotty answered for the group. "Questioned all the nearby neighbors, searched every outbuilding for blocks around. Mrs. Driscoll was well known. If anybody had seen her, it would've been noted."

"Nobody heard anything suspicious? Shouting? Barking dogs, nothing like that?"

"Nothin' out of the ordinary, no, sir."

"What about Mrs. Driscoll's friends? Have you checked with them?"

"The doc knew of only two people she might visit. One's the preacher of the Lutheran church. He hasn't seen her since last Sunday's service."

The other was the local librarian, who'd told the deputy she hadn't seen Mila Driscoll in a while, but had reassured him that none of the books she'd checked out were overdue.

"What about her family?" Bill asked.

"None closer than down around New Braunfels. Stands to reason."

Stood to reason because it was a predominantly German town. "Have you checked with them?"

"Her parents are deceased. Doc said her uncle is the designated head of the family. We're waiting on a long distance call to go through."

Bill nodded absently and turned back to the doctor, who was still holding his head between his hands and moaning disconsolately. "Gabe." He waited until the distraught man looked up at him. "Do you have any idea who this man was?"

"No."

"Based on the description of him—"

"It could fit a dozen men, Bill. A hundred."

He was right, so Bill didn't press him. "Mrs. Driscoll didn't mention having a visitor today?"

"He came asking about lodging. We used to rent out a room."

"Did she appear afraid, apprehensive, upset?"

Even before he finished the question, the doctor was saying, "No, no. She was her usual self. Maybe a little more subdued than usual, but I think she was sensitive to my mood."

"You were in a mood?"

"Distracted. I ran a rural route today. One of my patients had gone into labor. The baby was breech. Her sister was with her. She told me she'd assisted in breech births before, that she could handle it. I had several other people to see, so I left them.

"But I was worried about the danger to both the mother and child that a difficult delivery like that could be. It wasn't something I wanted to discuss with Mila, not with her being in her condition. As it is, she's nervous, this being her first."

"When's the baby due?"

"Two more months."

Bill took a deep breath. "So she read your mood and was a bit subdued. Anything else out of the ordinary?"

"No. We had supper. I went into my office and did some paperwork. She was crocheting."

"When did you last see her?"

"Around ten o'clock. We were getting ready for bed. I got an emergency call."

"The breech birth?"

"No." He cast a nervous look around the room. "Lefty's. One of the, uh, waitresses got worked over by a customer."

Bill took a visual survey of his deputies, who gave him various versions of a shrug. One said, "First we've heard of it."

"Gert wanted it kept quiet," Gabe said.

Lefty's was a roadhouse that had the best burgers within fifty miles. Also the best whores. Sheriff Amos couldn't vouch for that personally, but that was the general consensus known by everybody.

Lefty flipped burgers while his wife, Gert, oversaw the more lucrative side of the business. A ruckus of one sort or another was frequently incited by one of the "waitresses." Inevitably those incidents resulted in somebody bleeding.

Bill reasoned that Gert wanted this incident kept quiet so not to draw the law's attention to the place. Bill was well aware of the copious amount of bootleg liquor now being served in Lefty's back room. He would need to get out there and deal with that, but it took a back burner to Mrs. Driscoll's disappearance.

"You took care of the girl?" he asked Gabe.

"Yes."

"Is she going to be all right?"

"In time. Can all this wait?"

The doctor's patience was fraying. Bill had to keep him centered. "I've got to establish a time line, Gabe. What time did you get home and discover Mrs. Driscoll gone?"

"Late. On my way back into town, I stopped in to check on the breech birth. The baby had turned at the last minute. The delivery went fine. I checked out the mother and baby." His voice hitched. "While my own wife and baby—"

"Gabe." Bill spoke his name brusquely to keep him on track. "What time did you get home?"

"A little after one o'clock. I was exhausted, but hungry. I made a sandwich and ate it before going upstairs." He looked down at his hands as though they held the answers. "Mila wasn't in bed. Not in the bathroom. I turned the house upside down, searched the yard. When I couldn't find her anywhere, I called here. That's it." When he looked up at Bill, his chin was quivering. "She wouldn't have left on her own."

"I don't think so, either," Bill said, briefly laying his hand on Gabe's shoulder. "But let's not panic. Backtrack a little. Was she in bed when you left for the roadhouse?"

"Yes. She wanted to get up and send me off with a thermos of coffee, but I wouldn't let her. She needed the rest."

"When you got home was there any sign of a disturbance? Broken latch? Anything like that?"

"No."

Scotty chimed in. "We searched the house. Looked like nothing had been touched. No break-in. Led us to believe that Mrs. Driscoll let in whoever snatched her."

Gabe Driscoll lunged to his feet. "Are you implying that my wife invited—"

"He's not implying any such thing, Gabe," Bill said. "Sit down."

"I'm not going to sit down," he shouted. "What's wrong with all of you? Why are you just standing around? Why aren't you out looking for her? She could be hurt. Dying. She could be—"

Suddenly the door was pushed open with a lot of impetus behind it. When Bill saw who filled the doorway, he thought, *Shit!* Drolly, he said, "Mayor."

The Honorable Bernard Croft came inside and shut the door, bristling with self-importance. "Bill, what in hell is going on? Is it true? Mrs. Driscoll is missing?"

On a good day, Bill resented the city official's meddling in the affairs of his department. The mayor had a way of creating a hullabaloo even when one wasn't warranted, for his own aggrandizement.

Bill asked, "How'd you get wind of it?"

"Miss Eleanor Wise called me."

"For what purpose?"

With condescension, Croft replied, "For the purpose of saving Mrs. Driscoll from the man who abducted her, Bill."

"It hasn't been established that—"

"Have you identified him yet?"

"Until you blazed in and interrupted, I was compiling the facts of the case."

"How many facts do you need? Miss Wise described him to a tee."

Everyone in the room gaped at him, Bill included. "What do you know about him?"

"I know I mistrusted him on sight," he said. "I was reluctant to send him over there to your house," he said, addressing Gabe. "But the ad was right there in Hancock's window."

Gabe placed his fingertips to his forehead. "Ad? For the room? I'd forgotten it was there."

"He asked me for directions." Then, in a defensive tone, the mayor added, "If I hadn't told him, the next person he asked would have."

"We stopped taking in a boarder a while ago," Gabe said.

"I'm sure Mrs. Driscoll explained that to him, which means he had to look somewhere else for a place to stay." Bill shouldered past the mayor and reached for his hat. "Scotty, stay with Dr. Driscoll. The rest of you, let's go. Harold, bring a shotgun. Bernie, you can go on home."

"You'll need me to identify him." Seeing that Bill was about to object, the mayor added, "Unless you'd rather take along Miss Eleanor Wise."

NINE

———◦◉◦———

When Thatcher had fallen asleep, it never crossed his mind that he would be awakened by having a gun barrel jammed against his cheekbone.

A German infantryman somehow had survived the no-man's-land between his trench and the Americans', and intended to chalk up at least one doughboy to his credit.

Thatcher flung up his hand and slammed the barrel of the shotgun into the soldier's face. Flesh squished. Cartilage crunched. The man hollered.

Thatcher used that instant of the soldier's shock and pain to come up out of the bed and leap over the foot rail, where he barreled into another of the enemy, previously unseen. This one was stocky and strong, but Thatcher had enough momentum to drive him back against a wall.

From behind, another wrapped his arms around Thatcher, pulled him off the stocky one, and wrestled him facedown onto the floor.

But there were more than just these three. Two others joined the melee. The five of them surrounded him, all shouting and grasping at him from every side, trying to secure his arms and legs. One had a hand on the back of his head, holding it down, his cheek against the floor.

He fought them with savage will. They may shoot him, bayonet him, but he was not going to be taken prisoner by these bastards.

He managed to throw off the hand holding his head down and escaped the others' hold long enough to flip onto his back. Instinctually, he thrust his hands straight up into the face of the man straddling him. He had a thick mustache and a white cowboy hat.

Cowboy hat?

There was a five-pointed star badge pinned to his shirt. Engraved on it: Sheriff.

Jesus. The war was over. This wasn't France. He was back in Texas. The men surrounding him weren't German infantrymen. But he sure as hell had been in a life-or-death combat with them.

Before he could surrender himself, the backs of his hands were flattened to the floor on either side of his head. He took stock of the men encircling him. They were all breathing hard from having exerted themselves to restrain him. But even at that, he didn't know what he'd done to warrant their judgmental bearing. They stared down at him with unsettling disdain.

All were strangers save one. Thatcher recognized the gold pocket watch chain strung across his vest. He was the most heavyset. Thatcher figured it had been him he'd crashed into and rammed into the wall.

He was the first to speak. "That's him, all right."

"You're sure?" asked the one wearing the sheriff's badge. He planted his hand on the center of Thatcher's chest and pushed himself off him and to his feet. "What have you got to say for yourself, young man?"

"I woke up with a gun to my face. I was defending myself."

"Or resisting arrest."

"Arrest?"

The only light in the room spilled through the open doorway from the hall. These apparent lawmen cast long shadows across the bed and onto the ugly papered walls, enhancing the menace they conveyed. They meant business.

Thatcher repeated, "Arrest? What the hell for?"

"You're sure this is him, Bernie?"

"Positive," said the man with the gold watch fob. "I recognize him, and I recognize that bag. He had it with him."

He motioned toward Thatcher's army issue duffel bag, which he'd placed on the seat of the room's one chair after deciding last night that he could delay unpacking till morning.

"Gather up all his belongings, put them in the bag, and bring it," said the sheriff.

"You bet." One of the uniformed men turned away to do his bidding.

The sheriff said to another, "Question everyone in the house. See if anybody knows anything about him."

"Yes, sir." That man edged past the footboard and left the room.

Another moved forward and bent over Thatcher. His nose was bleeding. It and his eyes were beginning to swell. He was holding a shotgun, no doubt the one Thatcher had smacked into his face.

The man grinned with malice. "Thought you'd just drift into our town and haul off with one of our women? Think again, hotshot."

Then he flipped the shotgun and smacked the butt of it against Thatcher's skull. The blow hurt like hell and made his vision go dark and sparkly for a moment, but it didn't knock him out.

"Hey, go easy, Harold," the sheriff said. "We need him able to talk."

He extended Thatcher his hand and helped him up. The man who'd struck him—Harold—watched smugly as Thatcher struggled to regain his equilibrium. He made blurry eye contact with the man he recognized by his gold pocket watch. He also was leering with self-satisfaction.

"I'm Sheriff Bill Amos. What's your name?"

"Thatcher Hutton."

The sheriff repeated his name as though committing it to memory, then gathered up the clothes Thatcher had hung on a wall hook before going to bed and passed them to him. "Get dressed."

After he did, he was handcuffed. Then without further ado, the sheriff said, "Let's go."

Thatcher dug his heels in. "I have a right to know what you're arresting me for."

None of them seemed to think so. With the barrel of the shotgun against the base of his spine, he was prodded out of his room and into the hallway.

It seemed that he was the only boarder in the house who'd been taken unawares by the arrival of the posse. Everyone else had emerged from their rooms, all in pajamas or underwear, watching as the procession trooped down the two sets of stairs.

Few of them met Thatcher's gaze directly, but the smart aleck, Randy, who earlier had heckled the older man on the porch, winked at him. And when Thatcher passed the flashy dresser who'd introduced himself to Randy as Chester Landry, he gave Thatcher a sly, speculative look as though they shared a dirty secret.

The landlady stood at the front door, arms crossed over her bony chest, lips tightly pursed. "Don't expect no refund on your rent."

Once outside, the sheriff dispatched all the deputies except Harold to "rejoin the search." Thatcher asked, "The search for what?" but, again, he was ignored.

When Harold manhandled him into the officially marked automobile, he was showy with the shotgun, but careless with his gun belt, which was within easy reach of Thatcher's cuffed hands. However, to go for the deputy's pistol would be foolhardy. They would soon determine that they had the wrong man and release him. Until then, he'd go through the process without making more trouble for himself.

"Mayor, I guess you'll have to ride with us," the sheriff said, and the man Thatcher had met outside Hancock's store—the mayor?—climbed in along with them.

———

Harold drove them to a single-story limestone building that headquartered the sheriff's department. No one said anything during the brief ride. When they piled out of the car, the sheriff gripped Thatcher's arm just above his elbow. Together they entered the building.

It smelled of cigarettes and scorched coffee. The main room was crowded with the standard desks, chairs, and filing cabinets of any law enforcement office. Wall-mounted gun racks were impressively stocked. Two large maps, one of the county, the other of the state, were tacked to the far wall, along with numerous wanted posters and a notice of a missing cow.

Seated in side-by-side chairs were a man in a deputy's uniform and a man with a pale complexion, a dark five o'clock shadow, and wavy hair. The instant he saw Thatcher, he came hurtling toward him like he'd been shot from a cannon. If the deputy hadn't acted swiftly to restrain him, Thatcher thought for sure the man would have gone for his throat.

"Gabe!" the sheriff barked. "None of that business. Scotty, haul him back and keep him back."

"Yes, sir."

Though the man resisted, the deputy managed to wrestle him back into the chair.

The mayor went over to him and laid a hand on his shoulder. "Found him sleeping like a baby, Gabe. Can you believe that?"

Glaring at Thatcher, the man said, "Has he told you where she is?"

"Not yet, but he will." The mayor brusquely signaled the deputy, Scotty, up out of his chair, then the mayor sat down in it.

Thatcher, wanting to ask what the hell was going on, thought better of saying anything just yet. Harold shoved him down into a chair. He pulled a handkerchief from his pocket and wiped at the blood dripping from his now misshapen nose. One of his eyes had almost swollen shut.

Thatcher returned his glare with a mask of indifference and said, "I still owe you for the clout on the head."

The deputy gave him a fulminating look, but he walked away, slung Thatcher's duffel onto a table across the room, opened it, and began to paw through the contents.

No longer wearing his hat, Sheriff Amos drew up a chair and stationed it in front of Thatcher's, pulling it close enough that Thatcher could see the individual whiskers in his thick salt-and-pepper mustache. He said, "Son, save us all a lot of time and trouble. Tell us right now where Mrs. Driscoll is."

TEN

Laurel had been awake for most of the night, walking a fussy and feverish Pearl around the shack, trying to soothe her infant even as she fueled her resentment against Derby's selfish suicide, her present plight, her unknown future, and her absent father-in-law.

She had whipped herself into a high snit by the time she heard his truck clattering up the incline shortly before dawn. As soon as he cleared the door, she lit into him. "Where in the world have you been?"

He looked haggard and none too agreeable himself. "That's my business."

"It's my business, too! I was worried to death, afraid something had happened to you, in which case Pearl and I would have been stuck here. What have you been doing all night?"

She was accustomed to his being away most days, all day, often from sunup to sunset. This was the first time he had stayed away all night. Though she would rather die than own up to it, she had been afraid to be alone after the sun went down. With only a sliver of a moon, even the surrounding limestone hills had become indiscernible. She couldn't see the road from the shack. The darkness had been all encompassing, except for the lantern she had kept burning all night.

He plopped down on his seat on top of the barrel and rubbed his bad hip, wincing with discomfort. Mollifying her tone, she said, "I saved you some cornbread and bacon."

"I ain't hungry."

Laurel stood directly in front of him, making it impossible for him to ignore her. "I believe I deserve an explanation, Irv."

"You kept me occupied half the day teaching you how to drive. *Trying* to teach you how to drive."

The series of lessons had been intermittent, carried out during Pearl's brief naps between bouts of coughing. Laurel had never sat behind the steering wheel of an automobile. The sequence of necessary steps one had to perform with both hands and feet had been more difficult to coordinate than she'd anticipated. She was right-handed, so naturally she'd reached for the crank with that hand, when Irv had told her repeatedly to always use her left on the crank unless she wanted her "damn arm broke."

They had wound up being frustrated and fractious with each other.

She asked now, "Did you stay gone all night to punish me for not mastering how to drive?"

He gave her a withering look. "What do you take me for?"

"Then why didn't you come home?"

"I had a project to finish up."

"In the middle of the night?"

"How's Pearl?"

"She's sick, Irv. *What project?*"

"Putting up a wall inside an old house. It was just sold to a family moving here from Waco. The wife wanted to divide one room into two so that her daughter would have a space separate from her brothers."

"You're lying."

He glowered and looked guilty at the same time.

"You went into too much detail," she said. "Just like Derby did when he was lying."

He got up and headed for the other side of the room, but she caught him by the arm.

"What?" he asked, pulling his arm free.

"Do you have a . . . Is there a woman you see?"

He huffed a humorless laugh and continued on his way over to the sink where he pumped water into a glass and took a long drink. Laurel waited until he'd turned back to her before quietly apologizing. "I'm sorry. I had no right to ask that. It isn't any of my business."

He gave that same dry laugh. "I've loved only one woman in my lifetime. Derby's mama. And it damn near killed me to watch her die in misery. Don't go thinking I've got a romance going."

"No project, either, I'm guessing."

Looking done in, he returned to his seat and bent down to unlace his shoes. "No, I had a project all right." He looked up at her from beneath his bushy eyebrows. "That fellow that came here this morning."

"What about him?"

"I don't know, and that's why I'm worried. What the hell was he doing way out here?"

"I told you, he—"

"I know what he claimed, but I ain't buying it. I went around tonight, checked in with people I know, asked if they'd seen him."

"What people?"

"People."

She let his curt reply pass. "Had anyone in town seen him?"

"Nobody I talked to."

"He probably hitched a ride on the highway and is long gone."

"Maybe," he grumbled. "But him snooping around gave me an itch I can't scratch."

"What snooping? He was lost and asking for directions, that's all."

He gave a snort and focused his attention on Pearl, who Laurel had been holding against her shoulder, rocking gently. She'd slept through their conversation.

"You say the baby's sick?"

"She's running a fever again. I want to take her back to the doctor."

"I saw him tonight."

She stopped her swaying motion and looked at Irv with surprise. "You went to see Dr. Driscoll?"

"Naw, naw. He was at the roadhouse, you know, the place where I pick up burgers on occasion?"

"You told me it isn't a respectable place."

"It ain't. But Lefty fries a damn good burger, and he's also a fountain of information. Knows everything happening in and around here. I went to inquire about our visitor today."

"He didn't know anything?"

"Said he didn't. But he was dealing with a problem of his own. One of his, uh, girls got crosswise with a customer. He beat her up pretty bad."

Understanding dawned. "It's that kind of place?"

"It's full service, all right." Irv shook his finger at her. "Don't you ever darken the door of it. It draws all sorts of lowlifes. The girls who work there . . . Well, let's just say that most are experienced and tough enough to take care of theirselves. Lefty's wife, Gert, is the meanest of them all. When she saw her girl there, beat up and bleeding, she went after Wally—the guy who hurt her—with a meat cleaver.

"Lefty had to literally peel Gert off him. He turned him over to his cousins—them Johnsons cavort in a pack—then tossed the whole sorry lot of them out. They called Doc Driscoll to come patch up the young lady. By the time he got there, Lefty had calmed Gert down. Some. It was quite a scene."

Laurel listened with incredulity to Irv's account of the brawl and marveled at the matter-of-fact way in which he'd related it. She marveled even more to think of Dr. Driscoll's being in such a place.

During her one brief meeting with the doctor, she had thought him to be wholly professional, even a bit cool. Of course, she had been frantic with worry over Pearl, so, by comparison, anyone would have come across as composed and somewhat detached. She couldn't imagine that man tending to a patient in a brothel.

She said, "Despite his late night, I hope he maintains office hours tomorrow. I can't drive well enough yet to go into town. You'll have to take us."

"Sure, sure. Whenever you want to go."

"First thing after breakfast." She hesitated, then asked if he had any fix-it jobs lined up.

"A couple. Why?"

"I was thinking that as long as we're in town, and if Pearl isn't too fussy, we could look around, see what might be for rent."

He gave her a crooked grin. "You're not as smart as you think. I wasn't lying about the old house. I knew of it, sought out the landlord and talked him into meeting me there after he finished his supper. It's a big ol' rambling place, but it's stood empty for years on account of the back of it is built into a wall of limestone."

"Built into the rock?"

He shrugged. "Wouldn't take much to make it habitable. I could do the work myself. But if you don't like it—"

"The least I can do is take a look. Thank you, Irv."

"Don't thank me till you've seen it."

The house couldn't be more of a nightmare than this shack she was living in. She appreciated that her father-in-law had listened to the concerns she'd raised with him this morning, and had taken her ultimatum seriously enough to act on it.

In gratitude, she smiled at him. "You look worn out. Try to get some rest." She then retreated behind the partition with Pearl, who had become restless again and was mewling pitiably.

ELEVEN

———◆———

Thatcher repeated the sheriff's confounding words. "Tell you where Mrs. Driscoll is?" He looked over at the man who'd tried to attack him. "Are you Dr. Driscoll?"

"Yes, you son of a bitch. And I want to know what you've done with my wife."

"Nothing but talked to her. Why? What's happened?"

Sheriff Amos said, "She's missing."

"*Missing?*"

"It's feared she was abducted from her home sometime between ten o'clock p.m. and one o'clock a.m."

Thatcher glanced at the wall clock. It was going on five. He looked at each man in the room in turn, and the reason for their judgmental glowers took on meaning. The hairs on the back of his neck stood on end. "That's why I'm here? You think I know something about it?"

"You were seen talking with her today on her porch."

"I said as much. I was looking for a room to rent. You can ask him." He tipped his head toward the mayor.

"Mayor Croft told us that he gave you directions to their house."

"A decision I regret," the man boomed.

The sheriff, looking irritated, turned his head partially toward the mayor and said in an undertone, "Bernie, I'll handle this." Coming back around to Thatcher, he said, "Where'd you get the bruises, Mr. Hutton?"

"Your deputy Harold there poked me in the face with that pump-action."

Harold, who was still rifling through his belongings, shot him a dirty look over his shoulder.

"Not the bruise on your cheek," the sheriff said, "the one on your noggin."

"Oh." He reached up with his cuffed hands and touched the discolored goose egg at his temple. "I jumped off a freight train, had a hard landing, rolled down an incline."

The sheriff tilted his head and eyed him speculatively. "When was that?"

"This morning. Early. Before dawn."

"Where?"

"Eight, nine miles southeast of here. The middle of nowhere. I walked to town."

"You were bumming a ride?"

Given the circumstances, he felt that admitting to one malfeasance would be to his advantage. "Yes."

"Where were you headed?"

"Amarillo. Or as close to there as the railroad goes these days."

"What's up there?"

He explained his long-time connection to the Hobson Ranch. "I was making my way home, back to the ranch and my job."

The sheriff took it all in, then said, "If you've got a job waiting for you in the Panhandle, why'd you jump off the freight train way down here?"

He came clean about the poker game and the ill will it had created with those sharing the boxcar. "They were sore losers."

"Did you cheat?" Sheriff Amos asked.

"No. I have a knack."

"For winning at cards?"

"For reading people."

The sheriff glanced over at the others as though to verify that he'd heard correctly. Thatcher could tell that they were all skeptical of his boast, as well as of his story, so he didn't volunteer anything else.

When the sheriff came back to him, he said, "What happened when you got to the Driscolls' house?"

"I took one look and knew it was out of my reach." He told them about Mrs. Driscoll's coming out onto the porch and catching him as he was about to leave, and saying she wanted to thank him for coming by. "She called me up to the porch and brought out some fresh shortbread."

The doctor said in a strained voice, "At least that much is the truth. Mila baked it this morning. We ate some after supper."

"She gave me a second piece to take with me," Thatcher said. "I wrapped it in my handkerchief. It left a butter stain. You can check it. Right pocket."

He raised his cuffed hands, inviting the sheriff to withdraw his hand-kerchief from the pocket of his jacket. When he shook out the folded cloth, a few crumbs fell to the floor. The greasy spot was clearly visible.

"That doesn't mean he didn't go back later and do her harm," the mayor said.

The sheriff frowned. "Doesn't mean he did, either."

Recalling Mrs. Driscoll's friendly smile and hospitality, it bothered Thatcher to think that she was in a direful situation of any kind. "Mrs. Driscoll was as nice a lady as I ever met. We chatted there on the porch while I ate the shortbread. When I took my leave, she suggested I try to find a room at the boardinghouse. I thanked her and left. If something bad has happened to her, you're wasting your time talking to me. You ought to be out beating the bushes, looking for her."

Driscoll surged to his feet. "Or maybe we'll beat the truth out of you." Hands fisted, he made a lunge for Thatcher and took a wild swing.

Sheriff Amos shot out of his chair. "Dammit, Gabe. Sit down, or it'll be *you* I'm locking up."

The mayor took hold of the doctor's arm and dragged him back to his seat. "Can't say as I blame you, Gabe," he said, casting a glare in Thatcher's direction. "It's clear he's lying."

Thatcher didn't give a damn about that blowhard's opinion. The distraught husband was another matter entirely. "I'm telling you the truth, Dr. Driscoll. What call would I have had to repay Mrs. Driscoll's kindness by hurting her?"

The mayor answered for him. "I think you took advantage of her *kindness* and got her to open the door of her house to you tonight."

"I didn't," Thatcher said, but he addressed the denial to the sheriff, not to the mayor.

Harold came stalking across the room. When Thatcher saw what he was bringing with him, his stomach sank. It was a set of postcards that he had brought home from France. Harold had removed the string that bound them.

Smirking at Thatcher, he passed the cards to Sheriff Amos. "Found these in the bottom of his bag."

Each of the cards featured a photograph of a half-naked woman in a provocative pose. The sheriff fanned through them without comment or reaction, then formed a neat stack of them and set it facedown on the nearby desk.

Thatcher didn't offer any apology or explanation for them. Was there a man in the room who wouldn't enjoy taking a peek?

The sheriff leaned back in his chair and tugged at the corner of his mustache while he studied Thatcher. Thatcher wished he knew what was going through the lawman's mind. Apparently, so did the mayor. Above the loud ticking of the wall clock's brass pendulum, he prompted him. "Bill?"

Seeming to be in no hurry to respond, the sheriff waited another fifteen seconds, then indicated the torn shoulder seam on Thatcher's coat. "How'd that happen?"

"One of the men on the train made a grab for me."

"You really believe he jumped off a freight train, Bill?"

That from the mayor, whom the sheriff again ignored. He said, "You could've broken your fool neck. Why didn't you stay on the train and fight it out?"

Thatcher glanced around. All of them were poised, waiting for an answer. He addressed the sheriff. "I did."

"Did what?"

"Fought it out."

"Three against one?"

"Wasn't my choice."

The sheriff reached for his hand and turned it palm up. "How'd you get that cut?"

"One of the men came at me with a knife. I was defending myself."

"Against Mrs. Driscoll," the mayor said.

The sheriff didn't acknowledge the remark. "Back there in your room, you came at us like a vandal."

"I told you. I woke up with a shotgun to my head. I reacted."

"Violently," the mayor said.

The sheriff kept his attention on Thatcher. "Three against one. Five against one. Where'd you learn to fight like that?"

"A bunkhouse."

"He's obviously a dangerous individual, Bill."

"I'm not a danger to a woman," Thatcher fired back at the mayor. "Sure as hell not one in the family way."

The doctor choked back a sob and held his fist against his mouth to contain others.

Thatcher looked directly at the sheriff. "Look, hopping the freight? Guilty. I was just trying to get home, and the army didn't pay me enough to get there. I wasn't looking to fight the men on the train, but they would have killed me if I hadn't fought back. Fought y'all because I've been to war and temporarily mistook you for the enemy.

"The last time I saw Mrs. Driscoll was midafternoon as she was bidding me goodbye. That's the God's truth. I would never raise a hand to a woman or harm one in any way if I could help it."

He flashed to how he'd startled Laurel Plummer as she was hanging out her wash, but decided not to mention that encounter. Approaching two women who were strangers to him, on the same day, might compound their suspicions.

"What did you do after leaving the Driscolls' house?" the sheriff asked.

Thatcher told him about renting the room, then seeking out Mr. Barker. "He hired me."

"As a mechanic?"

"No. He's paying me to train a horse."

The mayor guffawed. "That horse in the paddock behind Barker's place?"

"If you're referring to a bay stallion, yes," Thatcher said.

"He's a brute, Bill. Others have tried. No one can get near him."

"I can," Thatcher said, still speaking directly to the sheriff and trying to ignore the butt-in. "That'll be easy enough to check with Mr. Barker. By the time I left his place, the sun was going down. I stopped by a secondhand store he'd recommended, but it was closed. I got back to the boardinghouse a little before seven o'clock. After supper, I went out on the porch and sat for a spell. A dozen men can vouch for that.

"Mr. Henry Hobson would vouch for me, too. When I left for the army, the ranch didn't have telephone service yet. It was out too far. They may have gotten it by now. If not, by hook or crook you could get word to Mr. Hobson." As an afterthought, he added, "When you do, ask him to please send me my gear. It's locked in a trunk in the bunkhouse. He'll know."

He forced himself to relax his shoulders and sit back in his chair. He'd been as honest and earnest as he knew how to be.

But they locked him up anyway.

For the next two hours, heated discussion filtered through a door that separated the main room from the cell block. Thatcher had been placed in the last cell. He was too far away to catch all the words, but he heard enough to piece together what was happening.

The mayor—Bernie Croft was his name—overstepped the duties

of his office. Sheriff Amos resented his interference and told him so, although it did no good.

Dr. Driscoll cycled between frustration, rage, and despair.

The highway department was alerted to be on the lookout for Mila Driscoll. It would be a hostage situation; she couldn't drive.

It was suggested that the Texas Rangers be brought into the investigation, but none seemed enthusiastic about the prospect and postponed making a decision.

Boats had been launched to search every body of water within a twenty-five-mile radius.

Volunteers on horseback and in motor vehicles, many with dogs, had converged on the sheriff's office, creating chaos and a lot of noise, until they were organized into groups and dispatched to search assigned areas.

Soon after their departure, the deputy named Scotty brought Thatcher a cup of coffee, a biscuit, and a sausage patty from a nearby café. Thatcher thanked him, but the deputy didn't acknowledge it.

Thatcher heard his name repeated hundreds of times beyond the door, but hadn't always been able to discern the context in which he was mentioned. He could guess, though.

On paper, he looked like a stranger of limited means, who'd wandered into town after having been in a fight, and was seen being friendly with a woman who was now missing. It added up.

It adds up had become the mayor's refrain. But the sheriff had been reluctant to act on a supposition, especially since they didn't have a witness to a crime or one iota of evidence on which to base a charge against Thatcher Hutton.

"We don't even know that a crime has been committed," Thatcher had heard the sheriff exclaim.

That had been followed by the doctor's hoarse shout, "Then where is she?"

Now, as Thatcher lay on the bunk staring up at the low ceiling, he heard the telephone ring, but it had been ringing often, so he didn't place any importance on this call until Scotty reappeared and instructed him to put his hands, wrists together, through the bars of the cell.

After being cuffed, he was guided back into the main room. He knew he must look disheveled, but he had fared the intervening hours better than Dr. Driscoll had. There were dark circles under his eyes. His unknotted necktie lay against his chest, which seemed to have been scooped out like a watermelon. He sat stoop-shouldered, his listless hands dangling between his knees, vacant eyes staring at the floor between his shoes.

Thatcher had seen men fresh from a days-long battle looking just like that, like they'd been to hell and back, and were wondering if having survived it was for the better or worse.

Hulking Harold was absent.

The mayor no longer looked smug, but rather like he'd eaten a bad tamale.

Sheriff Amos merely looked tired. He had one hip hitched on a corner of the desk with his nameplate on it. He smoothed his mustache as Thatcher came in. "Mr. Hutton, I just got off the phone with the Potter County sheriff. I explained our situation here. Telephone operator told him there's no line that goes out to the ranch, so he's sending a man to track down Mr. Hobson. He said it's a far piece out there, so it will take a while before we hear back."

Thatcher nodded.

"In the meantime, Fred Barker backed up what you'd told us. So did several men at the boardinghouse. One had noted that you left the porch and went inside at around nine-thirty. He remembered because he used the bathroom right after you and saw you go into your room. No one saw or heard you sneaking out after that."

Thatcher shifted his feet. "So I can go."

"Well," the sheriff sighed, "seeing as we——"

Suddenly the door flew open and Laurel Plummer burst in, clutching a baby to her chest. Wild-eyed, she scanned the room, drawing up short when she saw Thatcher. "*You?*"

The old man who followed her inside looked Thatcher over, noticed the handcuffs, and harrumphed, "Didn't I tell you he was up to no good?"

TWELVE

———◆———

Considering the short amount of time that Thatcher had planned to be in Foley, he had doubted he would ever see Laurel Plummer again. He certainly never would have predicted their next encounter would be under these circumstances, him in handcuffs, her looking like a woman on the verge of hysteria.

The dress she had on was only a little better than the one she'd been wearing yesterday morning. One of her shoelaces had come untied. Her hat looked as though it might have been an afterthought, put on to conceal how untidy and insecure the bun on her nape was.

The baby was alternately crying and making strangling sounds.

Thatcher guessed the old man who'd followed her in was her father-in-law. Yesterday, all Thatcher had seen of him was his shotgun. He didn't have it with him today, but he was squinting at Thatcher with malevolence. He asked the room at large, "Wha'd y'all get him for?"

The sheriff blinked with surprise. "You know Mr. Hutton?"

"Seen him."

"Where?"

"He came up to our place yesterday morning. He—"

Laurel said, "Never mind that," and rushed across the room to Dr. Driscoll. "Thank God you're here."

The Plummers' sudden and disruptive entrance had roused the doctor from his stupor. He stood up unsteadily. "Mrs.....?"

"Plummer. My baby, Pearl. Remember? You treated her for croup a week and a half ago. I gave her the cough syrup, but it hasn't helped. She's worse. You've got to help her."

He seemed at a loss. "I——"

"We went to your house," she went on. "No one answered the door. An old lady who lives across the street saw us and came over. She told us that your wife disappeared last night. I'm sure she got that wrong, but she said that you would probably be here. You've got to examine Pearl." She'd spoken so rapidly and breathlessly, she had to pause and inhale deeply before adding, "Please."

The doctor didn't react, only looked at her blankly, as though he hadn't sensed her anxiety or understood a word she'd said.

The mayor interceded. "Mrs. Plummer, was it? I'm Mayor Croft. Dr. Driscoll is indisposed. He's not seeing patients this morning. I could recommend several fine physicians who——"

"I tried that," Irv said, interrupting. "She was bent on finding Doc Driscoll on account of he'd treated Pearl before. There was no sayin' no to her. The baby's in a bad way."

"She can hardly draw breath." Laurel looked pleadingly at the doctor, but, as before, he seemed to be in a trance. With a soft cry of desperation, she turned away from him and took in the scene as though just now grasping the significance of the situation she'd barged in on.

"His wife really has disappeared?" She addressed the question to Sheriff Amos.

"Last night. A search is underway, but currently Mrs. Driscoll's whereabouts are unknown."

"The neighbor lady said she'd been abducted."

The mayor loudly cleared his throat. "We're trying to ascertain that. From Mr. Hutton."

When Laurel's gaze moved to Thatcher, embarrassment bloomed hotly inside his chest. She focused on the handcuffs, then looked up into his eyes with misgiving. "I thought surely the old lady was senile, talking nonsense."

Thatcher said quietly, "You told me where to look for the advertisement. I went to the address on the card."

"It was Dr. Driscoll's house?"

"I was seen talking to Mrs. Driscoll."

Laurel's father-in-law made a grunting sound, as though this news was confirmation of the low opinion of Thatcher that he'd already formed.

The sheriff said, "Mrs. Plummer?" She shifted her attention away from Thatcher and back to Bill Amos. "We met on the occasion of your husband's demise. It was such a difficult time for you, I wasn't sure you would remember."

"Of course I do."

He nodded solemnly, then gestured toward Thatcher. "What can you tell me about Mr. Hutton?"

She scooted the baby up onto her shoulder and tried to shush her. "Nothing, except what Irv already told you. He showed up at our place yesterday."

"What time was that?"

She thought on it. "Around eleven, but it could have been thirty minutes either side of that."

"How did he get there?"

"On foot."

"From which direction?"

"I didn't see, but I guess from the south. The railroad is in that direction from us, and he told me he'd jumped off a freight train."

"Did you believe him?"

She hesitated, then said, "It made no difference to me if he was lying or not."

"It did to me," Irv said. "Poking around where he didn't belong."

The sheriff turned to him. "He poked around?"

"No, he didn't," Laurel said, giving her father-in-law a look of asperity. "He asked for a drink of water. I gave him one, and told him how to get to town, then sent him on his way." The baby began to cough. Laurel patted her on the back. "That's all I know, Sheriff Amos. I've got to get Pearl to a doctor."

"A couple more questions. You told Mr. Hutton about the Driscolls' room for rent?"

"I didn't know it was theirs. I just remembered seeing the notice in Hancock's window, and mentioned it to him when he asked if I knew of somewhere he could stay." She cut a glance at Thatcher, then said to the sheriff, "This really has nothing at all to do with me."

Without a blink, the sheriff continued. "Altogether, how long was he there?"

"No more than a few minutes. Ten maybe."

"Did he look beat up, like he'd been in a fight?"

"He had a bump on his head. His hand was wrapped in a hand-kerchief. The shoulder seam of his coat was ripped."

"What was his demeanor, Mrs. Plummer? How did he act toward you?"

She took another quick look at Thatcher, and he figured this was where she would tell them about the rooster's attack and what had happened after. But she didn't relate any of that.

She said, "He didn't act any particular way. He thanked me for the water and the information and left." She pressed her palm against the baby's forehead. "I must go now and find another doctor."

"Doc Perkins is right down the street," Irv said, opening the door. "Come on, Laurel."

She walked quickly to the door, then stopped on the threshold and turned back and addressed the doctor. "When I brought Pearl to your office, Mrs. Driscoll treated me kindly. I'm very sorry for what you're going through. I hope you find her soon. And that she's safe."

Her eyes connected with Thatcher's for a split second, and then she was gone.

After they left, the doctor's knees folded and he dropped back into the chair. The mayor said, "Gabe is exhausted. He can't even stand, much less think straight. He should be allowed to go home for a while and rest."

"No, no," he said. "I want to stay here, be here, in case something...something..." Unable to finish the thought, he rubbed his forehead.

"You see?" the mayor said. "I'll see him home."

"Scotty will see him home," Bill Amos said.

The mayor seemed about to argue, but, instead, bent down and placed his arm around Driscoll's shoulders. In a murmur usually reserved for priests and undertakers, he began reassuring the doctor that he was going to stay on top of things.

The sheriff turned to his deputy and spoke in an undertone, but loudly enough for Thatcher to hear. "Don't let anybody talk to him. There'll probably be a parade of church ladies bearing food. You take it at the door and thank them on behalf of both the doc *and* Mrs. Driscoll. If they start asking questions, say you're not at liberty to talk about an ongoing investigation, and that if you do, I'll have your ass chicken fried and served on a platter. And I will, Scotty."

"I understand, sir."

"Anything turns up, I'll come directly there and inform Gabe of it myself. Anything anyone else tells you, regard as rumor or fabrication."

"Yes, sir."

"Get to it."

Scotty crossed the room and, after nudging the mayor aside, took Driscoll gently by the arm, lifted him up, and guided him toward the door. The doctor went along without objection. He looked like a sleepwalker.

As Scotty pulled the door closed behind them, Mayor Croft

hitched his chin in Thatcher's direction. "What are we going to do with him?"

"You're not going to do anything with him. He's going back to his cell, and I'm going to make some calls."

"To whom?"

"To whomever I damn well please, Bernie. This is my desk, my office, my department, and my investigation." Reining in his anger, he said, "Thank you for your help this morning." He motioned toward Thatcher. "Identifying the suspect."

"It was the least I could do. To my knowledge, nothing like this has ever happened in Foley."

"You can't say that yet because we don't know what's happened."

"I want to be apprised as soon as—"

"News has a way of getting to you, Bernie. I'm sure you'll be among the first to hear of any developments."

"I'm depending on you to see that I do."

The sheriff gave a nod that could have been taken either as acquiescence or could have signified nothing at all, and Thatcher figured the latter.

With self-importance, the mayor headed for the door, but when he came abreast of Thatcher, he stopped. Meeting him eye to eye, he said in a low and sinister voice, "I don't care who you mistook me for. If you ever put your hands on me again, you *won't* live to regret it. Do we understand each other?"

Thatcher met his threatening stare head-on. "Oh, I think so."

Croft held his gaze as he said, "I'll be checking in, Bill," then he strode to the door and left.

The sheriff's relief over seeing him go was obvious, even though that left him alone with Thatcher, who'd been referred to as "dangerous" and "the suspect."

He lifted the metal ring that held the keys to the jail cells off a nail on the wall. "You gonna give me any trouble, Mr. Hutton?"

"No. But I could use the toilet." He'd seen a door at the far end of the corridor marked as such.

"Can't afford you the privacy when I'm the only one here. There's a chamber pot under your bunk." He signaled for Thatcher to precede him.

Once back inside his cell with the door locked, Thatcher stuck his hands between the bars. The sheriff removed the handcuffs.

Thatcher said, "I don't know what's happened to Mrs. Driscoll. I had no part in it."

The sheriff backed up and propped himself against the wall opposite the cell. "Why'd you choose that ratty old shack of Irv Plummer's to stop at?"

"It was the first place I'd come to. I needed a drink of water and directions to the nearest town."

"You ever been to Foley before?"

"No, and I wasn't headed here. Like I told you, I was aiming for the Hobson ranch. But I needed a town to get myself together, earn some money before continuing on."

"You had your poker winnings."

"They didn't amount to much."

"They did to the men who lost."

"If they couldn't afford to lose, then they shouldn't've been gambling."

The sheriff snuffled. "True enough." He studied Thatcher as he thoughtfully stroked his mustache. "Irv seemed to have taken a dislike to you. How come?"

"I have no idea."

"Y'all didn't have a run-in of some kind yesterday?"

"I never even saw him. When I got there, Mrs. Plummer was in the yard hanging out her wash. I didn't know for certain that anyone else was around until he called to her from inside the house. He didn't show himself."

Deliberately he neglected to tell the sheriff about the shotgun, although he couldn't say where his reluctance to mention it came from. "Do you think the baby will be all right?"

"My boy had croup a couple of times when he was little. Sounds worse than it is."

"What's Plummer do for a living?"

"He's a handyman. Drives an old truck."

"It was parked in the yard."

"It's full of tools and gadgets, jangling around. You can hear him coming from a mile away. He's quite a character."

"I gathered." Thatcher debated whether or not to leave it there, but decided to be up-front. "I know that Mrs. Plummer's husband died by his own hand just a few months ago. Mrs. Driscoll told me." He recounted how that conversation had come about. "She didn't go into detail. Told me only that he shot himself."

"He put a Colt forty-five under his chin and pulled the trigger."

Jesus. Thatcher hoped Mrs. Plummer hadn't been the one who found him. "That was an awful thing to do to his family. He leave a note?"

"No." The sheriff lowered his head and stared at a spot on the floor between him and the cell. "When I questioned Mrs. Plummer about it, she told me her husband had come back from the war a different man, that he never recovered from his service over there, and that's what drove him to kill himself."

"It can happen."

The sheriff kept his head down but lifted his gaze to Thatcher, looking at him from under a pair of eyebrows that matched his salt-and-pepper mustache. "Did it happen to you? See, Mr. Hutton, I recognize the buttons on your coat. My boy wore the same uniform."

He lowered his gaze to the floor again. "I know the name of the town in France where he's buried. Can't pronounce it, but I can't see it matters much. I doubt I'll ever get there.

"And, anyway, if I were to, there's a bunch of Company B boys all buried together. They couldn't really tell one from the other, they said. Made separate graves...Well, impractical, I guess."

He coughed behind his fist. Thatcher heard him swallow. Then he raised his head and looked Thatcher in the eye. "Were you witness to atrocities like that?"

"Damn near every day. Even after the armistice, I was left over there to clean up messes that folks who haven't seen can't imagine."

"You didn't feel the effects of seeing things like mass graves stuffed with unidentified body parts?"

"Yes, Mr. Amos, I felt the effects, all right. But they didn't make me lose my mind, or tempt me to blow my brains out, or drive me to abduct women." His hands closed around two of the bars. "Seeing all that death only made me determined to get back home and go on living out the rest of my life as best I can."

Their gazes stayed locked for a time. The sheriff was the first to break away. He turned and started down the corridor. "Try to get some shut-eye."

"How long can you hold me without charging me?"

"I don't think you'll have to worry about it."

"With all due respect, I do worry about it."

Bill Amos stopped and turned. He subjected Thatcher to a long, assessing stare. "There's a lot about you I'm trying to figure out. But it's occurred to me to wonder why you would spend ten minutes or more with a young woman who you thought was all alone way out yonder, and leave politely without laying a hand on her, then walk five more miles, on a hot day that topped eighty, meet another woman who's seven months pregnant, and decide to sneak back in the dead of night and carry her off. On foot."

THIRTEEN

———⊰⊙⊱———

Laurel spent an anxious hour pacing the waiting area of the doctor's office, trying to comfort Pearl. Her coughing spasms were relieved only when she could draw enough breath to wail.

When they finally were called into the examination room, the elderly physician peered at them through his wire-rimmed eyeglasses and asked, "What seems to be the problem?"

Laurel wanted to smack him.

With a maddening lack of urgency, he went about examining the screaming baby while asking Laurel pertinent questions. In the hope of moving things along, she kept her answers brief and precise.

He listened to Pearl's chest and, when he removed the earpieces of the stethoscope, asked if she'd been born early.

"By three weeks."

He ruminated on that, then used a medicine dropper to dose Pearl with powdered aspirin dissolved in water. "This will bring down her fever. And this," he said as he similarly administered a dose of sweet smelling syrup, "will help with her cough." He gave Laurel a small bottle of the cough remedy and a packet of the aspirin to take with her.

Irv had waited in the car. When he saw her coming from the building, he got out to help her and Pearl into the passenger seat. "Is it the Spanish flu?" he asked. "Pneumonia?"

"He didn't say."

He tilted his head and looked at Pearl, who was lying in Laurel's arms. "She seems better already."

"He gave her paregoric."

He frowned. "That's dope, ya know. You'd've been just as well off funneling some whiskey down her throat."

Laurel agreed. Her mother had given her paregoric whenever she'd suffered a stomachache or diarrhea. However, rather than easing her symptoms, the opiate had always nauseated her, making her throw up.

She didn't like the idea of the stuff, and would be very stingy with the doses she gave Pearl for her cough. Now, however, she was grateful that the baby was no longer struggling for every breath. Pearl's eyes were blinking sleepily, and sleep would be as good a remedy as anything.

Laurel kissed her daughter's forehead, then whispered to her, "Things are going to get better, Pearl. I'm going to make them better. I promise." After Irv had started the car and gotten behind the wheel, she said, "I want to see that house for rent."

<hr />

As they drove through town, Irv reopened the subject of the scene in the sheriff's office. "That fella Hutton. What do you think?"

"I don't think anything."

"I mean in connection with the doc's wife gone missing."

Rather than answer his question, she asked, "How was the mayor involved? Is he a close friend of the Driscolls?"

"Naw, he just sticks his big nose into everybody's business."

"Well, this is his business. He's a public official, and a woman in his city went missing overnight."

"You think that Hutton took her?"

"I don't know, Irv." Her tone reflected how tired she was of his seeming obsession with Mr. Hutton. Since he'd ventured into their yard yesterday, no matter what topic they were talking about, Irv always circled back to him. Every time she'd asked what had made him so suspicious of the man, his answer was usually the same. "Just don't trust a tall, dark stranger who drops out of nowhere."

As now, he muttered, "Don't trust him as far as I can throw him."

He would trust Mr. Hutton even less if he knew that he'd placed his hands on Laurel's arms and held her against him. She'd taken his hand!

By doing so, she'd given him an opportunity to force himself on her if he'd been of a mind to. No, they had to be wrong to suspect him of molesting Mrs. Driscoll in any way. He'd done nothing in the manner that Sheriff Amos's question had suggested, nothing to make her fear that he meant her harm, or that his intentions were dishonorable.

The worst he'd done to her was to make it impossible for her not to think about those moments when they had touched. She feared that seeing him again, even in those circumstances, had prolonged the time it was going to take for her to forget them.

⁂

The house was as Irv had described: rambling. It appeared to have been broken apart at one point and pieced back together incorrectly. Even more uniquely, it backed up to a sheer wall of limestone.

But it was actually better than Laurel had expected. "Can we see inside?"

Irv wasn't completely sold on the idea of moving into town, but he turned off the truck's motor, grumbling, "Landlord said he'd leave the key under the porch in a sardine tin."

They found the key. The front door's hinges screeched when Irv pushed it open. The interior smelled like mildew with an undertone of dead mouse, but Laurel reasoned that if the front windows were open, the southerly breeze would dispel the odor.

Flanking the central hallway were a parlor to the left and a staircase to the right. Laurel stepped into the parlor. The wallpaper was shabby and stained, but it had tall windows and a pretty Victorian carved wood spandrel that demarcated the parlor from the dining room. A door on the far side of it led into the kitchen.

"The icebox is the old-fashioned kind," Irv said. "You'd have to have ice delivered. But the stove's electric." Gesturing to the rusty faucets in the sink, he added, "It's tapped into the city water. You won't have to pump no more."

"Is there a bathroom?"

Irv led her to it. Obviously a late addition, it was tucked under the staircase. The fixtures needed a good scouring, but she was delirious at the thought of no longer having to use an outhouse.

"Upstairs?"

"Two bedrooms and a sleeping porch. Some of these steps are rotted, so be careful."

The front bedroom faced south. Sunlight shone through the dirty windows, from which she could see the tallest buildings of downtown. Having been isolated for months, the thought of having a view of nearby civilization was comforting. She could make this a pleasant room for Pearl and her to share.

The sleeping porch was a screened-in, long and narrow space. She would have to think on how best to utilize it.

Beyond it was a small, claustrophobic room that had only one east-facing window. The ceiling slanted downward to meet the far wall. "This'll do me fine," Irv said. "I don't require much space."

"But you'll have to climb the stairs," Laurel said. "That won't be good for your hip. I have a better idea."

She led him back downstairs and into the kitchen. "Build a wall on this end of the kitchen to enclose the keeping room. It has a window. It would easily convert into a bedroom."

He scowled. "Where'd you get that notion?"

"From you. You shouldn't have lied about dividing one room into two for a family from Waco."

He swore under his breath, but Laurel could tell that the idea appealed to him. The new room would give him access to the rest of the house without having to use the stairs. The back door leading from the kitchen to the outside would also enable him to come and go freely.

She pointed that out to him, then stood by waiting hopefully as he mulled it over. For an eternity. "If it's a matter of money—"

"It ain't."

"I plan to pitch in."

"I told you, I ain't destitute."

"I still have my money."

"Keep it. I owe you this."

"How so?"

"It was my boy who skipped out on you."

Whenever the subject of money came up, they argued, and Irv was cranky for days after. She supposed it was a blow to his pride for her to question him about finances.

But she suspected his obstinance on the matter went deeper than that. The guilt he felt over leaving Derby in an orphanage weighed even more heavily on him since the suicide. It was too late for him to make restitution to his son. Instead, he had dedicated himself to taking care of Pearl and her.

She was strongly opposed to the idea of being accountable or indebted to anyone, even to her well-meaning father-in-law, but she didn't want to scotch renting the house by quarreling with him now. "When can we move in?"

He hooked his thumbs under his suspenders and ran them up and down as he took a slow look around.

"Well?" Laurel said.

"I'm taking stock."

"You're stalling."

"We don't have any furniture."

"We don't have any now!" she exclaimed, causing Pearl to stir. "Why are you so opposed to this, Irv?"

"I ain't."

"Good. We'll move in tomorrow."

Before he could say anything further, she turned on her heel and left through the front door. By the time he had followed, locked the door, and returned the key to its hiding place, she was in the car—in the driver's seat.

He hobbled around to the passenger side and opened the door. "What do you think you're doing?"

"Pearl's asleep. You can hold her while I drive."

"You need a lot more practice."

"I'll have five miles' worth after driving home. Now get in."

FOURTEEN

—◦◉◦—

Thatcher was confined to the jail cell throughout the day, although after deputies returned, he was allowed two visits to the lavatory. Harold grudgingly provided him with a bar of soap and a towel so he was able to wash up.

He heard people entering and leaving the building where briefings were held in the main room, but for most of the day the door at the end of the hall had remained closed, so he was unable to hear everything that was being said.

The telephone rang frequently. He supposed updates on the search for Mrs. Driscoll were being called in to Sheriff Amos, but Thatcher didn't sense a thunderbolt from any of the incoming information.

Darkness had fallen and the hubbub in the office had died down before Sheriff Amos came through the door. Thatcher hadn't seen him since their conversation that morning.

Apparent to Thatcher immediately was that the stressful day had taken a toll. Bill Amos probably had twenty-five years on Thatcher, but for a man of his age, he was fit. Tonight, however, he looked like he was under a lot of strain and weary to the bone.

Thatcher got up from the bunk and met him at the bars. "Any news?"

"We'll get to it." He hefted a lidded enamel pot by its wire handle. "Hungry?"

"I could do with something."

"Chicken and dumplings." He unlocked the cell and passed Thatcher the pot. "Take it by the handle. It's hot."

Thatcher took the pot, lifted the lid, and sniffed. "From the café?"

"One of Martin's specialities." He took a spoon and napkin from his shirt pocket and passed them through the bars. "Don't dig an escape tunnel with the spoon."

He said it with a smile that Thatcher returned. He carried the pot over to the bunk, where he set it down carefully so not to spill. The sheriff didn't withdraw, but stood just beyond the bars, staring at nothing, thoughtfully smoothing his mustache. Thatcher went back over and waited him out until he was ready to reveal the cause of his furrowed brow.

He began by saying, "There's news only about where Mrs. Driscoll isn't. Nothing about where she is. None of her kin has seen or heard from her. Her uncle and aunt drove up from New Braunfels. They took over for Scotty, staying with Dr. Driscoll."

"How's he doing?"

"At wits' end. Several times he tried to leave his house and join the search. Wrestled with Scotty and the uncle when they stopped him. Last I heard, they'd persuaded him to take a sleeping draught."

"What about me? Are you going to charge me or let me go?"

"The district attorney has taken it under advisement."

"What's that mean?"

"It means that even though we don't have a body or any sign of foul play, Mayor Croft is putting pressure on him."

"What kind of man is the district attorney? Hard or soft?"

Amos snickered. "Flexible."

"The mayor's ready to hang me from the nearest tree. I can't figure why."

Amos took a long, pondering look at him. Thatcher sensed they had arrived at the reason for the sheriff's frown. "Mr. Hutton, how familiar are you with the Anti-Saloon League?"

"Not familiar at all. Must've been formed while I was overseas. But the name sort of explains itself."

"Quite aptly. It's an organization of lobbyists, movers and shakers, zealots."

"Teetotalers."

"They don't merely choose to abstain themselves. Their goal is to rid the earth of every drop of alcohol, along with the people who make it and sell it."

"Then they must've got what they were after when Prohibition was made law."

Bill Amos gave a wry grunt. "Backed by our fire-breathing governor, the League succeeded before that. Last year, Texas passed laws that are stricter than the federal ones. They've made even minor infractions felonies, which carry much stiffer punishments."

"Did that curb consumption?"

Sheriff Amos gave a soft laugh. "Just the opposite. Since these laws went into effect, moonshining and bootlegging have become booming businesses."

Men wanting a drink would find one. Thatcher thought back on the two men at the boardinghouse who'd left together in search of booze. Hell, he remembered soldiers in the trenches fermenting whatever they could, making undrinkable concoctions which they drank anyway.

The sheriff continued. "Some members of the Anti-Saloon League, the governor included, are of the opinion that we local law enforcement agencies and personnel are soft on transgressors, that a large number of us are corrupt, and that we're doing a lousy job of helping them accomplish their goal of making Texas one hundred percent dry. So they've devised a way to 'assist' us in identifying, capturing, and prosecuting offenders."

"How's that?"

"By recruiting what the governor has termed 'innocent bystanders.'"

Thatcher said, "What the hell?"

"In order to convict a bootlegger, state law requires a third party eyewitness to testify to the illegal sale. Since an innocent bystander of such a transaction is rarer than hen's teeth, the League is—"

"Recruiting them."

The sheriff nodded. "Men to work undercover. They infiltrate areas where moonshiners are thriving. They make friends with the culprits, pretend to be one of them, gain their trust—"

"Then rat on them."

"In court and under oath." The sheriff took a deep breath and met Thatcher's gaze. "I think the reason our mayor took an immediate dislike to you is because he suspects you might be one of these official snitches." He raised his eyebrows. "I suspect it, too."

Thatcher gave a short laugh. "Me? I didn't even know there was such a thing. Only undercover agents I've ever heard of were Pinkerton men."

The sheriff stared at him, unfazed by his denial.

"Nobody sent me here," Thatcher said. "When I jumped off that train, I didn't even know where I was. It was dumb fate that I even wound up in this town."

"You're telling me the truth?"

"Damn straight."

"Texas Rangers didn't send you here to make sure I'm square and enforcing the law?"

"No."

"I wouldn't hold it against you."

"Swear to you, sheriff. And I'll tell you something else." He held up his hand, palm out so the cut was visible. "I'll defend myself against a guy wanting to knife me, but I wouldn't tattle on somebody that I'd befriended. That would go against my grain."

Amos assimilated that, then said, "All right, then. I'll take your word for it, and if Bernie ever voices his suspicion again, I'll tell him I already confronted you about it, and you flat out denied it."

"If the mayor suspects I've been sent to rout out local moonshiners, wouldn't he favor that? Why's he hostile?"

"Because he ramrods the most prosperous bootlegging operation in the region."

Thatcher took that news like a clip on the chin. "Son of a bitch," he said under his breath. "Why don't you arrest him?"

The sheriff grimaced. "That'd be messy."

Thatcher didn't press him to elaborate. He felt it possible that arresting the mayor would create a conflict of interest for the sheriff. The ethics of these men were no concern of his. Even if the sheriff dealt dirty on some matters, Thatcher felt that he was a basically good and conscientious man.

"Well, the mayor won't have to worry about me for long," Thatcher said. "I'll be heading up to the Panhandle soon. Assuming you let me go. I thought you'd've heard something from Mr. Hobson by now."

"Sheriff called me back. They had a hell of a sandstorm up there. The deputy dispatched to go out to the ranch got lost."

"I've experienced storms like that," Thatcher said. "You can't see a foot in front of you."

"Well, the fellow turned around and managed to make his way back to Amarillo without crashing into something. He'll try again tomorrow."

That was disappointing. Henry Hobson Jr. had been more than simply the man he'd cowboyed for. He'd been his mentor. Mr. Hobson was a man of his word. A character reference from him would go a long way toward clearing Thatcher of suspicion.

The sheriff was absently plucking at the corner of his mustache. Thatcher had come to recognize the signs. The sheriff wasn't done with him yet. Eventually he said, "There's something niggling me."

Thatcher thought it best not to ask what.

"When we brought you in here and started questioning you, why didn't you tell us you'd stopped at the Plummers' place?"

Thatcher's guard went up. "Didn't seem worth mentioning."

"Bullshit. It was damn worth mentioning because Laurel Plummer could have attested that you had the bruise, the cut, before you ever made it into town and met Mila Driscoll. You relied on Fred Barker to back you up. People in the boardinghouse. But you deliberately omitted mention of her. Why?"

Thatcher shifted his stance, knowing that it probably gave away his uneasiness. "I'd approached two women that day. They were strangers to me, and, best to my knowledge, alone. I thought if y'all knew about Mrs. Plummer, in addition to Mrs. Driscoll, it would look bad."

"It does. It looks bad that you didn't volunteer the information, and I don't think you're being completely honest with me now, are you? What happened out yonder at her place?"

"Not a thing. It was just like she said." She'd left out what had happened out by the water pail. Obviously she was embarrassed by that, and didn't want anybody knowing about it, so Thatcher wasn't going to give it away. But he could tell the sheriff the truth about the rest of it.

"In the short time I was there, it was plain to me that Mrs. Plummer had reached the end of her rope. I got the sense that she'd had more than her fair share of hard knocks lately, and I didn't want to heap on another problem for her."

"You felt compassion for her."

"I guess you could put it like that."

Amos took his measure, then exhaled heavily. "If you're indicted, I advise you against putting it like that. The mayor, the D.A. would pounce on it."

"I don't follow."

"You felt sorry for Mrs. Plummer, so you got your drink of water, your directions into town, and left her alone. Then you met Mila Driscoll. It could be surmised that you felt no compassion for her." He let the implication sink in, then nodded toward the bunk. "Don't let your supper get cold."

FIFTEEN

Wallace Johnson had been born with a pair of jug ears like none other. Not only did they exemplify the term, they sat low on his head and were pointy on top. This manifestation of a problematic gene pool had made him a target for torment by his passel of siblings, by his mother when she got on one of her infamous tears, and by his classmates during all six years of his schooling.

He dropped out at the age of twelve and went into the family business, for which limited literacy wasn't a drawback.

By the time Wally had reached his late teens, the ridicule he'd suffered in his youth hadn't made him timid and fainthearted as one might expect. Instead he was arrogant, aggressive, and meaner than hell.

Somewhere along the way, he had learned to wiggle his ears, making them even more notable. Nowadays, when teased, he used this talent to distract from his reaching for brass knuckles, which he then vigorously applied to the individual who'd insulted him.

One of Gert's whores, who was relatively new to Lefty's and didn't hail from the area, was unaware of Wally Johnson's reputation for a short temper and violent bent.

She was fully aware of it now.

Which was why Gert had left her husband to tend to a middling crowd and had taken back roads out into the countryside to where two clear-running, spring-fed creeks converged, making it an ideal spot for one of the Johnson family's distilleries.

Wally was the family member assigned to operate and protect this particular still. Sometimes a kid cousin helped out with heavy lifting or needed repairs, but Wally preferred to work alone.

He lived in a lean-to tucked beneath a shelf of limestone, which helped shelter him from the elements. The geological configuration also hid the fire required to keep the sour mash cooking at a low boil, thus making the still unlikely to be detected. Wally's great-granddaddy Hiram had chosen the location for just that reason. The still had been producing corn liquor uninterrupted for decades.

When she was still a distance away, Gert rolled her Model T to a halt and blinked her headlights twice, slowly, then three times in rapid succession, signaling that she was a customer and not a hostile competitor or the law.

Wally emerged from his lean-to, cradling a rifle in the crook of his elbow, but, having recognized Gert's vehicle, motioned her forward. She drove up to within yards of where he stood, stopped, and climbed out.

She motioned toward the still. "Why ain't you cookin' tonight?"

"Didn't have a mind to," Wally replied. "You bring my money?"

She planted her hands on her broad hips. "Dammit, Wally, I'm as pissed off at you as I can be at a person, and that's sayin' somethin'."

"What for?"

"What for? I'll tell you what for. Thanks to you, I got a whore who's out of commission."

"You told me to do something that'd guarantee getting Doc Driscoll out to the roadhouse, and that's what I did. Saw him arrive myself."

"I told you to rough up the girl a *little*. You broke her arm, her jaw's out of whack, and her eye's all swole up and ain't sittin' right."

"She told me she'd as soon fuck a bat as me. Which I reminded her of, she said."

Gert gave a snort. "You've heard worse."

He held out his hand, palm up. "Twenty bucks, Gert."

"I ought to subtract what her ruint appearance will cost me in lost revenue." She looked over at his stockpile of moonshine. "But, because I'm a forgivin' person, I'll take a jar for the road, and we'll call it even."

He cursed her under his breath, but went over to a straw-lined crate, lifted out a mason jar of white lightning, and brought it back to her. She screwed off the lid and took a swallow. "You're one ugly son of a bitch, Wally, but you do make good 'shine."

"Twenty bucks." He held out his hand again.

Gert screwed the lid back onto the mason jar and tucked it in her left armpit, then reached into the pocket of her dress, took out a pistol, and shot Wally in the forehead. She bent over his supine form, stuck the bore of the pistol into one of his ears, and fired again.

As she was getting back into her car, she muttered, "Pissant cost me a week's worth of work out of that girl."

SIXTEEN

Shortly after noon the next day, Harold came to Thatcher's cell.

His looks hadn't improved since Thatcher had last seen him. He might have explained that he'd mistaken him for a German soldier and apologized for messing up his face, but the deputy radiated so much hostility as he said, "They want to see you" that Thatcher didn't bother.

After being handcuffed, he was prodded out of the cell block and into the main room.

Mayor Croft was standing in front of a window, a position that cast him in silhouette, obscured his face, and made him the most imposing presence in the room, which Thatcher figured was his intention. If he thought Thatcher would be intimidated by either his public office or his bootlegging, he was wrong. Thatcher looked him square in the eye.

Sheriff Amos motioned Thatcher into a chair. "Coffee?"

Thatcher accepted.

The sheriff filled a mug from a pot simmering on a hot plate, then brought it over. When he bent down to place the mug in Thatcher's bound hands, he said under his breath, "Don't volunteer anything."

Then he straightened up, sat down on the corner of his desk, and commenced another interrogation. Beginning with the fight and Thatcher's leap from the freight train, they rehashed Thatcher's account of that day. The sheriff's questions were straightforward. Following his advice, Thatcher stuck to the facts and didn't expand on any of his statements.

Bernie Croft didn't pose any questions, but expressed his skepticism of Thatcher's truthfulness with snorts and harrumphs and dry coughs covered by his fist.

Thatcher finished with, "I went to bed, fell asleep, woke up with a shotgun in my face and y'all surrounding my bed."

The sheriff waited a beat, then looked over at Croft, who had remained in his spot by the window, but was now rocking back and forth on his heels like a man trying to keep his temper under control.

Bill said, "We don't have one iota of evidence implicating him, Bernie."

"Except that he was with Mrs. Driscoll earlier that day."

The sheriff dismissed that with a shake of his head. "Circumstantial. The D.A. has declined to indict him based on that alone."

"Something could still turn up."

"Mrs. Driscoll could still turn up."

"Dead."

"Let's pray that's not the case. But if, after further investigation, we discover something that does implicate Mr. Hutton in any wrongdoing, I'll be on him like a duck on a June bug."

The mayor scoffed. "He'll be long gone."

"He doesn't plan to leave town immediately."

"So he says."

Thatcher said, "Mr. Barker and I shook on me training that stallion before I leave."

"That's hardly a binding contract."

"It is to me."

Thatcher's words fell like four bricks into the room. Croft's face turned red, but he didn't respond. No one said anything. Then Sheriff Amos broke the taut silence.

"I've got to release him, Bernie. But I'll do so with the provision that he doesn't leave town. If not a suspect, he's still a material witness."

"Fine. But you're gambling with your reelection."

"Every damn day I'm in this office."

Because his warning didn't have the desired cowing effect on the sheriff, Croft strode across to the door, yanked his hat off the coat tree, and stormed out, pulling the door closed so hard, it rattled windowpanes.

Amos signaled to Harold. "Uncuff him."

With obvious disgust, the deputy lumbered over and removed the handcuffs.

Sheriff Amos said, "Mr. Hutton, you heard the condition of me letting you go. Don't run off."

"What if Mrs. Driscoll never turns up? I can't stick around here forever. I want to get home. No word from Amarillo?"

"Not yet, but it's early. It'll be a round trip for whoever drives out to the ranch, and you said it was a far piece from the city."

Thatcher acknowledged that, then said, "As much as anybody, I want to know what happened to Mrs. Driscoll. Not just for my sake. I hate to think."

"Me too," the sheriff said. "I've moved past hoping she'll turn up unharmed and with a logical explanation for her absence." Giving Thatcher a keen look, he said, "I'm letting you go. Don't betray my trust." Then he glanced over his shoulder at Harold. "You have his bag ready?"

The deputy carried over Thatcher's duffel and dropped it at his feet. "Everything's there, including the nudie pictures."

Thatcher gave him a sardonic grin. "Good. They're souvenirs I'm taking to the other hands at the ranch." He shouldered the strap of the bag and walked out.

Bill went home for lunch. He was halfway into his meal when the telephone rang. He left the table, went into the hall, and answered.

A deputy identified himself. "Wally Johnson's been found dead. Two bullet wounds through his head."

That was more than enough to spoil Bill's appetite. He pulled his napkin from his shirt collar and blotted his mouth. "Who found him?"

"A cousin."

"Where?"

The deputy described the scene. "The still was intact, there was a stockpile of product, barrels of mash were fermenting. Only thing spoiled was Wally."

"What's the cousin's name? Besides Johnson."

"Elray."

"He owned up to moonshining?"

"Kid's only fourteen. He was scared shitless that whoever did in Wally was going to come after him, too. Said he'd rather be in jail as in Wally's shoes."

"How do I get there?"

The deputy gave him directions. "I'll wait for you at the turnoff. Otherwise you might miss it."

"Has the J.P. been notified?"

"He's on his way. Not that we need an official pronouncement. Wally's deader'n a doornail. Shot through one of his ears."

Sighing over the ill-concealed mirth in the deputy's voice, Bill hung up. But no sooner had he turned away from the telephone than it rang a second time. He picked it up again. "This is Sheriff Amos."

———⊙———

Gabe Driscoll sat at the dining table, force feeding himself from the plate of food Mila's aunt had insisted he eat.

He had met these relatives of Mila's only once before, and that had been on his wedding day. Whenever Mila had gotten homesick for her extended Teutonic family, with whom he had nothing in common, not even language, he would put her on a train and cite a heavy patient load as his excuse for not accompanying her.

Yesterday, these family ambassadors hadn't so much arrived as *descended*. They had been beside themselves with worry over Mila's fate. But it had come as an unwelcome surprise that they were equally worried about him and his fragile condition.

They'd smothered him with platitudes, advice, sympathy, and affection, which he didn't want, and certainly hadn't earned. His only means of escape had been to lock himself in his bedroom with a "sleeping draught," which had been a bootlegged bottle of bourbon.

This morning, when he'd come downstairs looking even more haggard than he had yesterday, the older couple seemed intent on convincing him that whatever had become of Mila, her leaving hadn't been voluntary.

He'd said, "I'll admit that I wondered if she'd had a man in her life before she met me. Maybe she had heard from him and—"

They chorused a swift denial. She hadn't had a serious beau before him. She wouldn't have forsaken him or broken her marriage vows, not their Mila. She loved Gabe dearly and wanted desperately to be a mother. He'd coughed a sob and held his head between his hands. "Of course I know that. I *do*. I'm certain she didn't leave of her own accord."

Now, having eaten enough to pacify the aunt, he thanked her for preparing lunch, excused himself from the dining room, and barricaded himself in his office, where he poured himself a bourbon.

He carried the drink over to the sofa, took off his shoes, and reclined, covering his scratchy, burning eyes with his forearm. He hadn't slept in two nights. His cuffs were loose, his collar button undone, his trousers wrinkled from having been wallowed in.

If he caught a glimpse of himself in a reflective surface, he barely recognized the image. He looked like a bum, bearing scant resemblance to the self-possessed physician who people relied on for healing and succor.

He very much doubted that he would ever regain the high regard and status that he'd had before his wife had gone missing. Even if

Mila had abandoned him of her own volition, her mysterious disappearance would leave a stain on him as permanent as a port wine birthmark.

That distressing thought was interrupted when he heard an automobile approaching. Sheriff Amos? That deputy, Scotty, again? Had they found her?

Heart thumping, he drained his bourbon, rolled up off the sofa, and padded over to the bay window. Peeking around the edge of the drapery, he watched a shiny black touring car come to a stop in front of his house. Around town, it was a familiar automobile. As was the driver, whose name was Jimmy Hennessy. He got out and assisted Bernie Croft from the backseat.

The mayor strutted up Gabe's walkway, chest thrust out like a despot about to watch a parade of his military might.

Hennessy stayed with the car, a daunting, pugnacious presence against the backdrop of Miss Wise's Victorian house and bright petunia beds.

The doorbell jingled. Mila's uncle went to answer. Gabe heard him quietly explaining that the doctor was unavailable to visitors and wouldn't be seeing patients until further notice.

Bernie, of course, was having none of it. He declared that the doctor would see *him*. Over the uncle's objections, Bernie came inside. Gabe followed the sound of his footsteps, which stopped outside his office door.

There was hard knocking. "Gabe, it's Bernie."

Gabe's head dropped forward, and he maintained that helpless pose until the door was rapped on again, this time more imperiously.

"Open up."

Gabe trudged to the door, flipped the lock, and pulled it open. Looking beyond Bernie, Gabe addressed the apologetic uncle. "It's all right. Mayor Croft is a friend."

The uncle retreated. Bernie forged in. Gabe closed the door.

Bernie went straight over to the ledge of the bookshelf where he helped himself to the bottle of bourbon, splashing some into a tumbler. When Bernie turned and extended the bottle toward Gabe, he shook his head.

Noticing the empty glass on the end table beside the sofa, Bernie said, "Just as well, I think. Appears you've already been imbibing."

Gabe didn't reply, but returned to the sofa and slumped against the back cushions. Mila had spent months painstakingly doing the crewelwork on them.

The mayor made himself comfortable in an armchair. "You should open a window, Gabe. You stink. The whole room reeks of you."

He could smell his sour odor himself. Since having to report Mila missing, he hadn't washed, hadn't shaved. With indifference, he'd observed himself becoming more and more disheveled, but had done nothing to stop the deterioration.

"That's what you came to tell me? That I stink?"

Bernie took a sip of whiskey. "The D.A. has declined to indict Hutton. He's been released from custody."

That was hardly surprising, as no evidence had been found to implicate him. But that he'd been eliminated as a suspect wasn't welcome news, which Gabe supposed was the reason Bernie had come to break it to him personally.

"No other persons of interest?"

"None. Of course they're continuing the search. But sooner or later the zeal will begin to flag, and, eventually, they'll stop looking. I'm sure you realize that."

Gabe nodded morosely.

The mayor crossed one leg over the other and propped his glass of whiskey on his knee.

Alerted by the feigned casualness, Gabe sat up straighter. "What?"

"Do you recognize the name Wally Johnson?"

"Of the infamous Johnsons?"

"More infamous than most. It was Wally who beat up that whore at Lefty's. The one you were summoned to treat."

"So?"

"His body was found this morning. He'd been assassinated. My sources in the sheriff's department tell me it was ghastly. Carrion birds and such."

Gabe just looked at him with dispassion.

After an ahem, Bernie said, "The reason I bring it up, this homicide will divert attention from your wife's disappearance. Now that Bill Amos has a murder to solve, and seeing as how it involves a pack of jackals like the Johnsons, he'll be focused on that. The missing person's case will fade into thin air."

Gabe plopped back onto the cushions. "What happens then?"

"You resume your practice. And you begin working for me."

Gabe dug his middle finger and thumb into his eye sockets. He mumbled, "I don't think I can."

Around a soft laugh Bernie said, "You can. You will. Consider this a swift kick in the ass."

Gabe lowered his hand from his eyes. "It's too soon. I'm not over the shock of Mila yet."

"Get over it. Patience isn't my strong suit."

"Look at me, Bernie. I can barely function, much less take on... additional responsibilities."

Bernie tossed back the rest of his whiskey and, with a decisive thump, set the glass beside Gabe's empty one on the end table. "This whining won't do, Gabe."

With desperation, he said, "I can't just snap my fingers and have things return to any kind of normalcy. It's going to take time."

"Of course, you're right." Smiling, the mayor got up and walked over to the sofa. He set a heavy hand on Gabe's shoulder and gave it a paternal squeeze. "You have two weeks."

It was nearly four o'clock in the afternoon before Bill made the return trip to town. It was a long drive, allowing him time to mentally review what he'd observed at the scene of the homicide and what he knew about the Johnson clan.

They were notorious for thumbing their noses at the laws against their industry. If a family member was caught plying his trade, he paid his fine—and, more often than not, a granny fee to empathetic officials. These payoffs were considered a cost of doing business. The additional expense was passed along to the consumer, and the offender and his kinfolk continued making moonshine with impunity.

But in the months since the Volstead Act went into effect, and the ensuing crackdown on offenders, culprits were getting prison time in addition to being fined.

However, the possibility of stiffer punishment hadn't seemed to deter or unduly concern Wally Johnson. Crates of his product were stacked in plain sight outside his hovel, with no apparent attempt having been made to hide it from whomever had killed him. His rifle was still lying in the crook of his arm.

Evidently Wally's young cousin Elray wasn't from the most stalwart branch of the family tree. He blubbered unedited answers to all Bill's questions, providing the names of Wally's friends as well as his sworn enemies.

When asked if he had any idea who would have wanted to murder Wally so ruthlessly, Elray had dragged his sleeve across his snotty nose and replied, "Any of 'em. He wasn't generally liked, ya know. But everybody was mad at him over that girl. It drew unwanted attention."

"What girl?"

"Corrine, I think her name is. Out at Lefty's."

Bill was still mulling over Elray's explanation as he approached the Quanah Parker Creek bridge, a town landmark and one of Mayor Croft's crowning achievements, which he unabashedly advertised.

Fred Barker's auto garage was just this side of the bridge. Guessing he would find Thatcher Hutton there, Bill pulled in. Fred and his assistant mechanic were changing a tire. Seeing Bill approach, Fred wiped his hands on a shop rag and met him halfway.

"What brings ya, sheriff? Hutton?"

Bill noticed the apprehension in the other man's voice and said, "I didn't come with a warrant."

"I'm glad to hear it. A deputy came by yesterday, asked could I back up Hutton's story. I did. Down to the letter. He showed up a while ago, and apologized a dozen times for being two days late for work." Barker chuckled and the sheriff smiled.

"Is he still around?"

Fred told Roger to keep at what he was doing, then struck off toward the stable. Bill fell into step with him.

"Thatcher worked with that ornery stud for a bit," Fred said. "Then asked if he could inventory my tack, see if anything needed repair or replacement. He's conscientious. Not like Roger," he mumbled and spat out a chunk of tobacco. "I saw him come out of the stable a while ago. He's probably back here."

Bill was led around the stable to the corral. Thatcher and the stallion were in the center of it. Thatcher was lightly dragging a wound lasso in an unhurried and unending circuit along the horse's back, down his flank, across his barrel to his shoulder and back up again to his withers. During one of these rotations, the animal got spooked for no good reason Bill could discern. Thatcher spoke softly and stroked him with his hand, settling him before applying the rope again.

He acknowledged their arrival with a glance over his shoulder. "Getting him used to the sight and feel of a rope."

"Never thought I'd see it," Barker said, sounding proud.

"We've got a long way to go," Thatcher told him. "At this point, he trusts me only so far."

Thrasher hung the lasso on his shoulder and rubbed the stallion's neck with both hands while softly commending him for being so cooperative. "But you've had enough for today." He stroked his forehead and muzzle, then left him and joined the men outside the corral.

"Impressive," Bill said.

"You know horses?"

"Know enough to stay off them unless I can't help it."

Thatcher grinned. "I'm happy to give you some pointers."

"Sheriff!"

The three turned in unison to see Harold jogging toward them and Roger rounding the corner of the stable.

The next sequence of events happened with lightning-bolt suddenness.

Thatcher's right hand smacked his right thigh, then, in a single, fluid motion, he jerked the Colt six-shooter from Bill's holster and fired at Harold, who fell back onto the ground.

Fred Barker slapped his hand against his heart.

The stallion went berserk.

Bill heard the report before it had even registered that Thatcher had disarmed him and fired his weapon.

By the time he gathered his wits and realized what had happened, Thatcher had lowered his gun hand. He calmly turned to Bill and extended him the pistol, grip first.

Barker blurted, "What in tarnation?"

The gunshot had stopped Roger in his tracks. Now he ran over to where Harold lay prone and called to them excitedly, "His head's blowed clean off."

SEVENTEEN

Roger bent down and picked up the dead rattlesnake lying within inches of Harold's size thirteen boots. The deputy struggled into a sitting position. Thatcher ran over to him. He didn't even glance at the snake, but gave Harold a helping hand up. "There was no time to warn you. You all right?"

Stupefied, Harold nodded.

Roger was as energized as if he'd been plugged into an electrical socket. "Six feet if he's an inch." He dangled the limp, headless body, looking at Thatcher with bug-eyed admiration. "Never saw shooting like that."

Bill had never seen anything like it, either. Not in all his days. And he'd grown up in a family of excellent marksmen, skilled with both long guns and pistols.

"Can I keep the skin?" Roger asked Thatcher.

"Makes no difference to me."

Assured that Harold was all right, Thatcher went back to the corral and directed his concern to the stallion as he thrashed around the paddock, his eyes crazed, whinnying at a high pitch.

Fred Barker said to Bill, "I've had about all the excitement I can stand for one afternoon. I'll leave you to ask your questions of Mr. Hutton. After witnessing what you just did, you prob'ly have a few more."

He motioned for Roger to go along with him. They walked off together with Roger chattering nonstop about Thatcher's incredible shot and his prize snake skin.

Bill turned to Harold, who still hadn't said a word. Bill guessed he hadn't quite regained his senses, and who could blame him? "What did you come out here for, Harold?"

"Oh, uh, to tell you that the J.P. turned Wally's body over to the undertaker."

"I want to take another look at him before he's embalmed."

"Figured that. I told the undertaker to hold off till you got there." Harold looked over at Thatcher. "Guess I owe him a thanks."

"No, go on. Tomorrow will be soon enough."

Appearing both relieved and humbled, Harold turned and walked off in the direction of the auto shop.

For several minutes, Bill watched Thatcher talking soothingly to the stallion, then walked over to join him. The horse had been kicking at the fence as he bucked and reared. He'd settled down somewhat, but his ears were still flattened back. As Bill sidled up to Thatcher, he asked, "Did he hurt himself?"

"I was afraid he might've. So far, though, no signs he did. I didn't stop to think how the gunshot would booger him."

"You reacted out of reflex."

"I saw Harold about to step right into that rattler and..." He trailed off, raising a shoulder.

"Where'd you learn to shoot like that?"

"On the ranch. Part of the job."

Bill looked at him skeptically. "Quick draw?"

"Never know when you'll have to fend off a predator."

"Of every sort, I would imagine."

"You name it. Wolves. Coyotes. Rattlers."

"Rustlers?"

Thatcher looked at him, his eyes hard and alight with anger. "What? You think I'm a hired gun or something?"

Bill didn't back down. "Are you? Have you ever killed a man, Mr. Hutton?"

"Plenty. I was a hired gunman for Uncle Sam." He spoke with soft but angry emphasis, then turned back to watch the stallion. "I think he'll settle. He just got spooked. I'm calling it a day." As he turned away from the paddock, Bill fell into step with him.

"Did you come straight here from the jail?"

"Yeah."

"Where's your duffel bag?"

"In the stable."

"Get it. I'll drive you."

"No thanks, I'll walk."

"I'll drive you."

———

Once underway, the sheriff said, "Strange day."

It was clear to Thatcher that Sheriff Amos still harbored some suspicion of him. If it hadn't been for that goddamn diamondback...But it had happened, and the sheriff had seen it, and now he'd tossed out a remark that Thatcher didn't think was offhanded. Unsure of how he was expected to respond, he didn't.

"For instance," the sheriff continued, "on my way to the office this morning, I came across Irv Plummer. That old truck of his was pulled off to the side of the road."

"Broken down?"

"Overloaded."

Thatcher was curious, but pretended not to be.

The sheriff said, "He was moving."

"Moving what?"

"Domiciles."

Thatcher looked over at him then. "Domiciles?"

"He's rented a house out on the north side of town. With a sickly grandbaby, he thought it best to be closer in."

"They were moving today?"

"He said his daughter-in-law had put her foot down."

It would be a small foot, but Thatcher could envision her planting it firmly and issuing an ultimatum, spine stiff, chin angled up. It was an image he would enjoy dwelling on if he were alone. He said, "Did he say how the baby's doing?"

"They took her to Dr. Perkins. He gave her some medicine." The sheriff made a right turn and honked at a spotted dog that was trotting down the center of the street.

"Then," he said, picking up where he'd left off, "after releasing you, and while I was at home having lunch, I got two telephone calls. The first was to notify me of a homicide."

Thatcher's heart thumped. "Mrs. Driscoll?"

"No. No sign of her yet, and the search parties are getting weary."

"They can't stop looking."

"My office won't. But volunteers are just that: volunteers. They've got businesses to run, farms to work, cattle to tend. In all truth, Mr. Hutton, we may never know what happened to her."

"People don't just vanish."

"Actually they do."

That was a depressing thought. Not only because of the effect the unsolved mystery could have on his future, but it distressed him that he might never know the kind woman's fate.

"A fellow named Wally Johnson."

Thatcher had to clear his mind of Mrs. Driscoll before the sheriff's words sank in. "Sorry?"

"The murder victim. Well known around here." The sheriff went on to describe the volatile temperament of the deceased and the disreputable family that had spawned him.

Thatcher took it in. "Sounds like you need to find the killer before his kinfolks do. Cream doesn't rise to the top. Bad blood does."

"There you're right. If ever a pack of miscreants adhered to the an-eye-for-an-eye system of justice, it's the Johnsons. If a competing moonshiner is suspected of killing Wally, it'll be like lighting a short fuse to a powder keg. It's happened before. One rival shoots another. People take sides. Old grudges are reignited. Bodies start stacking up. It's all-out warfare until a truce is negotiated."

"Is Bernie Croft one of the Johnsons' competitors?"

The sheriff smiled across at him. "Bernie would never do his own killing." He pulled to a stop near the railroad depot, fifty yards shy of the boardinghouse. "If I took you to the door, it would look official."

"This is fine. Thanks for the ride." Thatcher reached for the door handle.

"The logical conclusion to draw," the sheriff said as he shut off the engine, leaned back in his seat, and began stroking his mustache, "is that another, probably less successful, competitor killed Wally out of jealousy or spite."

Thatcher resettled in his seat, accepting the sheriff's implied invitation for him to stay while he did his thinking out loud.

He looked over at Thatcher, hesitated for a moment, then said, "You're a good listener. I've noticed that about you, because, in that way, you remind me of my boy. Other ways, too."

"Was he your only son?"

"Only child."

Damn. "Did he have a family?"

"Not yet. He was keen on a certain young lady but hadn't declared himself. I heard recently that she's engaged. I'm happy for her, of course, but I can't help wondering, wishing..."

He gave Thatcher a rueful smile, then began to describe the position Wally Johnson's body had been in when found, and the ruthless nature of the wounds. He told Thatcher about the teenaged cousin who'd made the gruesome discovery.

"Elray says he got to the still early this morning prepared to put in a day's work. Saw Wally spread-eagled on the ground. 'Drawing flies,' he said. He drove to the nearest gas station and used the telephone to call it in. I caught up with him and deputies already at the scene. The kid was as skittish as that stallion you're trying to train. Least little sound, Elray would jump three feet."

He paused before continuing. "What I can't figure is this. If it was a competitor, or any perceived enemy, why was Wally found lying flat on his back, holding a rifle that hadn't been fired? The shot to the ear was overkill. He was already dead. The shot that killed him was fired point-blank."

"He and his killer were face-to-face."

"If Wally felt anything at all, it was a split second of shock."

"No resistance?"

"Looks like none."

"Then he knew the person, trusted him to get that close."

"That's what I'm thinking."

"Well, you're probably right, sheriff. I hope you catch the culprit soon. Thanks again for the lift." Thatcher opened the passenger door and put his right foot on the running board, but got no farther before the sheriff waylaid him again.

"None of the Johnsons are geniuses. As book-learning goes, they're ignorant. But they're cagey, wily, and came out of the womb lying. Even so, I believe Elray was telling the truth. Too scared not to, I think. And he told me something that I keep going back to."

"Something niggling you."

"Exactly that." The sheriff gave him a crooked smile and shook his index finger at him. "See? I noted that you're a good listener. Anyway, Elray told me that he and Wally were at Lefty's Roadhouse night before last. You know Lefty's?"

Thatcher shook his head.

"It's a blind tiger."

Thatcher couldn't contain his surprise. "A speakeasy here in Foley?"

"I see you're familiar with the term."

Thatcher shrugged with chagrin and pulled his foot back into the car. "In Norfolk, when we got off the troop ship, some buddies and me were ready to let off steam."

The sheriff smiled in a way that didn't pass judgment. "Your first stop off the boat was a speakeasy."

"One of the ship's crewmen who'd been to this one gave us the password. Never would've known it was there otherwise."

"What was the front?"

"A haberdashery. Family owned, established 1898. There was a black-and-gold sign above the door."

"A family of smart entrepreneurs, it seems. These days booze is selling hotter than tweeds."

Thatcher chuckled. "We didn't go there for tweeds."

"Good stock of liquor?"

"Nobody left thirsty."

"Ladies?"

Thatcher didn't say anything, but he figured his expression was telling enough.

The sheriff chuckled. "Was it a nice place?"

"Nice enough for us. We'd come off a troop ship. We didn't care whether or not it was high-toned."

"Well, Lefty's isn't high-toned. Not by a long shot. It's a roadhouse, a typical diner that serves fat hamburgers. It's also a cathouse. Gert, Lefty's wife—probably common law—oversees that aspect of their business.

"It was a popular watering hole, but since Lefty can't sell liquor legally anymore, customers have to enter through a rear door into a back room. Bootleg booze and locally made moonshine flow as steady as Quanah Parker Creek during a heavy rain."

Thatcher didn't see how any of this concerned him, so he didn't comment.

"Now, I don't meddle in Lefty's business so long as the peace is kept and nobody bleeds overmuch. But Wally died with his brains in the dirt. Approximately twenty-four hours earlier, he was at Lefty's where, according to his cousin, he got a little too amorous with one of the girls upstairs. She didn't favor him, turned him down in terms to which he took exception, and he beat the hell out of her.

"This afternoon, I dropped by there to ask her about the incident, to see if it had any relevance to Wally's murder. He'd bashed in her mouth and broken her arm. In time, those will heal, but she'll be lucky not to lose sight in one eye." He shook his head and made a sound of profound regret. "She's seventeen."

A train came rumbling into the station, spewing steam, its brakes squealing. The sheriff let the noise die down before resuming. "The reason it's bothering me is that Dr. Driscoll went out to Lefty's that night for the purpose of patching up that girl."

Thatcher reacted with a start. "The same night Mrs. Driscoll disappeared?"

"That's why she was alone in the house. Gabe had told me about the incident at Lefty's. He didn't name Wally Johnson as the offender. He might not have known. But that connection is what niggles." The sheriff shrugged. "It's thready, at best. May be nothing. Could be something."

Thatcher turned his head aside and watched passengers disembark from the train. Some were greeted, others not. A porter unloaded luggage. The engineer climbed down from the locomotive and stood on the platform, stretching his back.

The atmosphere inside the sheriff's car had become weighty, although, if pressed, Thatcher couldn't have said why. Sensing that the sheriff was waiting for a response from him, he said, "It's probably just a coincidence."

"Probably. An interesting one, though."

After a lapse, Thatcher said, "Well, my landlady is a stickler for clearing the sideboard on the dot. I don't want to miss supper. Thanks again for the lift."

"Thatcher?"

He'd been about to step from the car, but pulled up short when the sheriff addressed him by his first name, something he hadn't done before. He turned back to him.

"I told you I'd received two telephone calls during lunch. The second was the one you've been waiting on from the sheriff's department in Amarillo. I hate telling you. Truly, I do. Some while back, Mr. Hobson passed away."

EIGHTEEN

B ill Amos didn't soft-soap it. Not that it mattered how delicately he broke the news. To Thatcher it came as a heavy blow.

Mr. Hobson had suffered a stroke. His son Henry Hobson III had sold the herd, sold the ranch.

Learning of Mr. Hobson's passing was dismantling enough, but Thatcher listened with disbelief when the sheriff told him that the ranch, his home for fifteen years, no longer existed. "Trey *sold* the ranch?"

"Not the land itself," Bill explained, "but what's under it. Oil leases. Dozens of them. Everybody's punching holes in the ground up there, looking for oil."

Thatcher couldn't bear the thought of the sweeping plains being dotted with drilling derricks instead of beef cattle. But he wasn't surprised that Henry III's eye was on the future rather than the past.

Much to Mr. Hobson Jr.'s disappointment, his son never had desired to take over the ranch and had wanted nothing to do with the operation of it. When Thatcher had left for Europe in 1917, Trey had already moved to Dallas and was serving in a managerial capacity in a bank, on his way up.

"What happened to all the ranch hands?"

"I don't know, Thatcher," the sheriff replied. The intimate conversation had established a first-name basis between them. "I guess they scattered. The deputy who went out there said the place was deserted except for a dog that looked half wolf, and an old Mexican man."

"Jesse," Thatcher said. "He was born on the ranch. His daddy worked for the first Mr. Hobson, Henry senior. His mother cooked for the family."

"Well, Jesse was still out there, living in the bunkhouse. He told the deputy he would stay until somebody forced him off, or he died. He preferred the latter."

That sounded like Jesse.

"He was glad to learn that you'd survived the war," Bill said. "He's been safeguarding your trunk and saddle. He sent the trunk back to Amarillo with the deputy so he could put it on a train. He was reluctant to send the saddle, though. Didn't trust it to arrive undamaged or not at all."

Thatcher nodded absently. He would make arrangements to reclaim it later. In the meantime, he struggled to take in that Mr. Hobson was gone.

"I'm awfully sorry about this, Thatcher," the sheriff said.

Thatcher replied by rote, "Thanks."

He retrieved his duffel bag from the backseat of the sheriff's car and returned to the boardinghouse. He hadn't been back since being hauled out in handcuffs. He ignored Landlady May's glare and the sidelong glances of the other boarders, and, skipping supper, went straight upstairs to his room, where he weathered a sleepless night remembering the kindness and generosity of the man under whose wing he had spent formative years of his life.

The next morning, shortly after breakfast when all the other boarders had cleared out, he used the telephone in the central hallway to place a long-distance call to the bank in Dallas where Trey Hobson worked. He had to wait for five minutes for the local telephone office to get through.

A lady with a smooth and polite voice answered with the name of the bank. Thatcher asked to speak to Mr. Hobson. "May I ask who's calling?"

Thatcher gave her his name. "He knows me. Up till the war, I was a hand on his daddy's ranch. I didn't learn about Mr. Hobson till yesterday. I phoned to tell Trey how sorry I am."

"Please hold on, Mr. Hutton. I'll get him to the phone."

She came back about a minute later, still smooth and polite. "Regrettably, he's in a meeting, Mr. Hutton, and can't talk right now, but he said to tell you that he's relieved and glad to know that you made it back from the war, and that it was very kind of you to call about his father."

"Okay. I have a number here, if he gets a chance to call me back. It's in Foley."

He gave her the information and hung up, disappointed but not surprised that Trey was unavailable to talk to him. Mr. Hobson had shared more interests with Thatcher than he had with his son. Although Trey never would have wanted to switch places with Thatcher, Thatcher felt he might have resented the relationship that had developed between Mr. Hobson and him. But then again, Trey had never warmed to any of the cowhands, regarding all of them as nothing more than hired help.

His trunk arrived two days later. Thatcher picked it up at the depot and opened it in the privacy of his room. He'd placed his most cherished possessions on top, so they were the first things he saw when he raised the lid: a tooled leather gun belt with holster and a shiny Colt revolver with a stag horn grip. They'd been Mr. Hobson's gift to him on his eighteenth birthday. From that day forward, he'd strapped it on every day until he'd packed it in the trunk. The pistol had been what he'd reached for when he saw the rattlesnake poised to strike Harold.

For the next week, he went about his business, but without enthusiasm. He slogged through each day, the finality of his mentor's death catching him at odd times, and he would experience the crushing impact of the news all over again.

The more permanent residents of the boardinghouse continued to be standoffish. He sensed that they still harbored doubts about his innocence regarding Mrs. Driscoll. He didn't mind them keeping their distance. He didn't feel like making meaningless conversation.

However, one evening after supper, he was invited to join a round of poker being played out on the porch. The stakes were diddly, but a dollar was a dollar, so he anted up. He won five hands straight. Then, to avoid antagonizing the others, he lost the next two hands on purpose before excusing himself.

The landlady made no secret of her dislike and mistrust of him, but she accepted his rent money for the second week.

<hr>

Laurel was certain the preacher knew the appropriate scriptures by heart. He was old. No doubt he had performed this rite hundreds of times.

Nevertheless, he held his Bible open in the palm of one hand and pretended to read the passages. Although they came from several books of both the Old Testament and the New, he never turned a single page. It would have been awkward for him even to try. In his other hand, he was holding an open umbrella above his head.

Rain drummed on it so loudly, it made his creaky voice nearly inaudible.

Low, dark clouds had created a false dusk at midmorning. The rain fell straight down in oppressive monotony. Even so, Laurel welcomed the miserable weather. On the day she was burying her daughter, even one ray of sunshine would have seemed obscene.

Pearl had died less than twenty-four hours ago, but there had been no reason to postpone her interment. There was no one to host a wake, and no one to invite even if one had been held. The undertaker had an infant coffin in his stockroom. The plot next to Derby's was available. No purpose would have been served to delay the inevitable.

The preacher closed his Bible. "Please join me in prayer."

Beside her, in spite of the rain, Irv removed his hat before bowing his head. Because she couldn't bear seeing the tiny coffin being pounded by the rain, she bowed her head and tightly closed her eyes as she joined the preacher and her father-in-law in reciting the Lord's prayer.

Two grave diggers hunched inside rubber rain capes had been standing by. They moved in immediately after the amen and began lowering the casket. Laurel, unable to watch it being buried, turned away.

The bleak trio made their way back to their cars. Irv had driven them to the cemetery in her roadster. When they reached it, they thanked the preacher, who looked relieved that the brief service wasn't being prolonged. He made a hasty departure.

Irv and she rode home in silence. Their footsteps echoed in the hollow silence of the house as they let themselves in. "You want me to put the kettle on, make you some tea?"

Laurel wanted to decline the offer, but Irv looked so distraught, she thought that perhaps he needed a task to alleviate his despair. "That sounds nice. Thank you."

She removed her hat and sat down at the table. He brewed her tea. He took his secreted jar of whiskey from the cabinet. "A touch of this wouldn't hurt you."

"No thank you."

He poured some of the moonshine into a glass for himself. "You hungry?"

She shook her head. He sat down across from her. They sipped their beverages. After a lengthy silence, he said, "I was tore up when Derby died. But nothing like this. This hurts something awful."

Looking across at him, she watched his eyes fill.

"Derby died of his own choosing," he said, gulping a breath. "That baby girl didn't."

Then a terrible sound issued from deep in his throat, and he began to cry. Laurel left her chair in a rush, knelt beside his chair, and placed her arms around his shoulders, drawing him to her. They clung to each other as he wept. She murmured to him all the banalities that would cause her to scream and run mad if anyone were saying them to her. Yet he seemed to derive comfort from them.

He cried himself out. As he wiped his wet face with the large handkerchief he always carried in his back pocket, he looked embarrassed.

"I haven't carried on like that since Derby's mother passed. It helped a little to get it out. What can I do for you, Laurel?"

"Nothing, thank you. I'm going up to my room."

"I understand. But you'll let me know if you need anything?"

"I will."

"The hurt will never leave you, but you learn to tuck it away," he said, tapping his heart, "and get on."

She gave him a wan smile. But as she climbed the stairs, she doubted that she would survive the night. She would surely die of grief.

At first, Thatcher had been too aggrieved over Mr. Hobson's demise to give much thought to how it would affect his future. But soon he had to face the reality of his situation and figure out a way to make money. Even living frugally, he'd gone through his poker winnings from the men on the freight train and at the boardinghouse. He couldn't live for long on a dollar fifty a day.

One afternoon, Thatcher approached Fred Barker. "I'm making progress with the stallion. But I've got to scare up more business for myself."

"What's on your mind?"

"You've got five empty stalls that aren't earning you a cent. If I can get some horses to work with, how much will you charge me to stable them here and use your paddock?"

They struck a deal that Thatcher thought favored him. But it wouldn't matter how good the terms were if he couldn't fill the stalls.

He put in another few evenings of poker at the boardinghouse, won the largest pot each night, and invested his winnings in having handbills printed. He spent the next Saturday afternoon going around town nailing them to utility poles.

That's when he spotted Laurel Plummer on the other side of Main Street. Her hair was in a long braid hanging down her back out from under a wide-brimmed straw hat. She was dressed in a dark skirt, a white blouse, and a pair of black gloves. She was trying to secure something on top of the trunk of her Model T with a leather strap. Looked to Thatcher like the strap wasn't cooperating.

He hit the head of the nail he'd been hammering one final time, then, taking the sack of nails, hammer, and handbills with him, he crossed the street. "Need a hand?"

She let go of the strap and whipped around. As before, her features were taut, her expression guarded. They relaxed only slightly when she recognized him. "Oh. Mr. Hutton."

"Hi."

"Hi."

"Seems you're always wrestling with something." He gestured toward the strap. He saw now that she'd been trying to get the ends to meet so she could buckle it.

She looked him up and down, taking in his cowboy hat, faded shirt, and dusty boots, then turned away and resumed pulling on the strap. "My father-in-law told me they had released you from jail."

"They had no reason to hold me in the first place."

"Mrs. Driscoll is still missing."

She yanked hard on the strap as she glanced over her shoulder at him. If she had meant that as an implied accusation, he wasn't going to honor it with a denial. "I heard you moved into town."

"That's right."

"Do you like your new house?"

"It's a far cry from new, but it's better than where we were. How's your hand?"

He held it up, palm out. "Healed. How's your little girl?"

She gave the strap another yank. "She died."

The ground seemed to give way underneath him. Her blunt statement had left him dumbfounded, and she must have sensed it. She stopped grappling with the strap and faced him.

"Please don't feel like you have to say anything, Mr. Hutton. Actually, I would rather you didn't."

"All right."

"It's just that it's difficult for me to talk about."

He nodded. "I can see where it would be."

She wet her lips, then pulled the lower one through her teeth.

He squinted up at the sun and readjusted the brim of his hat to shade his eyes.

After several awkward moments, he set the sack of nails, hammer, and handful of flyers on the hood of the car, then stepped around her and easily buckled the strap over several bundles of what looked like household goods. He gave it a test tug. "That ought to hold."

"Thank you."

"You're welcome."

He looked down at her. The straw brim of her hat cast a patterned shadow over her face that intrigued him. Or, he just liked looking at her. Her eyes were green. And skittish. They looked everywhere except back at him.

A strand of hair had escaped both the braid and her hat. She pushed at it with the back of her wrist, the small knob of which barely cleared the curled edge of her worn leather glove. He didn't remember ever seeing a wrist that delicate or a gesture that feminine.

But if he weren't mistaken, the collarless shirt she wore was a man's garment. It was way too large for her. The sleeves were rolled back, forming bulky cuffs against her thin forearms. The top button had been left open, exposing the triangular hollow at the base of her throat and making it about the most tempting patch of skin on the planet.

Her darting eyes eventually landed on the handbills. She tilted her head in order to read the bold printing upside down. "You break and train horses for a living?"

"Trying to."

"That explains the cowboy clothes." She glanced down at the ground. "The boots make you taller."

Pleased to know that she'd noticed anything about him, he lifted his foot and looked at the scuffed riding heel. "I reckon so. I never thought about the height thing because I've always worn them. Only recently have I been without. These didn't catch up to me until a few days ago, and it was like meeting up with old friends."

He explained about the trunk. "It had been up there waiting on me, but turns out I won't be going back to the Panhandle, after all."

"No?"

"No. Circumstances up there changed while I was gone. Anyhow, these britches are more suited to my occupation." He grinned. "The seat of my suit pants ripped the first time I got thrown."

"Thrown? You mean bucked off?"

"That's what I mean. The horse I'm working with now—his name's Ulysses—is spirited, to say the least."

"Were you hurt?"

"A knock or two. Nothing to speak of."

"He could do it to you again."

"Oh, you can count on it."

"You're not scared?"

He hesitated, then said, "I'm not that easy to scare off. He's a bit touchy, but he'll learn to trust me."

He could tell by the way she dropped her gaze that she'd caught his underlying meaning. "I have to go," she said. "Good luck with Ulysses."

"There's no give in that strap."

"What?"

He tipped his head toward the bundle on top of the trunk. "You're gonna have trouble unbuckling it without some help. If your father-in-law isn't around, I'll be glad to lend you a hand."

"I can manage."

"I don't doubt that, but why turn down my offer to help?"

"Because—" She broke off whatever it was she had been about to say and turned her head aside.

"Oh. I get it." He took a step back. "Mrs. Driscoll is still missing."

She came back around and said quickly, "No, no. That's not the reason. Not at all." She clasped her hands together, then, as though realizing she was still wearing the gloves, took them off, and tapped the pair of them against her palm. "I don't want to be beholden to you, Mr. Hutton."

"You wouldn't be."

"I don't want to be beholden to anybody."

She looked like she meant it, and he didn't want to provoke her by trying to change her mind. He supposed a young widow would be sensitive to becoming indebted to a single man. Though knowing that didn't make him any less sorry that he couldn't get near her without her bristling.

He motioned toward the driver's door. "At least let me crank the motor for you. Climb in." He extended his hand to help her onto the running board.

She hesitated only briefly before setting her hand in his. It was the one with the cut across his palm. She looked into his eyes, swiftly, then reclaimed her hand and stepped into the car.

He went around to the front of it. After she'd adjusted the spark and throttle levers on the steering column, he turned the crank twice. She switched on the battery, and the engine sputtered to life.

He collected his things from the hood, came back to the driver's side, and passed her one of the handbills. "In case you come across anyone with a horse that needs to be taught some manners."

She took the sheet from him and gave him a small smile. "I'll pass it along."

"I'd sure appreciate it. Thank you."

He looked at her for maybe a couple of seconds longer than was easy on either of them. Long before he wanted to, he brushed the brim of his hat. "Take care, Mrs. Plummer." He started back across the street.

"It was pneumonia."

Her blurted statement brought him to a halt. He turned around.

She was off by five degrees of looking him directly in the eye. "Pearl came early. Her lungs probably weren't finished developing, Dr. Perkins said. They were too weak to fight off the infection."

He let his breath out slowly. "You asked me not to say anything. Just as well. I don't have the words."

She did look straight at him then, her expression stark with pain.

Then she bobbed her head, put the car in gear, and drove away.

NINETEEN

———◦《◉》◦———

Bernie stood at one of the four windows in his office. It was on the second floor of City Hall, affording him a bird's-eye view of Main Street. From this advantageous point, he could monitor who was doing what, sometimes to his amusement, sometimes to his consternation.

Presently he was watching Thatcher Hutton make his way along the thoroughfare, going from utility pole to utility pole, nailing a notice to each one.

"What does it say?" Bernie asked and held out his hand.

Hennessy passed him one of the flyers. Bernie scanned it, then said to his bodyguard, "Thanks. That's all for now."

Hennessy left the office and closed the door.

"Does he ever speak?" Bernie's associate asked.

"He doesn't need to."

"No, I guess the scowl does speak for itself. What about Mr. Hutton? What does his handbill say?"

Bernie turned away from the window and sat down at his mayoral desk. "It's an advertisement for his services. Read for yourself." He pushed the printed sheet across his desk toward the man sitting facing it. "This indicates to me that he's sticking around."

"He paid our charming landlady another week's rent."

"What do you make of it?"

Frowning in thought, Chester Landry needlessly straightened his perfectly tied bow tie. "I would suspect, as you do, that he's a spy for the Anti-Saloon League in conjunction with a law enforcement agency. May they all roast in hell. Although, if they get their way, that's where we're destined."

"Bill Amos swears up and down that Hutton appears to be exactly what he claims. A cowpoke without a herd. A straggler of a dying breed."

"Well, the sheriff may be right." Chester told Bernie about the arrival of Hutton's trunk. "He dragged it up two flights of stairs, declining assistance from several who offered, myself included. The following morning, he came down for breakfast wearing common cowboy getup." He dusted an imaginary speck of lint from the knee of his trousers, a lazy gesture Bernie privately regarded with scorn.

Chester Landry fancied himself a dandy. His hair was slicked down with enough pomade to pave the highway from here to El Paso. The side part looked like it had been carved into his scalp. He was always dressed to the nines, favoring patterned vests and brightly colored bow ties that Bernie wouldn't have been caught dead in. The man also had a gold upper molar that glinted whenever he flashed his wolfish smile.

He was Bernie's partner in business. He was also a pain in Bernie's ass. Bernie couldn't get moonshine out of the county and into the speakeasies in Fort Worth and Dallas without it going through Chester Landry's manicured hands. Nor could he get bootlegged liquor smuggled into the county without Landry. He brokered the deals on both ends, and the percentage he demanded for each transaction was downright usurious.

But without him and his "powers of persuasion," Bernie's business wouldn't run as smoothly. Or as covertly. Which brought him to a matter of importance. "Is that loudmouth still at the boarding-house?"

"Randy Wells? Yes. As talkative and obnoxious as ever. His hobby is goading the teetotalers, and the most pious among them can't resist the bait. It results in some lively give-and-take."

"He hasn't told you who he buys his whiskey from?"

"It remains his secret."

"Dammit, Chester, I want to know who it is."

"Well, the choices are limited to either one of the Johnsons or to someone in our organization."

"Or it's a lone wolf who's selling cheaper and undercutting all of us."

"In other words, someone not playing by the rules as set by you."

"You're damn right."

Landry chuckled. "Should we try to unionize?"

"I'm thinking more of monopolizing."

Chester raised his brows. "Hmm. An interesting prospect."

"It would be good for everybody."

"Especially you."

"And you."

Landry conceded that with another languid gesture and sly smile.

"Get me the identity of this Randy's source."

"I'm working on it."

Chester's smile remained in place, but his voice suddenly had a bite, and that didn't sit well with Bernie. The bootlegger was a necessary evil, but Bernie never would allow him to get the upper hand. He feared that most of Landry's posturing was just that: posturing. He wasn't nearly as insouciant as he pretended to be.

"These things require finessing, Bernie," he said, speaking smoothly again. "I can't press Randy on it, or seem overeager, and he doesn't want to reveal his source because he's acting as his own middleman. I'm not his only customer. For every jar he sells, he jacks up the price and takes a cut for himself."

"Everybody and his dog takes a cut."

"If you don't like the system, you should have invested in another enterprise."

"As it is now, the *system* is taking money out of my pocket."

The gold tooth flashed. "But by anyone's standards, they're still awfully deep pockets."

Bernie grumbled in response, then said, "It takes only one hotshot like your pal Randy to put all of us in jeopardy. Advise him to keep his fat mouth shut."

"I'll put it more diplomatically, but consider the problem of Randy's loquaciousness solved." With that, he shot his cuffs and straightened his cuff link. "Anything happening toward finding that missing woman?"

"Nothing."

"How's the doctor getting on?"

"He isn't. He's holed up in his house. He hasn't resumed seeing patients." Bernie didn't add that he wanted to throttle the man. Gabe was a veritable wreck. He needed to be brought up to snuff. Soon.

"What was his missus like?"

"You're speaking in the past tense."

Chester shrugged negligently.

Bernie said, "She had butter-colored curls, a round, rosy face, and big jugs. A *fraulein*. So anybody with an axe to grind against the Germans could have wished her harm. Including our sheriff. He lost a son to the war."

"He's cleared Hutton as a suspect."

"He hasn't *cleared* anybody." Frustrated, Bernie got up and moved to the window again. "Speaking of." Across the street, Hutton was engaged in conversation with Irv Plummer's daughter-in-law.

Chester joined him at the window. "Who's she?"

Bernie filled the bootlegger in on what he knew about the woman's history and described the scene that had taken place in the sheriff's office. "Stunned us all that she and Hutton had met, but she backed up everything he had told us about his random arrival here."

"Well, then," Chester said, "I don't think we need to worry about him working undercover."

"I worry," the mayor said. "I live here. I don't flit in and out like you do."

"Flit?" Landry said, taking umbrage. "Don't forget that I represent a line of quality women's shoes. I have a vast sales territory to cover."

Bernie snorted. "Shoes."

"Shoes. Just today, I arm-twisted Hancock into placing his largest order yet. It's not like I come here to relax and enjoy the quaintness of the boardinghouse."

Down below, Thatcher Hutton was helping the recent widow with something on the back of her auto. Bernie thoughtfully fingered the chain on his pocket watch. "How's he act around the other boarders?"

"Polite but not engaging. Keeps his head down. Never offers an opinion unless asked, and then he hedges."

"What do they say about him?"

"They're split down the middle. Half think he was the victim of circumstance and wrongly accused. The other half aren't so sure. But they all agree on one point. No one wants to cross him."

"Has he made a single friend?"

"No."

"Does he socialize at all?"

"He's played cards a couple of times."

"And won big."

Landry looked at Bernie with surprise. "How did you know?"

"He told the sheriff he had a knack." The mayor turned his head and met the bootlegger's gaze. "A knack for reading people."

"An enviable talent."

"A problematic one." Through the window, Bernie focused again on their subject. "When we startled him awake in the boardinghouse, he came up out of that bed as though he'd been catapulted."

"It was quite a commotion," Landry said. "I'm on the second floor. I was afraid the ceiling would collapse."

"It took five of us to subdue him. And have you heard about the rattler?" Chester hadn't. Bernie related the story that had been circulating. "He doesn't get flustered. He fights with ferocity and shoots with awe-inspiring skill."

"He's a surprise to you, Bernie. That's all."

"I hate surprises. I'm not discounting that he's more than an ordinary cowboy, which is why I'm going to keep a close eye on Mr. Thatcher Hutton. And, if you're as smart as I think you are, Chester, you will, too. In fact," he said, smiling, "the man is in want of a friend."

A knock on the door forestalled any rejoinder Landry might have made. Bernie consulted his watch and called out, "Bill?" Sheriff Amos opened the door and came in. "Right on time," Bernie said. "In fact, we were just talking about you."

"Anything good?"

"You tell us." Bernie pointed him into a chair and Landry returned to the one he'd been occupying. As Bernie sat down behind his desk, he thumbed over his shoulder and said to Bill, "We were observing Mr. Hutton out there on the street and speculating on his future."

He picked up the handbill on his desk and pretended to reread it. "As a horse trainer at Barker's? What happened to going home to the ranch in the Panhandle?"

"He suffered a misfortune." Bill took off his hat and set it on his crossed knee. "Finds himself adrift. He knows horses and, until something better comes along, he's got to eat. What were you speculating about?"

Landry said, "Bernie fears that Mr. Hutton is an agent of some sort, who could put a crimp in our, uh, profitable endeavor."

"I asked, he denied it, I believe him."

Bernie said, "I think you're being naïve, Bill."

"And I think you're needlessly fixated on Thatcher Hutton when you should be concerned about Wally Johnson's murder and the hell that's sure to rain down because of it." He was fuming. "You talk about a *crimp*, Mr. Landry? I'm talking about *castration* if Hiram finds out that you two killed him."

Bernie barked a laugh. "Don't be ridiculous. I wouldn't go within a mile of that freak."

"Then who'd you send?"

"Nobody."

"Hennessy?"

"Neither Chester nor I had anything to do with it."

Landry raised his hands. "No blood on these, Sheriff Amos."

"No, but I would swear your nails are buffed," Bernie said. The two of them laughed.

The sheriff, however, didn't find either of them funny. To humor him, Bernie clasped his hands on his desk and spoke with exaggerated seriousness. "Though Hiram would never admit it, he's probably secretly glad that Wally is no longer an embarrassment to the family as a testament to their inbreeding. What motive would I have had for killing him and, in doing so, putting my manhood at risk?"

"Because the Johnson clan is making inroads into markets you covet."

Bernie tried to keep his expression schooled. "True. I'll admit that they've got a relay route up to the oil towns that I wish I had. But it would have been petty to kill Wally over it."

"The more mischief you make for them, Bernie, the more ground you gain. Don't insult my intelligence, or their vengeful mentality."

"I didn't order Wally's execution."

"I haven't heard you sound that sincere since your swearing-in speech." The sheriff snuffled a laugh as he stood up and put his hat back on. "But it's not me you've got to convince. It's the bloodthirsty Johnson tribe."

Supremely annoyed by Bill's amusement as his expense, Bernie said, "Wait a minute, Sheriff Amos. You don't want to forget this."

He opened the bottom drawer on the left side of his desk and took out an unopened bottle of Jim Beam and a letter envelope bulging with cash. He pushed both to the edge of his desk. For ponderous moments, the sheriff stared at both. Then he did something he had never done before.

He took only one of them and left the other.

TWENTY

Laurel hadn't believed she would live through the night after Pearl's burial. She had, but the days and nights that followed were just as difficult to endure. She'd sequestered herself in her bedroom, holding Pearl's baby clothes against her face, inhaling the familiar scent, using the soft garments to muffle her continual keening.

She'd bound her breasts. Eventually her milk had stopped coming.

Irv had checked on her periodically, delivering plates of food she hadn't wanted. Those trips up and down the stairs must have pained his hip, but he didn't complain, and, although he was visibly concerned about her well-being, he didn't admonish her to hurry along her grieving process.

One morning, she had opened her eyes and realized that tears were no longer blurring the sunlight coming through her window. The pain in her heart wasn't as sharp. When she went down and joined Irv in the kitchen for breakfast, his smile was worth the effort it had taken her to bathe and dress.

Later that morning, she'd sealed all Pearl's clothes and baby things inside a box and slid it beneath her bed. That dreaded rite behind her, she'd pushed through the remainder of that day, fearing that if she didn't, she would remain inert and languish until she died.

Damned if she would give Death that satisfaction.

She'd attacked the leased house as though it were an embodiment of all her recent misfortunes. She dipped into her nest egg money to buy items that would spruce it up, then had thrown herself into every chore—scrubbing, painting, repairing—in order to keep her hands busy and her mind from reverting to debilitating heartache.

She'd made the bedroom she had expected to share with Pearl into a retreat for herself, complete with a cozy sitting area. Once Irv had built the wall to enclose the keeping room, she'd made it as comfortable for him as he would let her, although he'd told her repeatedly not to fuss.

He'd brought his barrel seat from the shack. It was an eyesore, but she'd said nothing when he'd rolled it into his room and turned it right side up in a spot of his choosing. He'd declined her offer to make him a new cushion for it.

She'd painted the kitchen cabinetry white, which had brightened the drab room considerably. She'd bought a dining set in a second-hand store and varnished it to a new shine. Irv had complained of the bathroom being so sanitary he was reluctant to do his business in it.

She'd given the parlor and formal dining room thorough cleanings but had left them unfurnished. They weren't needed for living space, because she and Irv each enjoyed spending time alone in their private quarters. When they were together, both were content to remain at the table in the kitchen.

Another area of the house that she'd left alone was the cellar. She'd discovered it one day while trimming a thick honeysuckle vine that blanketed the exterior wall of the kitchen. Behind the dense foliage was a door, which she'd had to use a crowbar to pry open.

She'd lit a lantern before venturing down an unstable set of steps. The cellar was musty-smelling, but not as damp as one would expect. The dirt floor was well-packed and firm. Cobwebs clung to the ceiling, and a few castoff articles had been abandoned there, but otherwise the space was remarkably unlittered. It attached the house to the limestone hill. The far wall was solid rock, the edges of it sealed with a clay-like matter.

That evening she'd told Irv about her discovery. "Did you know it was there?"

"Landlord mentioned it, but he didn't take me down there."

Nothing more had been said about it.

Day by day, the house had become more livable. Eventually Laurel had completed all the projects she had planned for herself and had begun nagging Irv to finish the list of undertakings she'd assigned to him.

This night, as she was clearing the table after their meal, she asked him for the third time to repair an electric light fixture in the ceiling of the central hallway. She said, "If I need the bathroom during the night, I have to feel my way."

"You could carry down a lamp."

"And you could fix the electric light."

"Can't tonight. I've got something else to do."

Her impatience boiled over. She shook her handwritten list at him. "If I could do these things myself, I would. I can't reach the ceiling, even with a ladder. I tried."

"You got up on that rickety stepladder? It's a wonder you didn't fall and break your neck."

"Well, I didn't. Don't change the subject."

He ran a hand over his bald pate. "I'm keeping food on the table by repairing other people's light fixtures, Laurel. Work is a blessing, and in my whole life I've never backed down from it, but I've got more than I can handle right now, and I'm tuckered out of an evening."

She piled their dishes in the sink and turned on the taps, muttering, "Not too tuckered out to leave and stay gone for hours on end."

"What was that?"

She turned off the water and faced him. "I hear you sneaking out three or four nights a week, Irv. Where do you go?" When he remained stubbornly silent, she pressed on. "Keeping an eye out for Mr. Hutton is an excuse that no longer holds."

"It should," he retorted. "They haven't found nary a trace of that woman."

"They didn't find nary a trace of evidence against him, either."

Irv gave a grunt of distaste.

Immediately after her encounter with Thatcher Hutton on the street, she had regretted having told him the circumstances of Pearl's death.

Even Irv, who'd had that one crying jag following the burial, avoided talking about it with her. Perhaps he sensed that her sorrow was too raw, too personal to be shared.

Which was why she hated herself for exposing it to Mr. Hutton. Now he would look at her with pity, when she didn't want him looking at her at all.

Each of their chance meetings, the last one in particular, had left her discomfited. On the surface, they spoke as courteous strangers, their dialogue commonplace and harmless. But it seemed as though they were actually communicating in an unspoken language which he understood, but which escaped her.

She couldn't fault his behavior or criticize his manners. He was just too observant for her to feel comfortable around him. When he looked at her, she feared he was detecting more about her than she was willing to reveal.

Fortunately, there would be few, if any, opportunities for them to cross paths. Her last sight of him might very well be of his walking away, the straps of his braces forming a large letter Y tapering from his shoulders and down his lengthy spine, his walk the slightly bow-legged saunter of a man who had spent most of his waking hours astride a saddle.

That retreating image of him was scandalously stirring. She conjured it with irritating frequency, and it always brought with it an ache that was paradoxically pleasurable. Averse to acknowledging that forbidden sensation for what it was, she always forced it from her mind.

As now when it had distracted her from finishing this squabble with her headstrong father-in-law.

"I'm not going to argue with you about Mr. Hutton, Irv. In fact,

I'm not going to argue with you at all." She turned back to the sink and braced herself against the rim of it. "I'm tired, too."

"Tired, hell. You're exhausted. You tear around here every day like your hair was on fire, paintin' this, scrubbin' that, wearin' yourself to a frazzle."

"Yes. I do." Feeling tears welling in her eyes, she kept her back to him and began to wash the dishes with ruthless efficiency.

He sighed. "Where'd you leave that damn ladder?"

An hour later, with her holding the ladder steady for him, he twisted a new bulb into the repaired fixture, flooding the hallway with light. "Leave the ladder here," he said as he climbed down. "I'll take it out in the morning."

"Thank you." He waved off her thanks, but she touched his arm to keep him from dismissing her. It was important to her that he knew how genuine her gratitude was. "I apologize for being short-tempered, Irv. It's not you I'm mad at. It's—"

"Life. I know. I'm sorta put out with it myself." His smile was empathetic. "I'll get around to those other chores, Laurel. I promise. But I do have something else to do tonight."

He left and didn't return until the wee hours.

Only a few days after their spat over his mysterious nighttime excursions, Laurel learned of something else he'd been keeping from her: a money shortage.

Because she shopped in Hancock's store so frequently, she'd come to know the head cashier by name. Mr. Hamel was always chatty and friendly. Today, when she placed the items she wished to purchase on the counter, he looked askance, stammered a greeting, then hastily excused himself.

At least two minutes went by while other customers ready to check out stacked up behind her. She became hotly self-conscious of their malcontent over the delay she was causing.

Mr. Hamel returned, followed by another of the store employees, who took over the register, while he drew Laurel aside. He wore an agonized expression and spoke in an undertone.

"I'm terribly sorry, Mrs. Plummer, but Mr. Hancock refuses to extend further credit until your father-in-law brings his account current. It's months in arrears."

"What? You must be mistaken."

"I'm afraid not."

Her cheeks flamed. "I'm certain it's an oversight."

"Oh, I'm certain of that, too," he said hastily. "As is Mr. Hancock. It's just that..." He wrung his hands. "You understand."

"Of course. Of *course*."

She asked the amount of the balance due, and when he told her, her knees went weak. She opened her pocketbook and removed the small change purse in which she carried her nest egg money when she was on an errand.

She rapidly counted the bills folded inside it. They covered only half the amount owed to the store, but she gave what she had to Mr. Hamel. "I'll bring you the rest later today."

Still looking pained, he said, "Should I restock the goods on the counter?"

Aware of people nosily staring, she forced herself to smile. "I wouldn't have you go to all that trouble. If you'll please sack them up, I'll pay cash for them when I return." Then, with as much dignity as she could muster, she exited the store.

As promised, she returned with cash in an envelope addressed to Mr. Hancock. In it, she included a note of apology and assured him that it would never happen again.

But getting current with Hancock's had taken a huge bite out of her nest egg.

She was loaded for bear when Irv came home for supper. But he looked weary to the core, and, without her even asking, he undertook the first to-do task on her list.

She didn't have the heart to relate the humiliating experience she'd suffered, or to demand an explanation for the embarrassing delinquency. Perhaps he'd bitten off more than he could chew by renting the house. If so, whose fault was that? Hers.

Although it wasn't like Irv to be absentminded, maybe the unpaid account *had* been a mere oversight. That night she went to bed praying that was the case.

However, the next day while he was away working, she entered his sanctum and opened the lidded cardboard box he referred to as his filing cabinet. To her dismay, several recent bills had balances carried over from previous months.

How had he gotten them into these straits? When he went out at night, was he gambling? He could have been lying when he denied seeing another woman. Was he supporting a mistress in addition to Laurel?

She couldn't tell him how to live his life. But—to hell with his pride—she would relieve the financial burden she had become.

To supplement Derby's paltry income from the army while he was overseas, she'd taken a job clerking in a drugstore. She'd enjoyed the sense of purpose and independence employment had given her.

But once Derby got back, he'd insisted she resign. He was the breadwinner, he'd said. Taking care of him would be her full-time job, he'd joked. After Pearl was conceived, the issue was never again addressed, not even when he couldn't hold a job for more than weeks, sometimes days, at a time.

She was *not* going to give up another home in order to spare a man's ego. If Irv couldn't afford for them to live here on what he earned, then she would subsidize the household income. And not only for the short term, not just long enough to bring their bills current. She must begin thinking long range, to the time when Irv was too old and infirm to provide for her to any extent. She must plan for a future without him.

Without *anybody*.

Because she had resolved never again to hand over the reins of her life to someone else, as she'd done with Derby. She would be self-supporting, thank you.

Making that resolution was one thing, implementing it quite another, and she had no time to waste. Days passed, bills piled up. Without Irv's knowledge, she went around to local vendors, paying them out of her nest egg only enough to pacify them and buy herself a little more time.

In secret, she began perusing the local newspaper's want ads. She wasn't qualified to teach school. The telephone company had more applications for operators than they had switchboards.

Other jobs open to women required secretarial skills like typewriting and shorthand. She could learn to do both, but not without Irv's knowledge, and she didn't want to raise the subject with him until she had something already in place, giving him no opportunity to argue with her about it.

She also began keeping count of the nights he left the house and how long he stayed away. He was entitled to a private life, of course. He was a man, after all. But if he was gambling money away, or spending it on a woman, or women, instead of keeping their household bills current, she had a right to her say-so on the matter.

She planned and prepared to follow him at a moment's notice the next time he slipped out the back door.

The night arrived. When she heard the back door closing behind him, she hurried downstairs and watched him from the kitchen window as he climbed into his truck and drove away.

She rushed outside, frantically cranked up her car, and, miraculously, it started the first time. She followed the taillights of Irv's truck, never getting too close. He had repaired the faulty headlight, so she didn't have to worry about a winking one giving her away.

Once he cleared the streets of town, he took the familiar highway that led to the shack. Maybe he simply missed his solitude and came out here to be alone. But when they reached the drive leading up to the old place, he drove on past.

The farther they got from town, the more uneasy Laurel became. Where on earth was he going?

When he turned off the highway, Laurel dropped farther back and switched off her headlights before carefully taking the same turn. But her ploy didn't work. She topped a rise, and, there in the middle of the road, was Irv's truck. He was standing in front of the tailgate with his hands on his hips. She pulled to a stop.

He walked up to her car, scowling. "Did you think I wouldn't notice I was being followed?"

"Where are you going?"

"Dammit, Laurel!"

"*Where are you going?*"

He stewed, cursed under his breath, then said, "You want to know so bad? Come on then."

He stalked lopsidedly back to his truck, climbed in, and pushed it into low gear. After a couple of miles, he turned onto another road, narrower and more rutted than the previous one. It wound its way between the hills. As they rounded a curve, Laurel saw flickering firelight ahead.

Irv pulled his truck off the road and drove cross-country toward the fire. The old truck jounced over the rugged ground, its headlight beams eerily bouncing off stands of cedar trees and rock formations. Laurel, with her teeth clenched to keep them from being jarred loose, followed and pulled up behind him when he braked and killed his engine.

He got out of his truck and waited as she picked her way over the rocky ground to join him. He extended his arms from his sides. "Well? Satisfied?"

She looked beyond him at the glow of the fire. "You camp out here?"

"Damn, girl. Wha'd'ya think? I'm making whiskey."

TWENTY-ONE

Muttering imprecations, Irv turned and led her toward the contraption being attended by a man she'd never seen before. As Irv and she approached, he stayed where he was, but stopped what he'd been doing and gaped at the two of them, slack-jawed.

He was holding onto a long stick that extended out of a pear-shaped metal vat, the rounded bottom of which was nestled in the center of a manmade stone pit. An opening had been left in the pit's base in order to stoke and fuel the fire smoldering inside it. The fire's smoke drifted out of a flue on the back side of the pit and curled up the face of a limestone outcropping, which formed a natural backdrop for the still, which seemed to Laurel to have been haphazardly engineered.

"Meet Mr. Earnest Sawyer," Irv said. "Ernie, this is my *nosy* daughter-in-law, Laurel."

The other man let go of the stick and doffed the brim of his newsboy's cap. "Ma'am. I've heard a lot about you."

"Me and Ernie worked together on the railroad," Irv said. "Known and trusted each other for years. He's from Kentucky. Knows everything there is to know about making corn liquor. So, when I retired, Ernie said to hell with the railroad and quit, too. We partnered up—"

"This is why you've been sneaking out at night?"

"You thought I was seeing a woman, didn't you?"

"You're making moonshine?"

"Good moonshine."

"It's illegal!" Her voice echoed off the surrounding hills, making both men cringe.

"Pipe down," Irv said. "Sound carries out here. And, yes, it's illegal, but it's a living. A damn good one. How do you think I'm affording that rent house?"

She was presently too flabbergasted to cite the past due bills. She took in her immediate surroundings, which, by all indications, was a permanent encampment. In addition to the components of the whiskey-making apparatus, a tent had been erected at the edge of the clearing. It was dark in color and camouflaged by cedar boughs.

She took a closer look at Ernie Sawyer. He was as thin as a string bean; his overalls hung straight from the shoulder straps, seeming to touch him nowhere else. He wasn't nearly as young as she, but not nearly as old as Irv. He was watching her with misgiving.

"You stay out here in the tent, Mr. Sawyer?"

"Yes, ma'am."

"All the time?"

"Mostly, yes, ma'am. Always when we're doing runs."

Laurel looked to Irv for clarification.

"A run is the process that starts with cooking the mash and ends with a jug of distilled whiskey. Ernie oversees the making of, I distribute. We split the revenue fifty-fifty."

The pride with which he spoke left Laurel at a loss for words. Resuming her survey of the area, she noticed a number of metal barrels lined up. "What's in those?"

"Mash. Fermenting till it's ready to cook."

"And all that?" She indicated a pile of what appeared to be building supplies.

"Materials to make our second still," Irv said. "We're duplicating this one, based on Ernie's great-granddaddy's design. It would already be assembled and doubling our production, but I had a *list*."

She let that shot pass without comment. "What about your fix-it business?"

"A front. Don't get me wrong. I fix plenty, I'm good at it and in demand. But driving around hither and yon, going from job to job, allows me to—"

"Distribute your product."

"Secret-like. There's a false floor in the bed of the truck. You can't hear the jars clinking together with all my tools rattling around. Plus, I'm old and have a crippled hip."

"He plays that up," remarked Ernie.

Irv shot him a dirty look, then said to Laurel, "I've got the perfect cover."

Still disbelieving, she rubbed her forehead, wet her lips. "It's not only against the law, it's dangerous. A local moonshiner was murdered recently. At his still. I read about it in the newspaper."

"Wally Johnson," Irv said with a snort of disdain. "The world's better off, believe me."

"They's all sorry, them Johnsons," Ernie said. "Sorry and mean. We're smart enough not to cross 'em."

Earnest was befittingly named. He spoke with perfect conviction. However, Laurel questioned his smarts. "Why didn't you set up shop in Kentucky?" she asked him. "Isn't it known for moonshining?"

Irv spoke up ahead of his partner. "So's this area. Texas's best held secret. There's stills all over these parts." He made a broad sweep with his hand. "Lot of hills to hide them in. Unlimited cedar and oak for the fires. Cedar gets it to going good, oak keeps it burning low and even.

"Hear that gurgle?" He angled his head toward the wall of limestone. "A natural spring flows out of that. Unlimited supply of cold, clean water, filtered by Mother Nature herself. You gotta have good water to make good 'shine."

He pointed toward a wooden barrel with a spout close to the bottom which emptied into a glass jug with a funnel acting as a stopper. "Ernie's great-granddaddy preached filtering and testing. First, filtering makes the whiskey smell and taste better. Testing prevents accidents."

Ernie chimed in. "No Sawyer in my branch of the family tree has ever poisoned or blinded nobody. We don't turn out popskull, neither."

"Popskull is—"

"I don't care what it is, Irv," Laurel snapped, cutting him off. Then she took a deep, calming breath. Her father-in-law and his crony had obviously lost their marbles, to say nothing of their morality. She must make them see reason. "The consequences of what you're doing could be dire."

"Dire?"

"Dire. Who owns this land? Tell me it's not government property."

"No, me and Ernie own it. He chose this spot, saying it was as ideal a place for a still as he'd ever seen. The previous owner, a cotton farmer who'd lost three crops in three years straight to the boll weevil, was happy to get rid of some of his land that wasn't fit to grow nothing. Ernie and me pooled our savings and relieved him of ten acres.

"The tract is long and skinny. Shaped sorta like a fishhook." He drew one in the air. "We're here, at the bottom of the bend. The shack is up here on top."

She'd never thought to ask about who owned the shack and the plot it was on. "It seems farther than that."

"Nope. The road loops and meanders around. But as the crow flies, the shack is just over that hill. Didn't you ever notice the smoke coming from this direction?"

"I thought it was another house." She'd had distractions, God knew, but her own gullibility fanned her temper. "You could get caught, Irv."

"Haven't yet, and we've been at it going on five years."

"Yes, but now Prohibition is in effect."

"Increasing the demand for whiskey," he said, giving her a shrug that emphasized the practicality. "That's why we want to double our production."

"You could go to jail!"

"Not for the first offense. We'd be fined, is all."

She flung her hand back toward their vehicles. "You drive around in that rattletrap, which is always breaking down, and it's loaded with jars of moonshine? That's...that's begging to be found out."

"I stage most of the truck's breakdowns, so all its rattling is convincing. As for being found out, I'm in plain sight every day. People are used to seeing me."

"Who do you sell to?"

"I have a route of regular customers that I keep supplied."

"Someone, anyone, who buys from you could turn you in."

"What kinda damn fool getting corn liquor delivered straight to his door would turn me in? Wives, now, are another thing. Gotta be careful of them, but that ain't my problem."

Infuriated by the logic of his arguments, she lashed out, "I should turn you in myself!" She pivoted and gave the two of them her back, hugging her elbows to her body.

Ernie hissed, "Shit, Irv. Have you gone plumb crazy, bringing her out here?"

"I didn't bring her. She followed me," Irv whispered back. Apparently both had forgotten how well sound carried.

On top of Derby's suicide, on top of Pearl's cruel death, on top of everything, *THIS*? Her father-in-law was committing a federal crime, with nonchalance and no shame, and for months she had been living off the profits of it, oblivious.

Dear God! When would enough be enough? What was she supposed to do about this?

"Laurel?" Irv said softly and with hesitation, "Are you gonna—"

She raised her hands, fingers spread, in an unspoken but emphatic demand that he not say another word. He fell silent.

She looked above at the panoply of stars. There was only a fingernail moon. The sky was very black. Somewhere in the distance a coyote yapped. While living out here in the shack, she'd gotten used to hearing them.

Now that she thought about it, it was remarkable how much she had gotten used to in the months she had been here. She was a different person from the woman who had left Sherman, clinging to the fragile hope that Derby and she would be happy together, or at least that their situation would improve. How naïve she'd been about love, loyalty, life, about a lot of things.

She looked down at the ground, pressed a loose rock deep into the chalky soil with the toe of her shoe, then turned her head and looked back at the still.

It was an odd configuration; all the separate parts of it looked crudely assembled, wrongly angled, and disjointed. She wandered over and went up the slight incline toward the limestone backdrop where Ernie had resumed using the long stick to stir the contents of the cooker.

Still regarding her with apprehension, he said, "It's just beginning to bubble. We'll be capping her soon."

Laurel peered down into the simmering mixture, then looked over at the empty glass jug sitting on the ground beneath the spout of the barrel, waiting to be filled with a product in huge demand. She thought of the "file cabinet" full of unpaid bills.

She met Ernie's nervous gaze, then turned to Irv.

"What's the recipe?"

TWENTY-TWO

When Sheriff Amos strolled into the stable late one afternoon, Thatcher was in the center aisle grooming a mare that had been brought to him the day before.

"Another bucking bronco?" Bill asked.

"No, this one just needs to be taught that it's not up to her when she's ridden. Her owner has to chase her down. She has him trained, not the other way around."

"I've seen your handbills all over town."

"They've paid off. I've got only one empty stall."

"Good for you. When you're done there, let's take a walk."

Thatcher lowered the currycomb and looked over at the sheriff, whose grave expression indicated that this wasn't a social call. He asked the first question that came to mind. "Has she been found?"

"No."

Thatcher waited, but when the sheriff didn't expand on that, he said, "Time to quit anyway."

After returning the mare to her stall and putting away the grooming utensils, he walked with Bill toward the bridge. They didn't cross. Instead the sheriff led him down the grassy embankment to the water's edge. The creek's current was sluggish.

Bill removed his hat and fanned his face. "This spot isn't as cool as I thought it would be. Not much of a breeze."

"Doesn't bother me if it doesn't bother you."

The sheriff turned his head and gave Thatcher several moments of intense scrutiny. "Does anything bother you, Thatcher?"

"Lots of things."

"You don't show it."

Thatcher raised a shoulder, not knowing how else to respond.

"What about people's opinion of you?"

Thatcher shifted his stance and tilted his head to one side. "One thing that bothers me is for someone to beat around the bush."

"All right." Bill hiked up his gun belt and took a deep breath. "I officially called off the search for Mila Driscoll today. It's been three weeks. Volunteers have petered out. I can't spare the manpower to keep up the search.

"I informed Gabe in person. I promised to hop on any leads that turned up, but I'm not hopeful there'll be any. The case remains open-ended."

Thatcher was quick to catch on to the reason for this visit. "This leaves me the one and only suspect."

The sheriff backed up to a butt-high boulder, propped himself against it, and folded his arms. "I don't think you had anything to do with it, Thatcher. None at all. But people are funny."

"It'll be like a shadow of doubt following me around."

"I hope not, but people—"

"Need somebody to blame."

"It's human nature."

Thatcher knew Bill was right. An unsolved mystery was like a sore tooth. It couldn't be left alone. He was the logical solution to this mystery, and, no matter what he did, in the back of some folks' minds, he would continue to be.

He supposed he could leave town as suddenly as he'd arrived, but that would look like running and only justify suspicion. And where would he go? He could probably be hired on at another ranch, but that would somehow seem disloyal to Mr. Hobson. City life held no allure for him.

Wildcatters were actively soliciting for roughnecks to work in the new oil patches, promising good pay. But he'd be living in a men-only camp and doing a dirty and dangerous job. If that lifestyle had held any appeal for him, he would have stayed in the army.

For the time being, staying in Foley was his best option. But he knew the prejudice he would come up against every day, and that rankled. "Damn. There'll always be those who think I'm guilty, won't there?"

"Until proven otherwise. What do *you* think happened to her?"

"What difference does it make?"

"Venture a guess."

"What for?"

"Why not?"

Thatcher hesitated, then squatted down, picked up a rock, bounced it against his palm a few times before pitching it overhanded into the creek. The plop sounded loud in the still air.

He squinted up at the sheriff from beneath the brim of his cowboy hat. "My guess? I'd say the doc had her with him when he left the house that night."

The sheriff assumed a contemplative expression. "She wasn't with him at Lefty's. Or with him when he made the stop to check on that breech delivery."

"Breech delivery?"

"I haven't mentioned that to you?" Bill explained Dr. Driscoll's second stop that night. "All had gone well, but because of that additional delay he didn't get back home until after one o'clock when he discovered that Mrs. Driscoll wasn't in their bed where he'd left her."

"Nobody can vouch for that."

"Except for the old biddy across the street who put Mayor Croft on to you. She says she saw their bedroom light go off around nine-thirty. That's consistent with what Gabe told me about their bedtime. The light came back on around ten, then went back off only a few minutes later. Eleanor Wise saw him collecting his medical bag from his office. That light went off. He backed his car out of the driveway a few minutes after that."

"Is watching other people all that old lady does?"

"Apparently."

Thatcher looked out across the creek to the opposite bank where a black-and-gray-striped cat was stalking something in the tall grass. "Did the old lady see the doctor walk from the house and get into his auto?"

"He keeps it parked around back."

Thatcher brought his gaze back to the sheriff, but he didn't say anything.

Bill said, "You're thinking Mrs. Driscoll was dead, and he carried out her body without Eleanor Wise seeing him."

"I'm not accusing anybody of anything."

"Understood, understood. We're just talking off the top of our heads here."

Thatcher didn't contradict him, but the truth was, he'd given this a lot of thought. Based on what he knew for fact and not scuttlebutt, he'd dismissed the various theories that had been disproved already or were too outlandish to put stock in.

The process of elimination always left Thatcher with only one plausible explanation for Mila Driscoll's disappearance.

"If she'd died accidentally," Bill said, musing aloud, "like if she'd fallen down the stairs, something like that, Gabe would have reported it."

"Um-huh."

"If they'd had a quarrel that got out of hand, if he flew off the handle and struck her—"

"A quarrel between them wouldn't have gone that far."

Bill's sharp look invited Thatcher to explain why he thought that.

He said, "When she talked about him, her cheeks turned rosier than normal."

"A woman in love."

"A woman who worshiped the ground her husband walked on," Thatcher said.

"Do you have a lot of experience in that area?"

Thatcher smiled. "No. Just wish I had a woman light up when she talked about me like Mrs. Driscoll did when she told me how fond her husband was of her shortbread. I doubt she ever said a cross word to him. But if they did have a squabble, she would've given in early. It would never have reached the boiling point."

Looking troubled, the sheriff ran his hand over his mouth and mustache. "Here's the thing, Thatcher. If a man kills his wife, it's usually in a fit of passion. Fed up with her nagging about his multiple failures, he loses his temper and, while teaching her a hard lesson in who's boss, he kills her, intentionally or not.

"Or a husband finds his beloved in bed with another man, goes blind with rage, kills them both. Afterward, he feels either justified for doing it—'They had it coming. I'd kill them all over again.'— or mortified, and he lives out the days till they hang him eaten up with regret.

"Of course some wife-killings are plotted. Another woman catches a man's eye, he disposes of the spouse who's blocking his path to greener pastures."

Bill paused and took a breath. "Over the course of my career, I've seen all that many times. What I haven't seen is a man killing his *pregnant* wife, his *very* pregnant, devoted wife who thought the sun rose and set in him. Not accidentally, not in a burst of violent rage, but with cold calculation. To take her life as well as his unborn child's, to do that with aforethought, would call for a total absence of soul. I just can't feature it."

Not wanting to interrupt the sheriff's thought process, Thatcher held his peace. He picked up another rock and tossed it from hand to hand.

"And anyhow," Bill went on, "it couldn't have been premeditated. The doc didn't know he was going to get called away from the house that night."

"It would help to know the length of time between the emergency call from the roadhouse and his arrival there."

"No more than half an hour, Lefty said."

"What's it usually take to drive it?"

"Roughly that. Gabe would have had to plan a perfect murder and implement it in a matter of minutes before racing out to treat the young prostitute who got beat up."

Thatcher looked at him intuitively. "You already asked this Lefty about the timing of the doc's arrival?"

Bill nodded.

"So this isn't a sudden notion of yours. It had crossed your mind that the doc had a hand in Mrs. Driscoll's vanishing."

Bill's sigh was as good as an admission. "He's the one link between Mrs. Driscoll's disappearance and Wally Johnson's homicide. The more I thought about it, the less coincidental it seemed."

"I thought so all along," Thatcher said.

"So did I."

"I just didn't want to say so."

"Me either." Glumly, Bill added, "I wish you'd scoffed at the idea. Doesn't make me feel any better to learn that it had occurred to you, too."

"Are you going to arrest Driscoll?"

"Without any evidence? No. It's still all speculation."

"That didn't stop you from arresting me."

The sheriff put his hat back on and slapped his thighs as he stood up. "I had that coming."

"You sure as hell did." Thatcher also came to his feet.

"Cut me some slack. Hauling in a drifter for questioning is one thing. Hauling in a highly respected pillar of the community is another." The sheriff started up the embankment. "But I could make it up to you. That is if you're willing."

"Willing?"

When the ground leveled off, the sheriff took advantage of the shade cast by the steel grillwork of the suspension bridge. "I've thought of a way to relieve you of suspicion."

"How's that?"

"I'll deputize you."

Thatcher laughed. "Come again?"

"You heard me. It would be a show of the faith I have in your innocence. If you wore a badge, folks would start looking at you in a different light."

Still amused, Thatcher shook his head. "Thanks for the offer, and the show of faith, but I don't want to be a lawman."

"You've got a natural aptitude for it. You're cool-headed. You listen more than you talk, and you yourself boasted of having a knack for reading people."

"In a game of poker."

"Bluffing at cards is a form of lying. Detecting it is a talent. You'd sense when a witness or suspect was giving me the runaround."

When he saw that Thatcher was about to argue, he held up a hand. "Besides all that, Mrs. Driscoll's fate is eating at you. You want to know what happened to her."

"So does everybody."

"But not everybody has a personal stake in solving the mystery. You've dwelled on it."

"In my idle time."

Bill grinned. "That speaks volumes. I'm headed out to talk again with that woman who had the breech birth. Maybe she'll provide some insight into the doc's frame of mind that night. Why don't you come with me, listen in? Give it a trial run."

Thatcher shook his head. "It won't do any good to go on about it. I appreciate your trying to improve people's opinion of me, but I don't want to be a deputy. All I know is ranching and horses."

"You could still do your horse training. You wouldn't be on staff. Just, you know, every once in a while, I could use an extra set of eyes and ears and—"

"And?"

"I've seen you shoot." After the blunt statement, he waited a beat. "I count on needing extra firepower soon, because I fear all hell's about to break loose. The Johnsons have sworn vengeance for Wally. I've heard rumblings that they're going to start sniffing out their competitors, and they're going to keep at it until they find and execute Wally's murderer."

"How will they know when they've got the right man?"

"When they've killed all of them."

He couldn't have hammered his point home any harder, and Thatcher felt the impact of it. Nevertheless, he had no aspiration to wear a badge. "I hope it doesn't turn into a bloodbath, Bill. But a war between moonshiners isn't my fight, and I'm staying out of it."

The sheriff held his gaze for several seconds. "We'll see."

They walked back to the stable together but said nothing more until they parted there with exchanged goodbyes.

As Thatcher watched the sheriff walk away, the words *we'll see* echoed in his head. He wasn't struck by the words themselves so much as by the way Bill had said them. Not with disappointment over being unable to change Thatcher's mind. But with the shrewd confidence that he would.

TWENTY-THREE

The morning following her discovery of the still, Laurel plunged headfirst into her study of the centuries-old art of making sour mash whiskey. The more product they had to sell, the more money they could make, and the sooner she could settle their outstanding accounts.

In addition to the pressing financial necessity propelling her was a personal goal: As long as she was embarking on an illicit business, she wanted to excel at it.

Under pain of death, Ernie confided in her his family's recipe for the mash: unsprouted corn kernels, malted barley, water, sugar, yeast, and pot-tail.

"But," he warned, "you gotta know how much of each ingredient to add. You gotta know what stage to add it, and it has to be the right temperature. You gotta know when the mash has reached the perfect stage of fermentation. If your mash ain't good, your whiskey ain't gonna be."

"How do you know when it's fermented long enough?"

"When it gets foamy on top. But I dip my finger in and taste it just to be sure."

Many of his instructions went that way. "What's pot-tail?"

"Also called slop. It's what's left in the cooker at the end of the run."

"And when is the run at an end?"

"When the liquor breaks at the worm and won't hold a bead. After that it's distilling less than a hunerd proof liquor. You stop cookin' and pour out the pot-tail right then so it won't burn. Hogs love it if you want to use it for feed. Chickens, too. But save some to start another batch of mash."

"Oh. Like sourdough bread."

"I reckon. Never heard of that. Is it like cornbread?"

She had a lot to learn, beginning with Ernie's vast glossary of moonshining terminology. Thumper. Backings. Goose eye. Popskull. "That's low-quality 'shine that gives you headaches for days on end," Ernie explained.

A swab-stick was what he'd been using to stir the mash as it had begun to cook. It was different from a stir-stick, which had a forked end with a wire strung between the points. That was used to stir the mash as it was fermenting, which usually took four to five days. "Longer when the weather's cooler."

The referred-to "worm," she learned, was slang for the copper tubing coiled inside the wooden barrel she'd noticed the night before. The hot vapor created by the cooking mash rose up to the cap and made its way through the cap arm into the worm, where the steam was cooled by circulating water inside the barrel. The condensed result that funneled out of the worm into the container outside the bottom of the barrel was corn liquor.

Because of his down-home way of speaking, Laurel's first impression of Ernie was that he was simple. Most would still have that impression of him. In actuality, Earnest Sawyer was a chemist, who prided himself on the quality of his product.

"You only gotta poison one or two customers and your business is did for." To guard against contaminants or toxins, he held to a rigid standard of filtering their moonshine three times before bottling it. Grinning widely, he'd told her, "I sample each run my ownself just to be sure."

He walked and talked her through their next run, letting her observe the entire process. She asked a lot of questions. She even took one sip of the white lightning. Ernie and Irv laughed at the face she made. Eyes watering, coughing, she said she would leave them in charge of testing their whiskey's quality.

Although she had no intention of taking over the distilling process, she'd wanted to have a rudimentary understanding of the science behind it.

Of course, it was also essential to learn how not to get caught. That was a science she must master.

One evening when Irv skipped going out to the still, she brought up her fear of being found out. The two of them were seated at the kitchen table enjoying a coconut meringue pie she had baked earlier that day.

Around a bite of pie, he said, "You don't have to be fearful, just careful. There's dyed-in-the-wool abstainers, sure. But a lot of folks around here turn a blind eye to moonshining because they understand the farmer's plight brought on by the boll weevil. They switched from cotton to corn because corn is a boon market. And that's because of whiskey-making. It's basic economics."

"It's basic crime."

"Yeah, well, tell that to a sod buster trying to keep his kids from going hungry. These people aren't outlaws, Laurel. They're hardworking, poor folk striking while the iron is hot."

"I don't think you take the potential dangers seriously enough, Irv."

"All right, I'll admit that things have clamped down since Prohibition. Before it, many lawmen ignored the illegal whiskey trade. Others adhered to 'if you can't beat 'em, join 'em.' They lined their pockets with bribes. Now, though, they're getting squeezed by federal revenue officers and the Texas Rangers."

He raised his fork for emphasis. "That bunch is serious about upholding the law, no matter how unpopular it is. They can muscle their way past local and county officials, clean or crooked.

"Rumor is," he continued, "the Rangers and other agencies are recruiting men to snitch, and typically these snitches are former moonshiners and bootleggers who know the business inside out. They swapped sides in exchange for clemency. Or maybe they found religion and reformed. Who knows? What I do know is that it's happening.

"Which is why I was leery of that Hutton when he showed up at the shack, what with our whiskey still being just over the hill. He raised the hair on the back of my neck."

"You still suspect him of being one of those snitches?"

"He looks the type."

"What type?"

"Like Pinkerton agents. I used to see them in depots. Could spot 'em a mile off. All had the same traits. Polite. Quiet. Calm. Deadly."

"*Deadly?*"

"One of my regular customers? His boy Roger works for Fred Barker who has the auto garage and stable just across the bridge from downtown."

That was where Mr. Hutton's handbills said he did his horse training. But she hadn't told Irv about their meeting on the street, so she said, "I know the place."

"Well, Roger saw this Hutton, if that's his real name, shoot the head off a rattlesnake poised to strike a deputy sheriff. Faster than a blink, Roger said."

He described the incident to Laurel as it had been told to him. "They were all dumbfounded, none more than Sheriff Amos, who'd been disarmed before he realized what was happening. The deputy had dirty drawers.

"But Roger claims Hutton took it in stride, never broke a sweat, like he was accustomed to beheading rattlers with one shot from twenty yards, firing a pistol he'd never touched before." After taking another bite, he'd added, "This is damn good pie, Laurel. Save some for Ernie."

"Of course."

She wished he would elaborate on Thatcher Hutton without her having to prompt him with questions. However, he said no more about him, and returned to the topic of avoiding detection.

Days ago she had proposed to her partners that she take over half of Irv's "regulars" route, giving him more time to work on the new still. "It only makes sense," she had argued, stressing that she had time on her hands, and that the new still was essential to increasing their production. After a lengthy back-and-forth with the two men, she'd gotten them to agree.

But since she was now an active participant, actually transporting the product, Irv seized every opportunity, like tonight, to emphasize how careful she must be to avoid pitfalls.

"Don't make a track that leads off-road. Lawmen look for them. One of Ernie's cousins got caught by creating a trail with his truck that led through the woods straight to his still."

"But to get to our still, we have to drive over ground."

"So never turn off at the same place twice. Also, lawmen are on the lookout for anybody buying copper. It's a dead giveaway. I was lucky to sneak in mine for the new still. Bought the copper sheets from an outfit in Weatherford, then smuggled them in on the bottom of my truck."

He had already explained that the purchase of the copper had coincided with their leasing the house. That was why their other bills had gone unpaid. He had planned to make up the temporary shortfall soon by doubling whiskey production. Her "list" had limited his time to work on it.

"You trust the copper seller not to report you?" she asked now.

Irv laughed out loud. "He ain't gonna tell. He's supplying every moonshiner west of Fort Worth. See? The business is good for everybody."

"How's the still coming along?"

"About finished. Soon's the cap passes Ernie's inspection. He's persnickety about the tapering. Says even before it's sealed during a run, it's gotta fit into the cooker as tight as a..." Clearing his throat, he'd left the analogy unspoken and simply said the fit had to be airtight.

He then circled back to other giveaways. "Don't be caught with a stockpile of mason jars or sugar. Nobody needs twenty or thirty pounds of sugar at a time unless they're making moonshine."

"Where do you buy your supplies?"

"From my trusted suppliers, who will remain nameless."

"Nameless to me?"

"Especially to you. For your own safety as well as theirs. They're making money hand over fist, too, but they can't be too obvious about it and jeopardize their legitimate businesses."

"They could trust me."

"The system doesn't work that way, Laurel. Their trust in me doesn't rub off on you. You'll have to earn it yourself."

"All right. But what's the risk to me?"

"Competition for goods is fierce. Men have had knock-down-drag-outs over bags of Dixie Crystals. That might've been what got Wally Johnson killed."

"The man who was murdered?"

"Gossip is that he hijacked a hay wagon loaded with contraband sugar that was meant for somebody else. I don't know if it's true, but it stands to reason. His family have recently upped their production to meet the demand in Ranger and Breckenridge."

"Oil boom towns."

"Yep. Populated by hundreds of thirsty men that the Johnsons intend to keep quenched."

"Not you, though."

"Hell no," he said. "Those are lucrative markets, all right, but they come with risks Ernie and me aren't willing to take. The men working on those drilling rigs are a tough crowd. They'll shoot each other over a roll of dice, a perceived insult, or a whore. Pardon the mention."

"I can hardly take offense, Irv. I'm a moonshiner, in no position to judge how another woman makes her living."

"Well, around here they don't walk the streets like in the boom towns. Mostly they ply their trade at Lefty's."

"The roadhouse."

"That's why I told you not to go near it. If a man is so inclined, he can take his pleasure in the rooms upstairs. Or get skunk drunk in the back room. Lefty's is a regular den of iniquity. A blind tiger."

"A what?"

He'd explained the term, and she was astonished.

"A speakeasy? *Here?* Where there's a church on every corner?"

He snuffled. "Me and Ernie, and every moonshiner around, love nothing better than a tent revival that goes on for days. We raise more spirits selling corn liquor on the parking lot than the preachers raise under the tent. Make more money than what's dropped in the offering plate, too."

They laughed together before he turned solemn again. "When this new still is up and running, I'd like to expand the business. But those boom towns...naw," he said, shaking his head. "I'm too old for all that rowdiness. And, if I was to poach on the Johnsons' territory, they'd cut out my heart and feed it to a mad dog.

"Just as scary," he went on, "are the government agents on the hunt for bootleggers and moonshiners. And it's open season. They patrol every road going in and out of those oil towns, armed to the teeth. More and more of them are getting those new submachine guns. And even if it weren't for the guns, Ernie and me don't have a vehicle fast enough to outrun theirs."

They fell into a ponderous silence, each lost in thought. Laurel picked up a piece of pie crust left on her plate and crumbled it between her finger and thumb. Her mother had taught her the technique of making it flaky. She remembered standing on a footstool in the kitchen, watching as her mother combined the ingredients and added cold water, one drop at a time, until the dough was the perfect consistency to roll out on the floured surface.

She often felt a wave of nostalgia for her mother. But never for her father. The condemnation he would heap on his daughter, the moonshiner, perversely deepened her determination to succeed at it.

"Tell me more about Lefty's," she said.

"It does a brisk business. Folks come from all round."

"Who keeps him stocked?"

"A bootlegger out of Dallas. Or so I'm told. He's talked about, but not by name. Lefty also supports the local economy, though."

Laurel raised an inquisitive eyebrow.

All Irv said was, "Lefty and me have an understanding and do just fine by each other."

"Who else does he have an understanding with?"

"That's his business."

"It's *our* business, Irv. Our bills are caught up, but I don't want to be just caught up. I want to make money, and my stock-in-trade is moonshine whiskey." She leaned forward across the table. "Maybe Lefty—what's his last name?"

Irv scratched his cheek. "You know, I don't recall ever hearin'. It's always just been him and his wife, Gert.

"Could Lefty be enticed to buy more from you if you discounted the price per jar?"

"Jug."

"He buys by the jug?"

"He does, and I'm leaving well enough alone, missy. We'll make enough profit without taking a baseball bat to a hornets' nest." He ended on that note, pushing back his chair and announcing that he was beat. "Thanks for the pie. I don't think I've ever had better."

She wished him a good night. He retreated to his bedroom and shut the door, but Laurel was too keyed up to go to bed. Over the course of their lengthy conversation, several things had become crystal clear to her.

One. The new still would double their production, but it was unlikely that Irv's regulars would correspondingly double their consumption—especially under the watchful eyes of their wives. In order for the new still to pay for itself, they must increase their customer base.

Two. Ernie's talent was distillation and controlling the quality of their product. Thus far Irv had proved to be a crafty and capable distributor of it. However, neither thought like an entrepreneur. Growing the business would be her contribution, and she was eager to start.

It galled her to think that the Johnsons had a foothold in the boom towns. But any attempt to compete with cutthroat big-timers like them would be foolish and potentially hazardous.

And, realistically, neither Irv, nor Ernie, nor she could make the long and dangerous trips up and back to the oil patch towns, hauling hooch. In newspapers, they were portrayed as fertile fields for every form of wickedness. One was either a purveyor of it, or a victim, but no one was immune to peril.

If the immoral climate and fearsome competition weren't enough cause for trepidation, there were the heavily armed lawmen who couldn't be outrun.

Surely there was a safer, saner way to conduct business. But how, when the manufacturing and selling of their product were illegal? These inherent dangers wouldn't abound if they were making and selling hat pins, or sachets, or...

She drew focus on the coconut meringue confection in the center of the table.

Eight hours later, she was still seated at the table, but the pie had been replaced with the scattered contents of the recipe box her mother had given her when she married. She'd filled sheets of paper with scribbled notes, jotting down ideas as they occurred to her. Various lists had grown longer as the night had stretched into morning.

"What the hell's all this?"

Not having even noticed that Irv had emerged from his bedroom, dressed and expecting breakfast, Laurel looked at him and declared, "I'm going to need more than twenty or thirty pounds of sugar. A lot more."

TWENTY-FOUR

———◦◉◦———

For days after his discussion with Bill Amos at the creek, Thatcher couldn't shake everything they'd talked about. He accepted that suspicion would shadow him until it was confirmed that someone else had abducted Mrs. Driscoll. His bet was on the doctor. Sheriff Amos was leaning that way, too.

But Thatcher was no crime-solver, and he rejected having to pin on a badge in order to convince skeptics of his innocence.

Nevertheless, the specter of suspicion continued to weigh on him.

At least on this night, he had something to take his mind off of it for a while. He was going out to dinner. It would be a distraction, but not one he particularly looked forward to.

After work, he washed up and changed into a fresh white shirt, dark tie, and his black suit. He'd had it dry-cleaned, the tears in his pants and shoulder seam sewn up, and his shoes shined. He put on his fedora.

The cracked mirror above the dresser in his room reflected a man who looked like he had a lot on his mind, but one presentable enough to go to supper with Mr. Chester Landry.

The shoe salesman's invitation had taken Thatcher off guard. Except for renting rooms in the same boardinghouse, he and the city slicker from Dallas had nothing in common that Thatcher could see.

But when Landry had approached him the night before and invited him to join him for a dinner out, he'd felt obliged to accept.

Landry was waiting for him out on the porch. He too was wearing a dark suit, but his bow tie was the color of bile and his satiny vest was striped. Thatcher caught a glimpse of a gold jaw tooth when the salesman smiled in greeting and informed Thatcher that he would drive them to the café.

As they motored through the streets of Foley, Landry kept the conversation flowing, commenting on aspects of the town and how it compared to others on his sales route.

Thatcher wasn't the least bit interested in either women's footwear or the salesman's travels, but he listened attentively and made polite inquiries that encouraged Landry to keep the chitchat on himself and off Thatcher, which was precisely Thatcher's intention.

Most of the locals stuck to the more agrarian schedule with which they'd been reared and tended to eat their larger meal at noon. Consequently, Martin's Café wasn't all that crowded at the dinner hour.

But parked in front of it was a long, black Ford, the most expensive of this year's models. As Landry pulled in beside it, he said, "I see the mayor is dining here tonight."

"That's his car?"

"It is."

"You know him?"

"We've met. Chamber of Commerce meeting, I believe it was. I attended as a guest of Mr. Hancock."

Seated in the driver's seat of the town car was a man with the bill of a newsboy cap pulled low over his eyes. Thatcher asked, "Who's that?"

"Mayor Croft's *chauffeur*," Landry said, adding tongue-in-cheek, "and if you believe that, I'll sell you the Brooklyn Bridge."

They alighted from Landry's car. As they walked toward the entrance of the café, Thatcher got a closer look at Croft's chauffeur. He had bulky shoulders and the face of a boxer who'd gone a thousand rounds.

As Thatcher and Landry reached the door of the café, Bernie Croft emerged from it. Upon seeing them, he pulled up short. His eyes sawed between them, lighting on Landry. "Mr. Landry, isn't it?" He stuck out his hand and Landry shook.

"Thank you for remembering, Mayor Croft. Allow me to introduce—"

"I know who he is." Croft settled a brittle gaze on Thatcher. "Mr. Hutton."

Thatcher tipped his head.

Croft hooked his thumbs in the pockets of his vest. "Your companion is well known for his derring-do, Mr. Landry. And his amazing skill with a six-shooter." Then to Thatcher, "I heard you saved a deputy's life."

"A lot of agony, anyway."

"Well, splendid marksmanship."

"Thanks."

Landry stepped in. "What do you recommend from the menu, Mr. Croft?"

"You can't go wrong with the fried chicken." He doffed his hat. "Enjoy, gentlemen. 'Evening."

Landry murmured a response, then entered the café. Thatcher followed, but as he stepped inside, he looked over his shoulder to see the chauffeur holding the rear seat door open for Bernie Croft. Both were looking back at him.

———◆———

Clyde Martin was a rotund and cheerful man who took obvious pride in his establishment and its longevity. It had occupied the same corner on Main Street since the turn of the century, serving breakfast through dinner. Salt, pepper, and sugar shakers, along with bottles of ketchup and Tabasco, were kept on the tables.

Mr. Martin welcomed the new arrivals personally and ushered them to a table. Thatcher took the chair with its back to the wall, giving him a view of the entire room. This was his habit. But also, from the moment he'd noticed Landry loitering in the dark corner of the boardinghouse porch, unobtrusively observing the others as he smoked, Thatcher had determined that he would never turn his back to this man.

Was it Landry's sly grin and oily manner that put him off? His pomaded hair? Was it the gold tooth, tucked into his jaw like a kernel of secret knowledge waiting to be exposed and used to someone's disadvantage?

Thatcher also had gotten the sense that he was better acquainted with Bernie Croft than either had let on.

Thatcher couldn't specify what it was that caused him to question Landry's integrity, but on matters as important as trust, he relied on his gut. The salesman's friendly overtures toward him seemed a little too polished to be genuine or spontaneous.

Now, as Landry cut into his thick slice of fried ham, he said, "I am as tired of the other boarders as I am of Mrs. May's uninspired cooking."

"Why do you room there then?"

"It's cheap. But the company is dull. Their conversation isn't exactly scintillating, is it? Or even interesting."

"You seem to get on with Randy all right."

He smiled. "He isn't bad company. He can tell a good dirty joke. He's just young."

"Outgoing."

"Yes, he's gregarious. But underneath all the braggadocio, he's as shallow as this pool of redeye gravy." He dipped the slice of meat into it. "Unlike you."

Thatcher had chosen a T-bone. "Unlike me?"

"The strong, silent type." Landry intoned the statement like a stage actor.

Thatcher speared a bite of steak and put it in his mouth.

His failure to comment didn't deter Landry. "You keep your own counsel, Hutton." He wagged his fork at Thatcher. "You never give away what's going through your mind."

"Usually because it's not worth knowing."

"Oh, I doubt that. I seriously do." He appraised Thatcher as he broke off a piece of dinner roll and spread it with butter. "Tell me about yourself."

Thatcher gave him a sketchy biography, sharing nothing of importance. "Mustered out, was making my way back, wound up here."

"Where you got stuck and now plan to stay for a while. Is that about it?"

"Just taking it one day at a time."

"A man with no plan."

"In the trenches I saw men die in mid-sentence. Planning your next breath is a wasted effort."

"Strong, silent, *and* a philosopher."

Flashing the wily grin that instilled Thatcher with dislike as well as mistrust, Chester held his stare a beat longer, then continued eating. When he was done, he leaned back in his chair, patted his stomach, and sighed with contentment.

"Must say, that was tasty. I'll have to trust the mayor's endorsement and try the fried chicken next time."

"Have you had a hamburger at Lefty's?"

The salesman cocked his head. "Lefty's?"

"It's a roadhouse. Out a ways. I've heard the burgers are worth the drive."

Thatcher couldn't say what had prompted him to drop a mention of the roadhouse into the conversation. It had been a gambit, like placing a large opening bid only to see how the other player at the table would react.

Chester Landry didn't take the bait. He gave a *hmm* of disinterest, and signaled to Mr. Martin that they were finished. Thatcher noticed that they were the only two diners remaining. They passed on dessert but ordered coffee.

As Mr. Martin served it, he said, "Take your time, gentlemen. There's plenty in the pot for a refill."

Thatcher sipped his coffee piping hot and black. Landry added cream and sugar to his and stirred it for longer than necessary. When he lifted the spoon from the cup, he clinked it against the rim several times.

He said, "It's such a shame that you were—associated—with the investigation into the missing woman. That couldn't have been a pleasant experience."

"It didn't last long."

"Even so."

Thatcher sipped his coffee, saying nothing, hoping the subject would die.

Landry wagged his spoon just as he had his fork earlier. "See, Hutton? That's what I'm talking about. Most men would be furious, railing at the sheriff, at everybody who would listen about the unfairness of your detention. You act unaffected, but I wonder if behind the steely veneer, you're seething. Or are you truly this slow to rile?"

Before Thatcher could answer, motion toward the back of the café drew his attention. The swinging door into the kitchen was being pushed open. By Laurel Plummer. By Laurel Plummer's bottom. Her very shapely bottom.

She was attempting to wedge through the door with both hands raised, each supporting what looked like a baking dish draped in a dish towel. It was a precarious balancing act.

In an instant, Thatcher was out of his chair. Mr. Martin was late to respond because he'd been behind the counter matching the day's receipts with the money in his till.

Thatcher pulled wide the door.

"Thank you, Mr. Martin," she said as she was turning. "I shouldn't have tried to—" She came to an abrupt stop and blinked up at Thatcher. Several seconds passed without either of them speaking, then she mumbled a thank you and sidestepped to go around him.

He reached for the dish in her left hand. "Let me take this one."

"No thank you. I've got them."

Mr. Martin rushed around the end of the counter. "Mrs. Plummer, forgive me. My people working in back were supposed to tell me when you got here."

"It's quite all right. They were busy." She took a breath and gave a shaky smile. "As ordered, a pecan pie and a peach cobbler."

She handed them to Mr. Martin in turn. He set the baked goods side by side on the counter and whisked off the muslin towels with the flourish of a magician over a top hat. "Ah, they look scrumptious. Beautiful, too. My wife, God rest her soul, always got the crust too brown."

Laurel looked pleased but self-conscious over the compliment. "I hope your customers approve."

"I've got two gents here now who turned down dessert, but I'll bet they'll reconsider." He winked at her. "Gentlemen, Mrs. Plummer has started baking for me, and her pies are out of this world. The cobbler is still warm. Can I tempt you? I'll add a scoop of ice cream on the house."

"You've sold me," Chester Landry said. He had pushed away from the table and was standing with his napkin in his hand. "Mrs. Plummer, Chester Landry." He touched his chest and gave her a nod.

"How do you do."

"Actually, I regretted that my dinner partner—oh, forgive me. This is Mr. Thatcher Hutton."

The introduction required her to acknowledge him again, something she had avoided doing since her stunned reaction to another unexpected meeting with him. Having recovered, she now said coolly, "Mr. Hutton."

"Mrs. Plummer."

Landry said, "As I was saying, to my disappointment, Mr. Hutton had declined dessert, so I felt compelled to do likewise. Thank you for coming to my rescue."

"I hope you enjoy the cobbler."

Landry pulled an empty chair from beneath the table. "Would you care to join us?"

"No." Then, as though realizing how curtly she'd answered, she added, "I can't. I have other deliveries to make."

She turned back to Mr. Martin and spoke to him in an undertone. Thatcher didn't catch her words, but Martin said, "Of course, of course," and bustled back around the counter to the cash register.

Laurel meticulously folded the dish towels and tucked them beneath her arm. When Mr. Martin returned to her, she extended her hand, and he counted out bills into her palm. She slipped the money into a pocket of her skirt. "Do you want to place an order for Thursday, Mr. Martin?"

"Can you do another apple? And people are still raving about the lemon meringue."

"I could make another lemon, of course. Although..." She dragged out the word, capturing the café owner's attention. "I also do a chocolate meringue."

"One apple, one lemon, one chocolate."

She reached across the counter to shake his hand. "Thank you. I'll see you before closing on Thursday."

She turned and gave Chester Landry a nod, which looked token to Thatcher. He outdistanced her to the swinging door and pulled it open for her. "I'll walk you out."

"No thank you. I'm in a hurry."

He suspected her of fibbing about having more deliveries to make, but there was no way to gracefully call her on it.

"Then good night, Mrs. Plummer."

"Good night."

He watched her wend her way through the kitchen, where two women were washing dishes, and a man was chopping up raw chickens. After Laurel disappeared through the rear exit, Thatcher let the door swing shut. Mr. Martin was behind the counter spooning Landry's cobbler into a bowl.

Landry himself had remained standing, his hand on the back of his chair, smarmy smile in place. Thatcher walked over and resumed his seat.

As Landry sat down, he said, "I was wrong."

"About what?" Thatcher sipped his cold coffee.

"One sometimes *can* guess what's going through your mind." He cocked an eyebrow in a one-man-to-another leer.

Thatcher gave him a long, unwavering stare from which most men would back down. Landry's grin only widened enough to reveal his gold tooth.

Thatcher badly wanted to knock it out.

Instead he called over to Mr. Martin, "I'll have a slice of the pecan pie, please. No ice cream."

His attempt to deflect Landry's interest only seemed to amuse the man more. But the salesman didn't pursue the subject of Laurel Plummer. Instead he asked Thatcher about his horse training technique.

Each bite of the rich pie melted in Thatcher's mouth.

As they left the café, Thatcher declined the ride back to the boardinghouse. "I need to stretch my legs. I'm going to walk back." Giving Landry no opportunity to quibble, he stuck out his right hand. "Thanks for dinner."

Chester Landry shook hands. "Don't get used to it. Next time it's Dutch treat."

Thatcher, planning for there never to be a next time, smiled as expected, then turned and headed down the street in the opposite direction from which he intended to go.

He waited until Landry's car was out of sight, then doubled back. He looked in Hancock's storefront window. The advertisement was still there.

He continued on, following the directions Bernie Croft had given him that first day.

Along the way, he kept to the shadows. Five minutes later, the picturesque facade of the Driscolls' house came into view. Lights were on in some of the downstairs rooms, including the parlor with the bay window, the doctor's office.

Aware of Miss Eleanor Wise's seemingly uninterrupted vigilance, Thatcher didn't go any farther, but took cover behind the catty-corner neighbor's detached shed. He slid down the exterior wall of it, worked his butt around until he'd created a depression for it in the ground, and settled in to wait.

What he was anticipating, he couldn't say. The sudden reappearance of Mrs. Driscoll? A surefire giveaway of the doctor's guilt?

He was irrationally annoyed with Bill Amos for lending credibility to his notions about the physician. If the sheriff had instead laughed himself silly over them, Thatcher wouldn't be sitting here in the dark, swatting at mosquitoes, accomplishing nothing.

Time passed. He whiled most of it away thinking about Laurel Plummer. She'd charmed Mr. Martin into increasing his order, and had seemed damned pleased with herself for having done so. Her features hadn't looked as strained as they had the other times Thatcher had seen her. The smile she'd given the café owner looked genuine.

She'd been dressed different, too. Her skirt was shorter than any he'd seen her in before. It was nipped in at the waist. And, right off, he'd noticed the good fit of her blouse.

He wished he'd thought of an excuse to touch her during the brief time she'd been in the café.

As mouthwatering as her pie had been, Thatcher was certain her mouth would be even more delicious.

He'd enjoyed the sight of her bottom wiggling its way through that door, and couldn't help thinking back onto what it had felt like when it had bumped up against his front during the rooster episode, as he'd come to think of it.

The contact hadn't lasted more than a few seconds, but it had flooded him with lust then, and remembering it did now, not for the first time. He meant no disrespect. He had no control over the fantasies about her that came to his mind, some so vivid and arousing they justified Landry's insinuating grin.

He wished he'd punched that sly mug.

As the lights in the Driscoll house began to go out, he pushed the image of Laurel from his mind. The last light to be turned off was on the second floor, the bedroom no doubt.

Thatcher stood up and looked toward the old busybody's house. "I guess we can get to bed now."

He slipped out of the cover of the shed and headed toward the boardinghouse, hoping he wouldn't be spotted walking the streets where he didn't belong, skulking around in the dark, like a criminal returning to the scene of his crime.

TWENTY-FIVE

Laurel pulled her Ford into the gravel drive that led around to the back of the house. Irv had told her always to park facing out toward the street in case she ever had to leave in a hurry. "It'll probably never happen, but...you know."

Tonight may be the night when taking the precaution would pay off.

Although it wasn't something easily done, she executed the three point turn and killed the headlights. She reached beneath the seat for the pistol Irv had insisted she begin keeping with her. She couldn't feature an instance where she would actually fire it, but it was a comforting weight in her hand now.

Her heartbeat thumped as she made a rapid sweep of her surroundings, then took more time to probe the shadows for a possible ambush, seeking out anyone who might have followed her from Martin's Café, which had been the last stop on tonight's round despite her claim of having more deliveries to make.

As she'd pulled away from the alley behind the café, she'd had no indication that she was under anyone's surveillance. Nevertheless, during the drive home, she'd half expected someone to roar up behind her.

She waited inside her car for several minutes longer, but no one showed himself, nothing stirred. Weak with relief, she dropped the pistol in her lap, placed both hands on the steering wheel, and pressed her damp forehead against the backs of them. She took deep breaths.

Of all people to happen upon: the perceptive Mr. Thatcher Hutton. While standing face-to-face with him, one of Mr. Martin's cooks was out back retrieving four jars of moonshine from the trunk of her car.

At the sight of Mr. Hutton, her heart had almost burst. But, despite the unexpectedness of their near collision, she'd recovered reasonably well, she thought now. Mr. Martin had kept his head and had given nothing away. Of course, he wasn't the novice that she was. Since the county had been dry for decades, Clyde Martin had been pouring illegal alcoholic beverages for drinking customers for as long as he'd been in business. Or so Irv had informed her.

Neither Mr. Hutton nor the man with him, whose name now escaped her, had seemed the least bit suspicious of her transaction with Mr. Martin, or of the order he had placed for three pies, which, in the coded language they'd worked out between them, translated to that many pies, plus twice that number of jars of corn liquor.

She'd taken her money and run, getting a nod from the cook on her way through the kitchen that the transfer of fruit jars from her car to a hidden compartment in the kitchen had been conducted without detection. Nothing had gone awry.

All the same, she felt she had escaped a close call.

Deciding it was safe to do so, she turned off the engine and got out. She let herself into the house through the back door and went directly upstairs to her bedroom, relieved that she didn't have to explain her shakes to Irv, who was helping Ernie at the still tonight.

As she entered her room, she left the light off, being more fearful of light than of the dark. She acknowledged that was standard criminal behavior.

Hands still unsteady, she set the pistol on the dresser. The handgun was small enough to fit in her palm, but Irv had assured her that the business end of it would give pause to anyone with harmful intent. He'd also assured her that it wasn't the one Derby had used to kill himself.

Feeling claustrophobic, she hastily undressed. When she was down to her chemise, she poured water from the pitcher into the wash bowl and sponged off a film of nervous sweat. Then, moving to the bed, she sat on the edge of it and bowed her head, if not in prayer, certainly in relief.

Over the past several weeks, she had become so wrapped up in her exciting new enterprise, that, at times, she had to pause and remind herself that she wasn't playing a high stakes game where she was merely trying to out-trick an opponent. She was breaking the law. If caught, the penalty was steep. She did not want to go to jail. Nor did she want to be responsible for Irv and Ernie being incarcerated.

When she'd first laid out her idea to use bakery goods as a cover for moving moonshine, Irv had responded with guffaws. Then he'd put up stubborn resistance, followed by pessimistic predictions. But after talking herself hoarse, she'd finally won his grudging support to try it.

"Just for a time. If it doesn't work, I'll stop."

He'd retorted, "If it doesn't work, we'll all be behind bars."

Clyde Martin, the restauranteur, had been the logical choice for their first prospective client.

"He used to keep a bootlegged stock," Irv had told her. "So long as it was only a state infraction, and a fine if caught, he poured bourbon and scotch on the sly and called it 'Mama's sweet tea.' He bought his moonshine from me. But the new law spooked him. He stopped buying, and, as far as I know, has gone completely dry. I don't figure he's a convert to abstinence, though. Might be worth me going to see him."

"Let me."

Irv had argued, but ultimately relented. "All right. But...Don't take this wrong, Laurel. When you go soliciting, wouldn't hurt if you girlied up some."

"Girlied up? What does that mean?"

"You know what it means. Every woman in the world knows what it means."

"I'm not soliciting at Lefty's."

"All's I'm saying is, you might want to throw away those baggy old shirts of Derby's and fix yourself up to be more...girlified."

She'd spent that evening taking in the waistlines of garments that she'd let out during her pregnancy. As an afterthought, she'd also taken up the hemlines an inch and a half. She'd ironed a blouse with a front placket flanked by strips of lace, and had dusted off her best hat.

She'd timed her arrival at the café during the lull between the midday meal and dinner. She gave the busboy her name and asked to see Mr. Martin. After getting clearance, he'd escorted her to a cramped office off the kitchen.

When she'd walked in, Clyde Martin had been standing behind his desk, looking the picture of benevolence. "Mrs. Plummer. I'd like to express my sincere condolences for your—"

She'd cut him off. "You're losing money, Mr. Martin."

"I...I beg your pardon."

"Try this." She'd taken a mason jar of moonshine from her tote bag, strode forward, and set it on the paper-littered desk.

"And this." Also from the tote, she'd produced a slice of apple pie wrapped in wax paper and set it beside the jar. "You need to be offering both in your café. I'll come back tomorrow to work out the particulars of a deal. Have a pleasant afternoon." She'd left him with his mouth agape.

When she'd returned the following day, Mr. Martin had been eager to negotiate terms. He'd soon learned that she was no shrinking violet, further weakened by grief. Settling on a price, he'd placed an initial order for two pies and 4 jars of moonshine. "I'll come by twice weekly to deliver the products and take your next order," she'd told him.

As they shook hands on the deal, he'd said, "I thought you were going to apply for a waitress job."

"This pays better."

Initially, Irv had kept up his route and the handyman cover, but once the new still was in operation, she'd suggested that she take over his deliveries. "I could drive your route on the days I don't bake."

"You can't drive my truck."

"Why not?"

"It's a truck."

She'd given him a roll of her eyes. "I could drive it, but you make a valid point. It would attract unwanted curiosity. Instead, what if you built some kind of false floor in my car, the way you did in your truck?"

He'd fashioned a false bottom in her trunk, creating a hidey-hole underneath, which she padded with an old quilt. Thus outfitted, she'd begun driving his route. As she became better acquainted with the roads and back roads in the area, she'd gone further afield, scouting for new opportunities.

She'd picked up two cafés in two different towns, both of which had been customers of Irv's before becoming gun shy of the Prohibition law. In addition to delicious pies, cobblers, and corn whiskey, she'd promised her customers utmost discretion.

As Irv was leaving one evening to work at the still, she'd approached him with another idea. "What about Logan's Grocery?"

"What about it?"

"As a possible broker."

"Hell'd freeze over first. A nicer man you'll never meet. Logan extends credit even to folks he knows will take a long time paying. But he's a staunch teetotaler. His wife was the standard bearer for the local temperance society."

"Does he sell fresh baked goods in his store?"

"Not that I know of."

"He should, don't you think? I'll pay him a call and take samples."

"I just told you, Laurel, he—"

"I saw a notice in his window that he offers delivery service for a small charge."

"That's recent."

"Who makes the deliveries?"

"A couple of young men. Twins, in fact. Davy and Mike O'Connor."

"Are they teetotalers?"

He'd scoffed. "They worked in the pool hall until it was forced to shut down. A campaign led by Mrs. Logan, by the way. I guess Logan felt bad about the twins losing their livelihood. He hired them to deliver groceries."

"Hmm."

It took several days for her to secure an interview with the busy grocer. As Irv had said of him, he was extremely polite, and highly complimentary of the samples of pie she'd brought for him to try. Even so, he'd declined.

"I would like to stock them, Mrs. Plummer, but the problem is a shortage of shelf space. I'm at full capacity."

She'd made a sound of regret. "That is unfortunate. Because I notice that all the baked goods you carry are factory-made and pack-aged." After a strategic pause, she'd added, "There's nothing wrong with that, of course."

At that, his smile had slipped a bit.

The next day, she'd gone back and told him, with rehearsed animation, that she had slept on his dilemma and believed that she had a solution.

"I could make up a menu of my pies. You display it and take orders. The pies will be delivered from my kitchen directly to the customer. You never have to touch the goods, and they won't take up your valuable shelf space."

"How would you get the orders?"

"You could telephone them in to me."

"Do you have a telephone?"

"I will by tomorrow." Her cheekiness had made him smile. "I think this idea is growing on you, Mr. Logan."

"You certainly have my interest, and I admire your initiative, which is rare in a young and recent widow."

"But?"

"But we haven't yet talked terms."

Acting *girlified*, she'd smoothed her hands over her skirt nervously, then had pretended to summon the courage to open the bidding. "For each pie order you submit, I'll give you ten percent."

"Fifteen."

"*Fifteen?*"

"My two deliverymen are kept busy during store hours. Your deliveries will have to be made after closing. I'll have to pay them extra."

After-hours deliveries were what she'd hoped for, but she'd pursed her lips as though she hadn't considered this stumbling block. "Perhaps just one could work overtime. Perhaps they could swap off."

"They're twins. Inseparable, and they work as a unit. One drives their truck and waits, while the other runs the delivery to the customer's door. It's a very efficient system. With the two of them working together, it takes only half as long to make the deliveries. Because they're paid by the hour, it's actually more economic to have both on the payroll."

She'd appeared impressed by his business savvy, but crestfallen by how it affected their deal. "I see. Well, I'll give you two percent more to cover that expense. For a total of twelve."

"Fifteen."

"Thirteen."

"Fifteen."

She'd been prepared to give him twenty. Her cash crop wasn't pies. It was whiskey. "You drive a hard bargain, Mr. Logan. I'll agree to fifteen percent."

He beamed.

Then she'd jerked the rug out from under him. "But we haven't yet shaken on it. There is a matter that concerns me, because I can't take any chances with my reputation as a businesswoman. I'm sure you understand."

"Of course. What's the nature of your concern?"

"Your deliverymen. My father-in-law told me they used to work in a pool parlor. Are they presentable? Do they have integrity? Can I trust them?"

"What Mr. Plummer told you is correct. They went through a wild phase, as young men are wont to do, but they've been tempered by my influence and that of Mrs. Logan. I've received no complaints from customers about their comportment. I wouldn't have them in the store if I thought they were dishonest. I'll summon them right now so you can meet them."

"No, if they know employment is riding on the introduction, they'll be on their best behavior, won't they? I'd rather see them in action, when they don't know it's an audition. As I leave, I'll pick out some grocery items and opt to have them delivered. If I approve their service and manner, you'll get your fifteen percent."

She'd straightened her backbone. "But if in my opinion they're unsuitable for any reason, I'll hire someone else and pay him out of my share, in which case, your percentage will be reduced to thirteen percent. That's the deal, Mr. Logan. Nonnegotiable."

"I'm agreeing because I'm confident that the O'Connor twins will work well for you."

Laurel had been confident of that herself.

That evening, Davy O'Connor had showed up at her front door, a box of groceries balanced on his shoulder. He flashed her a winning smile. "Mrs. Plummer, good evening. Whenever you come into the store, the very sight of you makes my day. But in this gloaming light, you look a vision. Your—"

"Cut it out. Mr. Logan went for it. Have Mike drive around to the back. I baked a strawberry and rhubarb pie for our celebration."

Her deal with the O'Connor brothers had been struck even before she had approached Logan.

Irv had been downright apoplectic when she'd advanced her idea to use the twins. "They're crazy kids. Rambunctious and reckless. Wish I'd never told you about them."

"Well you did. Please arrange a meeting."

Davy and Mike would have been interchangeable except for Davy's front tooth, which at some point in his boyhood had been chipped by a fist thrown by Mike. Both were handsome, flirtatious, and devilishly witty. Laurel liked them instantly.

Irv had informed them that the meeting was to discuss the peddling of moonshine. Already enticed, the two had been eager to hear what Laurel had in mind. Gathered around the kitchen table, she'd gotten down to business. "We need runners to move our product. You seem qualified."

"Count us in," Davy had said, winking at her. "We like excitement, right, brother?"

"We only went to work in that bloody store because we need to eat."

Laurel had explained why they would need to continue working at the store. "At least for the time being. We need the cover of a legitimate business."

The twins had looked at each other, obviously troubled. Speaking for both, Davy had said, "You know the Logans walk the straight and narrow."

"I've told her that," Irv had said.

"Mrs. Logan is trying to save our souls." Mike had grinned when he said that. "Being Catholic is failing in that regard, according to her."

"So when I approach Mr. Logan I should—"

"Act the prude, lady Laurel."

"I'll keep that in mind." When she'd told them her plans for expanding the business, they'd surprised Irv and her by contributing ideas of their own.

"All those men who used to hang out at the pool hall have worked up powerful thirsts, Mrs. Plummer. We can sell them your whiskey, whether or not they buy the baked goods."

"But we'll push your pies, too," Mike had said as though pledging fealty.

As hoped, Mr. Logan's customers had gone wild for Laurel's pies. The twins delivered them after hours and, while at it, peddled moonshine to standing customers. Two weeks into their sideline, the twins had asked for another meeting with Irv and Laurel.

Davy had acted as spokesperson. "One of our friends from the pool hall is working up in Ranger. He says if we deliver your pies up there, he could sell them for a dollar a slice."

Irv had dismissed that with a harrumph. "That ain't worth the bother or the price of gasoline. It's seventy miles one way."

Mike had said, "If, along with the pies, we delivered five gallons of whiskey—"

"Five *gallons*?"

"Every other day." Davy had turned to Laurel and winked.

Irv and she had given the O'Connors the go-ahead. Wearing their Saint Christopher medals for protection, they'd begun making trips to places where angels feared to tread. Irv and Ernie had difficulty keeping up with the demand.

And so had Laurel. A second oven had become necessary. She'd applied at the First National Bank for a loan. The bank officer, a long-standing customer of Irv's moonshine, had approved the note. To accommodate the new appliance, Laurel had moved their dining table from the kitchen into the unfurnished dining room.

Between making deliveries and baking, she'd become so busy that hours would go by without Pearl crossing her mind. Her marriage to Derby seemed to have belonged to another woman in another life far removed from the one she was living. But as exhilarating as this venture was, it came with constant threats to her newfound independence, even to her life. She'd had a shocking reminder of that tonight when, once again, she'd crossed paths with Thatcher Hutton.

Recently, on a trip out to the still to deliver supplies to Ernie, as they passed the cutoff to the shack, she'd casually remarked to Irv that it seemed a long time ago since Mr. Hutton had wandered into the yard asking for directions.

Irv had said, "*If* he wandered, and *if* it was directions he was after."

Her father-in-law still had Thatcher typed as a man who was polite, quiet, calm. And deadly.

Now, as she huddled on the side of her bed, Laurel wondered if the cowboy who broke horses was a guise for a government agent who broke up stills.

On the front page of today's newspaper had been a picture of a still in northeast Texas near the Arkansas line that had been discovered and destroyed by state and federal law enforcement officers, unsmiling men with firearms and stern resolve.

They'd been grouped around the disassembled still and busted casks, spilled corn liquor pooling around their boots and the hand-cuffed men sitting on the ground. The photograph had been staged to make a point, to send a warning to current or aspiring distillers of illegal whiskey.

Was Thatcher Hutton one of the snitches that Irv had warned her to be wary of? Had he come to the shack that day looking for a still? Did he suspect her of doing precisely what she was doing? Was that why he always regarded her with such intensity?

Despite the summer heat that had collected in her bedroom during the afternoon, her arms broke out in gooseflesh. She clumsily removed the pins from her bun and let it unfurl down her back. Ordinarily the release felt good. But tonight the scene in the café had left her nape and shoulders knotted with tension.

She folded back the bed covers and slid in beneath the top sheet. She settled her head on her pillow, closed her eyes, and tried willing herself not to dwell on the encounter.

But her mind replayed the incident anyway. Had she done any-thing that might have given her away? Should she tell Irv about it? No. Absolutely not. He would make far more of it than it warranted. He would say that she hadn't just bumped into any man during a delivery, she'd bumped into *that* man.

As reluctant as she was to admit it, her father-in-law would be right.

Whatever else he was, Thatcher Hutton was no ordinary man.

And neither was her middle's flighty reaction to the very sight of him.

TWENTY-SIX

W hat are you doing out here?" Randy asked as he clomped up the front steps of the boardinghouse.

"Too early to go to bed. Just taking in the air," Chester Landry replied. He lazily fanned himself with a folded newspaper. "You appear to be drunk."

Randy laughed and plopped down into the chair beside Landry's. "As a skunk."

"Fun evening?"

"Fun and frolic, my friend." He chortled over his alliteration.

Landry shushed him. "Lower your voice. Everyone else has turned in for the night." Everyone except for him, Randy, and Thatcher Hutton, who'd yet to return to the boardinghouse since they'd bade each other good night at the café.

Landry couldn't help but wonder if his dinner guest had cut out on him in order to follow the widow home. He made a mental note to pursue that later, but, right now, his focus was more on the indiscreet and talkative Randy Wells.

"Who were you frolicking with?"

Randy leaned across the arm of his chair and crooked his finger. Landry moved closer. Randy said, "The public library hosts a Bible study every Tuesday night for young singles."

"What's to whisper about?"

Randy giggled. "What's to whisper about is what happens after Bible study."

Landry pretended that was the most delicious piece of information he'd ever heard. "Do tell."

"Those young ladies who sing in church choirs on Sunday are just dying to be led astray on Tuesday. So me and some other guys—"

"Like who?"

"Davy and Mike O'Connor? Know them?"

"I don't believe so."

"You'd know if you did. They're twins. Anyhow, they've joined the Bible study because they work for Deacon Logan, and his wife is practically a missionary. She..." He hiccupped, then waved his hand. "Doesn't matter. Tonight, we treated a few of those young ladies to all the sin they could handle."

"You and these O'Connor brothers?"

"They are my kind of folk. If you know what I mean?" He bobbed his eyebrows.

"Drunk and disorderly?"

Randy roared with laughter.

"Shhh!"

"Oh, sorry." He pressed his index finger vertically against his lips.

"You know what?" Landry said, as though he'd had a sudden inspiration, when actually he'd been planning this since his talk with Mayor Croft about Randy and his loose tongue. "I could use some diversion. I had a rather dull evening tonight with Mr. Hutton."

"Tight-lipped, isn't he? Good at cards, though. Do you think he cheats?"

"If he does, he's good. I haven't caught him at it."

"No, me neither. Lost five bucks to him."

Landry pushed out of his chair. "Come on."

Randy stood up swaying. "Where're we going?"

"For a drive. Did you sinners drink all your hooch?"

"Still have half a jar under the seat of my car."

"Then let's go in it." He threw his arm across Randy's shoulder. "But I'll drive."

TWENTY-SEVEN

———◆———

Dusk was easing into full-blown darkness when Bill Amos came out of his headquarters and headed toward his car. Thatcher had been waiting for this opportunity to speak to him in private.

"Bill?"

The sheriff turned as Thatcher materialized out of the wide band of shadow under the eaves of the building. "Hey, Thatcher. What's doing?"

"Got a minute?"

Bill glanced back toward his office, hesitated, then asked, "Have you had supper?"

"No."

"Me neither, and Mrs. Amos is hosting bridge tonight. Get in."

Thatcher went around to the passenger side. Once on the road, he asked, "What's your wife's name?"

"Daisy. Her bridge club meets one night a month."

"Does she know how to play poker?"

Bill laughed. "Not with you, she doesn't." After a beat, he said, "I'm glad she's having the group at the house tonight. She doesn't entertain as often as she used to."

That had sounded like a loaded statement. Thatcher waited for him to expand.

Bill cleared his throat. "Daisy isn't always up to socializing. She has...declines. A heart condition."

"I'm sorry to hear that."

"Yeah, well, you know. Life." He gave Thatcher a weak smile. "How's it been treating you lately?"

"Can't complain. Me and Ulysses have finally resolved our differences. His owner is picking him up later this week."

"Will he take to another rider?"

"We'll see."

Bill chuckled. "I wouldn't want to be the first to try. Did you fill that last stall?"

"I've got a waiting list."

Bill removed his pocket watch and checked the time. "I have a hankering for a juicy hamburger. Have you been to Lefty's yet?"

Thatcher shook his head.

"Then you're past due." He tucked his watch away and settled into his seat. "Did you wait in the dark to see me so you could ask my wife's name?"

"Naw." Thatcher exhaled heavily and propped his elbow on the door ledge. "I was wondering if you had talked to that woman, Dr. Driscoll's patient who had the breech birth."

Bill gave him a sharp look, swerving in the process. The driver of an oncoming vehicle tooted a warning. Bill waved an apology as he passed a jalopy of a truck with two young men inside.

"Mrs. Plummer's delivery boys."

Thatcher reacted with a start. "Her delivery boys?"

Bill told him about the arrangement Laurel had made with Logan's Grocery. Although Thatcher turned his head aside and pretended to be absorbed in the passing scenery, he listened with avid interest.

"I hear her pies are selling like hot cakes," Bill said. "No pun intended."

"I knew she'd gone into the business. One night last week, I had supper in Martin's Café. While I was there, she came in to deliver an order."

"Really? To Clyde?"

"Um-huh."

"Huh."

"What?"

"Nothing. Just that Clyde has always used his own cooks for everything."

"I guess he prefers her pies to theirs."

"Guess so. Have you sampled her wares yet?"

Thatcher looked over to see if there was an innuendo behind the question, but Bill had his head turned away, signaling to make a left turn. "I had a slice of pecan pie."

"Was it good?"

"Damn good."

Bill had turned onto a road leading away from town. "We've got a ways to go before we get to Lefty's," he said. "Tell me why you asked about Gabe Driscoll's patient."

"I've been watching his house every night for a week."

Bill looked across at him with both consternation and curiosity. "What for?"

Thatcher started by telling him about his dinner out with Chester Landry. "He's a shoe—"

"I know who he is and what he claims to be."

"Claims to be?"

"Are y'all pals?"

"Hell, no," Thatcher said. "I don't trust that grin of his."

"So why'd you go to dinner with him?"

"I didn't have a reason not to."

Bill gave him a knowing glance. "You want to find out what he's hiding behind that grin."

He was right, but Thatcher didn't want to admit it. "Anyway, that's why I was in the café when Mrs. Plummer came in. By the time Landry and I had finished our desserts, I'd had about all of his company

I could stomach. I opted to walk back to the boardinghouse. But I didn't go straight there. I circled around to the Driscolls' place."

"Again, what for?"

"Shit, I don't know. But after you and I talked about the doc, the coincidences that took place that night, I couldn't get it off my mind. I just felt led to go over there, take a look-see. I didn't really expect to uncover anything, didn't even know what I was looking for. But I went back the next night, and I've been going back." He paused. "Did you question that woman again?"

"Her name is Norma Blanchard, and, yes, I went straight from our conversation by the creek to talk to her about that night."

"And?"

"Have you changed your mind about becoming a deputy?"

"No."

"Then I shouldn't be discussing an open investigation."

"You called it open-ended. Doesn't mean the same as active, does it?"

Bill waved that away with annoyance. "Speak your mind, Thatcher."

They were in the countryside now. They passed barbed wire–fenced pastures with horses and cattle grazing, farmhouses lit by lamps and lanterns instead of incandescent bulbs, chalky rock formations.

Thatcher took time to choose carefully what he was going to say and how he was going to phrase it. He turned slightly in his seat to better address Bill and gauge his reactions.

"Describe Norma Blanchard."

"Late twenties, I'd say. Dark hair, parted down the middle, all knotted up in back. Not pretty, but…Just say men would take to her better than women would."

"She came to the doc's house last night."

Bill gnawed on that as Thatcher figured he would. "After office hours?"

"At eleven twenty-eight."

He shrugged. "Could've been an emergency."

Thatcher said nothing, just looked at him.

"But you don't think so."

"No, I don't, Bill. She was dropped off at the street, and seemed in perfect health, best as I could tell by the way she walked."

"How'd she walk?"

"Like she owned the place. Knocked on the door the same way. The doc was up, or at least his bedroom light was on. Drapes were drawn but there was light around the edges of them, which was why I hadn't left yet.

"He came to the door in his pajamas and a bathrobe. It appeared to me that he wasn't altogether happy to see her. In fact, when she tried to step inside, he blocked her. They didn't raise their voices, or tussle, but there was a lot of angry gesturing. Eventually, he let her in."

Bill kept his eyes on the road and didn't comment, so Thatcher continued. "I don't know where they spent their time while inside, because no other lights in the house came on. If she'd come for medicine or something, they'd've gone into his office, don't you think?"

"How long did she stay?"

"Almost an hour. The car came back at twelve-fifteen. She walked out to it and got in, it drove off. A few minutes later, the upstairs bedroom light went off."

"She didn't have the baby with her?"

"No. Could have been in the car, I guess."

"Did you see who was driving?"

"Another woman."

"Her sister, no doubt. Patsy Kemp. They live together. Mrs. Kemp's husband is off working somewhere. Montana, Alaska, somewhere like that. Which is why Norma is living with her, I guess."

"Norma isn't married?"

"I didn't ask, but she wasn't wearing a wedding band and no reference was made to a husband."

"Did you see the baby?"

"He was sleeping there in a basket in the living room. She showed him off to me. If he was born out of wedlock, she gave no sign of being ashamed about it."

"What did she tell you about Dr. Driscoll?"

"What she'd told Scotty when he questioned her, which matched what Gabe had told us. He paid her a house call earlier in the day while she was still in labor. On his way home from Lefty's, he stopped there again to check on her. In the meantime, she'd given birth and all was well."

Thatcher took off his hat and ran his fingers through his hair. "I feel like a damn peeping Tom."

"It feels like that sometimes."

"What feels like that?"

"Detective work."

"That's not what I was doing."

"Then you are a peeping Tom. Swear to God, Thatcher, I ought to arrest you again."

Thatcher shot him a look.

"Well then, tell me what's compelled you to go over there every night for the past week?"

"I wish now I hadn't. I wish I'd left it alone."

"No you don't."

Thatcher gave him another hard look, which didn't dent Bill in the slightest. He said, "If you had wanted it left alone, you wouldn't have told me about Norma's late-night visit."

Thatcher didn't have a chance to form a comeback. They had arrived at the roadhouse. There were twenty or thirty vehicles parked around it, and yet only weak light shone through the screened windows. Built of unpainted clapboard, the structure was as square as a box of saltines and totally without character. A set of warped wood steps led up to the entrance.

It looked nothing like the speakeasy Thatcher had been to in Norfolk, which had had the classy veneer of the haberdashery and an aura of intrigue.

"You seem let down," Bill remarked.

Thatcher shrugged. "Doesn't have much atmosphere."

"Oh, it's got atmosphere." He reached beneath his car seat and came up with a Colt revolver. "A hostile atmosphere."

TWENTY-EIGHT

———◦———

Bill passed the pistol to Thatcher. "It's loaded."

"Will I need it?"

"Depends." He didn't say on what.

Even though Thatcher had been told the gun was loaded, he checked the cylinder before pushing the pistol into his waistband and buttoning his jacket over it.

He and Bill got out of the car and walked toward the porch steps where two men sat smoking. As they went around them in order to reach the door, Bill addressed the men by name. They kept their heads down and replied to his greeting with surly mumbles.

The instant they stepped inside, the low rumble of conversation died. Bill acted as though he didn't notice and pointed Thatcher toward an empty table. They sat in adjacent chairs, both facing out into the room, their backs to the wall.

Thatcher was about to take off his fedora, when Bill said, "Leave it on. Bad manners, I know, but the brim shades your eyes. Nobody can tell where you're looking."

Following Bill's example, Thatcher left his hat on. Once his eyes had adjusted to the dim interior, made even foggier by tobacco and grease smoke, he surveyed the place, trying not to noticeably move his head.

The bar ran almost the full length of the back wall, but behind it, the shelves were stocked with bottled soft drinks only. A gramophone in the corner emitted scratchy, tinny music. Only a few of the tables were occupied.

Thatcher remarked on the small crowd. "Doesn't match the number of vehicles outside."

"And you say you're no detective."

A steep staircase was attached to the far wall. Thatcher noticed a hulking figure leaning against the bannister halfway up, smoking a cigarette, and staring at him through the haze.

Bill said, "I see you've captured Gert's attention."

"That's Gert, the madam?"

"What did you expect? A red velvet dress and hourglass figure?" Lowering his voice, Bill added, "Careful how you answer. Here comes her other half."

The man approaching their table had the proportions of a praying mantis and the lips of a lizard. They formed a tight seam between his beak of a nose and pointed chin. A smile would have looked out of place on such a face, but, in any case, he didn't fashion one.

"Sheriff. Been a while."

"Hello, Lefty. How're things?"

He jutted his chin toward Thatcher. "Who's he?"

"Meet Thatcher Hutton. He's new to town."

"Hutton. You're the one what shot the snake."

"He's a horse trainer," Bill said amiably.

"Horse trainer." He said it like he'd been told that Thatcher performed a high-wire act in the circus. "Well, welcome to Lefty's."

Thatcher didn't say anything, just gave a bob of his head.

Bill placed their order for two hamburgers and cold Coca-Colas.

"Comin' up."

Thatcher watched Lefty's progress back across the room. Midway, he was intercepted by his wife. They had a brief exchange, then

Lefty continued on toward the grill behind the bar while Gert made her way toward their table. Through the soles of his boots, Thatcher could feel the vibration of her heavy tread.

Unlike her husband, who looked like he could be snapped in two as easily as a toothpick, Thatcher didn't think Gert could be knocked over with a tank like those he'd seen on the battlefront.

When she reached them, she sized him up. "Thatcher, huh?"

"Yes, ma'am."

"Never knew nobody with that name. Who're your people?"

"You wouldn't know them."

"Try me."

He gave her a one-sided smile that didn't show teeth. "*I* wouldn't know them."

Still appraising him, she took a drag of her cigarette, then leaned over and ground it out in the ashtray in the center of their table. She blew a plume of smoke out of the corner of her mouth.

Turning her attention to Bill, she said, "What are you doing here?"

Bill, who'd checked his watch again, pocketed it. "Hello to you, too, Gert. I'm here for a hamburger. Also to ask after the girl."

"Which?"

"You know which, Gert."

She huffed a gust of stinky breath. "That Wally Johnson. Jug-eared little bastard ruint her face, her arm's healing all crooked, and she cain't see out one eye."

"Is she still here?"

She hitched a thumb over her shoulder. Thatcher and Bill looked in the direction she'd indicated. A young woman with her arm in a sling was flipping meat patties on the grill while Lefty was uncapping Coke bottles.

Gert was saying, "Her name's Corrine. Out of the goodness of my heart I'm keeping her on even though she ain't much use to me upstairs no more. But some men if they're that hard up ain't all that particular about looks." She gave Thatcher a sly glance. "You interested? You can have half an hour at a cut rate."

Bill said, "Gert, if you openly solicit, I'll slam down your operation upstairs." He spoke in a low voice that thrummed with warning.

Her eyes, set in folds of ruddy fat, narrowed to slits. "Lessen you forgot, you and me have a deal, sheriff."

"Only as long as we both keep up the pretense that this isn't a low-rent whorehouse."

"Beg your pardon. It ain't low-rent."

"All I'm saying is, don't forget the terms of our deal, or I'll forget we have a deal. I'll close you down, and you'd lose a shitload, what with all the roughnecks racing down here from Ranger every Saturday night." He looked over at Thatcher. "They've struck oil up there."

"Yeah, I've heard."

"Despite the distance they have to drive, the oil field workers have been a boon to Gert's business."

"I don't know what you're talking about," she said.

Bill snickered. "The hell you don't. They're a wild bunch, those boys. I hear you've got them lining up in the hall and making them bid on who goes next. That's begging for trouble." Then, after a beat, he said in a steely undertone, "Keep things under control, Gert, or our deal is off."

She took a challenging stance. "I got iron control."

"You didn't the night Wally battered that girl." Bill eyed her keenly. "Or *was* that under your control?"

Looking up at her from beneath the brim of his hat, Thatcher noticed an instantaneous slackening of the woman's smirk, her rapid blinking. Bill had struck a nerve, but she recovered quickly.

"Chew good, sheriff. It'd be a damn shame if you choked to death on your burger." She looked again at Thatcher. "Any of my girls would be tickled to see you." She turned and lumbered off.

"Why, Thatcher. I think she took a shine to you," Bill said. He was still laughing under his breath when Lefty brought over their food.

After one bite, Thatcher understood why the burgers had earned their reputation. He'd polished his off in no time and was about to comment on the tastiness, when the crack of a gunshot silenced him.

Reflexively he dropped sideways out of his chair onto the floor and pulled the pistol from his waistband.

Much more calmly, Bill stood up and drew his weapon. "That was only the warning shot, Thatcher. But any from now on, you should take seriously."

"Warning shot?"

"We're raiding the back room."

Bill left him and began swimming upstream of all the patrons who were hotfooting it toward the entry. "I could use some help," he shouted back at Thatcher.

Thatcher was furious at Bill and at himself for being so goddamn gullible, but he followed, pushing people aside before they could trample him.

When he and Bill drew even with the staircase, Gert leaned over the bannister and screamed, "I won't forget this, sheriff! Fuck you!"

Ignoring her, Bill slid into a narrow space behind the bar that accessed a door. He knocked on it twice with the butt of his gun. It was opened by Harold, who was breathing heavily. "Hell's broke loose."

From beyond the doorway came the sounds of pandemonium: swearing and shouting, grunts of pain, the splintering sound of breaking furniture, glass shattering.

Bill turned and slapped his hand over Thatcher's chest. "Pin that on and consider yourself deputized."

Thatcher fumbled the star-shaped badge, pricking his finger on the pin. "You son of a bitch."

"Well, I guess I am, but—"

A barrage of gunshots drowned out the rest.

"Dammit!" Bill barged through the open doorway.

Thatcher slid the badge into the breast pocket of his jacket as he followed the sheriff. Holding the Colt at shoulder level, barrel toward the ceiling, he entered the fray.

Scotty had the man obviously responsible for firing the gunshots pinned facedown on the floor. Bill was trying to wrestle away the man's handgun before he could fire another round.

Harold was dodging the uncoordinated jabs of a broken beer bottle wielded by a man so drunk he could barely stand. Thatcher rushed over and bonked the drunk on the back of his head with the grip of his pistol. The man dropped the broken bottle and landed on the floor like a sandbag, face first.

Harold said, "That's twice I owe you. Thanks." Then he dashed off to help other deputies whom Thatcher recognized but didn't know by name. They were swapping blows with some of the angrier, drunker customers.

Others trying to avoid arrest were overturning tables, chairs, and each other in their mad scramble to exit through the single door at the back of the room. Some were making their escape by jumping through windows. Along with their male counterparts, a few women were kicking and clawing their way toward the nearest way out.

A dozen or more people had bottlenecked at the exit. Thatcher noticed in the midst of them a familiar head of hair, so pomaded it looked like it had been painted onto his scalp. No sooner had he identified Chester Landry than the man managed to squeeze through the congested exit to the outside.

Thatcher fought his way toward the door. Harold, he realized, was following in his wake, apprehending the people Thatcher shoved back toward him.

When Thatcher reached the door, he bolted outside and tried to catch sight of Landry. Mad confusion was made even worse by the darkness, and by the sudden blinding glare of headlights as people made it to their cars and peeled out in every direction.

A car without headlights came speeding out of the darkness, missing Thatcher by a hair. Thatcher saw two autos collide in their haste to leave the area. Some drove over ground in the opposite direction of the road, leaving clouds of dust that further obscured vision.

He didn't catch sight of either Chester Landry or his automobile, which Thatcher probably couldn't have identified anyway. But one vehicle did catch his eye, and it caused his heart to lurch. He ran over to it; no one was inside.

He replaced the Colt in his waistband and ran full-out back into the building, where the chaos continued. The deputies and Sheriff Amos were trying to restrain those still bent on escaping and to keep corralled those they'd halted. Above the cacophony, Gert was bellowing profane threats. Lefty was swinging a full bottle of whiskey at the head of a man he was calling a goddamn snitch, which his victim was frantically denying as he ducked each hazardous arc of the bottle.

On his first sweep of the room, Thatcher didn't see whom he sought, but there were several men down, lying on the floor either wounded or dead of gunshot. He rushed over to the first, who was cursing and clutching his thigh.

He yelled, "I'm shot!"

Thatcher squatted down and took a look. "It would be spurting if it had clipped an artery. You have a handkerchief?"

The man nodded.

"Use it as a tourniquet. Tie it tight. You'll be all right."

"I'm dead," he wailed.

"You're not going to die."

"Hell I ain't. My wife's gonna kill me."

Thatcher left him and moved to another person lying motionless nearby. He was on his side, facing away from Thatcher. Fresh blood was spreading a dark blotch on the back of his shirt.

There was no mistaking the bald pate, as round and shiny as a cue ball, fringed by wiry gray hair. Thatcher knelt and eased Irv Plummer onto his back.

His eyelids fluttered open, but when he saw Thatcher, he scowled. "Did you shoot me?"

"Where're you shot?"

"Under my arm." He raised his left arm, or tried to. But pain drained his face of color and he gnashed his teeth. "Hurts like a son of a bitch."

"Put your right arm around my neck."

"I can make it my ownself."

Thatcher swore at him, then hooked Irv's right arm around his neck, put his shoulder to Irv's middle, and stood up with Irv draped over him. He felt the old man go limp. He'd fainted.

Thatcher wove his way through the overturned tables and chairs toward the door, but it was slow going. The floor was littered with broken glass, and slick with spilled liquor and blood. He'd almost reached the exit when, "Thatcher!"

He turned to face Bill Amos, who asked, "Irv Plummer? Is he dead?"

"No, but he's been shot."

"How bad?"

"I don't know. I'll take him to a doctor."

"Put him in my car."

"His truck is outside. I'll drive him in that. Can't leave it here, it's his livelihood."

"Thatcher, he—"

"I'm driving him." He turned to go, but Bill caught his sleeve.

"When you told me that this wasn't your fight and that you were staying out of it, I knew better."

Thatcher didn't waste time arguing with him. He pulled himself loose and left through the door. Most everyone had cleared the area. Only a few stragglers remained. He carried Irv over the rough ground with as little jostling as possible.

When he reached the truck, he opened the tailgate and eased Irv off his shoulder and into the bed of it. Thatcher shook him slightly. "Where's your key?"

Irv groaned, but he'd understood the question and patted his right pants pocket. Thatcher fished out the key, then adjusted Irv's legs and feet to clear the tailgate.

"I saw you sittin' with the sheriff."

Thatcher turned quickly. Standing behind him was the young prostitute in the arm sling. She said, "You law?"

"No."

"Gert said you prob'ly was."

"She's wrong." The badge in his breast pocket seemed to be branding him through his shirt.

With a tip of her head the girl indicated Irv, who was moaning and muttering incoherently. "Is he gonna die?"

"I don't know."

"If you'll take me away from here, I'll help you with him."

"No thanks."

"I'm a good helper."

"Thanks, but—"

"Don't make me go back to Gert, mister. Please."

Thatcher took in her misshapen jaw and the damaged eye. He mouthed a vulgarity used frequently in the trenches. "Get in."

TWENTY-NINE

———※◎※———

Laurel was accustomed to Irv's truck clanking into the drive at all hours of the night, so when it did now, her subconscious registered that he had made it home, but she didn't fully wake up until there was thunderous knocking on the back door.

She threw off the sheet, grabbed her housecoat, and pulled it on as she rushed downstairs. She didn't even bother to turn on the kitchen light before running to the back door and yanking it open.

Even having been certain that the knocking didn't bode well, she still wasn't prepared for the sight that greeted her. Thatcher Hutton stood on the other side of the threshold. He was wearing the familiar black fedora, a bloodstained Henley undershirt, and dark trousers with a pistol stuck in the waistband. He was carrying Irv over his shoulder.

"Your father-in-law has been hurt."

Laurel stepped around him to better see Irv, who hung limply, his arms dangling lifelessly. "Irv?" She turned his face toward her and repeated his name. When he didn't respond, she cried out in alarm.

"He's not dead, just unconscious."

"He's bleeding!"

"He was. I stanched the wound."

"*What wound?*"

"He was shot."

Aghast, Laurel looked down at the pistol in his waistband.

"Not by me," he said. "Let's get him inside, see how bad it is."

"We already know it's bad. He needs a doctor."

"He refused a doctor."

"Refused? How could he refuse if he's unconscious?"

"Where should I put him?"

"Back in his truck. I'll drive him myself."

He took a breath, then in a voice that brooked no argument said, "Where to?"

He seemed immovable. Realizing that further argument would be a waste of valuable time, she motioned. "The room behind the kitchen."

Thatcher stepped inside and headed in that direction. She reached out to close the door, but a young woman with her arm in a sling was coming through. "The old man threatened to chop off Mr. Hutton's pecker if he took him to a doctor."

She scuttled past Laurel and followed Thatcher into Irv's room. Laurel shut the door, then rushed to follow them, reaching the room just as the girl switched on the overhead light. Thatcher eased Irv off his shoulder and lowered him onto his back on the bed.

Out of sheer desperation, Laurel prayed, "God, please no." She elbowed Thatcher aside and sat down on the edge of the mattress. She took hold of Irv's hand, squeezed it tightly, and exhaled in relief when he opened his eyes.

"Hi, Laurel."

"What in the world happened?"

"Ain't Hutton told you?"

"You need a doctor."

"It ain't gonna be that bad."

"You don't know that."

"Fetch that jar of 'shine from my dresser drawer."

"Which drawer?" Thatcher asked.

"Bottom."

On his way over to the dresser, he pulled the pistol out of his waistband and set it on the cushion atop Irv's barrel, then took off his hat and placed it over the gun. He eased his braces off his shoulders and let them fall to form loops over his hips.

He found the jar of corn liquor, brought it over to the bed and screwed the lid off, then held it against Irv's lips while he sipped.

After a few swallows, Irv relaxed his head on the pillow. "Don't fret, Laurel. Pour some of this whiskey in the bullet hole, smear it with a little coal oil, and cover it with a bandage. In a day or two, I'll be right as rain."

"Coal oil?"

"Cures everything." Irv gave her a woozy grin and helped himself to another sip of moonshine when Thatcher pressed the rim of the jar to his lips, then gave a grunt of satisfaction and closed his eyes. "Get on with it."

Thatcher turned to the girl. "Corrine, think you can put a kettle on to boil?"

"Sure."

"While you're waiting on it, gather up some things. Towels, tweezers, rubbing alcohol, bandages, some—"

"I don't have any bandages," Laurel said, interrupting him. She resented his taking charge of *her* emergency with *her* father-in-law in *her* house. "You'll have to cut strips of bedsheets," she said to the girl. "Fresh ones are in the cupboard in the upstairs hallway." She rattled off where the girl could find the other items.

The girl repeated the instructions to make sure she'd gotten them all, then turned to leave. In her haste through the door, she bumped into the jamb. Laurel had noticed that her right eye was swollen and partially closed. She was curious about her, but for the time being, she shelved her curiosity and asked the question uppermost in her mind.

"How did this happen?" She was afraid that Irv had been assaulted at the still. What of Ernie?

Irv made a limp motion with his hand, ceding the explanation to Thatcher, who asked her, "Do you know about Lefty's?"

She gave a brusque nod.

"The back room?"

"I've heard about it."

"Well, the sheriff raided it tonight. It was bedlam. Someone started shooting."

"At Irv?"

Although his eyes remained closed, Irv answered, "No."

Laurel looked to Thatcher for confirmation. He said, "I don't know for sure, but I think it was random. He caught a wild shot. I got him out of there quick as I could."

"I appreciate that, Mr. Hutton. Thank you for seeing to him, but you don't have to stay. I'll take over from here."

"You'll need help."

"I'll manage."

"I don't think the bullet is still in there, but the wound needs to be cleaned out. Have you ever dug around in a bullet hole?"

The thought of it made her queasy. She gave a tight shake of her head.

"It's nasty business," he said, "and through some of it, he'll probably have to be held down."

Laurel was still clutching Irv's hand, though his had gone slack. His face was ashen. She understood that Mr. Hutton was right. Giving in to him smarted, but it wasn't only her pride at stake here. Irv's life was at risk. "All right. I accept your offer to help."

"Good."

She swiveled her head to look up at him. "But I don't like it."

"I know. You don't want to be beholden." His gaze stayed steady on hers for several beats, then he turned his attention to Irv. "Let's get him out of his shirt."

The cloth had turned stiff with drying blood, front and back. Whenever they had to readjust his position to work his arms free of the sleeves, he hissed through clenched teeth. When the garment was off, Laurel wadded it up and tossed it into a corner.

"This isn't going to be pretty," Thatcher said.

He lifted Irv's left arm and removed a balled-up shirt from his armpit. It was more blood-soaked than Irv's had been. "Yours?" she asked, as she sent it the way of the other.

"It was the only thing I had handy." He gave his shirt no heed as he assessed the raw, gaping wound. "This is where the bullet came out."

"And went in where?"

"On the back of his arm. Help me roll him over."

Following his directions, she went around to the other side of the bed and helped him turn Irv toward her. Her father-in-law wasn't too drunk to spew some colorful expletives.

"Sorry," Thatcher said to him. "Bullet went straight through a fleshy part of your arm. Best I can tell, it missed bones. All told, you're lucky."

"Told ya it weren't gonna be bad. But right now, I ain't feelin' so lucky," Irv grumbled. "Where's the whiskey at?"

───────

The girl moved like a whirlwind. She made several trips in and out of the room, depositing everything that she'd been sent to scavenge. She placed them on a table that Laurel had cleared for that purpose and had moved close to the bedside.

Thatcher put the tweezers and scissors in a washbowl and poured boiling water over them. While he organized the things they would need, Laurel stayed at Irv's side and plied him with moonshine from their own still.

At one point, as Thatcher was packing towels beneath Irv's left side, he said to her, "Go easy on that whiskey. We'll need it for later."

"There's plenty more." Then, realizing her slip, she added, "He keeps another jar hidden in the bottom of that barrel. He doesn't know that I know."

Thatcher gave her a wry grin. "Before we're done, you and I may need a swig."

"Don't be giving away my whiskey, Laurel," Irv mumbled into his pillow. "Or my secrets."

She leaned down and whispered directly into his ear, "*Our* secrets. And I won't."

When everything was ready, and Irv was good and looped, Thatcher and she bathed their hands with rubbing alcohol. They worked on the entry wound first since it was the minor one. Irv remained stoic.

But when they repositioned him on his back, placed his arm above his head, and began to clean the exit wound, Thatcher had to restrain him while Laurel tweezed out a scrap of his shirt fabric from deep inside. Irv yelped, swore, then fainted. He remained blessedly unconscious while they continued.

At last, Thatcher said, "I think that's the best we can do."

"We're going to leave the wounds open?"

"You want to close them with stitches?"

She shuddered. "I dread the thought, and I'm not sure closing them would be best anyway."

"I don't advise it," he said. When she looked up at him, he gave a small shrug. "One time one of the ranch hands got shot by a rustler as we were chasing him. The boss, Mr. Hobson, sent for a doctor. The doc got the bullet out and wanted to stitch up the hole. Mr. Hobson wouldn't let him. He said the cowboy might survive the blood loss, but then die of infection."

"Did he live?"

"Yeah, he did fine. Well, until he tried to ride a bull on a dare. He got gored. Bled to death after all."

Laurel looked over to see if he was joking, but his brow was furrowed with concentration as he flooded Irv's wound with rubbing alcohol.

She stood by to blot up the runoff, then covered the bullet holes with folded patches of cloth. Only then did the tension drain from her shoulders.

Thatcher must have felt similar relief. He leaned against the wall and wiped his perspiring hairline with the back of his hand. "He's a tough old coot."

"He is." Laurel regarded the sleeping Irv with affection as she sponged dried blood off his arm and torso. "But I don't know what I would have done without him."

Thatcher let that hover for a moment, then said, "Tomorrow when you change the dressing, it probably wouldn't hurt to apply a little coal oil."

"I planned to," she said around a light laugh, "but I wasn't going to admit it. My mother swore by its healing properties."

"Keep the moonshine handy, too."

"I also planned to do that." She used a clean towel to dry Irv's damp skin where she had washed.

"Ready to wrap?" Thatcher asked.

The girl had left them with neatly stacked bands of cloth. Together she and Thatcher began winding them around Irv's torso, being as gentle as possible when they rolled him from one side to the other.

The room Irv had created for himself wasn't that spacious, but the quarters had never seemed small to Laurel. Until now. When sharing it with Thatcher Hutton.

As they wound the bandage, their movements were so in sync they could have been choreographed. Or perhaps they were just keenly attuned to each other, so attuned they read each other's mind.

Occasionally their fingertips brushed. When even a whisper of contact was made, she felt his eyes on her, but she didn't have the nerve to look into his. She kept her head down and pretended that her concentration was solely on their task.

But her awareness of him was breath-stealing. The five-button placket on his undershirt was open, revealing a wedge of dark chest hair that looked soft. The long sleeves had been rolled up to above his elbows, tightly cuffing his arms just beneath his biceps. Plump veins ran down his forearms all the way to the backs of his hands, which she watched now as long, strong fingers tied a knot to secure the bandage.

"It's snug," he said, "but keeping pressure on it tonight will keep the bleeding down."

"Thank you for stanching it when you did." She glanced over at his discarded shirt on the floor in the corner. "I'll wash it for you."

"It isn't a favorite."

"That one is worse for wear, too."

He looked down at the streaks of blood on his undershirt. "It'll soak out."

Looking away from him, she rested her hand on Irv's forehead. "He doesn't feel hot now, but I'll keep checking for fever."

"If the wounds get red and puffy, or start to stink, call in a doctor. Only, please don't tell Irv I was the one who suggested it."

Remembering what Irv had threatened to do if Thatcher took him to a doctor, Laurel bit back a smile.

THIRTY

Laurel had learned that the girl's name was Corrine. She had been very useful, eagerly fetching and carrying, handling everything with remarkable efficiency considering that she had the use of only one arm and limited eyesight.

She reentered Irv's room now. "There was a pie in the pie safe. I cut each of y'all a piece and started a pot of coffee. Take a breather, I'll sit with the old man. Irv's his name? Never mind that bloody water in the washbowl. I'll pitch it out the winda."

"Did you help yourself to some pie?" Laurel asked.

"It looked too good to pass up. I hope you don't mind."

"Not at all. You've been extremely helpful tonight. Thank you."

Corrine shrugged off the thanks, and with her free hand made a shooing motion for Laurel and Thatcher to leave the room. Irv was snoring loudly through his open mouth. Laurel didn't think she would be missed.

Thatcher followed her into the kitchen. When they were out of earshot of Corrine, she asked quietly, "Who is that girl? Where did she come from?"

"She works at Lefty's."

Laurel looked toward Irv's room, then back at Thatcher. "Not upstairs, surely?"

The look he gave her said otherwise.

"She's just a girl."

"Seventeen."

She was about to say more, ask more, but then remembered that Thatcher had been at Lefty's tonight when it was raided, and that what he was doing in the company of a teenage prostitute was none of her business.

He stood there, looking down at her as though waiting for her to pose questions she had thought better of asking. Then, stepping around her, he said, "I'll be right back," and went out through the back door.

She loaded a tray with the slices of pie Corrine had prepared, cups of coffee and the fixings, and carried it into the dining room, where she laid two place settings on the table. Since she and Irv had begun eating their meals here, she'd bought a secondhand sideboard. At each end of it, she'd placed matching kerosene lamps with milk-glass chimneys. Preferring their glow to the glaring overhead electric light, she lit them now.

As she leaned down to adjust the flame, her long braid swung forward. *Lord!* Throughout the ordeal with Irv, she'd lost sight of the fact that she was in her nightclothes, barefoot, her hair plaited for bedtime.

But it was too late to correct these oversights. The back door squeaked open. She made certain her housecoat was fully buttoned, flipped her braid over her shoulder, and called, "In here, Mr. Hutton."

He must have gone to Irv's truck to get his suit jacket. He'd put it on over his undershirt. His braces were no longer lying loose against his hips, so she assumed he'd pulled them back onto his shoulders. He might also have smoothed down his hair, although it seemed to have a will of its own. In spite of the bloodstains on his undershirt, he looked more respectable and suitable to the setting than she did.

They sat down across from each other. She tucked her bare feet beneath her chair, then pulled it closer to the table in a belated attempt to hide her dishabille.

She placed a napkin in her lap. As she poured a dollop of cream into her coffee, she noticed that he hadn't yet started on his pie. His hands were loosely fisted on either side of the plate, and he was studying it. "You don't like peach?"

"Oh, a lot. I was just wondering how you get the crust to wave like that at the edge."

"I flute it."

He raised his head and looked over at her.

"Like this." She used her fingers to demonstrate. "To the dough."

"Huh." He picked up his fork and began to eat.

After a full minute of strained silence—at least to Laurel it seemed strained—she asked, "Have you been thrown from a horse again?"

"Only once today."

"I was being serious."

He gave a lopsided grin. "So was the horse."

She laughed softly and shook her head. "I don't know how you do that."

"Well, I don't know how to flute pie dough."

They smiled across at each other, then she set her fork on the rim of her plate and clasped her hands in her lap. "You were right, Mr. Hutton. I—"

"Why won't you call me Thatcher?"

For a moment she was thrown by his interrupting her to ask that. She picked up her fork. Set it back down. "It wouldn't be appropriate for us to use first names."

"How come?"

"Because we're not that well acquainted."

"Using first names would be a start in that direction, wouldn't it?"

All things taken into account, not the least of which was the privacy of this moment, relaxing the rules of etiquette was a risky step she was unwilling to take. Once a boundary was breached, it was difficult, if not impossible, to reestablish. Breaching boundaries with him seemed particularly chancy.

"I think we should leave things as they are."

He didn't respond immediately, but ultimately made a gesture of concession with his shoulder. "You were saying?"

It took a moment for her to remember what she'd been saying. "I apologize for the curt way I turned down your offer to help with Irv. I couldn't have adequately tended to him by myself. Thank you for getting him home; thank you for staying."

"You're welcome, Mrs. Plummer."

He didn't smile, but his eyes—the bluish-gray color of storm clouds—glinted with humor. His amusement made her feel silly and prudish for making first names an issue. But it would take on greater significance if she amended her position on the matter now.

Instead, she changed the subject. "I grew up on a farm. The nearest doctor was ten miles away, at least. Accidents happened frequently. Even as a girl, I patched up cuts and scrapes, bound up sprains, things like that. I don't faint at the sight of blood. But I never had to deal with a bullet wound before. I hope I never have to again."

"How ammunition can rip through a body can be ugly, all right."

"You're referring to the war? I'm sure you saw some horrific things on the battlefield."

"And in the hospital. Some of the men brought in might've been better off dying on the front. In the hospital, they were just made to suffer longer."

"You were wounded?"

He shook his head. "Spanish flu. I was laid up with it for three weeks. Three miserable weeks."

"I lived in constant fear of Derby being blown to bits, or dying of exposure to mustard gas, something war-related. But I was just as scared that he would die of flu."

"Thousands did."

"In some ways that seems a crueler death than being killed during a battle. Little glory. Less heroic."

"More of a waste." He focused on tracing the curved handle of the coffee cup with his fingertip. "I'm sorry about your husband."

His somber tone indicated that he knew how Derby had died. Foley was a small town. Through someone, he would have heard the circumstances by which she'd become a widow. She nodded an acknowledgment of his condolence, then gestured to his empty plate. "Would you care for another piece?"

"No thanks. Sure was good, though."

"I'm glad you liked it. The peaches came from Parker County. It's famous for them."

"I didn't know that. They must be special if you went all that way to buy them. How long a drive is it?"

When she realized the dangerous territory she'd carelessly wandered into, her throat seized up. "Well, I didn't go myself."

"You sent Irv?"

"No. A couple of young men who deliver my bakery items were up in that area several days ago. They stopped at a roadside stand and brought a bushel of freestones back for me. It was very sweet and thoughtful of them."

"Hmm."

She could kick herself for bringing that up, and then for blabbering on about it. Hadn't she warned Irv that telling too much was the best way to get caught lying? Although she'd essentially told the truth. The O'Connor twins *had* brought her back a bushel of peaches, but their primary errand had been to deliver several gallons of whiskey to the man in Weatherford who'd sold Irv the copper to make the new still.

Mr. Hutton seemed to detect that she was nervously dancing around something. He continued to stare at her over the rim of his cup as he drank the last of his coffee. He returned the cup to the saucer. "Your father-in-law is going to mend."

She smiled. "I'm relieved."

"He'll be ornery for a week or so."

Her smile broadened. "I expect so. He's fiercely independent and doesn't like to be fussed over."

"I got that about him."

He shifted in his seat, stretched out his long legs at an angle to the table, then drew them back beneath it. He turned his head aside and studied the spandrel with much more absorption than it warranted.

Evidently he wanted to say something, but was hesitant. She waited.

Finally, his meandering gaze came back to her. "I hated having to give you a scare tonight."

"You mean when you arrived?"

"I knew it would shock you, seeing your father-in-law like that, the blood and all, but there was just no way to make it easy. At least, I couldn't think of a way."

"No, there wouldn't have been an easy way. My heart was in my throat."

"You must've thought the worst had happened."

"'Not Irv, too.' That's what flashed through my mind."

"I saw the fear in your face."

"Was it that obvious?"

"It was to me."

The four words, softly and solemnly spoken, had an immediate and noticeable effect on the atmosphere. He said nothing more, for which she was glad. Except that, moments into the ensuing silence, during which they just sat there looking at each other, she wished for more dialogue, or a movement, no matter how slight, anything to relieve her awareness of him, which had become both terrible and tantalizing.

Her nightclothes were made of summer-weight cotton, old and soft from so many washings, but they began to feel like chain mail against her chest, equaling the pressure collecting behind her breastbone.

When she could stand it no longer, she said, "I had better check on Irv." She pushed back her chair and came out of it so quickly, she tripped on the hem of her housecoat.

She hadn't quite made it out of the dining room when he touched her arm from behind. "Laurel, wait."

She didn't upbraid him for using her first name. Of greater consequence was that he had covered the distance from the table in half the time she had and was now standing close behind her. So terrible and tantalizing that she kept her back to him.

"What, Mr. Hutton?"

"Why didn't you ask me about Corrine?"

"I did ask you about her."

"You wanted to know more."

"No, I didn't."

"Yes you did." He reached for her hand and turned her around, then kept his fingers clasping hers as they faced each other. "Why didn't you ask how come she was with me?"

"Because it isn't any of my business."

"Yes, it is."

He drew on her hand, bringing her closer to him, close enough for her to feel his body heat. Denying to herself that she felt anything at all, she kept her head lowered and whispered insistently into the open placket of his undershirt, "No, it *isn't*."

"Well, it's about to be."

With his other hand, he tipped her chin up. His eyes moved over her face, pausing momentarily on each feature. He brought his hand up to her cheek and rested it there. His thumb stroked her chin, coming close enough to her lips to make them tingle. He lowered his head, then more, more still, until his face filled her field of vision and she felt his breath drift warmly over her lips.

Her eyes closed.

His lips met hers softly, whisking back and forth, sipping gently, teasing her so maddeningly that she came up on tiptoes to secure the connection.

He made a low sound as his arm curved around her waist. The hand against her cheek slid beneath her chin, supporting her jaw and neck as he tilted her head and realigned their lips.

His were parted. Hers responded in kind.

Tongues touched, shyly and fleetingly, but electrically. Breaths caught and were suspended. He waited. For her it was agonizing, this indecision, this self-denial, this wanting, wanting, but fearing.

But then he spoke her name on a ragged breath, and something inside her that had been fettered for a long time broke free and took flight.

He sensed it immediately and deepened the kiss with hunger and heat, a low growl, his tongue searching. His arm tightened around her waist until their bodies met where his was straining and hers was aching.

He nudged the dip between her thighs, and stayed, and pressed, and still it wasn't close enough. She placed her hands on his chest, clutched handfuls of his jacket...

And then gave a cry of sudden pain.

He released her immediately and backed away. "God, Laurel. What's the matter?"

She looked down at her right hand where a drop of blood beaded up out of her palm. "I don't know." Mystified, she looked up at him. "Something in your pocket?" She reached into his left breast pocket and came up with a star-shaped badge.

She gaped at it, then dropped it as though the pin had pricked her again. The badge clinked against the hardwood floor. She looked up into his face, her breath rushing in and out. "You're a deputy sheriff?"

"No. Not officially."

She backed away from him, drawing her housecoat more tightly around her. "Were you in on that raid?"

"Not by choice."

"Either you were or you weren't," she said, raising her voice. "If there hadn't been a raid, Irv wouldn't have gotten shot."

"If he hadn't been in Lefty's back room, he wouldn't have gotten shot."

"You're blaming *him*?"

"No. All I'm saying is that he was at the wrong place at the wrong time, and so was I."

"Oh, were you? If Irv hadn't been shot, would you have arrested him?"

"Wasn't up to me. I didn't arrest anybody. I hauled your father-in-law out of there, carried him to his truck, and drove him home."

"For which I've thanked you. Now I want you to leave."

"It wasn't my doing, Laurel."

"Don't use my name!"

"I got railroaded into taking part, *Laurel*. Sheriff Amos—"

"I don't care."

"Sounds like you do. Sounds like you care one hell of a lot."

"Will you just go?"

"What difference does it make to you if I was official or not?"

"None. Absolutely none. You...your...nothing you do is any of my business. Or didn't I make that clear to you not three minutes ago?"

He leaned forward and said with emphasis, "It was an eventful three minutes."

True. With desire spreading through her like warm syrup, all sorts of *events* had taken place in intimate places. To cover her mortification, she went on the offensive. "Why did you keep that badge concealed? It makes me wonder what else you're hiding."

"Yeah? Then that makes two of us. Because I don't think it was the kiss that has got you coming apart."

Anger and fear were potent emotions. In the throes of either, one could speak ill-advisedly. In the grips of both, one would be foolish to say anything at all. She'd gone far beyond that, but if she didn't stop now, she could dig herself in much deeper.

Drawing herself up to her full height, she said, "You prevented Irv's condition from getting much worse. Possibly you even saved his life. Thank you. But I want you to leave now and, from now on, stay away from us. Away from me."

He remained as he was just looking at her, then bent over and scooped the badge up off the floor. "Thanks for the pie." He turned and disappeared around the corner into the kitchen. The back door was soundly pulled shut.

Laurel walked backward over to the table, groping blindly for her chair, and when she located it, landed hard in the seat. She squeezed her eyes shut and covered her mouth with her hand. Her lips were still damp from his kiss. She could taste him. Her breasts felt heavy, full, tingly. She didn't know whether to scream with fury, wring her hands with anxiety, or weep because she could never be near him again.

"Miss Laurel?"

She started. Corrine was standing only a few feet away, looking at her with uncertainty. "Did he leave me here?"

Laurel laid her forehead on the table and hiccupped a sob tinged with hysteria. "So it would seem."

THIRTY-ONE

———◦◦◦———

"...and like a damn fool, I believed every word out of his lyin' mouth and ran off with him." Corrine finished a slice of bacon and licked the grease off her fingers. "It was romantic and excitin' and all. I kept tellin' myself that Mama and Daddy wouldn't miss me, that they'd be glad to have one less mouth to feed. There's eleven of us kids. I'm second oldest.

"Anyhow, on the night Jack and me had set, I snuck out of the house and walked to the crossroads where he was waitin'. We hit the open road, laughin' and carryin' on, waitin' to see where destiny would take us. It took us to Lefty's. You gonna finish that?"

The sudden question, asked out of context, roused Laurel from her woolgathering. "Pardon?"

"You gonna eat what's left of your breakfast?"

"Oh. No. Help yourself." She pushed her plate across the table. Corrine broke a biscuit in half, spooned jam onto it, and popped it into her mouth. At least that silenced her for several seconds.

Laurel didn't know where the girl found the energy or wherewithal to chatter. Both of them had been up for most of the night, taking turns sitting with Irv, waiting and watching to see if he would take a bad turn. He was in obvious pain, but he'd showed no signs of worsening. Except for some spotting on his bandage, there'd been no further bleeding, no fever.

At sunup, Laurel had gone to her room to wash and dress for the day. She'd undone her braid and brushed her hair, then plaited it again and wound it into a bun on her nape. As though her loose braid were responsible for her lapse in good judgment last night, this morning she had mercilessly jabbed the hairpins in to secure it.

What other excuse did she have for allowing Mr. Hutton to kiss her like that? The crisis with Irv had left her emotionally vulnerable, yes. But she'd always disparaged members of her sex who blamed stupid behavior on frayed emotions.

When she had returned downstairs, Corrine was in the kitchen frying bacon. Biscuits were baking. Laurel had been embarrassed by the girl's industry, because she felt completely wrung out.

When she'd murmured an apology to that effect, Corrine had said, "You got saddled with me. I'll make myself useful till you kick me out."

When Corrine had been left behind in the middle of the night, Laurel would never have insisted she leave. But now she didn't know what to do about the girl. Or really what to do about any aspect of her predicament.

Throughout the night, Irv's condition had been her primary concern. However, dawn had brought with it jarring realizations. He'd survived the gunshot, thank God. But the repercussions of it, chiefly his convalescence, created practical problems to which Laurel must find solutions. Soon.

"... so what I think is that he outright sold me to that old bitch."

Laurel's thoughts were so deeply troubling, her attention had again drifted away from Corrine's running monologue. "Sorry?"

"Gert," Corrine said. "When I came back after a visit to the outhouse, Jack was gone. He'd hightailed it as soon as my back was turned. Gert said I could stay, but I'd have to earn my keep and pay back her 'investment' in me.

"I caught on quick, though. I could spend the rest of my life on my back, and I would never make enough to earn my 'keep' plus repay whatever chickenshit amount of money she'd given Jack. But I didn't have nowhere else to go, so..."

She gave a shrug which, to Laurel's amazement, conveyed more resignation than rancor. The girl seemed to have accepted being prostituted better than she herself had being intentionally widowed.

"Most of the time it wasn't so bad," Corrine continued, "but after the hullabaloo that creep Wally Johnson caused, Gert—"

"Wally Johnson? The man who was murdered?"

"Yeah. The night after he did this to me." She pointed to her face and patted her arm in the sling. "The sheriff came out to Lefty's and asked did I know anything about his killing. I told him nothing except I was glad he was dead."

Laurel remembered Irv telling her that he had seen Dr. Driscoll at the roadhouse, attending a girl who'd been beaten. Things had come full circle.

"Anyhow," Corrine continued, "all ol' Gert cares about is money, money, money. I thought she was gonna beat the tar out of Wally for ruinin' what she called my 'earnin' capacity.' Now he's dead, she's takin' it out on me that my face is messed up and my eye has gone wonky. She's gotten meaner by the day. So, last night, when I saw a chance to get away from her, I took it."

"With Mr. Hutton."

"Um-huh. He sure is nice. Handsome, too. I clapped eyes on him the second he walked into Lefty's. I thought to myself, now there's a man that might be worth droppin' drawers for. Gert must've thought so, too. The bitch pounced, offerin' her wares, I'm sure. He didn't go upstairs, though.

"Then, after the shootin' started, I ran outside like everybody else. I saw Mr. Hutton come out carryin' the old man. He laid him in the back of the truck. I ran over, took in what was happenin', offered to help if he'd let me tag along. He cussed somethin' fierce. You know how a man does when he's had about all the aggravation he can tolerate? But then he said okay and told me to get in the truck.

"I didn't give him time to think twice. I hopped in, put your daddy-in-law's head in my lap, so it wouldn't be bangin' around while we was driving. Along the way, though, he started bleedin' real bad. I hollered at Mr. Hutton to stop. He came back, took a look, and that's when he pulled off his shirt and stuffed the bullet hole with it. Are y'all sparkin'?"

These sudden questions of Corrine's continued to throw Laurel. When she realized what the girl was asking, she replied with a definitive *no*.

Corrine giggled like she knew otherwise, then scooted her chair back. "You go see to Irv. I'll clean up the kitchen."

"Really, Corrine, you don't have to do that. I don't expect anything from you."

"Neither did Mr. Hutton, which is why I think he's right decent. And real serious like, ain't he? Go on now, before the ol' man gets cranky. I took him some breakfast. He's probably finished it by now."

Laurel tapped once on Irv's bedroom door before pushing it open. He was half sitting up, a tray on his lap. His lined features were compressed into a frown.

As Laurel entered, she asked, "Are you hurting?"

"I've felt better," he groused, "and that girl didn't put enough sugar in the oatmeal."

"I know that you know her name. You failed to mention she was the one brutalized by Wally Johnson and treated by Dr. Driscoll."

"You didn't ask."

Laurel removed the tray from his lap and set it on the dresser. Despite his complaint, she noticed he'd eaten everything. She went back over to the bed and laid her palm against his forehead. He didn't feel feverish. "Have you used the chamber pot?"

"The girl's already emptied it."

"Did you have trouble getting out of bed?"

"No. I'm limber as a ballerina. Did a coupla twirls while I was up."
At her look, he added, "What do you think? Yes, I had trouble. Took
twenty minutes to take a piss."

He was way past cranky. "I'll bring you a jar to use in the bed."

"The girl already offered. I told her hell no. I'm not an invalid."

Laurel restrained herself from commenting on that. "I need to
change your bandage."

"That can wait." He motioned toward the end of the bed. "Sit
down so I don't have to crane my neck. We gotta talk."

She did as requested. "What's on your mind?"

"You have to ask?"

He would become even more irascible if she pretended not to
know what they needed to talk about, so she went straight to the
point. "I don't know how we're going to manage things while you're
recovering. I haven't figured it out yet."

"You're already toting more than your fair share, Laurel. Damn
me for getting my fool self shot."

"It wasn't your fault, but what were you doing at Lefty's?"

"Negotiating that new deal you proposed."

"Did he go for it?"

"He listened, but we hadn't shook on it before the deputies came
busting in. One fired a pistol into the air. He got everybody's attention,
all right. Caused a stampede."

"You could've been killed."

"Well, I wasn't. But it served as a reminder to me that you're in
constant danger."

"So are you."

"But I've been at it longer, and I'm old. If I got killed, some would
say it was past time. But if something was to happen to you, I'd never
forgive myself. This ain't a lark, you know."

"I do know that, or I wouldn't have agreed to carry a pistol. I
realize the dangers and accept them as part of the venture."

"What about him?"

"Who?"

He lowered his chin and looked at her from beneath his bushy eyebrows.

She somehow kept herself from squirming. "If you're referring to Mr. Hutton, nothing about him. He extended us a kindness. I think he would have done the same for anyone."

"He didn't, though, did he? There were others hurt. Several shot. I was the only one he slung over his shoulder and brought home. Why do you think he singled me out?"

"Well, not because he suspects something. To him you were just another customer having a drink in Lefty's back room."

"He said that?"

"He didn't say otherwise."

"That's not quite the same, though, is it? In fact, I've noticed he doesn't say much of anything unless it's called for. Did he tell you that he was there with Sheriff Amos?"

"He mentioned him."

"Strange that he was out there with the sheriff at that particular time."

"He said he got railroaded into it."

"Railroaded into what?"

"Into . . . I don't know, Irv." It irritated her that her father-in-law was fixated on the one subject she definitely did not wish to talk about. "Never mind him. Let's focus on us."

"All right, I'll drop it for now. And, anyway, we won't have to worry about secret agents or incarceration if we don't make and sell product."

"Exactly. It'll take weeks for you to fully recover."

"Only one."

"At least two, possibly three."

"Well, we'll see. In the meantime, our daytime activities will continue pretty much as they have been. You'll keep baking and delivering as usual."

"I can certainly do that."

"How big's our stockpile of product in the cellar?"

"Fair. But with the business the O'Connors are generating, it won't last long."

"Ernie's got some inventory stashed away," he said. "You trust those twins enough to send them out there for it?"

She liked the young men. They were charmers, and had given her no reason to mistrust them. But she didn't trust them enough to reveal the location of the stills. "No."

"Me neither. One's moony over you."

"Davy."

He looked surprised that she knew. "Has he professed himself?"

"No. I've sensed that he's infatuated, but pretended not to notice. Please, can we get back to the subject? I'll go out to the still today, bring back Ernie's stash, and transfer it to the cellar. It'll have to last until you're back on your feet and we resume production."

"*Resume* production? *Resume?* We ain't shutting down, Laurel. Not for any length of time. As of yesterday, we've got twenty barrels of mash fermenting. You planning on just pouring it out, wasting it?"

"All right. Ernie can do a run when a barrel becomes ready, but until you're up and about we won't mix more mash, and we'll cut back to just one still."

Irv shook his head. "We've got customers to keep supplied. New ones that you yourself courted. If we stop delivering as promised, they'll start buying from someone else."

His arguments against shutting down were considerations she had already taken into account. "I'll have to help Ernie then. But on the nights I'm at the still, I worry about leaving you here alone and helpless if anything were to happen."

"What could happen?"

"The house could catch on fire, and it takes you twenty minutes to use the chamber pot."

"Well, you can't be baking all day and then driving back and forth to the still in the dead of night, either."

"Why not?"

"Because I said so."

"Irv—"

"Laurel, we're not arguing over this. I'd bust up both stills myself before I'd put you at risk like that. What I propose," he said before she could raise another objection, "is this." He grimaced as he shifted his position. "Situate the girl out there."

"Corrine?"

"Set her up in the shack. It'll look like you've taken her on as a charity case. You rescued her from a life of iniquity. She's young and spry. She could walk back and forth over that hill between the shack and the still with no problem at all. She can help Ernie."

"Help him make moonshine? That's not rescuing her from a life of iniquity, it's setting her up to commit a crime."

"What she's been doing at Lefty's is a crime."

"That was imposed on her."

"All the more reason this arrangement will be better."

Laurel rubbed her forehead, which had begun to throb. "Does she know anything about making whiskey?"

"Haven't asked her yet. I wanted to run the idea past you first. Whether she does or not, she can stir mash. She can seal jars. She can box them."

"With a broken arm?"

"It's almost healed. She took her sling off and showed me how she can rotate it. As for the process, she'll catch on quick enough with Ernie teaching her. She can't read, but she's bright enough."

"She can't read?"

"No, but she can talk. Damn can she ever. She's got magpie in her blood. Before I told her to put a sock in it, I heard her whole life story."

"Why can't she read?"

"No schooling. She had to stay at home and help her mother tend the brood. Her two ambitions in life are to learn to read and to see a moving picture show. Anything else you want to know?"

"Yes. Why aren't you worried about her safety at the still the way you're worried about mine?"

"Because she ain't my kin, and because she's had to live by her wits, and, considerin' how young she is, she's fared pretty good, survivin' Wally and Gert and all. You can't bake your pies in that old stove at the shack, and if you weren't seen around town, everybody would wonder where you went off to. Especially that Hutton. I'd bet my left nut on him being first to ask where you was at. And you hate that shack."

It was a speech that sounded suspiciously rehearsed. "You have given it some thought."

"Wasn't nothin' else to do last night except to hurt and think. I don't see another solution. Now, send the girl in here. I'll lay it out for her, but I know she'll jump at the chance. She's scared you're gonna cast her out for being a fallen woman."

"I wouldn't do that." She went over to the dresser and picked up the tray. "I'll be back shortly to change your bandage."

"First," Irv said, "you need to drive out to the still and tell Ernie what's happened. He was expecting me out there last night after my visit to Lefty's. He'll be worried."

"That'll take me an hour."

"My arm ain't gonna rot off in that amount of time." To make his point, he tried to raise it and winced. In a growl, he said, "Next time you see that Hutton fella, tell him I'm grateful. I don't trust him, but I owe him my thanks."

"I won't be seeing him anymore."

But when she walked into the kitchen with the tray, he was standing on the back door threshold in conversation with Corrine.

THIRTY-TWO

Thatcher wasn't feeling too gracious toward Laurel this morning, and when she saw him, he could tell by her sour expression that the feeling was mutual.

The tray she was carrying was set on the drainboard with a dish-rattling thud. "Corrine, Irv wants to talk to you." Her tone didn't invite discussion or argument.

"Can't wait to hear what he's gripin' about now." Corrine shot Thatcher a parting smile, then scuttled around Laurel and out of the kitchen.

Laurel waited until Irv's bedroom door was closed, then said in an angry whisper, "I told you to stay away from us."

"Only reason I'm here is to get what I left behind last night."

She propped her hands on her hips. "Corrine?"

He didn't blame her for being mad about that. He'd been so miffed when he left, he'd forgotten all about the girl until he'd reached the boardinghouse. He sure as hell wasn't going to come back for her then. "I didn't mean to dump her on you."

"What *did* you mean to do with her?"

"Well, I really didn't have time to mull it over. What with keeping your father-in-law from bleeding and all."

"Tell me, deputy, did you save him last night only so you could arrest him this morning?"

To hell with this. He had things to do that didn't include swapping snide remarks on her doorstep. "I came for the pistol. I could've bought another hat, but the gun isn't mine. I need to return it to its owner."

"And who is that?"

"Can I have it back, please?"

She stood there seething, then said, "It's been in safekeeping. Wait here."

She went into the dining room. He heard her open one of the sideboard's drawers then slam it shut. She reappeared with his hat in one hand and the Colt in the other. She thrust them at him.

He caught them both against his chest. "Thanks." He placed his hat on his head and pushed the pistol into his waistband.

"You're going to walk around town with it poking out like that?"

"No. I'm going to ride around town with it poking out like that."

"Ride?"

He thumbed over his shoulder toward her backyard where he'd hitched a gelding to a post of her clothesline. She glanced past him, saw the horse, and remarked, again snidely, "He doesn't look like a bucking bronco to me."

"Far from it. He's lazy. His owner hired me to pump some spirit into him. Riding him over was a lesson in obedience."

"For him or for you?"

"I got him up to a canter. For me, it beat walking."

The scornfulness in her expression was replaced by one of sudden realization. "When you left last night . . . ?"

"Yeah, I was afoot. But I'm used to walking." He didn't see a need to belabor the point. "Corrine and I will ride double. Go get her, and we'll be out of your hair."

She hesitated, tugging at her lower lip with her teeth, and damn if he didn't want to be doing that. Sore as he was at her in his head, other parts of him hadn't gotten the message.

She said, "Did Corrine express a desire to go with you?"

"You mean just now? No. She was bringing me up to date on Irv. Sounds like he's doing okay."

"Ornery, as you predicted, but holding his own."

"Have you changed the bandage?"

"Not yet. But he isn't running a fever, so I don't think the wound is infected."

"Want me to stay while you check, then help you wrap him up again?"

"No, I wouldn't want to inconvenience you any more than you already have been." She clasped her hands at her waist and avoided looking him in the eye. "In fact, Irv asked me to tell you—on the outside chance that you and I met again—that he's grateful for what you did and to give you his thanks."

"He said that?"

"Specifically."

He propped his shoulder against the doorjamb and folded his arms. "Now I wonder who that pained the most? You for having to pass along his thanks? Or him for owing me his thanks in the first place?"

"My gratitude is sincere, Mr. Hutton. So is Irv's."

"Then he's changed his opinion of me?"

"Why would you say that?"

"When you two came into the sheriff's office while I was in custody, the second he saw me he said, 'Didn't I tell you he was up to no good?' Meaning that before he'd even met me, before he ever looked me in the eye, he'd drawn that conclusion and shared it with you."

He uncrossed his arms and pushed off the door frame to face her squarely. Watching closely to see how she would react, he added, "Which I guess is why he went for his shotgun that day I wandered into your yard."

"Shotgun?"

"No sense in lying. I saw him. Why'd he have that shotgun at the ready?"

Noticeably uneasy, she said, "He's leery of strangers."

"Overmuch, I'd say."

"He kept a shotgun handy as a precaution. To protect Pearl and me if the need arose."

"But I hadn't done anything out of line. You said so yourself. You told the sheriff that—"

"I know what I told him."

"Then why did your father-in-law feel he had to stand guard?"

His persistence had turned her uneasiness into annoyance. "Maybe it's your overall manner, Mr. Hutton."

"What manner is that?"

"The way you look at a person. Like you're trying to figure them out."

"Sometimes I am."

"Well, it's rude and unnerving. It makes people uncomfortable."

"You especially, I think."

Dander up, she said, "Not at all."

"Then why'd you go all jumpy last night?"

"I didn't go *jumpy*."

He snuffled. She'd played right into his gambit.

When she realized it, she looked away from him, then turned and looked behind her toward Irv's bedroom before coming back around to him. Her expression was now as prim as a nun's.

"You deliberately got us off the subject of Corrine," she said. "In good conscience, I can't send her back to the roadhouse and that Gert who has been so cruel to her."

"She wanted out of there, all right. But where can she go?"

"I'm willing to take her in. She'll have a place to live, and I'll pay her a modest salary to work for me. With Irv incapacitated, I could use the extra help with my business. Corrine is eager to improve her lot in life."

"Sounds good all around, but it seems sudden."

"Well, she was suddenly foisted on me, wasn't she? I thought you would be relieved. This will free you from any responsibility you feel toward her."

"Not entirely." He hitched his chin toward the bedroom. "How's Corrine feel about this arrangement?"

"Irv is talking it over with her now. He's confident that she'll jump at the chance, and so am I. It's certainly preferable to the situation she was in at Lefty's."

"How'd she wind up there? Did she tell you?"

"She was naïve and trusting of a man. She's paying the consequences of having stars in her eyes. They can be blinding." She looked down at her open palm and ran her other thumb over the pinprick in the center. Then she dropped her hand and hid it in a fold of her skirt, as though she'd been caught with it in the cookie jar.

"I shouldn't have let you kiss me last night, Mr. Hutton. But neither should you have taken advantage of me when I was in such a state, so we were both at fault for things getting out of hand. Don't even think of it ever happening again. The incident will never be mentioned. We'll pretend that it didn't happen. No, we'll *forget* that it happened."

He didn't say anything. She didn't look into his face but continued to stare straight ahead at the button on his shirt to which she'd issued the ultimatum about pretending and forgetting. He waited her out. Finally, she tilted her head back and met his eyes. "That's how it's going to be."

"Is that right?"

She went rigid with indignation and made a sound of disgust. "I knew you'd be difficult about it."

She elbowed him aside and went out into the yard. She strode over to the horse. The gelding shied, taking several cautious steps backward. She untied the reins from around the post, then tugged on them until the reluctant horse went along as she led him over to Thatcher.

"Here." She held out the reins. "Goodbye."

Thatcher took the reins, then caught her hand and walked her backward until she came up against the gelding's side, the back of her head resting against the seat of the saddle. Thatcher cupped the horn with his left hand and placed his right on the cantle, bracketing her with his arms.

He could tell the action shocked her, but he didn't give her time to counter. "You've said your piece, now I'm going to say mine. I like the look of you. Have since I first laid eyes on you. That soft spot right there where your lips meet was the first place I wanted to kiss."

He homed in on that spot, then his eyes trailed down her front and back up again. "I like the size and shape of you. I like everything. Even your sass. Mostly your sass," he said, his gaze dipping briefly to her lips again before returning to her eyes.

"As for not thinking about that kiss ever happening again, I've already thought about it. And more. I think about you unbuttoned and unhooked and with your hair loose. I have dreams where we're lying down together, and I hate like hell waking up."

He shifted his stance, still not touching her, but coming awfully close, and it was hard as hell not to give in to the urge to bring them flush like they'd been last night. "Now, Laurel, I've never taken advantage of a woman in my life. You damn well know that I didn't take advantage of you last night, and I won't. Ever."

He dropped his voice so she'd have to listen really close to this last part, because it was an ultimatum of his own. "But if you genuinely don't want me coming at you again, be careful you don't dare me."

He gave the words seconds to sink in, then lowered his hands from the saddle, moved her aside, put his boot in the stirrup, and swung up. He nudged the gelding with his knees and rode out of the yard without looking back.

Thatcher had another difficult encounter ahead of him this morning. He'd said what he'd wanted to say to Laurel, but in doing so had probably offended her beyond any hope of ever making amends. But if he had it to do over again, he'd say the same.

He feared things wouldn't go any better with Bill Amos.

The sheriff's car wasn't parked out front of the department, but Thatcher went inside to check if he was there. Three personnel were inside, but Harold was the only one Thatcher knew by name. All stopped what they were doing when he walked in.

Harold said, "Sheriff's not here."

"Do you know where he is?"

"At home."

"I have business with him."

"What kind of business?"

Harold had covered his back last night during the raid, but the resentment persisted, it seemed. "The kind that won't wait. Where does he live?"

The Amoses' house wasn't as picturesque as Dr. Driscoll's, but the second story roofline sported gingerbread trim. It overhung a deep porch with two wicker rocking chairs. The yard was shaded by a massive pecan tree loaded with clusters of green shucks that promised a good harvest come fall. Thatcher secured the gelding to a fence post, made his way up the limestone walk, and knocked on the front door.

The upper half of it had an oval glass pane through which Thatcher and the sheriff made eye contact as he approached. He was in shirt-sleeves and seemed a bit thrown to see Thatcher at his door. He greeted him by name with a question mark behind it.

"I stopped by your office first. Harold told me where you lived. Can I have a minute?"

The sheriff turned his head and glanced up the staircase attached to the right wall of the vestibule. He came back around, smoothing his mustache. "All right. Come in."

Thatcher took off his hat and stepped inside. On the wall opposite the staircase was a gallery of framed photographs, but the foyer was dim, and Thatcher couldn't make out who was in the pictures.

"How bad off is Irv Plummer?" Bill asked.

"He'll live. The bullet entered the back of his arm, here." Thatcher illustrated. "Came out through his armpit. Lost blood, but it wasn't as nasty as it could have been. What about the other injured?"

"Bloody noses and scraped knuckles, one broken finger. Four were shot, including Irv. None of the wounds were fatal or permanently crippling. Thank God."

"Who was the shooter?"

"Local boy. Preacher's kid. Stupid and blind drunk. He panicked, overreacted. Broke down and cried when we told him that his wild shots had found flesh. More scared of his daddy's punishment than jail time. We've got a dozen in the cell block sleeping it off until they can be arraigned later today. Lefty's lawyer has already posted bail for him and Gert. Routine," he said with a shrug. "How was Mrs. Plummer when you got Irv home?"

"Scared at first, seeing the blood. But once the shock wore off and she realized the wound wasn't fatal, she was fine."

"Third crisis in a row for that young lady."

"Another would be having the old man sent to jail. Do you plan on arresting him?"

"Not this time. But he should learn his lesson from getting shot and stay out of Lefty's."

Thatcher didn't comment on that. He pulled the pistol from his waistband and extended it to Bill by the barrel. "Wasn't fired. Wasn't needed after all."

"Why don't you keep it, Thatcher?"

"No thanks."

"Why not?"

"I've already got one. It was a gift. This one comes with strings."

With a sigh of resignation, Bill took the Colt and set it on the lengthy table that ran along the wall under the picture gallery. "Look, I can tell that you're upset about—"

"I'm not upset, Bill, I'm pissed off. You roped me into something I wanted no part of, and it's not like I hadn't told you flat out that I wanted no part of it."

"Guilty. But last night you only proved that you—"

"Bill?"

The feminine voice came from above. Thatcher looked up the

staircase where a woman hovered halfway down. She was of comparable age to Bill, maybe fifty. She was wearing a dressing gown and bedroom slippers. Her long, pale hair hung loose and tangled almost to her waist. She looked like a disheveled angel, a remarkably beautiful angel.

And she was regarding Thatcher with as much awe as he was regarding her.

With gentleness, Bill said, "Daisy, go on back upstairs. I'll be there in a sec."

She eased her grip on the bannister and continued her descent, but it was as plain as day to Thatcher that she was drunk or high on something. Her tread was so unsteady that if Bill hadn't bounded up to assist her down the last few steps, she surely would have fallen.

When they reached the bottom, she shuffled toward Thatcher, bringing with her a waft of whiskey. She laid her frail hand against her chest as she gazed up at him with a yearning that made Thatcher uncomfortable. He looked over at Bill, who was watching his wife with sorrow, pity, and love. The raw and tragic kind.

"Daisy, this is Thatcher Hutton. Remember I told you about him?"

In a breathy voice, she said, "For a moment there, I thought... With the light behind him, the angle of his jaw, he looked..." She trailed off, and, turning away from Thatcher, said to her husband, "They do make mistakes. I've read stories."

Bill placed his arm around her shoulders. "I don't think it's a mistake, Daisy."

She looked toward the photo gallery, then pressed her face into Bill's shirtfront, and began making keening sounds that made chills run down Thatcher's spine.

Bill shushed her, then turned with her toward the stairs, saying to Thatcher over his shoulder, "Wait for me on the porch."

Thatcher quietly slipped through the front door. *Fucking hell.* This was turning out to be some morning.

He sat down in one of the rocking chairs and stared at the gelding whose head drooped in the midmorning heat. He was too lazy even to graze at the patch of grass within nibbling distance. Thatcher actually preferred a horse that would stamp and rear and buck him off a dozen times to one he had to light a fire under.

Neither he nor the horse moved much in the ten minutes before Bill came through the door, pulling it closed behind him. He avoided looking at Thatcher as he dragged the other rocking chair over and lowered himself into it, settling heavily. He rested his head against the back of it and closed his eyes, his bearing one of utter despair and defeat.

Thatcher took his cue from Bill and remained silent.

After a time, Bill sat forward and placed his forearms on his thighs, linking his fingers between his knees and staring at the floor planks under his boots. "Daisy has a heart condition. You see? Her heart is broken. Shattered, actually.

"The 'declines' I told you about are actually drinking binges. When I got home late last night, she was passed out. I couldn't wake her up. Scares me shitless when I find her like that. I stayed home this morning, waiting for her to wake up, bathe, to eat something…" He made a rolling motion with his hand. "You get it."

Thatcher nodded, but Bill had yet to look at him, so he didn't see the nod. He said the first thing that came to mind, and it was in earnest. "She's beautiful."

Bill gave a sniff of rueful humor. "First time I saw her, swear to God I don't think I took a breath for five full minutes. It was at a community picnic on the Fourth of July. She had on a white dress and carried a parasol. I drew her attention by winning a shooting contest. She strolled over to congratulate me on my blue ribbon. I don't remember what we said to each other. I doubt I made a lick of sense."

He paused and smiled at the recollection. "Anyhow, I started courting her the next day. A few months later, I asked for her hand, and she said yes. I thought for sure she was taunting me, but no, she was in earnest. I marched her to First Methodist before she could change her mind. Our son Tim was born nine months later, almost to the day of the wedding."

During his next pause, his smile faded. "But after Tim, she couldn't conceive. That boy became the light of our lives. We loved him. Most everybody who met him did. The good die young, they say." He gulped, and it took a while for him to continue.

"We never saw his body, didn't have a casket. We put up a marker in the cemetery, but Daisy can't accept that he's gone. I know it was eerie for you, the way she was staring. I apologize. She thinks she sees Tim in every young man who's the right age and of similar build. You do resemble him that way.

"She drinks herself into stupors. Some last hours. Some for days. Every once in a while, she can pull herself together and make an effort to be her old self, the belle of the ball. But not often."

Thatcher shifted in his seat. "Have you thought of taking her to a sanatorium?"

"A thousand times a day. But I can't bring myself to do it, Thatcher. I can't do that to either of us. Being locked up might send her over a cliff to where I couldn't reach. I wouldn't have anything of her, and I'd rather have this than nothing."

"Where does she get the hooch?"

He looked over at Thatcher then, and in his eyes was a shameful confession. "That's why I told you it would be messy if I tried to charge our mayor with bootlegging. Not just messy, but hypocritical. He supplies me with the good stuff from Kentucky."

"He might not if he knew it wasn't for you, if he knew it was Mrs. Amos who was drinking it."

"Oh, he knows. He takes perverse pleasure in her addiction and our sad, sad circumstance." He gave Thatcher another rueful smile. "He was Daisy's escort to the picnic."

THIRTY-THREE

Chester Landry was in conversation with Mr. Hancock and one of his female customers. She was effusively extolling the quality and styling of her recently purchased shoes. With matching effusiveness, Landry complimented her on how well she wore them.

She simpered, Mr. Hancock suggested she buy an additional pair, and Landry's eye was caught by Jimmy Hennessy, who was paying for a purchase at the cash register. Croft's bodyguard tipped his head toward the door.

Landry excused himself from the merchant and the woman, telling them how badly he regretted being unable to stay longer, and exited the store. Hennessy was staring into one of the store's display windows and didn't even turn his head in Landry's direction as he said, "He wants to see you."

Five minutes later, Landry entered the municipal building through a back entrance and took a private staircase that led to a side door of the mayor's office, bypassing his secretary. This door was used only by Bernie's inner circle and individuals like Sheriff Amos who came to pick up their graft.

Landry tapped on the door and was told to come in. Concealing his displeasure over being marshaled, he said, "Good morning, Bernie." He walked over to his customary chair and took a seat.

Bernie, seated behind his desk, was fiddling with a sterling silver letter opener. Landry got the sense he was testing its worth as a weapon. He said, "I understand there was some excitement at Lefty's last night."

"Yes. Rip-roaring."

"Why didn't you tell me?"

Landry's head went back an inch. He cocked an eyebrow. "If you know, then obviously you didn't need me to tell you."

"I want to hear your account of it, Chester."

He raised his shoulders. "It was a raid. Typical in execution and response. People scattered and fled. Heads were knocked. I'm sure there were some arrests, but I have a lot of practice at avoiding arrest, and I succeeded in doing so last night."

"In company?"

"I was there by myself. Prior to the bust-in, I chatted with Lefty. He placed his standard order, but you'll be pleased to hear that I talked him into taking an extra case of that expensive Canadian." He paused, then said, "You still look perturbed."

"Thatcher Hutton was at Lefty's last night."

"Hutton? He wasn't in the back room, I'm certain."

"No, he was out front."

"He must've taken his own recommendation."

"Explain that."

"At dinner last week, he said he'd heard Lefty's hamburgers were good. I guess he decided to try one."

"He didn't go for a hamburger. He was there with Bill Amos."

That took Landry by surprise. "Are you sure?"

"Yes, I'm sure," Bernie replied testily. "Hutton took part in the raid, on the side of the sheriff's department. Not all of Bill's men are happy about it, either. There's grousing in the ranks. First Hutton is in cuffs, now he's in our sheriff's back pocket."

"And the sheriff is in yours," Landry returned mildly.

This was a development he hadn't foreseen. Last week, Hutton had claimed that he had no plans, that he was taking things one day at a time. His sudden change of course needed to be explored, but in a coolheaded manner. Bernie was fuming, and that bothered Landry. First because his anger was so apparent, and secondly because angry people made rash decisions in order to put a quick end to an unexpected problem.

He needed to talk him down. "Actually, Bernie, you should be relieved."

"Why in hell?"

"Because if Hutton is wearing a badge and carrying out raids, he isn't working undercover."

"Not necessarily."

"But improbably."

"Well, I don't like it. I don't like him. You two live in the same boardinghouse. Keep an eye on him."

"Hmm." Landry steepled his fingers and tapped them against his chin. "He's no fool, Bernie. He won't be as easily manipulated as Randy was."

"I'm confident you'll handle him with your usual finesse."

"I'm glad we agree on that."

Landry got up and went to the door. Hand on the knob, he turned back. "You were entirely right to tell me about Hutton's new status. I needed to know. But I disliked being summoned. I'm not one of the good ol' boys you have at your beck and call, Bernie. Don't ever send that mick lummox of yours after me again."

THIRTY-FOUR

Gabe Driscoll was appalled by Norma's recklessness. "What the devil are you thinking, showing up here in broad daylight?"

"I suggest you let me in. It wouldn't do for your nosy neighbors to see you refusing to examine a pediatric patient, no matter how closeted you are."

He glanced down at the bundle in her arms. "The baby's sick?"

"He's as healthy as a horse, but they don't know that." She shoved past Gabe and entered the house.

He took a furtive look up and down the street. Norma's sister's automobile was the only one in sight, but Patsy wasn't in it. He shut the door. "You drove yourself?"

"I wanted us to be alone." Without invitation, Norma went into the parlor. "This room is like a dungeon. Why don't you raise the shades and open the drapes?"

"Never mind the drapes, Norma. I told you not to come here."

"You gave me no choice. You haven't kept your promise to come see Arthur and me."

"I couldn't get away."

"What's keeping you occupied? Not your practice. The sign out front says you're still closed."

"People are watching me."

"People?" she said, sputtering a laugh. "What people?"

"All people," he shouted. "My every move incites speculation on what really happened to Mila."

"You're imagining things."

He chewed the inside of his cheek. "Maybe. To an extent. But we have to be discreet, Norma. Why can't you understand that?"

"I do understand it. I just hate being apart." She came toward him, her gait that of a stalking predator. He was easy prey. He swelled inside his trousers just as he had the first time he saw her.

Patsy had been suffering a wracking cough, and Norma had brought her to him for treatment. While he'd been pressing his stethoscope against her sister's chest and listening to her wheezing lungs, Norma had been toying with the strand of beads lying against her own chest and drawing his attention to her voluptuous, well-defined breasts.

When they left, Patsy had gone ahead of her. Hanging back, Norma had glanced toward the kitchen where Mila could be heard humming. Looking up at him provocatively, Norma whispered, "I hope the medicine doesn't work, and we'll have to come back soon. Or maybe," she'd purred, "you should spare my ailing sister the trip into town and make a house call."

The following day, he'd done that. He'd spent five minutes examining Patsy, then had spent an hour in Norma's cluttered bedroom examining every inch of her dusky nudity. She was without shame or modesty. She was exotic and carnal and sexually industrious, so unlike Mila and her conventional wholesomeness that he became besotted.

Or bewitched.

Because even now, when he was irritated with her, he was incapable of breaking the spell she had cast over him that first day. Sandwiching the baby between them, she leaned in and breathed against his lips. "I'm tired of doing without you, Gabe. I'm burning. I want us to be together all the time."

He placed his hands on her shoulders, squeezing. "We will be. Be patient. Please. Just a little longer."

"How much longer?"

"Until our being seen together won't arouse suspicion. We've come this far. We can't get careless now."

Beneath his hands, her shoulders relaxed. "Of course. You're right. I'm being selfish." She backed away, then went over to the divan, sat down, and opened the light flannel blanket wrapped around the infant. "Come say hello."

Gabe sat down beside her and looked at his son, whose dark eyes were open and alert. Gabe stroked his cheek. "He is a fine-looking boy."

"More than fine. He's perfect. I adore him."

"He does appear to be the picture of health."

"He eats well." Her eyes linked with Gabe's, she unbuttoned her dress, pushed down her chemise, and put Arthur to her breast. When the baby latched onto her nipple, the lust that surged through Gabe was rampant and consuming. During the past year, and with only token resistence from him, his sexual appetite for her had taken control of his reason. It had procured his soul.

He couldn't pinpoint the precise moment he had decided that he must kill his wife, but it had been around the time that Norma told him she was pregnant. His spontaneous reaction was to suggest an abortion. "I could send Mila to her kinfolks for a visit and perform the procedure in the office while she's away."

He'd done D and Cs following miscarriages, but had never aborted a living fetus. He wasn't certain that when the time came, he could go through with it. But his ambiguous reaction to the prospect was mild compared to Norma's tumultuous one.

She had collapsed on the spot. She'd wept bitter tears. Once he'd calmed her down, he'd determined that it wasn't their unborn child he needed to be rid of, it was Mila. She was the impediment.

Even Mila's pregnancy, which she had informed him of with unbridled joy, hadn't deterred him. Whenever his conscience got a tenuous toehold, Norma reminded him that their baby had been conceived first. His loyalty must be to it, not to the product of his loveless marriage. Wouldn't he choose true love over duty?

On the day he'd irreversibly chosen love, he had returned home from his rural route in time for supper. He hadn't entered the house thinking that this was the night he would commit murder. Mila had greeted him with a kiss on the cheek, her unsuspecting smile, and a glass of iced tea.

He'd relaxed in the parlor and read the newspaper while she'd puttered in the kitchen putting the finishing touches on their meal. When it was ready, she'd called him into the dining room. There was a bouquet of flowers in the center of the table. The linen napkins smelled of starch. From a china tureen, she'd served him pork roast with potatoes and carrots.

He remembered these small details later. That evening he'd taken them for granted.

While they ate, she'd kept up her happy prattle, telling him about the first shoots springing up in the vegetable garden, the fabric she thought would do nicely for the nursery curtains, and the man who had stopped by to inquire about the room to let.

"I think he was hungry. I had just taken da shortbread out of dee oven. I gave him two pieces. Are you ready for your dessert?"

He remembered looking down at his empty plate, surprised to find that he'd eaten his whole portion without tasting it. His mind had been on Norma and his infant son whom he had stopped by to see that day. Arthur had been born a month earlier, not that day. His birth had been easy, not a difficult breech. Those were lies he'd later told the sheriff.

During that afternoon's visit, Patsy had left him and Norma alone to admire their son. They lay on the bed with Arthur between them. Norma had wanted to make love, but he'd told her it was too soon for her after giving birth. She'd settled for playfully stroking his penis through his trousers and lauded it for the ideal son it had provided, a child untainted by foreign blood.

That was one of Norma's familiar refrains: His wife's German heritage continued to cost him patients even this long after the Armistice.

That's what had reeled through his mind that evening as Mila left the dining table carrying their plates into the kitchen, keeping up her running monologue about mundane topics. He didn't give a fuck about what color she'd chosen for the nursery curtains when he was stiff with the anticipation of fucking Norma again.

He'd gotten up from the dining table and walked into the kitchen. Mila had her back to him, cutting slices of shortbread for their dessert. He hadn't been nervous or hesitant. He hadn't paused to think: *I'm going to kill her now.*

He simply picked up a clean iron skillet from off the stove and swung it at the back of her head. The blow didn't even break the skin, but he heard the crunch of bone as her skull caved in. Never having known what had hit her, she'd gone silent and fell to the floor.

Later, he didn't recall how long he'd stood there staring at her inert form. Eventually he'd knelt down and checked to make sure her scalp hadn't bled. It hadn't. Not one drop. He'd felt her carotid. No pulse. No *breath*. Utter stillness. That's when he'd realized the magnitude of what he'd done, and he experienced a paroxysm of panic. He'd thrown up his dinner in the sink.

Even after retching until he was empty, he was dizzy. His ears were buzzing. His mind was spinning with possible explanations. But he couldn't land on one that sounded plausible. None would be believed. He would be charged and tried. During the trial, his affair with sexually unrestrained Norma would be exposed as an unquestionable motive. He would be sentenced to hang.

He'd witnessed a hanging once. His father had thought it would be good for his ten-year-old self to see firsthand the wages of sin. It had been ghastly. He didn't want to die shitting his pants and twitching at the end of a rope.

Clutching his head between his hands, he tore at his hair, and sobbed.

Then as spontaneously as the panic had seized him, it vanished, and was replaced with an incredible calmness. He thought through the idea that had suddenly occurred to him. He inspected it, looking for pitfalls. It wasn't without risks, certainly. But he didn't want to hang.

He'd stepped over Mila's body, went into his office, and picked up the telephone to call Mayor Croft.

"Gabe?"

The sound of his name jerked him back into the present. Arthur was no longer nursing, but sleeping on his stomach beside Norma on the divan. She frowned. "You were miles away. Were you thinking about *her*?"

"No."

She knew he was lying. The first night she had showed up on his doorstep, unexpectedly and near midnight, they had fought over the guilt eating at him. Then, after pitching a temper tantrum, she had cried and begged him to forgive her for being insensitive to his plight.

"You have a reputation to protect. You must preserve it. It's just that I miss you so much," she'd whispered into his neck.

That smoky seductiveness was in her voice now as she ran her fingers through his hair. "Thinking about it only distresses you. You did what was necessary for us to be together, Gabe. You see that, don't you?"

"Yes."

"It's done. We have Arthur. We have each other." Her lower lip began to tremble. "Would you want to change things back to the way they were before? With her?"

"No. God no. Of course not."

"Then stop punishing yourself. Instead, take advantage of the reason you did it." She unbuttoned her dress the rest of the way and laid it open. Except for the chemise wadded up around her waist, she was bare.

"We can't, Norma. It's too soon after the baby."

She gave him a sultry smile and drew him to her. "Mama needs you."

Afterward, when they separated, they were damp and listless and breathing heavily. Gabe slid to the floor and sat between her legs. He rested his cheek on her lap. "Did I hurt you?"

"Yes." At his start, she pressed his head back down and laughed huskily. "It was marvelous."

"Tease." He turned his face into her belly.

"You came like a fire hose. I hope it cleared your thoughts of Pointer's Gap."

He ceased the nuzzling and looked up at her with horror. "*What?*"

"Pointer's Gap. Where your dead wife is buried."

He gave his head a violent shake as though to deny hearing what she was saying. "How did you... Nobody knows that except me."

"And Bernie Croft."

Gabe forced himself to swallow before he choked. "He swore to me... swore that nobody would ever know."

She smiled placidly and stroked his cheek. "Surely you didn't think that 'nobody' included me."

THIRTY-FIVE

With Corrine assisting, Laurel changed the dressings on Irv's wounds. They showed no sign of festering, but, for good measure, she dabbed on some coal oil before wrapping him in a fresh bandage.

Once that was done, she left him to rest while she prepared to make the necessary trip to the still and to get Corrine settled in the shack. There was no question of her happiness over her new position. She celebrated by dancing a little jig.

They raided the pantry and icebox for foodstuffs that would last her for several days. As they carried the parcels from the house, Laurel said, "Don't forget your things. Did you leave them in Irv's truck last night?"

"What things?"

Laurel stopped and looked at her. "Your belongings."

Corrine swept her hand down her front. "What I got on is what I've got to my name. When Mr. Hutton stopped cussing and told me to get in, I got in. And anyway, there was nothing at the roadhouse I wanted bad enough to go back for."

"Clothes?"

"This is what I was wearing the night I ran off with Jack. Gert gave me some castoff dresses, but she's probably passed them on to another girl by now. Besides, I wouldn't want them back. They were whores' clothes."

Laurel motioned toward her auto. "Climb in."

She drove them to Hancock's, where she bought Corrine three changes of clothes, undergarments, and basic toiletries. Once on their way out of town, Corrine said repeatedly that she'd never before owned things so fine, and Laurel believed her. The girl clutched the package to her chest, often peering into it as though she feared the merchandise might disappear.

Laurel was touched that she took such delight in simple necessities. Their moonshining business might yet fail, but she was confident in her decision to rescue Corrine.

The girl was even inordinately pleased with the shack. "I've never had a place all to myself. Can I fix it how I want it?"

"Certainly."

She unwrapped her new hairbrush and other grooming items and lined them up just so on Irv's old three-legged bureau. Then, "What's this?" She pulled a tablet from the bottom of the package.

"What does it look like?"

"A schoolbook."

Laurel had added the purchase in secret before leaving the store. "That's right. It's a primer used to teach people the alphabet. Irv told me you wanted to learn to read. The first step is to learn the alphabet."

The girl ran her hand over the workbook's cover as though it were the costly first edition of a classic. "What if I'm too stupid?"

"Nonsense. I'll teach you. Let's start with your name."

"Right now?"

"There should be a box of pencils in the package. I asked the store clerk to sharpen them for us."

Fifteen minutes later, Corrine had followed the guidance of Laurel's hand to print her name. "Two of them?" she said, pointing to the r.

"That's right. You must practice printing all twenty-six letters as you see them in the example. Capitals and lower case. Next time, we'll go over the sound each letter makes."

"I'll practice. I promise."

"When Ernie doesn't need you. He'll be putting you to work, you know."

Corrine rubbed her hands together. "I'm ready."

Rather than drive to the still, Laurel left her Ford at the shack and showed Corrine the shortcut over the hilly, rocky terrain. Along the way, she dispensed advice.

"As the crow flies, it's about a mile, so if time is a factor, allow yourself at least half an hour to walk it. After dark, always bring a lantern with you, but only light it if you must. You don't want to signal someone that you're making this trip back and forth. I'll ask Ernie if he can spare you a firearm."

"To shoot at what?"

"You might come upon wildlife."

"Or them Johnsons."

"Same thing," Laurel said under her breath. "Alter your route a little each time so you don't create a noticeable path. If you see anyone showing an interest in the shack, or the same vehicle frequently driving past, be sure to caution Ernie."

"What's he like?"

Laurel hesitated. "Rustic."

Following their introduction, the moonshiner and the former prostitute sized each other up, and it was clear to Laurel that both found admirable traits lacking in the other.

Ernie had reacted to the news about Irv with the expected concern. Laurel had assured him that his friend would heal. "But I'm afraid it will be several weeks before he regains full use of his arm, if ever. While he's out of commission, Corrine will be assisting you in the distillation and bottling process."

A taut silence followed that announcement. Then Ernie said, "She whut?"

"It's a temporary arrangement," Laurel said. "She'll work with you only until Irv is able."

Corrine piped up. "Don't forget that he's old and already has a bum hip."

"I ain't forgot," Ernie snapped.

Laurel could have done without Corrine's contribution and Ernie's retort. She said, "The point is, his convalescence can't be rushed, Ernie. You wouldn't want him to return to work too soon and do further damage to himself."

"'Course not." He picked up a stir-stick and moved it around in a barrel of mash. He aimed his pointy chin in Corrine's direction. "Does she know squat about making whiskey?"

"I've got ears," Corrine said, "and I'm standing right here. You want to know something, ask me d'rectly."

"Do you know squat about making whiskey?"

"Irv said it was up to you to teach me. That's what Laurel said, too."

He harrumphed. "It ain't as easy as it looks."

"It don't look easy at'all. In fact, I've never seen a more rickety pile of junk as that still."

"It's my great-granddaddy's design."

Before Corrine could comment on that, Laurel stepped in. "Ernie, let me stir the mash. You walk Corrine through the process."

It took him an hour to explain all the still's components and their various functions. Lesson over, Corrine asked to be excused to seek a private spot to relieve herself.

Ernie said to Laurel, "Wouldn't have taken half as long if she hadn't asked so many dadgum questions."

"They were good questions, Ernie, about things she needs to know."

"She always rattle on that much?"

"You'll get used to it."

"I doubt it. What happened to her eye?"

"She took a beating from the late Wally Johnson."

He looked in the direction Corrine had gone. "She's the whore?"

"Don't use that word again." After her sharp rebuke, she set her hand on his arm in conciliation. "Listen, Ernie, when Mr. Hutton brought Irv home last night, I thought he was dead. I'm sure you were fit to be tied when he didn't show up for work. It was a rough night on all of us. Fair to say, we're feeling the strain?"

He nodded.

"I'm sorry to spring Corrine on you," she continued, "but it was actually Irv's idea, and at first even I was resistant to it." She recapped for him the conversation she and Irv had had early that morning. "We've got to keep up production or we'll soon be out of business. In fact, our supply is already low. I'll walk back to the shack and bring the car around. Irv said you had some crates stashed away. I need to take them back with me."

"They was stole."

Her breath escaped her. *"What?"*

"I wasn't gonna tell you, didn't want you worrying."

She backed up to an upended crate and sat down. "Well, I'm worried now. When were they stolen?"

"Night before last. I'd added a crate to the stash that day. Went back yesterday to add another one. They's all gone."

"How many?"

"Ten."

One hundred and twenty jars of one hundred proof. She did the math. Her heart sank over the amount of the loss.

Ernie said, "I would've told Irv last night, only he got shot." He raised his bony shoulders.

"Where was this stash hidden?"

"Over in that cedar break."

She looked in the direction he'd pointed. "That nearby?"

"Thirty yards, maybe. I'd dug a hole big as a grave, thought I had it covered up good with brush."

"Who could have gotten that close without your knowing?"

Another shrug. "I wasn't doing a run that night. Did some tinkering on the new still. Shored up the firebox with more rock. Crawled into the tent pretty early. Never heard a thing." He pushed his hands into the deep pockets of his overalls. "You trust those twins?"

"Yes." Then she gave a shrug of her own. "I suppose."

"Irv says they're half drunk half the time. Randy as goats. Lightning rods for trouble."

"Maybe, but we need them."

"What about that Hutton fella?"

"What about him?"

"How was it he brought Irv home from Lefty's?"

"It's a long story." She didn't want to mention the deputy's badge. "Irv thinks—"

"I know what Irv thinks." Her brittle tone stopped him from taking that subject any further. *Be careful you don't dare me.*

"Well," Ernie said, "somebody found out where we're at. If it'd been lawmen, they'd've poured out the hooch and busted up the stills."

"Unless it was corrupt lawmen."

"Could be. But…"

"But what, Ernie?"

"You don't need this on top of Irv."

"Don't spare me bad news. I hate surprises. Recent ones have been calamities."

"Well then, what I think? Whoever stole the 'shine was giving us a warnin'. It was somebody's way of saying we know who you are and where you're at, and you got off light with us just taking off ten crates instead of ten fingers and toes."

"The Johnsons?"

"So long as we're small timers, they'll leave us be. But if we start horning in on their profit…"

Again he didn't finish, but she got the message. "Maybe I shouldn't involve Corrine after all. What if they come back?"

"I've got two rifles, a side-by-side shotgun, a six-shooter, and a trap."

"A trap?"

"Jaw spring. Big enough to trap a bear. If some sorry sumbitch sticks his hand in that hidey-hole again, he'll come up with a stump."

Corrine reappeared. Both observed her as she walked toward them. When she got nearer to them, she stopped and put her hands on her hips. "Why are y'all lookin' at me like that?"

"Can you shoot a rifle?" Ernie asked.

"Damn good. Back home, I helped keep food on the table."

"You ain't back home, and you got only one good eye."

"Then I might have to use you for target practice."

Looking at Laurel, he mumbled, "I'll give her the shotgun. Tell Irv to take it easy and not worry about things. That mash needs stirrin'." He skulked off.

Laurel and Corrine watched him go. Laurel said, "Are you comfortable with me leaving you here?"

"Sure."

"Will you have trouble finding your way back to the shack?"

"I made note of things along the way. With my one good eye," she added with a scowl aimed at Ernie.

"Irv and I are counting on you to make yourself useful. Do you think you can do that without picking silly fights with him?"

Corrine looked over at Ernie as he dipped the stir-stick into the barrel. "One thing I can do is put some meat on his bones," she said. "I never saw a man who needed feedin' more'n him."

<hr />

When Laurel came upon the road sign, she slowed down then rolled to a full stop. She stared at the sign's uneven, hand-painted lettering, which was familiar because she'd passed it many times before. But the sign now had new, and more personal, significance.

She calculated how long she'd been away from the house, leaving her infirm father-in-law alone. She thought about the deal he had failed to cement with Lefty before the raid. She thought about Corrine and the abuse she'd suffered.

Before she could talk herself out of it, she made the turn. Earlier today, she'd been told she had sass. This would be a test of just how much.

The road was as corrugated as a washboard. Her tires kicked up dust as fine and white as talcum powder. It swirled around the Model

T when she brought it to a stop. As the dust settled, she studied the uninviting structure. It looked deserted.

She hesitated, thinking that perhaps this wasn't a good idea at all. She patted her pocket and, after feeling the reassuring weight of the Derringer, pushed open the car door and got out.

Warped steps led up to an equally uneven porch. The heels of her shoes tapped loudly on the planks and echoed in the crawl space beneath. The screen on the outer door was rusty and jaggedly torn in places, as though someone had taken a dull can opener to it. The wooden frame supporting it was splintery. It slapped against the solid door behind it when she knocked.

She heard muffled voices from within, and then a thudding tread as someone came to answer.

The individual who opened the door had to be Gert, because she was the female counterpart of an ogre. A cigarette was anchored in the corner of her lips, the smoke from it curling up around her face. She squinted against it, making her eyes appear even more hostile.

"We're closed."

"Not closed. Shut down."

"Then what are you doing here?"

"To discuss business with Lefty."

Gert took away the cigarette and barked a sound that was half laugh, half phlegmy cough. "I think your business is with me. You must've heard about the girl I lost to the raid. You figuring on taking her place?" She looked Laurel up and down. "There's men who don't mind small ones. What's your name?"

"Laurel."

"Pretty."

"Plummer. And my business isn't with you. It's with your husband. Is he here? Or in jail?"

"I'm here." A stick figure of a man materialized out of the dark and murky interior. "Plummer, you say? Kin to Irv?"

"His daughter-in-law."

"Huh. Heard your husband blew his brains out."

Laurel ignored Gert's cruel remark and focused on Lefty. "May I have a moment of your time?"

"What for?"

"It would be in your best interest."

Gert repeated the statement, mimicking the modulation of Laurel's voice. "Who do you think you are, a fuckin' Rockefeller?"

"Back off, Gert." Reaching past her, Lefty pushed open the screen door. "Come on in, but I already told Irv no deal."

"That's not what Irv told me," Laurel said as she stepped inside. "One of you is lying." She gave the hatchet-faced man an arch look. "I suspect it's you."

He turned and crossed the large room to the bar, where he motioned her onto a stool. He sat down, leaving an empty stool between them. Laurel pretended not to notice the shotgun lying on the bar.

Gert lowered herself into a chair at one of the nearby tables and lit a fresh cigarette. By the time she'd smoked it down all the way, Laurel and Lefty were sealing a new deal with a handshake.

As Laurel stood to leave, she asked, "Do you know the O'Connor twins?"

"Don't everybody?"

"Since Irv was wounded in the fracas last night, one or both of the O'Connors will take over making your deliveries. They'll know the terms of our agreement. Don't try to cheat me."

"Wouldn't think of cheating a lady," he said, grinning. If that's what you could call the exposure of his crooked teeth when he peeled his lips back.

"When do you think you'll be able to reopen?"

"Tonight," Gert said as she ground out her cigarette butt in the chipped ashtray on the table. She heaved herself out of her chair. "Smarty-pants, you keep undercutting people in this business, you're gonna start pissing them off."

"Thank you for the warning." Laurel headed for the door.

"You got gumption. I'll say that for you. If moonshining don't work out, I could always use you upstairs."

Laurel didn't acknowledge that. Rather, she kept walking until she reached the door, and only then turned and confronted Gert. "You didn't lose Corrine to the raid. She took advantage of the commotion to escape her imprisonment here."

Gert's face became bloated with rage. "That ungrateful little slut. Where's she at? If you know, you'd better tell me. She owes me money."

"While in your charge, she was disfigured, maimed, and half blinded. The only thing you're owed is contempt." She turned and stalked out.

The screen door banged against the exterior wall as Gert barged through it, but Laurel didn't turn to look back. Gert was bellowing obscenities, most of which Laurel didn't even know the meaning of.

She kept her head high and walked toward her car with purpose, although she was mindful of that handy shotgun. At any moment a blast from it could be the last thing she ever heard.

She made it to her car and thanked God that it started on the first crank. She drove away unscathed except for the blistering her ears had taken from Gert's profanity.

But midway to the highway, when no longer in sight of the road-house, fear and trembling caught up with her. Like the night she'd escaped from Martin's Café without being exposed as a moonshiner, she broke a cold sweat.

She braked her car, rested her forehead on the steering wheel, and gasped for breath as she willed her heartbeat to slow down. Hearing another vehicle approaching, she jerked her head up and looked behind her. But the sound was coming from ahead, not from the direction of the roadhouse.

She pulled out of the middle of the road, allowing the other vehicle to pass her. It was a newer model than hers by several years, the shiny black paint defiant of the powdery road, but she was relieved to see that it didn't have an official seal stenciled on the side.

She continued on her way and blessed the second she reached the highway without anyone in pursuit. Still shaken, but calmer than she had been, she pointed herself toward town.

THIRTY-SIX

⸺◈⸺

After leaving Bill Amos to deal with his situation at home, Thatcher rode the gelding back to Barker's, then put in a long day of work, exercising every horse in the stable and trying to correct whatever bad habit or stubborn trait each had.

He kept his distance from Fred and Roger. The youngster had developed a case of hero worship since the incident with the rattlesnake and often trailed Thatcher around like a puppy. Today the two picked up on his desire for solitude and stayed away from the stable and corral.

Learning of Bill's circumstances had left Thatcher with conflicting emotions that were equally strong and unshakeable. Throughout the day, he fluctuated between being angry and resentful over Bill's manipulation, while also feeling compassion for his personal torment.

And prior to that distressing conversation with Bill, he'd had the set-to with Laurel.

He was ready to see an end to this day.

He returned to the boardinghouse in time to fill a plate with what was left of the cold supper and ate alone in the dining room, even as the landlady was clearing the dishes and utensils off the long table with more clatter than necessary. When finished eating, he dodged the residents seeking companionship and headed for his room.

He'd almost reached the third floor when he was called to from below. "Hutton."

Chester Landry was rounding the landing on the second floor. His gold tooth caught the light from a wall fixture as he smiled up at Thatcher. "Hold up."

Shit. Chester Landry's intrusion was the perfect top-off to this crappy day.

He replied unenthusiastically to the salesman's greeting and was tempted to continue on to his room, but, in spite of himself, he was curious to see if Landry would refer to the roadhouse raid.

Landry reached him and took a moment to catch his breath. "You'd think I would be conditioned to climbing these infernal stairs by now." He inhaled deeply, then asked, "Am I keeping you from anything?"

"Bed."

"That kind of day?"

"And then some."

"Would you consider going out for a little refreshment? Grab a Coca-Cola at the filling station?"

"No, thanks. I'm ready to hit the hay."

"Well then, another time." He slid his hands into the pockets of his trousers. "I feel at loose ends tonight."

"Ask your buddy to go with you."

"Buddy?" He tipped his head and looked at Thatcher with puzzlement, which Thatcher thought was faked. "Oh, you mean Randy? He's moved on."

It occurred to Thatcher only now that he hadn't seen the young man around lately. "Where'd he go?"

"God knows. Greener pastures, I guess." He shrugged. "I missed seeing him around and inquired about him. Mrs. May said he left without notice. She went up to collect his rent, which was a day late. He'd cleared out in the dead of night." He chuckled. "Sounds like something impulsive and irresponsible he would do."

Thatcher thought Landry's dry laugh also seemed faked. When Thatcher didn't join in, Landry must have sensed his reserve. He glanced down the staircase to make certain no one else was around. No one was. Nevertheless, he lowered his voice to a confidential level.

"We're avoiding the subject we're both dying to talk about."

Thatcher just looked at him.

"Come on, Hutton." For the first time ever, some of Landry's polish dimmed and he showed annoyance. "I didn't see you, but I heard you were there last night."

"I saw you, running away."

"Yes, our perspectives were entirely different. We were on opposite sides of the bedlam." When Thatcher didn't respond, Landry said, "No comment on that?"

"What do you want to know?"

"From kidnap suspect to deputy sheriff is a very broad leap. You covered it in a matter of weeks. How did you manage to curry the sheriff's favor and become a deputy?"

"I didn't."

He declared it as a fact, but that damn badge was still in his breast pocket. After listening to Bill's tragic tale, witnessing the heartache, sorrow, and despair that he lived with daily, Thatcher hadn't had the heart to return the badge with the stern put-down he'd rehearsed.

"What I heard was that you were in the thick of it with the sheriff's men."

"I went for a hamburger, and got caught up in it." He stopped there, not feeling a need to explain or justify anything he did to this popinjay. "What were you doing there, Landry? Fitting the soiled doves with new shoes?"

Thatcher got a flash of the gold tooth when Landry threw his head back and laughed. "You have a sense of humor after all. I was beginning to wonder." Recovering from his laughter, he said, "God help any man who goes near one of those girls. I'm sure they're petri dishes for VD.

"No, I went only for a hamburger, too, but couldn't resist the enticement of a drink. You were the one who told me about the place, remember? Did you know about the back room?"

"I'd heard rumors." Thatcher paused, then asked, "That was your first time there?"

"Rotten luck to choose last night to try it out, huh?"

"I'd say."

"Having to escape arrest wasn't the worst of it. In the melee, I lost my pocket watch. I went back today to see if it had been found and turned in. The madam..." He raised his eyebrows. "...denied having seen it. I doubt that's true, but there was a shotgun within her reach, so I wasn't about to question her honesty."

"Good call."

Landry shuddered. "Lord, she's a species unto herself. To make the unpleasant encounter even worse, she was already in a foul temper when I arrived. I hope her ire wasn't provoked by Mrs. Plummer."

Thatcher felt like a bolt of lightning had shot through him, from the top of his head to the soles of his feet. Every nerve ending in his body sizzled. "Laurel Plummer?"

Landry grinned and winked. "The charming lady of the pies. She was leaving as I was arriving."

"Leaving Lefty's?"

"We met on the road. She pulled over so I could pass."

"You must have mistaken somebody for her."

Landry tapped him in the chest with the back of his hand and winked again. "Come now, Hutton, who could mistake that face?"

Thatcher wanted to lift him bodily and pitch him headfirst over the bannister. But he knew he was being baited, and that a volatile reaction was what this slick dude was after, so he forced one corner of his mouth to tilt up. "A blind man, maybe."

"There's an appealing air of refinement about her, too." Landry made a spiraling motion with his hand. "I can't picture her going to that ratty roadhouse for any reason other than it having something to do with her father-in-law getting shot."

"You're well informed, Landry."

"Small-town scuttlebutt," he said. "I couldn't go anywhere today without hearing about the raid and the fallout from it. It's all anyone was talking about."

Thatcher remained noncommittal and tried to look bored with the subject. He covered a yawn with his hand. "Sorry. As I said, I was off to bed."

Landry gave him a little bow. "Then don't let me detain you any longer. Good night."

"Good night."

"Sleep tight."

Landry's mocking lilt set Thatcher's teeth on edge. He went into his room, but not to sleep.

Laurel led the O'Connors down the steps into the cellar and set the lantern on the dirt floor. She gestured toward the stacked wooden crates. "The theft hurt us. That's our stockpile."

"That's it? No jugs?" Davy asked.

"As you see," she said. "Ernie had hidden ten crates of jars. Even those would barely have covered our orders. Now, they're gone."

"Thieving bastards," Davy muttered.

She had gauged the brothers' furious reaction to the news of the theft and didn't believe they would have stolen from her even if they'd known where the crates had been buried. They seemed to understand and appreciate that their enterprise was in dire straits due to the loss of product simultaneous with Irv's being incapable of working to replace it.

"Ernie is doing a double run tonight," she said. "In the meantime, this is the supply we have on hand."

Mike did a quick calculation. "Seventy-two jars. Those roughnecks will have that drunk before we get halfway back from delivering them."

"I can't help it, Mike. Nobody counted on these setbacks."

Davy sighed. "Let's get the haul into the car, brother, and make the best of it."

"When you have everything loaded, join me inside. There's another development to tell you about."

A few minutes later the two came inside. Davy was about to speak when Laurel put her index finger to her lips. "Softly, please. Irv was restless and grumpy all afternoon. I know he's in pain, but he's also fretting over our situation. I let him drink enough to tranquilize him. He's asleep, and I hope he'll stay that way till morning."

They carried cups of coffee into the dining room and gathered around the table. She served the twins slices of cherry pie. "None for you?" Davy asked.

"I was up all night last night. I've been baking since I returned from the still." While there, she'd made the trek over the hill twice, but she didn't tell them that. "My feet are tired, my back is aching, and the last thing I want to see is a piece of pie."

They looked at her with sympathy but dug into theirs.

As she watched them shovel in bites, humming enjoyment, she pushed her fingers into her hair and held her head. "It's just occurred to me that I should be putting up jars of pie filling while fresh fruit is in season." It was an exhausting thought, but their moonshining business was reliant on her pie trade as a cover. "But that's a worry for another day."

Lowering her hands, she met the twins' expectant gazes. "You don't have to tell me *how* you know her, but are you acquainted with a girl named Corrine who worked at Lefty's?"

"The whore?" Mike said.

Davy kicked his brother beneath the table. Mike drew back his fist.

Laurel held up her hands. "Stop it! We don't have time for that, but don't ever refer to Corrine that way again. Within or outside of my hearing."

Davy said, "We know she's the poor girl Wally Johnson beat up."

"That's right, and she's still suffering the effects. By a set of bizarre circumstances, she's now a member of our group."

The twins gaped at her with identical expressions of incredulity.

"Never mind how it came about. She arrived here last night with Irv. She proved herself helpful in any number of ways, and that gave Irv an idea." She went on to tell them about the present arrangement at the stills. "Ernie will teach her how to do the simpler tasks, and I trust her to work hard so that our shortfall will be made up for soon. And—"

"Jesus," Mike said. "There's an and?"

Laurel gave him a look. "*And*, I went to Lefty's today to renegotiate terms."

"You went to Lefty's?"

"Alone? Are you daft, Laurel?"

"Irv had laid the groundwork of a new deal with him, and I couldn't let that opportunity pass, especially in light of the theft. I got Lefty to triple his usual order."

"Bloody lot of good it'll do us, though," Davy said. "We've got no whiskey to sell, and Lefty's is shut down."

"Only until dark tonight." She glanced out the window at the darkened sky. "By now, they should be back in full swing."

"He greased somebody's palm," Mike said. "Somebody high up."

"I'm sure he did," Laurel said.

The twins cut glances at each other, but neither said anything.

"What?" she asked.

Davy shifted in his seat and cleared his throat. "Have you ever considered…uh…"

Mike cut in. "What numb-nuts is trying to ask is, have you ever thought of *approaching* someone who has *influence* to persuade him to be a tad less *influential*?"

"You mean pay him not to be? Absolutely not."

"It's the way business is done, darlin'," Davy said softly.

Mike added, "In order to stay in business, the owner of the pool hall had to give graft to damn near everybody."

"Look how far it got him," she snapped. "I won't stoop to bribery. And, anyway, we can't afford it." She pushed back her chair and stood up.

"This new order of Lefty's is a good one, and, as long as *he* continues to bribe officials, it'll be a standing order.

"All the more reason why Corrine's help is essential until Irv can resume his duties. Now, you need to be on your way to Ranger, and I must go to bed before I drop. Any questions?"

The brothers looked at each other again. Laurel braced herself for what might be coming this time, but Davy flashed her a boyish grin. "Can we take a piece of pie for the road?"

She gave them half the pie for themselves, and sent them off with the others she had baked and boxed that day. As he carefully placed the last one in their truck, Mike said, "We'll have them there well before breakfast. The men working the night shifts on the rigs love having pie for breakfast."

"And moonshine for dinner," Davy said.

The three were laughing together as she walked them out to their truck. She admonished them to drive carefully, but fast enough to return in time to start their shift at Logan's store. "You can't get fired."

"Ah, we won't," Mike said. "We're Mrs. Logan's pet project."

"She's urging us to get baptized," Davy explained. "She fears our infant baptism didn't take."

The three of them began laughing again, but there was no levity in Mike's voice when suddenly he asked, "Who is that?" and simultaneously pulled a pair of brass knuckles from his pants pocket.

THIRTY-SEVEN

———◦◉◦———

Alarmed, Laurel turned.

Just outside the fan of light provided by the kitchen windows, Thatcher was propped against the clothesline post where he'd hitched his horse that morning. To Laurel's dismay—and outrage—her heart thumped at the sight of his tall, lean silhouette.

She wanted to rail at him for not making his presence known, but she needed to defuse the O'Connors, who were a hairsbreadth away from a catastrophic overreaction. "It's okay," she told them in a murmur, then, "Mr. Hutton. You startled us."

He pushed himself off the post and strolled forward, but his seeming nonchalance didn't fool Laurel, and she doubted the O'Connors would be deceived by it, either. Beneath the brim of his cowboy hat, his eyes shifted from one twin to the other.

She was almost certain that Thatcher had seen the brass knuckles now bridging Mike's fingers, and surely he'd also noticed that Davy's right hand was at the small of his back, where she knew he carried a small pistol similar to hers.

When the twins first began delivering to the boom towns, she'd expressed concern for their safety. They'd shown her their weapons and assured her that they would never be without a means of protecting themselves. However, this was the first time she'd seen just how willing they were to act first with violence and ask questions later. The two weren't all smiles and blarney.

Thatcher stopped within five yards of them, planting his feet firmly, causing her to wonder if he was still toting the pistol he'd retrieved from her this morning and was about to draw it like a gunslinger in a dime novel.

He said, "I came to ask how your father-in-law is faring, but I saw that you had company and didn't want to break up the party."

She injected a lightness into her voice that she was far from feeling. "No party. These are the O'Connor brothers, Davy and Mike." She pointed out which was which. "They work for me."

"They brought you the peaches," he said.

"That's right. I'd forgotten I'd mentioned that." But he hadn't, and that was disconcerting. "Davy, Mike, this is Thatcher Hutton. He was the Good Samaritan I told you about, who brought Irv home last night after the raid."

Thatcher leaned forward only far enough to shake hands with the twins in turn, then all three of them returned to their guarded stances.

Mike looked him over. "Are you a cowpoke, Mr. Hutton?"

He asked it as a put-down, but Thatcher replied blandly, "You could say."

Laurel said, "He breaks and trains horses."

"Does he?" Again, his question sounded deprecating.

Davy shot his twin a warning look, then addressed Thatcher with a smile. "So, you were at Lefty's last night. Things were exciting, I hear. How did you avoid arrest, Mr. Hutton?"

"I wasn't in the back room."

"Occupied upstairs then," Mike said.

Thatcher slanted him a glance, but didn't even blink. "I was having a hamburger in the front room."

"Ah," Davy said, "what fortunate timing for you that was."

When Thatcher didn't respond, and no one else spoke, Laurel turned to the twins. "The night isn't getting any younger, and you have deliveries to make."

As boss, she really gave them no choice except to depart. With noticeable reluctance, they retreated to their truck. As they got in, the backward glances they gave Thatcher were blatantly hostile.

As soon as their truck had cleared the drive, Laurel turned to face Thatcher, feeling hostile herself and ready with an accusation of snooping.

He, however, got the jump on her. "Kind of late to be making deliveries, isn't it? Where are they off to?"

To equivocate would only make them all look guilty. "Ranger."

Obviously he was familiar with the town's reputation. His eyebrow arched. "That explains the hardware they're carrying."

"To be used only in self-defense."

He looked skeptical of that. "They go all the way up there to deliver pies?"

She resisted the impulse to rub her damp palms against her skirt. "It's worth the trip. The markup per pie is three times what I get here. Seems every roughneck has a sweet tooth."

"And a taste for other things, too." He waited a beat, then said, "Are the O'Connors always on edge like that, spoiling for a fight?"

"Yes, especially with each other." She gave a soft laugh.

Thatcher didn't join in. "What were you doing at Lefty's roadhouse today?"

She couldn't conceal her astonishment over his knowing that, and it robbed her of speech.

"So it *was* you he saw."

Although her mouth was dry, she attempted to swallow. "Who saw?"

"Chester Landry."

"Who is... Oh, your friend with the plastered hair."

"He's no friend of mine, Laurel, and I don't think he's one to you, either."

"I don't even know him."

"Well, he knows you, and he made a point of telling me about your visit to the roadhouse."

"Why would he do that?"

"I'm wondering that, too. Why would he?"

Trying not to appear bothered by his probing stare, she shrugged. "Would he need a reason? He knows we're acquainted. He saw me today and mentioned it to you in passing."

"Un-huh. He climbed three flights of stairs, huffing and puffing, to tell me." He came forward, crowding in on her, but she held her ground. "What the hell were you doing at Lefty's?"

"What business is it of yours?"

He lowered his head, bringing his face to within inches of hers. "Asking for another demonstration? I warned you not to dare me."

The thought that perhaps she was subconsciously angling for another kiss mortified her. Relenting on her resolve not to back away from him, she did, but only by one step. "I went out there to implore them not to give the sheriff Irv's name."

"Them?"

"Lefty and that horrid woman, Gert."

"What made you think they would give Irv over?"

"Based on what Corrine and Irv have told me about that pair, they're without scruple. I was afraid that if they were pressured to rat out anyone who was there last night in exchange for leniency, they would do it in a heartbeat. I went for Irv's sake, to plead on his behalf."

She'd made up the explanation as she'd gone along, but to her it had sounded perfectly plausible. She hoped it would to him. He was watching her in that incisive way of his.

After a moment, he said, "You could have saved yourself the trip. Irv isn't going to be arrested."

"How do you know?"

"I asked the sheriff myself."

"You did?"

"This morning. Directly after leaving here, I went to see him to give back his Colt and the badge."

"You really aren't a deputy, then?"

"No."

She inhaled deeply, but her relief was short-lived.

"But if I was," he said, "what would it matter?"

"It wouldn't."

"It did."

It had. She groped for a logical reason. "If you had shown me the badge, explained it...But you didn't, and that seemed underhanded. I like to know where I stand with people."

"Yeah, I like that, too."

There was no winning this argument, and she would only sink herself in deeper if she continued trying. She fixed her gaze on the loose knot that secured a bandana around his neck. "I appreciate your intervening for Irv with Sheriff Amos."

"He said maybe getting shot taught Irv a lesson." He looked beyond her toward the house. "How's he doing?"

"He was hurting all day, and that made him grouchy. This evening I let him sip his moonshine until he fell asleep."

"Sleep is the best thing for him."

She nodded. "I hope he sleeps through the night."

"Who does he buy his moonshine from?"

That was the second question he'd asked out of the blue. As before, she was momentarily dumbfounded before mumbling, "I'm not supposed to tell."

Thatcher just stood there looking at her, silently pressing for a more satisfactory answer.

The one that sprang to her mind was evasive, but actually the God's truth. "He doesn't have to buy it. A friend gives it to him in exchange for handiwork."

"Hmm," he said. "Well, Irv and his friend need to be careful. Obviously local law is cracking down on offenders."

"I'll pass along the warning, but I'm afraid Irv won't change his ways."

"I'm afraid of that, too."

It was a solemn and weighty statement, not a quip. The intensity of his stare held her captive without force, without even a touch. Perhaps Irv's sixth sense about him had been correct. Perhaps Thatcher Hutton was something other than the loose-limbed cowboy he played, someone who represented a threat, not only to her, but to the people whose welfare depended on her.

But no sooner had that upsetting possibility entered her mind than he relaxed his shoulders and eased away from her. "How's Corrine? Did she go for your idea?"

"Wholeheartedly. Just as I thought." She hoped he wouldn't ask to speak to Corrine or ask for details about living arrangements, etcetera. Lying to him had become increasingly hard on her conscience, and standing this close to him in the dark made it hard to breathe.

That inability became even more constricting when he took yet another step closer to her. "Those twins."

Bravely, she tilted her head up in order to look into his face. "What about them?"

"You seem friendly with them."

"I am. Why shouldn't I be?"

He frowned at her flippancy. "You know what I'm asking you."

She did know. "They're charming boys."

"They're men."

"And I'm a widow."

"A young and pretty widow."

"A very recent widow, who has morals and a reputation to uphold." Her cheeks went hot. She dipped her head. "Which makes my lapse last night all the more incomprehensible."

He didn't say anything for the longest time, then, "The O'Connors are troublemakers."

Her head came up. "Says who?"

"Sheriff Amos. He pointed them out to me last night as we were on our way to Lefty's. He called them a wild pair."

She didn't want to read too much into the sheriff's notice of her deliverymen, but it gave her a twinge of concern. "Davy and Mike can get into mischief, I'm sure. But they're hardworking and, at heart, decent. If I didn't believe in their integrity, I wouldn't have them working for me."

"It's not all work, though, is it?" He looked aside, staring into the empty darkness. "You were laughing."

"What?"

"You were laughing," he said, turning back to her. "I heard you all the way out here. They make you laugh."

"Sometimes." The hushed tone in which she'd spoken the word made it sound like what one would admit only in a confessional.

He bobbed his chin once and looked aside again, his jaw working. He took off his hat and tapped it against his thigh as the fingers of his other hand raked through his hair. He said a swear word under his breath.

She didn't dare try to guess what these manifestations of male agitation implied. Actually, she was afraid she knew. "It's late. I'd better go in, so I can—"

"Run away from me."

"I'm not running away."

"Those twins make you laugh. I make you nervous. You've been wound up since you saw me here."

"Yes! Lurking in the dark!"

"Are you jittery because of what I said to you this morning?"

Unbuttoned. Unhooked. Us lying down together. "I don't remember what you said this morning." Her voice lacked conviction and substance, and instead sounded raspy with desperation.

"You remember."

"No I don't."

He didn't grab her. She didn't even see him move. She had no warning at all before he was just there, his hands encircling her waist, his fingers tensing and drawing her against him. Flush against him. Fitting them together. He felt solid and strong, an ensuring and durable presence, safe except for the quickening in her center that he incited and the unchecked recognition with which her body responded.

His breath was damp and warm against her neck as he sighed her name, the one she had forbidden him to use but which sounded so sweet now as he nuzzled her ear and whispered, "Stay away from Lefty's."

She couldn't believe she'd heard right. She jerked her head back. "What?"

"Keep away from there, Laurel. It isn't safe."

She tried to escape his hands, but he held her fast. "Let go of me."

"Not until you listen. Don't go out there again."

"You're overstepping, Mr. Hutton." She pried his hands from her waist, but before she could move away, he cupped them around her face, bringing it up and close to his own.

"You're right, I am, and I'll tell you why. Chester Landry claimed that last night was his first time to go to Lefty's, but I don't believe that for a second."

She turned her head aside and was about to shout at him how little she cared, but he talked over her.

"He told me he went to Lefty's today to recover a pocket watch he'd lost during the raid. He's the flashiest dresser I've ever come across, but I've never once seen him sporting a pocket watch."

It finally sank in that he hadn't insulted her carelessly or maliciously. He'd wanted to secure her attention because what he was telling her held importance, at least to him.

She placed her hands over his where they still pressed against her cheeks. "Why are you preoccupied with this man you obviously dislike, and how does it relate to me?"

He withdrew his hands gradually, as though fearing that as soon as he released her she might sprint into the house. Which she probably should do. And bar the door. But when he said, "Just hear me out," she stayed where she was and gave a small nod.

"Landry palled around with a young man in the boardinghouse. A show-off. Obnoxious. Named Randy. One night, he up and moved out without notice, without telling anybody."

"So?"

He raised a shoulder. "Maybe nothing, but..." He raked his fingers through his hair again. "Landry made light of it. Shrugged it off. But I got the impression he knew exactly what had happened to Randy."

"If they were friends, maybe Randy had asked him to cover his trail."

"Maybe," he said, but it lacked backbone. "He claims to be a shoe salesman. He boasts of a wide territory he covers on a routine basis, but he's rarely away from the boardinghouse for more than a couple of days at a time."

"Men often exaggerate their success."

"True, but I think Landry downplays his. I think he's very successful, but not at selling women's shoes. He's dealing in something else."

"Like what?"

"Liquor. He's bootlegging."

Her heart skipped a beat, but when he paused to give her time to comment, she didn't say anything.

"There's money to be made," he said, "and a lot of it, but it's a dangerous occupation. There are few game rules and no such thing as honor among thieves. Double-crossers, poachers, and loudmouths— like Randy—usually wind up dead."

He paused and focused even more sharply on her. "If I'm right about Landry, he wouldn't want to be seen at a well-known speakeasy the night after a raid when it was closed to business. But he *was* seen. By you."

She took all that in and thought how closely it correlated to what Irv had told her about the hazards of the illegal liquor trade. But she couldn't tell Thatcher she'd heard it all before in cautionary sermons from her father-in-law. She carefully weighed how she would respond.

"The only two people I saw were Lefty and Gert. Not even a sign of the girls. On my way out, before I got to the highway, a car passed me on the road. I didn't see the driver. Even if I had, and had recognized Mr. Landry, I wouldn't have given it a second thought because I don't know him, and how he earns his living makes no difference whatsoever to me. So even assuming you're right and his business dealings are illegal, he has absolutely nothing to fear from me."

"But see, Laurel, you may have a lot to fear from him."

THIRTY-EIGHT

G ert knew that eyes had been on her since she'd turned off the highway. From the crevices of boulders, from behind foliage, from underneath the collapsed roof of a disused barn, she was being watched, probably through the sights of deer rifles.

Her arrival had been charted, but when she reached the house, it was in total darkness, and there was no one to greet her, not that she'd expected a welcoming committee.

A pack of mongrels was standing sentinel. They weren't barking, but she could hear their bloodthirsty growls as they stood alert and eager for the signal that would send them charging her.

She heaved herself out of her auto and moved to stand in the beam of her headlight where she could be seen. Cupping her hands around her mouth, she hollered, "Call off your mutts and your militia and invite me in."

Nothing happened. She stayed as she was, knowing that the head of the clan was taking his sweet time just to piss her off. "I ain't leavin' till we talk, Hiram."

From around the corner of the house, a Johnson materialized out of the darkness. She couldn't make out any distinct features except for the shotgun he held aimed at her.

"You're trespassing," he said. "Be on your way."

"Or what? You'll pull the trigger?"

"You make a sizable target. I couldn't miss with both eyes closed."

"If you shoot me, you'd just be provin' what everybody knows, and that's that all Johnsons are stupider than they are ugly, and that's sayin' somethin'."

"What do you want?"

"Like I said, to talk to the ol' man. Unless he's dead."

"He ain't."

"Figured that was too much to hope for. Tell him to show hisself or *he*'ll never know what *I* know about Wally's killin'."

Seconds ticked past. Then, no doubt acting on a cue from inside the house, the young man lowered the shotgun. The dogs backed down, whimpering in disappointment over being denied a mauling. The screen door squeaked open and a young woman came out onto the porch. "He says come on in."

Lamps flickered to life inside as Gert made her way toward the house. She paid the dogs no mind as she stomped past them and up the steps. The young woman lit a cigarette, eyeing Gert sourly as she shook out the match. "He's waitin'."

Gert pulled open the screen door and went inside.

It was a large, rectangular room. The collective glow from the recently lit lamps didn't reach the ceiling. Loitering around the perimeter of the room were a passel of Johnsons of both sexes spanning at least three generations, from a bald-headed baby straddling his mother's hip to a withered, toothless old woman, who Gert recognized as the reigning matriarch.

Gert muttered with scorn, "To think I'm related to this bunch."

"We ain't so proud to claim you, neither."

This from the man holding the place of honor in the corner of the room where he sprawled in an overstuffed chair. He held a coffee can propped on one knee. Looking at Gert, he raised it to his mouth and spat a string of tobacco juice into it.

Hiram Johnson had inherited his position as head of the clan from his father, and for the last four decades had ruled the family with an iron fist. His face was as crinkled as a dry creek bed in August. He had a dingy gray beard that covered his chest to the third button of his flannel shirt. A jar of moonshine and a flyswatter sat on the windowsill within easy reach of him. His bare right foot, missing toes and striated white with petrifaction, was propped on a footstool. A large, leather-bound Bible lay open in his lap.

"But I don't hail from the inbred branch of the family," Gert said.

Eying her with malevolence, Hiram spat into the can again and wiped stained spittle from his beard with the back of his hand. "Gettin' raided is bad for business, cousin."

"Couldn't tell it by the crowd we got tonight," Gert said. "The place was hoppin' when I left."

"You had some product stashed?"

"Enough for tonight, but the raid made a dent. I come to buy."

"Tup." Hiram raised his index finger to one of his offspring whose chair was propped against the wall, front legs raised. He was stropping a hunting knife. At the signal from the old man, the chair legs hit the floor. The man addressed as Tup came to his feet and slid the knife into a scabbard at his waist.

"Load her up," Hiram said to him.

He was on his way to the door when Gert said, "Ten gallons less than what we usually take."

Tup looked to Hiram for direction. Gert kept her expression blank. Never taking his eyes off her, Hiram said, "You heard her." Tup pushed open the screen door and went out, calling to someone unseen to come help him.

"How come you're cuttin' back?" Hiram asked.

Gert took a slow look around the room, as though taking inventory of the assembled relatives. They all appeared indolent and uninterested, but she knew better. They all had the trademark big ears, but not necessarily in the physical sense.

Hiram, grasping that she wanted to talk to him privately, flipped his hand at the room at large. "Git."

His offspring began to scatter, some going outside, others dis-appearing into other rooms. A teenaged girl helped the old woman out of her chair and supported her as she hobbled out.

Watching her leave, Gert said, "I thought she'd've died by now. You, too. And why don't you spare us all that stink and cut that damn foot off?"

Ignoring that, Hiram repeated his question about her order.

Gert seated herself in one of the vacated chairs. "While your boys have been keeping the roads hot between your stills and the oil patches, small-timers have been taking up the slack locally. You're losing ground, Hiram. You're being undercut."

"Nobody would dare."

"Fine. Don't believe me. But Lefty struck a deal today. I's sittin' right there when they shook on it. More hooch for a lot cheaper than you charge us."

"Rotgut."

"Nope. Good stuff."

"Labeled liquor?"

Gert shook her head. "'Shine."

"Whose?"

"I'll get to that. Let's talk about Wally."

He slapped his palm onto the open Bible in his lap. "God as my witness—"

"Which he ain't."

"—we're gonna get the sumbitch what killed Wally."

Gert crossed her arms over her massive chest. "You made any headway in that direction?"

"We'll get him."

"That means you got no idea who done it."

Temper sparked, Hiram leaned forward, nearly tipping over his spit can. "If you know something, you'd better tell me, or being my second cousin thrice removed won't mean shit. Kinship won't save your fat ass from being flayed."

She huffed an exhale. "The night before Wally was murdered,

he tore into one of my girls." No doubt Hiram had heard about it because he didn't dispute or defend it. "She weren't much count as a whore, but she was handy helping Lefty on the grill and serving drinks in the back room, so I kept her on."

"You're sayin' *was*. She die after all?"

"No. The ungrateful hussy run off last night, still owing me money for her upkeep. Slipped off during the raid. Today, I learned she's been took in."

"By who?"

"By the moonshiner who persuaded Lefty to squeeze you out of ten jugs per order." She leaned forward and tapped her temple. "I put two and two together. One bullet was fired into Wally's head for stealing that truckload of sugar and causing a shortage. The second bullet was payback for whippin' up on that whore."

Hiram picked up the Bible and brandished it. "He's dead meat."

Gert's smiles were as infrequent as blood moons. She gave Hiram Johnson a smug one now. "Ain't no he."

THIRTY-NINE

Irv scowled up at Laurel from his pillow. "Hutton dropped that on you, then just left?"

"Without another word." Now part of their morning routine, she tied a knot to secure the fresh bandage around his chest. "There."

"Does it have to be so tight?"

"Yes, because you work it loose as the day goes on. But the wound looks better today than yesterday, and it will continue to get better if you *rest*."

"I've done nothing besides lie in bed."

"And fret. Your mind needs rest, too. Stop worrying so much."

"First you tell me that Ernie's secret stash has been stolen, then that you took it upon yourself to go *alone* to Lefty's, and lastly about this doomsday message from Hutton. Now you tell me to stop worrying?"

"Do you know Chester Landry?"

"How would I know a guy who sells ladies' shoes?"

"Maybe more than shoes."

"What's he look like?"

She described him to the best of her recollection. "I only saw him that one time in the café, and I wasn't really paying attention." She'd been distracted by Thatcher.

Irv scratched his bristly chin. "I know the fella you're talking about. I've seen him in town."

"Where?"

"Here and there."

"At Lefty's?"

"No, and I think I would remember, considering those duds he wears."

"If you haven't seen him there, then it's possible Mr. Hutton's hunch about him is wrong."

"Just as possible that he's right, though, Laurel. Remember, I told you it was rumored that a bootlegger from Dallas was a big-time operator around here? Could be Landry's him. Hutton must think so, or he wouldn't've gone out of his way to tell you."

"That wasn't all he came to tell me. You'll be glad to know that Sheriff Amos is letting you off the hook, this time, in the hope that you've learned your lesson."

"And I hope you've learned yours." He shook his finger at her. "Out at Lefty's, you're in danger of more than bootleggers. Don't go there again."

"I won't." When he looked sternly doubtful, she stressed that she wouldn't. "I only went to seal your deal. The O'Connors will be making the deliveries."

"Larger deliveries."

"Which is what we were going for, Irv. Remember?"

"There's nothing the matter with my memory. But our gain represents a loss to competitors. I'm all for increasing our business, but not if it means that one or all of us will meet with bodily harm."

"I'll be doubly discreet and careful."

"Warn those twins not to be so damn cocky, but don't tell them why. Keep it general."

"You still don't trust them." .

"Never have trusted men with dimples."

She laughed. "What do you have against dimples?"

He went on as though she hadn't interrupted. "Ernie and Corrine need to be put on watch, too."

"Because of the theft, Ernie is already on alert."

"How'd Ernie take to Corrine?"

She hedged. "She'll grow on him."

He barked a laugh. "Don't count on it. He's used to his own company and silence. God knows he'll have precious little of that."

Laurel smiled. "I have pies to bake today, but I'll drive out and check on them tomorrow. Hopefully they'll have several crates of whiskey ready for me."

"Speaking of, I could do with a nip."

"At bedtime."

"I just woke up."

"At bedtime."

"I'm hurting now."

"Part of the healing process." She stood up and straightened the cover where she'd been sitting at the foot of his bed. He was idly scratching his chin again. "Your stubble is itching. Would you like a shave?"

"No."

"I'm happy to do it."

He waved off the offer. "I'm thinking, is all."

"Something's gnawing at you, Irv. What?"

"You say you introduced Hutton to the twins? How'd that go?"

"All right. After they shook hands, I sent the twins on their way."

In giving Irv an account of last night's visit from Thatcher, she had omitted certain details, one being the hostility that had crackled between him and the O'Connors. She also didn't tell him that Thatcher had questioned her about the deliveries the twins made to Ranger, or that Sheriff Amos had pointed the O'Connors out to Thatcher while referring to them as wild. Nor did she mention that Thatcher had asked who supplied Irv's moonshine.

Unabridged honesty could set his recovery back for weeks, which was how she justified those omissions. Even so, his forehead remained furrowed.

"This warning from Hutton about Chester Landry worries me," he said. "It should worry you, too, Laurel. My advice is to steer clear of the man."

"I plan to, whether or not he's into bootlegging."

Irv peered up at her through his lowered brows. "I wasn't referring to Landry."

Bernie Croft had eaten a late breakfast at Martin's Café. Rather than ride to his office, he'd chosen to walk the short distance and was almost there when a deranged individual lunged at him from out of a narrow alleyway.

He was grabbed roughly by the lapel of his suit coat, jerked into the space between the two buildings, and forcefully pushed against a brick wall. Hands closed around his neck and began to choke him.

Dr. Gabe Driscoll was barely recognizable. His eyes were bloodshot. His bared and clenched teeth looked feral. But his fingers were like steel clamps around Bernie's throat. "I'm going to kill you."

Bernie gasped, "Jesus Christ, Gabe." He planted his hands on the physician's chest and pushed with all his might.

Obviously in a weakened state, Gabe wasn't that hard to dislodge. He reeled backward and landed against the opposite brick wall, his shoulder catching the brunt of the impact. He clapped his hand over his rotator cuff and yelped in pain.

Hennessy came bounding in from the end of the alley. Bernie held up a hand. The bodyguard skidded to a halt. "I'm all right," Bernie said. "But don't let anybody wander in here."

Hennessy looked at Driscoll with misgiving. Bernie patted the air. "It's fine, Jimmy." Hennessy backed out of the alley and posted himself at the entrance to it.

Bernie returned his attention to Gabe, whose ferocity had

evaporated. He was slumped against the wall. "What the hell is wrong with you?" Bernie hissed. "It's ten-thirty in the morning, and you're pissing drunk!"

"Why did you tell?"

"Tell what?"

Gabe glared at him with maddened eyes. "You want me to yell it out loud? You want me to shout it out so everybody will know about Pointer's Gap?" Unmindful of Hennessy, he stumbled toward the street.

Bernie reached out, clutched a handful of his jacket, and yanked him back. Despite his rancid body odor and days-old breath, Bernie held him by the lapels and got right in his face, speaking softly, but with emphasis. "Nobody knows."

"You promised me that no one would, but you told Norma Blanchard. Why? *Why?*"

Bernie instantly released him and took a step back. He felt like his head might explode. Every blood vessel in his body began to throb with wrath. But he clenched his teeth in order to keep his features rigid and his expression impassive. He tugged on the hem of his vest, shot his cuffs, assumed his customary intimidating, confident posture, and said blandly, "Insurance."

Gabe blinked several times. "How did you even know about her and my...our..."

"Your grubby, adulterous affair? I make it my business to know who's fucking whom. It comes in handy on occasions just such as this, Dr. Driscoll. I've got you by the balls, you see. You killed your wife in order to take up with your mistress and bastard child."

Gabe flinched and gulped back a sob. "I came to you that night for help."

"You came to me panicked, beyond any hope of getting yourself out of a nasty fix without my assistance. You were out of your mind with desperation and fear, and I responded immediately."

"We made a vow."

"Yes, we did. We made a vow to help each other. Quid pro quo.

I held up my end of our bargain in a matter of hours. You, by contrast..." He sniffed with disdain. "Look at you. You're a wreck, a disgrace."

Gabe wiped his dripping nose with the back of his hand. "You swore to me that no one would ever know."

"But did you think that a man in my position would volunteer to get rid of your problem without holding some collateral? Did you think that, Gabe? Did you really? Are you that naïve? That dim?"

The man's shoulders sagged. His head dropped forward as though the pin of a hinge holding it onto his neck had been pulled.

Bernie let him suffer in humiliation and silence for several moments, then said, "I assume Miss Blanchard is using this information for leverage of her own?"

"She's come to the house twice," Gabe mumbled. "Once in the middle of the night. I lectured her on how foolhardy that was, but she came back. In daytime, no less. She even brought the baby. She wants us to be together."

Bernie made a sound of regret and sighed. "Typical female behavior. She's wanting to nest."

"It's too soon. People would become suspicious."

"Rightfully," Bernie said. "You must drill that home to Miss Blanchard. Or would you rather I speak with her on your behalf?"

Gabe raised his head and looked at Bernie with bleary eyes. "No, I'll do it."

Bernie gave Gabe's arm a fatherly squeeze of support. "I suggest that before you go calling on your ladylove, you get sober, take a bath, and shave. Get a haircut. Buy Miss Blanchard something nice. Take the baby a play-pretty."

Gabe nodded assent, but Bernie could tell that his heart wasn't in it.

With vexation, he said, "I gave you two weeks to sort yourself out, Gabe. Instead you've lost ground, and your time is up. You start tomorrow."

"What?"

"Hang out your shingle. Resume making house calls. Dispense pills, set broken bones, administer enemas. And, as agreed, begin your work for me."

"Smuggling bootlegged liquor on my rounds."

Bernie tugged on his lower lip. "Actually, since our last conversation, I've determined that any able-bodied person with half a brain can do that. I have plenty of them already on my payroll. You would be a wasted asset doing manual labor.

"No, what I have in mind for you now, Gabe, is something more complex, more suited to an austere and respected man who has a knowledge of science and the healing arts."

Befuddled, Gabe said, "What are you talking about, Bernie?"

"Poison."

FORTY

———◦◉◦———

Thatcher was working late. The sun had already set, making it dark enough in the stable to require a lantern. He moved it from stall to stall as he replenished water and feed for each of his charges.

The mare who had caused him to work overtime snuffled and tossed her head when he entered her stall. She had a bad reputation for kicking, so he waited for her to settle before closing himself in with her.

"I saved you for last because we need to have a talk." He moved to stand where she could see him. He stroked her forehead. "You kick another board out of Mr. Barker's fence, he may kick both of us off his property. I'd lose money. Your owner, who's already put out with you, would send you to the glue factory."

Her ears twitched. She was listening.

"What he would rather do is breed you with that handsome stallion he's got. If you keep acting unladylike, you'll miss out. He's hung like a racehorse," he whispered. "He *is* a racehorse. The other mares would give their eye teeth. Think it over."

He lifted a coiled lasso from a hook and began rubbing it over her with one hand while smoothing her coat with the other. Dryly, he said, "Of course, I'm nobody to be giving advice in that department."

He'd spent three restless nights since he'd gone to Laurel's house and had seen her with the O'Connor brothers. She thought they were charming. They had the gift of gab. They made her laugh.

This was Thatcher's first experience with jealousy, but it had sunk its claws in deep. He understood now how it could cloud a man's judgment and cause him to behave irrationally. But jealousy aside, he didn't see anything good coming from Laurel Plummer mixing with hell-raisers the likes of them.

Thatcher knew—damn his knack for reading people—that she didn't always tell him the whole truth. Some of that wiggling around certain topics and giving less than direct answers could be passed off as part of her prideful nature. She was fiercely determined to stand on her own. But he suspected that her sidestepping pertained to something besides protecting her privacy.

And that bothered him, because he didn't think she had taken his warning about Chester Landry seriously.

To get her to listen, to try and impress upon her how important it was that she heed his warning, he had held her and made out like he was going to kiss her again. The instant he'd put his hands on her, he'd gotten her attention, all right, but she'd for damn sure gotten his, too.

He'd counted on feeling a stiff corset or whatever it was women wore under their clothes to narrow this and plump that. But all he'd felt through Laurel's dress was Laurel.

Her waist had been giving, each dainty rib delineated. The heel of his hand had brushed the underside of her breast. Not to cup that soft crescent in his palm . . . He deserved some kind of medal. He—

The mare's ears twitched, and she restlessly bobbed her head at the exact moment that Thatcher heard a noise coming from the front of the stable. He lowered the lariat, but continued to run his hand over the mare's withers to keep her calm.

A rustle. The faint crunch of straw underfoot. Maybe some kind of critter? Mouse, rat, cat, possum?

Then a clangor that would raise the dead. An animal might

knock over an empty feed bucket, but it wouldn't cuss a blue streak when it did.

The mare began to stamp and neigh, as did the other horses in their stalls. Thatcher hooked the lariat over his shoulder, unlatched the stall door, and slipped through. But he had to take the time to latch it back so the mare wouldn't get out. Once it was secure, he ran to the wide stable door. As he cleared the opening, he caught sight of a fleeing male figure. Thatcher bolted after him.

It was full-on dusk, but Thatcher spotted the intruder skirting around the corral and running for the creek. Thatcher went after him, uncoiling the lariat as he ran. As the man began to slide down the steep embankment, Thatcher tossed the rope and lassoed him with ease, neatly dropping the loop over his head and trunk, pinning his arms against his torso.

The man gave a sharp cry as he was jerked backward and off his feet. When he landed butt-first on the rocky ground, he let fly another round of colorful profanities.

Thatcher walked toward him, taking up the slack in the rope as he went. The face that glared up at him was that of a young man still in his teens, about Roger's age.

"Fuck you, cowboy."

Thatcher planted the sole of his boot against the youngster's chest and pushed him onto his back, holding him down with his foot. "You know what happens to horse thieves?"

Still glaring, the boy remained stubbornly silent.

"They're hanged from the nearest tree."

The young man's rebellious, hostile expression wavered. "What I said, I didn't mean nothin' by it."

"Sounded to me like you did."

The kid peered up through the gathering darkness into Thatcher's face. "Heard about some cowboy who shot the head off a rattlesnake here in town. You him?"

"Um-huh."

"Oh, shit."

"Roger tell you?"

"Don't know no Roger. Just picked up word of it somewhere."

Thatcher tipped his head back toward the stable. "Horse thieves are a sorry lot."

"I was just lookin' around, is all."

"Bald-faced liars are just as bad." Thatcher removed his foot and hauled the kid up. "Before you kicked over that bucket and gave yourself away, you figured on helping yourself to a horse, didn't you?"

"I kicked over that goddamn bucket on my way out. I'd changed my mind about *borrowing* a horse."

"You saw my lantern?"

"Saw the horses. I thought they'd be saddled."

In spite of himself, Thatcher chuckled. "A sorry, thieving numbskull. What's your name?"

Thatcher's insults had put the chip back on his shoulder. "What's it to you, Billy the Kid?"

Thatcher looked around, his gaze landing on a large live oak. "That lowest branch ought to do." He started toward it, yanking on the rope, pulling the kid along behind.

He dug his heels in. "Wait! Wait! Hold it! It's Elray. My name is Elray Johnson."

Recognizing the name immediately, Thatcher stopped and turned back. The sheriff had told Thatcher about Elray Johnson's fearfulness following the murder of his cousin, Wally. Elray looked ready to jump out of his skin now. "Why were you trying to steal a horse, Elray?"

With no cockiness left in him, the kid choked up and gave a hard shake of his head. "You can hang me, mister, but I ain't tellin'."

Bill was summoned from home by Scotty. The deputy didn't share much information over the telephone except to say that the matter had to do with Elray Johnson. That didn't bode well.

When Bill walked into the department ten minutes later, he wasn't met with the chaos he'd expected. The wall clock's pendulum ticked loudly in the otherwise quiet room. Scotty was filing paperwork.

He said, "Sorry to bring you from home."

"What's the trouble? Where's Elray?"

"He's got him back there in a cell."

"Who does?"

"Your boy wonder."

Bill rebuked that remark with a stern look. "I assume you're referring to Thatcher."

"Are the rest of us supposed to consider him official?"

"Good question," Bill muttered as he hung up his hat. He entered the cell block where all the barred doors stood open. In the first cell, Thatcher was leaning with his back to the wall, one foot flat against it, his knee raised. He had a bead on Elray, who was sitting on the cot gnawing at his fingernails and jiggling his knees.

When he saw Bill, he shot to his feet and aimed an accusing finger at Thatcher. "He roped me like a damn calf. He was gonna hang me!"

Bill looked at Thatcher, who said, "He sneaked into Barker's stable to steal a horse. He bungled it, and I caught him. But that's not why I put him in here."

"Okay," Bill said, "I'm listening."

"He said he would rather me hang him than tell me why he needed a horse."

Bill hadn't seen Thatcher since the morning he'd come to the house. During their conversation on the porch, he'd told Thatcher more than was comfortable about his and Daisy's personal life, but he knew instinctually that his secrets were safe with this man of few words.

He also knew that Thatcher wouldn't have hanged the Johnson kid, but had scared him into thinking he would. Apparently Thatcher also had perceived that Elray's desperation might signify a need to flee. Bill thought Thatcher was probably right.

Elray had dropped back down onto the cot. His knees were bobbing again at a frantic rate. Bill asked, "What's going on?"

"Nuthin'."

"Did you intend to steal a horse?"

"Naw."

Thatcher said, "He admitted he was until he realized they didn't come already saddled."

Wanting to laugh, Bill managed a strict tone. "That true, Elray?"

Glowering at Thatcher, he said sullenly, "He didn't have to rope me and jerk me to the ground. It's a miracle my butt bone ain't broke. I'd've stopped running if he'd've asked me nice."

Bill said, "Where were you planning to go on horseback?"

"Just ridin'. I hadn't thought that far ahead."

Bill went over to the cot, motioned for Elray to scoot to the other end of it, and sat down where the boy had been. "My supper's getting cold on your account, and you dare to bullshit me? Now, where were you off to that was so important you'd steal a horse to get there?"

Elray's face muscles began working like a child's on the brink of tears. "Somewhere, anywhere, to lay low for a while."

"Why do you need to lay low?"

He choked on a sob. "If they find out I was here talking to y'all they'll...they'll...no telling what they'll do to me."

"Who?"

"Cain't say."

"Your family?"

Elray wiped his dripping nose on his sleeve. "Goddamn Wally."

"What about him?"

"He was always stirrin' up trouble, then skippin' out, leavin' it to everybody else to clean up his mess."

"Is that what's happening now? A cleanup?"

Elray didn't answer.

Bill said, "Has something come to light about who killed Wally?"

Elray's eyes darted between Bill and Thatcher, then he lowered his head and shook it *no*.

"Then why were you hoping to get away?"

"Just tired of everybody being all worked up over it, is all." He sat up straighter, gave a belligerent roll of his shoulders, and looked across at Thatcher before coming back to Bill. "He don't know what I wasn't at the stable only to take a gander at the guy who shot that rattler. I weren't in there more'n a few seconds and didn't steal shit. Anyhow, I got nuthin' more to say."

Bill looked over at Thatcher, who raised a shoulder and said, "He's not worth the trouble it would take to hang him. I doubt Mr. Barker would want to bother with pressing charges of trespassing."

"Then what do you suggest?"

He gave another laconic shrug. "Notify his kin to come take him off your hands."

Bill recognized it as a bluff, but Elray didn't. He surged to his feet again. "No!"

Bill grabbed him by the waistband of his britches and jerked him back down onto the cot. "What's got you scared, son? You tell me, or I'll hand-deliver you to your great-granddaddy. What's Hiram up to? Vengeance for Wally?"

Elray hiccupped several times, then said, "He's been on a rampage. He ordered all us to comb the hills. Every square inch we could cover. Any stills we found, tear 'em up, he said. 'Wreak havoc on anybody making moonshine who ain't a Johnson' is how he put it."

He made another swipe at his nose. "The other night one of my cousins—we call him Tup. Don't ask why. Me and him were explorin' and picked up the scent of wood smoke. We followed it to a still. Two, actually, but only one man was camped out there. What had drawn us was the smoke from his cookfire. He weren't doin' a run, just tinkerin' around.

"We watched him hide a crate of 'shine in a hole in the ground. After he went into his tent, we waited to make sure he was down for the night, then snuck up to the hidin' place, and took his whiskey."

"How much?" Bill asked.

"Ten crates."

"Ten *crates*?"

"It was a deep hole. Like a grave, only covered up good with brush. Had to make several trips to get it all back to our truck."

"Did you know the man?"

"Don't think so, but it was dark so I couldn't see him good."

"Do you think he saw you?"

"I know he didn't. He had firepower within reach. If he'd've seen us, he would've used it. We got away clean."

Stroking his mustache, Bill mulled that over. "Sounds to me like Hiram ought to be happy with you and your cousin." When Elray didn't respond, Bill asked, "Or isn't that the end of the story?"

Thatcher hadn't moved or taken his eyes off the boy. He said, "I don't think it is, sheriff. He's spooked."

"Is he right, Elray?" Bill asked.

"Things is gettin' crazy," he said, his voice cracking.

"This path of vengeance Hiram is on?"

Elray nodded several times. "Old Hiram—he ain't my great-grandaddy, he's my great uncle—he told Tup and me that those two stills we happened on sounded like easy pickin's. The 'shine we stole was quality, too."

"He wouldn't like that," Bill said. "Competition."

"Yes, sir. He told us to go back, steal all the liquor that was bottled, dump out the barrels of fermentin' mash, bust up the stills, and..." He lowered his voice. "And hurt whoever was there. Make 'em sorry they'd ever heard the name o' Johnson, he said."

"Wreak havoc."

"Yes, sir."

"You jumped to carry out his orders to hurt people?"

"I weren't given no choice, sheriff. And Tup, who has a mean streak a mile wide, was looking forward to it. So we went back last night."

"Who'd you hurt and how bad? Did you kill the moonshiner?"

"No! Tup and me waited till late and snuck up, same as before. Nobody was around. The cookers weren't thumping, and the cookfire had burned down to coals. We crept over to where the hole's at. Tup reached into the brush covering it and—" He stopped and swallowed several times. "I ain't ever heard a scream like that, not from nobody, not even from a woman."

"What happened to him?"

"Bear trap. Damn near chomped his arm in two. Then the shootin' started."

"How many shooters?"

"I didn't stick around to count. I ran like hell." His voice cracked again. "I got to our truck and took off, but after a few miles, I left it and struck off on foot."

"Afraid you'd be followed by the man at the still?" Thatcher asked.

He shook his head. "He already had Tup. He might've shown me mercy if I'd of given his whiskey back. But I knew that Uncle Hiram, all them, was gonna be wonderin' why me and Tup hadn't come back. I ran out on him, and that's somethin' a Johnson won't forgive, running out on kin. If they find me, they'll kill me. Slow and in misery."

Bill feared the boy was right. He and Thatcher exchanged a glance, and Bill could tell that he was of the same mind.

Elray's head was down. He was staring at the loose cuticle that he'd picked at until it had bled. "I've been hidin' all day, working my way into town, waiting for it to get dark. I counted on hopping a freight, but missed the last one out till tomorrow morning." He raised his head and looked at Thatcher. "I was gonna steal a horse so I could get the hell away from here."

Bill asked, "Do you think your cousin is dead?"

"Don't know. The shootin' stopped, but his screaming didn't. I could hear him all the way back to the truck. He might've died or been killed after I left."

He thought on it for a moment, then added, "Like I said, he's got a cruel temper, especially when he's drunk, which is usually, but I'm a damn coward for leavin' him. That's what Hiram will say, and what that ol' bastard says is law."

"Not in this office, it isn't." Bill stood up. "You sit tight while I call in some deputies, then we'll be on our way."

Elray sniffed back dripping snot and looked at him dumbly. "On our way where?"

"You have to guide us to those stills, Elray."

His eyes went wide and wild. "Please don't make me. Anyhow, I'd lose my way. I don't remember where they're at."

Ignoring that, Bill tipped his head toward the door into the main room and started moving in that direction. "Thatcher."

Thatcher pushed himself upright. "Hold on a sec." As he walked toward Elray, the boy shrunk back against the wall behind the cot. Frantic, he looked over at Bill. "Don't leave me by myself with him."

Thatcher stood over him. "Relax, Elray. If I'd've wanted to hurt you, I would have strung you up."

"Then what'chu want?"

"I want to know what you're lying about."

"I ain't. I owned up to stealing that whiskey, leavin' Tup, and—"

"Not all that."

"Then whut?"

"What's come to light about who killed Wally?"

FORTY-ONE

———◆◆◆———

Laurel turned off the highway and started up the familiar rutted drive to the shack, where she was dropping off supplies for Corrine before driving the remainder of the way to the stills to pick up product.

It didn't surprise her that the dwelling was barely detectable in the darkness. Corrine spent most of the nighttime hours working with Ernie at the still, rarely returning until daylight. But on the nights she was in the shack, it still looked unoccupied from the road.

Not wishing anyone to know that it was inhabited, Laurel had purchased a bolt of thick, black cloth from the general store in another town. Corrine and she had draped the shack's few windows with it, and tacked it over the interior walls to keep light from leaking through the cracks. Corrine used the cookstove as infrequently as possible to keep smoke at a minimum. When the season changed, and the potbellied stove was needed for heat, they would have to make adjustments, but Laurel had a few months to figure it out.

She pulled her car around to the rear of the building, out of sight of the road, and retrieved her parcels from the floorboard. It was a moonless night, but she knew where there were obstacles to avoid as she made her way.

One of them was the chicken coop, which reminded her of that malicious rooster. Before moving into town, she had made good on her threat to throw him into a stewpot—Ernie's. She'd given the laying hens to an old folks' home, the staff of which had been most grateful for the contribution.

Thinking of the rooster reminded her of the altercation she'd had with him the day she'd met Thatcher. And the reminder of Thatcher made her "truculent." That was the word Irv had used to describe her mood since their last encounter.

She'd neither seen nor heard anything further about Chester Landry, either to substantiate or dispel Thatcher's warning. When she'd asked the twins if his name was familiar to them, they'd told her they'd heard of the shoe salesman through their friend Randy. But Randy hadn't been around lately, and they'd never met his pal Chester.

The twins had begun delivering to Lefty's, so far without incident. Although, they'd told Laurel, since the raid, the sheriff's department had begun patrolling the roads around the roadhouse with regularity. Lefty had complained about the increased vigilance keeping customers away.

Since that night in the yard, Thatcher hadn't sought her out.

She considered the matter closed.

Out of politeness, she tapped on the door to the shack and softly called Corrine's name. Getting no response, she pushed open the door and went inside. As expected, Corrine wasn't there. Laurel set the parcels she'd brought on the table, leaving it to Corrine to put away the items where she wanted them.

On her way out, Laurel noticed two things about Irv's old bureau. To support the legless corner, Corrine had replaced the stacked catalogues with blocks of wood. And on top, along with her hairbrush and other personal articles, was the primer Laurel had given her.

She thumbed open the cover and was pleased to see that Corrine had been practicing. She'd copied several lines of the alphabet on the first page. The letters were imperfect, but by page three she was showing improvement. On page four she'd doodled a drawing. Beneath it, she'd printed ERNIE.

Laurel laughed softly. Maybe Corrine's drawing was an indecipherable death threat. Their relationship was still prickly.

She returned the primer to its place on the bureau, then stepped out and pulled the door closed. As she was retracing her way to the back, she heard the sound of an approaching automobile on the road. A set of headlights topped a hill. Another set of lights followed close behind the first. Then a third vehicle. All were traveling fast, maintaining their distance from each other, looking very much like a convoy with a mission.

Laurel's heart lurched and didn't stop pounding until they had passed the turnoff to the shack. She could easily have talked her way around being here. It was still Irv's property. She could say she had come to retrieve something he had left behind when they'd moved.

But then, a worse thought occurred to her: If the shack hadn't been their destination, where were they going in such an obvious hurry? Beyond here was no-man's-land, nothing out there except—

Not thinking twice about it, she began running toward the hill behind the shack. She forgot all the safety precautions she had hammered into Corrine. Her pistol was in her pocket, but she didn't have a lantern, and she wouldn't have lit it if she did. She didn't tread carefully. She didn't think about turning her ankle or slipping on loose rocks and plunging down a steep incline into a crevice where she could die of thirst before being found.

She heard the yap of a coyote, but it was far away, and the only predator that concerned her was Man. Lawmen. Or angry competitors. She didn't know which posed the greatest threat, and was loath to speculate on the consequences of the stills being discovered by either element. If indeed that's where the convoy was headed, she had to get there first. The stills might have to be abandoned, but Corrine and Ernie could escape.

Over the months that she'd been making this trek, she'd found routes that weren't so steep, that curved up the incline gradually. But they meandered and took more time, and she was aware of time running out. She went straight up.

She stumbled once and fell to her knee. Her skirt and petticoat helped to pad her kneecap, but she'd struck it hard enough to jar her teeth. She would bear a bruise.

Losing her footing a second time, she reached for a bush to break her fall. The brittle foliage scraped her arm. A night bird swooped low directly in front of her, its screech causing her to cry out in fright despite the need for stealth.

Her lungs began to burn, her heart felt near to bursting, but she pushed on, upward. If she was wrong, they would all have a good laugh over her frantic climb later. Much later.

But for now she must assume that her friends were in danger of being caught, captured, punished to the extreme. If she arrived too late, they might even pay with their lives.

Even in the darkness, she knew she was approaching the crest that overlooked Ernie's camp. She was panting hard as she scrambled up the last several yards. Sweat dripped into her eyes, causing them to sting. As she topped the hill, she closed her eyes to blink away the sweat, but also to postpone, even for a millisecond, what she would see below.

Praying for the best, expecting the worst, she opened her eyes.

What she saw caused her to stagger backward. She gasped for breath through her mouth, which hung open in disbelief.

Because there was nothing to see below. The clearing was empty.

FORTY-TWO

———◆———

The sheriff stood at the edge of the clearing with his hands on his hips in a pose of disgust. He watched while deputies used flashlights to search the area, which obviously had been recently vacated.

"Goddamn it."

Thatcher came alongside him in time to overhear his muttered blasphemy. "They just left with Tup. His given name is Thomas."

"How's he doing?"

"Hanging on. Doc Perkins gave him a shot of morphine. But up to that point he was vocal. Very. Cursed the sons of bitches who had laid the trap, cussed his sorry-assed cousin who'd abandoned him." Thatcher paused, then added, "Honestly, when we arrived, and there was nothing here, I thought Elray had been lying about all of it, even the stills."

Elray's memory of the stills' location had been miraculously restored when Bill again threatened to turn him over to his great-uncle Hiram. Shortly thereafter, three sheriff's department vehicles, one with Dr. Perkins as a ride-along, had set out from town with Elray giving directions. Because the night was so dark, he'd mistaken landmarks several times, and they'd had to double back in order to find turnoffs previously missed.

The various roads they traveled became progressively narrow and rutted, winding through hills that all looked the same to Thatcher. He had begun to suspect Elray of leading them on a wild-goose chase, when the kid had suddenly sat forward and pointed through the windshield.

"Over there. Behind them cedars."

Tup Johnson had been found in the grave-like hole that Elray had described. He was still alive, but if he didn't die of gangrene or sepsis, he would surely lose the limb, which was half-severed already, grotesquely dark and swollen, and had jagged broken bones protruding from it.

As Bill and his deputies had fanned out to investigate the scene, he asked Thatcher to remain with Tup and try to get from him as much information as he could. Apparently it had slipped the sheriff's mind that Thatcher had declined to become a deputy. But none of this would be taking place if he had let Elray go. So, having only himself to blame for his involvement, he'd done as Bill requested.

"No, Elray wasn't lying, Thatcher," Bill said now. "There were stills here, all right. Two, just like the kid claimed. You ever seen one before?"

"Only pictures."

"Those stacks of rocks are the fireboxes. Some of the charred wood is still smoldering."

"Cookers sat on top?"

"Right. Scotty figured the flues were backed up to the cliff face there, an old trick to disperse the smoke, keep it from being easily spotted."

"What about the man Elray and Tup saw working here?"

"Not a trace. All we know for sure was that he wasn't a Johnson."

"He had a partner," Thatcher said, bringing Bill around to him. "Yeah. Tup says there were two of them, but he never got a glimpse of either. While he was writhing on the ground, they came up behind him and put a burlap sack over his head. He thought for sure they would put a bullet through it. But one held his good arm while the other released the trap."

"No sign of it," Bill said. "Retrieved to use another day, no doubt."

"They lowered Tup into the pit. None too gently, he said. But they left him with a canteen of water and a full jar of moonshine. He admits that he yelled and screamed and cried for his mama. They ignored him and went about breaking camp. He managed to uncap the jar with one hand, drank all the whiskey, and eventually passed out.

"This morning when he came to, he knew they were gone. Dead silence, he said, except for the gurgling of the spring."

"Moonshiners capable of assembling a still are just as capable of rapidly taking it apart and relocating."

Thatcher smiled. "Not to a spot as good as this one. According to Tup, this is an ideal place."

"He would know."

Together, they watched deputies pick through a clump of dead brush to see what it might yield, but nobody cried *Eureka*.

Bill said, "Tup didn't see them, but what about their voices?"

"Never spoke a word. Neither of them."

"All night?"

"That's what he said."

"Huh. Moonshiners clever enough to keep their mouths shut."

"I guess."

"Anything else he remembers?"

Thatcher rubbed the back of his neck. "They were light-footed." He got another questioning look from the sheriff. "I don't know what to make of that, either, but Tup said they both had a light tread."

"So our suspects are clever, mute, light-foots." Bill sighed. "At least we know Elray was telling the truth."

"About this."

"You still think he's lying?"

"About something."

"How sure are you?"

"Royal flush sure."

Bill gave a grunt.

Thatcher watched the flickering flashlight beams sweeping across the ground. "The clearing has been pretty much covered. Has anybody checked for tracks leading away from it?"

"A couple of the men tried, but got nowhere. Are you any good at tracking?"

"Stray cows. Wolves, coyotes, bobcats."

Bill handed him a flashlight. "You're not looking for scat or paw prints. Don't venture too far in the dark. I don't want to have to search for you, too. I need to get home."

"How's Mrs. Amos?"

Bill turned away. "Meet me back at the car in ten."

Thatcher rejoined him in under ten minutes and returned his flashlight. "Too dark to see much."

"I'll send a team out after daylight, but I have a feeling our bear trappers are too savvy to leave an easily followed trail."

Elray had been so fearful of Tup's wrath, he'd pleaded with them to let him stay in the car to avoid being seen. He'd been hunched down in the backseat under a deputy's guard. Bill dismissed the deputy, then got into the driver's seat.

"Y'all find anything?" Elray asked. "I mean, except for Tup."

Bill didn't answer. Neither did Thatcher as he climbed into the back with Elray.

"I'm not ignorant enough to jump out of a moving car, Mr. Hutton. You don't have to ride back here with me."

At some point over the course of the night, the kid had begun addressing Thatcher respectfully, which amused Thatcher. He didn't think Elray was a genuinely bad sort, or ignorant, but more hapless than anything, like he'd had the rotten luck to be born into a family where he didn't truly fit. Which was probably why he was coming to like the kid.

But now, he followed Sheriff Amos's lead and gave Elray the silent treatment as he settled in beside him. He didn't feel like talking just now, anyway.

Their silence must've been unnerving, because Elray began to chatter. "Only law I broke was to steal another moonshiner's whiskey, and how can that be a crime? I won't see a nickel from that. Plus, I was actin' under orders to cause pain, but I didn't raise a hand to nobody."

When neither Thatcher nor the sheriff responded, he continued.

"Them stills was hid so good, weren't for me, y'all never would've found 'em. Y'all should be thankin' me, not..." He swallowed. "Not whatever y'all're plannin'.

"What I think is, what y'all ought to do, is keep me locked up in jail, maybe a jail in a faraway town. Just till the dust settles around here. Better yet, put me on that freight train tomorrow morning, and you'll never have any trouble out of Elray Johnson again. I have a hankering to see Arkansas."

Bill drove in stony silence.

Thatcher gazed out the window.

Elray gave up on engaging them and lapsed into a brooding silence.

Although by now they were on the main highway, there was little to see. When they passed the Plummers' place, Thatcher looked up toward the shack, but it was barely discernible against the black sky.

The day he'd come upon Laurel wrestling with the wet sheet, the sky had been purely blue behind her. She'd made quite a sight, one engraved on his memory. He figured he would think back on it for the rest of his life.

Under his breath, he cursed her.

———

"Dammit, Laurel. Your pacing is making me dizzy."

"The whiskey is making you dizzy."

Irv lifted the jar toward her. "You should have a snort. Maybe it would calm you down."

"I can't afford to be calmed down."

Since returning home and waking him up to report what she'd

seen—and hadn't seen—she'd been beside herself, unable even to sit. "You don't know what it was like, looking down and seeing nothing there. Everything just *gone*."

While she had been trying to grasp that her friends, the stills, the tent, everything had vanished, out of the corner of her eye she'd caught headlight beams sweeping across the smooth face of a nearby hill.

Not having had time even to fully regain her breath, she'd turned away from the abandoned site and had begun the return trip to the shack in a flat-out run. Most likely, whoever was in those approaching vehicles would spend more time than she trying to figure out what had happened there, and what the implications were. But that was a supposition, not something she could count on, and it was imperative that she not be caught in the vicinity. Not by anyone.

She'd also been frantic to share this news with Irv, who might possibly have some information unknown to her. Her most earnest hope was that he could provide an explanation for the site having been abandoned.

But, to her dismay, after she'd shaken him awake, he had listened to her breathless recitation of facts with astonishing and infuriating calmness. For the past hour, while she'd been whipping herself into a froth, he had grown increasingly mellow by sipping from a jar of moonshine.

"I'm sure Ernie's got it under control."

She spun around to him. "If you say that one more time, I'm going to hit you with something. You can't be sure of anything. They might have gotten away. They might even have gotten away with most of the equipment. But how far could they have gone carting all that?"

"Ernie's old truck—"

"Yes, Ernie's old truck." She stopped in her tracks and turned to face him, hands fisted at her sides. "Why wasn't I ever told that Ernie had an old truck?"

"Because we had no call to tell you."

"Until tonight!" she shouted. "If his truck is so well hidden in the hills, maybe they couldn't get to it. Carrying all that paraphernalia? How could they possibly?

"If the people in the three vehicles I saw launch a search...God!" She resumed pacing and wringing her hands. "Ernie and Corrine could be in custody. Or worse, dead. And any minute now so could we be."

"I'm sure Ernie's got it—"

Her glare silenced him.

He used the jar of moonshine to point at the article lying at the foot of his bed. "I still think that could be a message of some sort."

She picked up Corrine's workbook and slapped it against her palm. "Of what sort? It's squiggles and lines."

"Then why'd you'd bother going in after it and bringing it back? You must've thought those hen scratches the girl made meant something."

The return jaunt to the shack had seemed more hazardous because it was mostly downhill, and she'd run like the devil was chasing her, which she feared he was. By the time she'd reached the shack, her entire body had been about to give out on her. Muscles, lungs, heart, had been taxed to their limit. She'd collapsed against her Model T, her arms outstretched across its hood, hugging it like a pilgrim at a shrine.

She'd allowed herself one precious minute to slow her heartbeat and breathing. Partially restored, she'd willed herself to move and get into the Model T.

"I was backing into a turn so I could drive out when I remembered seeing this primer on the dresser. I honestly don't know what urged me to stop and get it."

She opened the workbook to the page where Corrine had drawn what looked like absentminded scribbles. She realized now that the printing of Ernie's name seemed beyond Corrine's present capabilities.

"Is Ernie literate?"

"Yes. He's no scholar, but he can read good enough to get by."

"Then maybe this is his doing, and Corrine left the primer where she knew I would see it."

"Let me take another look."

She rounded the bed where Irv was semi-reclined and handed him the primer. He studied the crudely drawn etching, tilting both his head and the workbook to various angles. Then a laugh began deep inside his chest before burbling out.

"What? What is it?"

He closed the primer and passed it back to her. "Go to bed, Laurel."

"Not on your life!"

"Turn out the light. Everything's fine. I know where they're at."

He refused to talk about it further, saying that morning would come soon enough. Frustrated, but exhausted, Laurel turned out his bedroom light and pulled the door shut on her way out.

Bone-weary as she was, she took a bath before retreating upstairs to her room, where she pulled on a fresh nightgown, took the pins from her hair, and gave it a good brushing. She plaited it loosely into her customary bedtime braid. She was about to extinguish the flame in the lamp when she saw his reflection in her dresser mirror.

Gasping, she spun around, her hand at her throat.

FORTY-THREE

D on't raise a ruckus."

"What do you think you're doing? Get out of here!"

Thatcher came into the room and quietly closed the door.

"If you don't leave in two seconds, I'll shoot you."

"With what? You keep your pistol in the pocket of your skirt."

"How do you know that?"

"I've noticed you're always patting at it."

Intending to mend and wash her tattered and soiled skirt in the morning, she'd left it on a hook on the back of the bathroom door, her pistol forgotten in the pocket. She didn't believe Thatcher meant to harm her, but she wished she had the Derringer to reinforce her point about his audacious intrusion.

"As you're well aware, Irv has a shotgun," she said. "He's right downstairs."

"Sawing logs. I could hear his snores as I passed through the kitchen."

"If you don't leave now, I'll yell for him."

"No, you won't. You don't want me confronting him with this."

"This what?"

He didn't answer. Instead, he took off his well-worn black felt cowboy hat and set it on a table. Then he took off his jacket and folded it over the back of a chair.

"Pick those right back up," she said. "I did not invite you to stay. In point of fact, I'm sick of you sneaking around me and my house. What gives you the right to do that, to show up at all hours of the night?"

"When you always seem to be awake. Awake and wound up like a top. I wonder why that is."

"If I'm wound up it could be because you appear out of nowhere and catch me unfit to receive a visitor." Yes, this was twice, wasn't it, that he'd caught her wearing only—

She didn't finish that thought, because, somewhat recovered from the shock of his being in her house, her bedroom, she realized that his demeanor was particularly solemn.

His gray eyes shone in the lamplight beautifully, but reflecting bleakness. His face was drawn, his expression taut, emphasizing the sharp ridges of his cheekbones. He looked as though he were about to undertake a dreaded task, like someone designated to deliver tragic news. She felt twinges of alarm. Why *was* he here?

It was then she noticed that his boots had been ghosted over with a fine, chalky dust, and she realized where he had been tonight before coming to her. Though her breathing turned quick and uneven, she struggled to keep her features schooled. She even managed to ask aloud the troubling question in her mind. "Why are you here?"

He reached down to his coat and took something from the breast pocket, then walked over and set it on the dresser. Instantly recognizing a silver barrette, her heart seized up. She swallowed. "I must've lost it in the yard."

Speaking quietly, he said, "I didn't find it in your yard, Laurel."

She didn't need to ask where he had found it. She knew. But she brazened it out and made an offhanded gesture. "Then it probably isn't mine."

"I've seen you wear it in your hair."

"Lots of women have that same clip. Hancock's sells them. Six to a card. You didn't need to bother to return it."

"Actually, I did."

"Why?"

"Because I've got something to tell you."

"About a hair barrette?"

"Have you seen Chester Landry around?"

The question was out of context. She replied with exasperation. "No. I told you it was doubtful I would." Thatcher didn't look convinced. She added, "I don't know the man. How many times do I have to tell you?"

"Was the O'Connors' trip up to Ranger successful?"

He was intentionally trying to rattle her. She couldn't allow being caught off guard. "Very."

"They didn't encounter any problems?"

"In fact they did. They sold out of pies in a matter of minutes and left some of the roughnecks disgruntled. I need to bump up production." If her flippant answer annoyed him, he didn't show it.

"How's Corrine working out?"

Involuntarily, she glanced at the barrette and could have kicked herself for doing so. "She'll be able to do more when her arm gets stronger."

She could tell by the way Thatcher was looking at her that he knew she was hedging every answer to these questions. On the surface they might seem casual and random, but she knew they weren't.

"Do you know Elray Johnson?"

That query genuinely threw her. "His name is vaguely familiar. Is he one of the—"

"Notorious clan, yeah. His cousin Wally was murdered recently. Elray discovered his body."

"That's it. I remember reading his name in the newspaper. What about him?"

He told her about the teen's aborted attempt to steal a horse from Barker's stable. "I took him to the jail and summoned the sheriff."

"That doesn't seem fair. You caught him before he stole anything."

"But I sensed that he had something else on his conscience. Turned out, I was right. He confessed to stealing crates of corn liquor from a competing moonshiner."

Those twinges of alarm became outright pangs. She was trembling on the inside, but managed to keep her voice steady. "From what I understand, that happens routinely."

"This theft might've been routine if it had stopped at that. But it didn't."

"What happened?"

"Last night, Elray and his cousin, Tup, went back to the same still. A decision they came to regret. There was an incident."

Her heart in her throat, she asked, "What kind of incident?"

"One that warranted investigation. Tonight, when Sheriff Amos organized a team of deputies to return to the scene with Elray, I was more or less recruited to go along."

That was the convoy she'd seen. Thatcher had been among those who'd discovered the location of their stills, and there he'd found the barrette she'd given Corrine.

Feeling that her silence might be a giveaway to her mounting anxiety, she said, "Like at Lefty's. You were roped into taking part in the raid."

He gave a mirthless smile. "Literally this time." He told her about lassoing Elray. "But that's neither here nor there. He was pressured into leading us to the site. Seemed like we covered miles of wilderness on roundabout roads. I thought the kid had been lying. But no, we found Cousin Tup."

"At the still?"

"In a hole in the ground with his arm mangled so bad you couldn't identify it as a human part." His eyes holding steady on hers, he said, "It had been snared in a bear trap."

By now her heart was pumping so hard, she thought she might faint. By a sheer act of will, she contained a sob pressing at the back of her throat. "That's horrible," she said hoarsely. "Was he dead?"

"Last I heard, he was still alive but short one arm."

The strength to stand up deserted her. She sank down onto the end of her bed and hugged her elbows close to her body. "How awful."

Thatcher sat down in the rocking chair in which she had planned to spend hours rocking Pearl in her lap, reading to her from storybooks, loving her. She had attached a cushion to the chair's back, so she'd have something to lean her head against during nighttime feedings that had never taken place.

Thatcher placed his head on that cushion now and closed his eyes. "Whoever was operating the stills—there were at least two of them—had cleared out, taking everything with them. Setting that trap to catch a man stealing moonshine seemed extreme, a cruel thing to do.

"But," he continued on a sigh, "Tup had stolen from them, and had gone back with every intention of stealing again and then destroying their property. He and Elray had been ordered by the family head, Hiram, to rain down hell on them. If they hadn't caught Tup in that trap, if they hadn't cleared out, chances are good they would be dead."

He rocked two or three arcs. "I used to think the difference between right and wrong was clear-cut. Law and justice meant the same thing. But I'm not sure of that anymore."

She studied him for a time. He looked like an everyday cowboy who lived from one day to the next, accepting and dealing with the vagaries of life without giving them much thought. Not so, Thatcher Hutton. Perhaps he thought too much, saw too much. "Who are you?" she asked in a hushed tone that conveyed her mystification. "Who are you, really? Where did you come from?"

He stopped rocking and looked over at her. "What do you mean?" She didn't say anything, only continued to search his face. Finally, he said, "I'm nobody."

"Parents?"

He went back to rocking, but rested his head on the cushion again and gazed into near space. "Well, I didn't hatch, but I don't remember either of them. I was told my father worked in a smithy, shoeing horses mostly. He was accused of laming a horse on purpose because he held a grudge against the owner. The horse had to be put down. My dad was tried and sentenced. He didn't survive prison. I never knew what exactly he died of."

"Is your mother still living?"

"I don't know. She ran off with my daddy's accuser days after he was convicted. They were never seen or heard of again." He glanced over at her and asked dryly, "Do you reckon that story about the lame horse might've been made up?"

Laurel was dismayed. "She just left you?"

"Appears so."

"Who took care of you?"

"I was placed with a family. Decent people. They took in orphans, kids like me. We were expected to do chores on their place, but they saw that we got schooling.

"When I was eleven, thereabouts, I heard that a Mr. Henry Hobson, who had a large spread, was looking for hands to drive his sizable herd to the nearest railhead, which at that time was Fort Worth. Mr. Hobson's age requirement for trail hands was thirteen, but I passed for that. He signed me on."

He smiled with one corner of his mouth. "Years later, he told me he knew I'd fudged on my age, but he saw how bad I wanted the job. Anyhow, after the drive, he made it permanent. I lived and worked on his ranch for the next fifteen years, till I was drafted into the army."

"Why haven't you gone back?"

"Nothing to go back to." He told her the circumstances, his gaze pensive and sad when he talked about his mentor's death and the change of fortune it had wrought for him.

"Mr. Hobson was the finest man I've ever met. I called his son up in Dallas and left word how to reach me. Haven't heard from him, though, and I don't expect to. Don't see that it makes much difference. Not now."

"Now?"

He broke his distant stare and turned to her. "Things have changed, Laurel."

"What things? Since when?"

"Since tonight."

He left the rocker and made a circuit of the bedroom. Pausing at one of the windows, he drew the curtain aside and looked out, before resuming his restless prowling. Ordinarily she would have resented his prying and this invasion of her personal space and would have told him so. However, being unsure of his reason for coming here, and made timid by his broodiness, she held her tongue.

He said, "Before they took Tup away, I had a chance to talk to him. He told me what he remembered about the two people working those stills. One trait he recalled was they were both light-footed." Now standing in front of her dresser, he looked down at the barrette he'd set there. "Where's Corrine?"

Believing it would benefit her to stick as close to the truth as possible, she said, "She's staying at the shack."

He turned and fixed his gaze on her.

"She was afraid if she didn't pull her weight, I'd kick her out, although I had assured her I wouldn't. But she was doing too much and not giving her broken arm time to heal properly. I took her out there to stay for a while."

"We drove past the old place tonight. Twice. The shack was pitch black dark both times."

"I guess she had turned in."

He came toward where she sat on the end of her bed. "If I went back out there right now, would she be there?"

"Why are you asking me all these questions?"

He captured her head between his hands, tilted it back, and brought his face close to hers. "Because I'm afraid we're gonna wind up on opposite sides of a bitter and bloody fight."

"What fight?"

"You know damn good and well what fight, Laurel. Why did I find your hair clip at the site of a still?"

She tried to look down, but he held her head, disallowing her to look away and making it impossible for her to lie to him anymore. With a catch in her voice, she implored him, "Please don't ask."

He stamped a hard kiss on her lips. "Please don't answer."

He placed his knee on the bed and took her down with him as he stretched out across it. He dug his fingers into her hair as his thumbs brushed across her cheeks. Looking into her eyes, he said, "You knew this was coming, didn't you?"

Understanding what he meant by "this," she whispered roughly, "Since that day we met on the street."

"I knew sooner than that. Also knew it was a bad idea. You're the damnedest, most complicated woman I've ever met. But I can't stop wanting you."

He kissed her again. This time it started out tender, but almost at once turned tempestuous. When she responded with the same degree of ardor, he placed one arm around her shoulders while the other encircled her waist. She folded her arm around his neck and clung.

Moaning unintelligible words of arousal, he wedged his knee between hers and pushed it up to separate her thighs, then splayed his hand over her bottom and secured her against him. She felt his want, hard and imperative, assertively male. Every feminine inclination in her being yearned to have that potency inside her.

When he began undoing the buttons down the front of her nightgown, she said faintly, "The lamp—"

"Stays on." He opened her neckline, slid his hand inside and lifted her breast clear of her nightgown. "Jesus." His warm breath drifted over her, as did his fingertips, feather-light. He lowered his head and rubbed his lips against her nipple, then swept it with his tongue.

She whispered his name and tunneled her fingers into his hair. He hadn't gotten it cut since she had met him. It was longer, thicker than then, and she loved the feel of it sliding between her fingers.

When he drew her nipple into his mouth, she closed her fingers, clutching at his hair. He tilted his hips and began moving against her. She arched up to meet the evocative thrusts.

Air stirred against her skin as he raised her nightgown up over her hip. He cradled the back of her knee in his palm, squeezed it with strong fingers, then began stroking her inner thigh. His touch was gentle but bold, dictating adjustments in position as he worked his hand up to where she lay open.

His exploring caresses brought her into stunning awareness of her own feverish, full achiness, of how wet she was. When he pressed a finger into her, she flinched. But reflexively she clenched, signaling a desire for more. He withdrew his finger, but where he touched her next caused her body to jerk in response.

He began drawing fluid circles upon that spot. When at the same time, his mouth tugged on her nipple, her body began to tingle throughout. It was wonderful. It terrified her.

She gasped, "What are you—?"

And then all control spun away from her. Her throat arched, her hips came up off the bed, seeking the cursive design of his strokes. If he stopped, she would die. If he continued, she would die. She ground against his hand in her desire to be engulfed by this tidal wave of sensation, even as she feared being drowned by it.

She panicked and cried out, "Stop!"

He did so instantly. He pulled his hand from beneath her nightgown and braced himself above her on one arm. "Laurel?"

"Don't." Using hands and heels, she madly pushed herself from beneath him, moving all the way up to the brass headboard. She crammed the hem of her nightgown into the vee of her thighs, grabbed a pillow and held it against her bared breasts. Her nipples were pinpoints of sensation.

Thatcher was looking at her with bewilderment and concern. "What?"

She couldn't speak for the currents that continued to ripple through her. Even as they ebbed, her breathing remained choppy.

"Did I hurt you?"

She shook her head and managed a gruff "No." She pulled down her nightgown to cover her legs. "I'm not like the French girls, that's all."

He frowned. "What?"

"I know about them. Derby told me. He admitted that he had been with a few women while he was over there. Only because of the horrible things he saw. I couldn't hold it against him, could I?"

He opened his mouth to speak, but she cut him off before he could.

"He told me the girls over there do things that are unheard of in America. Against the law, even. Not only prostitutes. Regular girls. I'm sure you had your share of them."

He looked down at the floor and ran his hand around the back of his neck. "Laurel—"

"Of course you did. That's none of my business, just don't expect me to be like them and do...things." She raised her chin toward the bedroom door. "Please be enough of a gentleman to leave now."

He looked like he wanted to argue, to say more, but he exhaled heavily and turned away from the bed. He picked up his hat and put it on, then pulled on his jacket. He went to the door but didn't open it. Looking back at her, he said, "I didn't finish my story."

"I don't want to hear it."

"Well, you need to."

"It doesn't concern me."

"I hope to God not. I really hope to God not, Laurel." He paused. "See, when we got back to the jail, the sheriff left straight for home. I volunteered to escort Elray inside and lock him up. Deputies were piling out of the other car. Some lit up smokes and jawed about the expedition, others went inside. I hung back with Elray and seized the opportunity to ask him in private what he'd been lying about."

"He'd told you the truth."

"But not all of it. I knew he was holding something back about Wally's murder, something that had recently come to light. He hem-hawed around but finally told me that a tip had come from none other than Gert. According to her, a competing moonshiner had done Wally in."

"That's not at all surprising."

"I didn't think so, either. But I sensed that Elray was still with-holding something. I kept pressing him about the identity of this bloodthirsty competitor, and he finally gave up what he knew."

"Which was?"

"It's a woman."

Laurel's breathing was suspended for a full fifteen seconds before Thatcher continued.

"I doubted him. I told him that either Gert was lying or she'd been misunderstood. Elray swore he was there when Gert named the culprit to his great-uncle Hiram. Naturally, I encouraged him to give me her name. And I believe he eventually would have. Except that somebody shot him through the head from the roof of the bank building."

Laurel exhaled in a burst. "Oh, my God, Thatcher."

He stared at her for several beats. "He was standing no more than a foot away from me. I saw his eyes go dead before he dropped."

She covered her mouth with a shaking hand. "I'm sorry."

"Yeah, so am I. He wouldn't have been there if it weren't for me."

He put his hand on the doorknob and addressed it rather than her. "Sheriff Amos predicted that there was going to be a bloody moonshine war. He said he could use an extra deputy and offered me the job. I turned him down, told him it didn't have anything to do with me, that it wasn't my fight, and I wouldn't be taking sides. That's the thing that changed tonight."

He reached into his pocket, took out the now familiar badge, and, looking back at her, pinned it to his lapel.

———————

Irv was standing in the kitchen, holding the shotgun aimed at the door through which Thatcher had to pass on his way out. When he saw Irv, he stopped. The two squared off, and when Irv spotted the badge, his scowl deepened.

He said, "Badge or not, I could shoot you for trespassing."

"You could. But just so you know, I'm unarmed. To a jury that might look like murder."

"I could murder you for messing with my daughter-in-law."

"I'd be dead. Laurel would be left to suffer a scandal."

"It's Laurel now, is it?"

"Yes." Thatcher walked forward until the barrel of the shotgun was inches from his belly. "It's Laurel. And hear me, Plummer. If you and your moonshining get her killed, I'm going to kill you."

He allowed time for the words to sink in, then he stepped around the old man and left through the back door.

FORTY-FOUR

———◆———

Norma was seated on a stool at her vanity table plucking her eyebrows when Patsy sauntered into the bedroom. "You're not even dressed yet?"

Norma yanked out the last wayward hair, dropped the tweezers onto the vanity, and swiveled around. "What's your rush?"

"I'm not in a rush. The man at the bank is, and he keeps bankers' hours."

"What is the problem?"

"Something to do with a signatory card. He was expecting us at one o'clock. It's thirty minutes after."

"Can't you handle it alone? I don't want to get Arthur up just to traipse in and out of the bank."

Five minutes later, Patsy left the house more noisily than necessary, probably in a spiteful attempt to wake Arthur from his nap. But he slept peacefully in his bassinet. Earlier Norma had placed it near the open living room window that provided a gentle southern breeze.

She was returning to her bedroom when she heard an auto braking out front. Thinking that Patsy must have forgotten something, she muttered, "Not a moment's peace around here."

But when she looked out the window, her irritation evolved into apprehension. Bernie Croft was climbing out of an unfamiliar automobile. It wasn't his long touring car, but a much smaller roadster. For once, his chauffeur, whom she secretly feared, wasn't with him.

She overlapped the sides of her silky, floral-patterned robe and tied the belt tightly around her waist. It was almost back to what it had been before the baby. Her curvy figure was coveted by women and lusted after by men. Arthur had been worth the temporary bloating, but she was glad to have her notable figure restored.

As Bernie neared the door, she opened it and, with more bravado than she felt, said, "This is a surprise."

"A good one, I hope."

"A delightful one."

She stood aside; he came in.

This being his first time ever to come here, he took a look around. Like the rest of the house, the main room was shabby overall. The wallpaper was faded. The window curtain sagged unevenly. There were stains on the rug.

In these surroundings, Bernie looked all the more immaculate and imposing.

"I'm a mess," she said. "Give me a sec?"

"Of course."

Norma rushed into her bedroom and inspected herself from the different angles provided by the tri-panel mirror. Dammit, she didn't look her best. Although it was after lunchtime, she'd spent a lazy morning and hadn't even powdered her nose. There wasn't time to pin up her hair, so she fluffed it around her shoulders. Grabbing a tube of lipstick, she applied a coating, then turned toward the door as Bernie strode in and tossed his hat into a chair piled with discarded clothing.

Embarrassed over the bedroom's messiness, she made a self-conscious gesture of helplessness. "The baby keeps me so busy, I don't have time to do much else." Then around a nervous laugh, she added, "Not that I've ever been much of a housekeeper."

"You weren't expecting company."

"Especially not such important company."

His affectionate smile relaxed her. Gabe wouldn't have been fool enough to tell Bernie that she was in on their secret about Pointer's Gap.

"Would you like something? Maybe some iced tea?"

"Nothing, thank you. Except privacy."

He shut the bedroom door with his elbow. She would have preferred that it be left open a crack so she could hear Arthur if he stirred, but Bernie was having to bat away the articles of clothing hanging on the back of the door that had swung outward and swiped his face, so she let it go.

"Did you see Arthur?"

"I took a look," he said, "but you're who I came to see."

Responding to the suggestiveness of his tone, she moved her shoulder enough to make the robe slip off it. "I hope you don't mind that I didn't consult you on the baby's name. Do you like it?"

"It'll do."

"Well, I couldn't name him after you, could I?"

He laughed. "God, no."

"He has your wide brow. I hope no one notices the resemblance."

"No one will be looking for one," he said. "If they look for resemblances to anyone, it will be Gabe."

"Yes, our marriage coming so soon after his wife's disappearance may raise a few brows, but I've come up with a tragic love story." She placed the back of her wrist to her forehead and struck a dramatic pose. "Arthur's father was taken too soon, I'll say, and give a delicate sniff-sniff. He never got to see his son, but he would be pleased to know that his child's stepfather is a prominent physician, a loving man who treats Arthur as his own."

He grinned. "You've got it all planned."

"I am a planner. But I do like surprises." She leaned back against her vanity table, letting her robe fall open, baring her legs.

Appreciating the view, Bernie walked toward her. "You're no pious-looking madonna, Norma."

She fluttered her eyelashes. "Thank you for saying so."

"How is motherhood?"

"Sleep-depriving. But I adore Arthur. He's a good baby."

Bernie fingered the silk lapels of her robe, then impatiently pushed them apart. "Are you a good mother?"

"I think so. I want to be."

"I'm sure you are." He covered her breasts with his wide hands and squeezed. "With these titties? I'm sure you excel. Arthur's a lucky little bastard."

She recoiled. "Don't call him that."

"That's what he is."

"It's an ugly word."

"I agree." He looked up from her breasts into her eyes. "So is *whore*."

Her lips parted in shock.

"And that's what you are, Norma."

"I'm not!"

"The word fits you to a tee."

His squeezes had become painful pinches. She pushed his grasping hands away and pulled her robe together. "You had better leave. Gabe wouldn't like knowing that—"

"That I was fucking you on the night he called me in a panic over killing his wife?"

"He never has to know about us."

"Maybe he should."

"No! Anyway, that phase of my life is over. I got what I wanted."

"A well-to-do husband with a lovely home."

"Yes."

"Respectability."

"Yes."

"Gabe hasn't married you yet."

"Soon, though."

"But the blushing bride-to-be welcomes me, naked except for that cheap, tacky robe and red lipstick."

"Before I knew you were going to be so horrid."

"You thought we would end our affair on a sweeter note."

"Yes."

"I hate to disappoint."

He pulled back his fist and slammed it into her face.

The pain was so excruciating she didn't even feel the center mirror of her vanity shattering against her back when she fell into it. He hit her in the face again, this time hard enough to knock her to the floor. She groped for the vanity stool to try and pull herself up and attempt some kind of defense, but he kicked the stool out of her reach.

She crawled on all fours in an effort to escape his hammering fists and the vile things he was saying to her and about her. Worse, he didn't shout the insults in outrage. He spoke them in a soft but repugnant parody of sweet nothings.

He kicked her in the ribs. Then he stopped and stood over her, breathing heavily. She thought that perhaps that was the end of it. He'd vented his rage. He was through.

But then he stamped on her, and the pain was unimaginable. She screamed.

He pulled her up by her hair and pushed her face-first onto the bed. He held her head down with one hand and used the other to shove her robe up above her waist.

He clamped the tops of her thighs and forced them apart. She tried to scream again, but the mattress beneath her battered face muffled the sound. She couldn't draw in sufficient air through either her nose or her split and bleeding lips. She feared suffocating.

But in a black and distant part of her mind, she wished she would.

His thrusts were brutal. His hands held her with bruising strength. His language was obscene, vicious, abasing. It seemed to go on forever.

Then, heaving and hot, he collapsed on top of her, leaden, compressing her lungs, making spears of the ribs he'd broken. But he lifted his hand from her head, allowing her to turn it aside and try to suck in air through her mouth, but nothing was functioning right. His sweat had combined with the cloying scent of his cologne, making her gag. She choked on blood.

Finally he pushed off of her. Standing beside the bed, he righted himself. She heard the rustle of his clothing, the jingle of his belt buckle, the clink of his watch fob. The floorboards creaked under his weight as he crossed the room toward the door. It whooshed open, the clothes hanging on the back of it swishing.

In a voice that was eerily detached, he said, "*If* you have the misfortune of surviving, and *if* you breathe a word of this, I'll tie that brat of yours in a sack and throw him in the Brazos."

He walked out of the bedroom. He left the house.

Norma was too benumbed to move.

FORTY-FIVE

Laurel baked all day. Recollections of what had happened between Thatcher and her last night were persistent distractions, and her feelings about them ranged from delirium to despair. Work helped to keep those troubling thoughts from swamping her, but they lurked at the fringes of her mind, teasing and tormenting.

While her last batch of pies was cooling, she delivered Clyde Martin's order to the café. By dusk when the O'Connors showed up, she had pies boxed and ready for them.

"Where's the whiskey?" Davy asked.

"We're fresh out. There's been some trouble. Our distiller had to shut down and relocate in a hurry. I'm hopeful he'll do a run tonight, but at this point, I just don't know. In the meantime, we're in the pie business exclusively."

The twins took the news with a surprising lack of despondency. "Don't worry yourself, lovely Laurel," Davy said. "In view of our recent shortfall, we've been courting another supplier to keep us in moonshine should another shortage occur. Which it has. Once we're up and running again—"

"Wait. What other supplier? Who?"

"Now, Laurel, you know better than to ask," Mike said. "We can't give you his name any more than we'd give him yours. It's all very discreet."

"Is he reliable?"

"Yes," Davy said, "but reliability is expensive."

"How expensive?"

They told her the terms of the deal they'd negotiated, and they were reasonable. Nevertheless, she was leery. "I don't like having to buy moonshine in order to sell it."

"A temporary necessity," Mike said.

His brother added, "And a smaller profit is better than none."

"Is his whiskey any good?"

"We thought so," Mike said.

His glazed eyes indicated that he had had more than a sampling, which reassured Laurel not at all. Dividing a stern look between them, she said, "You're sure of this?"

Davy answered for both. "We wouldn't let you down, sweetheart."

Reluctantly, she counted out the currency they would need to purchase the moonshine. "Just this once."

Before they set off, she pleaded with them, "Please, please be careful. A young man was killed last night right in front of the sheriff's office."

"Ah, we heard about that. Tragic for sure. But it's rumored that it was a family dispute. Nothing to do with us."

She could have argued that it wasn't any ol' family's dispute, it was a Johnson family dispute, and that if they discovered that it was her still where their kinsman Tup had been maimed, the clan would be gunning for her.

The less the twins knew of that, the better. She also didn't want them knowing that she was consorting with a lawman. Further discussion of Elray's slaying might lead to mention of Thatcher, a subject best avoided.

But no sooner had she thought that than Mike said, "Did you hear about your Good Samaritan Mr. Hutton?"

"What about him?"

"Ah, he was talking to the young man when it happened. A second shot missed Hutton by a hair."

Davy picked up. "But he took off running to the building where the shots came from. Couldn't be stopped, they said."

Laurel's hands had gone clammy. "Who said?" she asked huskily.

"The sheriff's deputies trying to hold him back, because he wasn't even armed. But that didn't stop him sprinting to the bank building. He was mad to catch the shooter. Those there said he never uttered a word, but that the look in his eyes was positively feral."

"He didn't catch him?" she asked.

"No," Mike said. "Lucky for the murdering Johnson."

Laurel put up a disinterested front, but she couldn't wait for the twins to be on their way. After they left, she felt more forlorn than she had since Derby's suicide and Pearl's death. She'd had no control over either of those life-changing events.

But rather than surrender to feelings of defeat, she had resolved never to be that defenseless against fate again. With sheer determination, she had persevered, had built a life and livelihood for herself.

Now, she felt control of that also slipping away.

Recent events had played out on their own, without her knowledge or oversight. Irv had been wounded. A man had lost his arm. A boy had lost his life. Ernie and Corrine and the stills were unaccounted for. Where had her tight grip on control been when all that was happening?

And when she was with Thatcher? Last night he'd come to her after what surely had been one of the worst experiences of his life. But his concern had been for her, not for himself. She recalled the sorrow in his eyes when he'd told her about his mentor's death and Elray Johnson's murder. She also remembered the determination in his demeanor when he'd pinned on the badge.

Some might mistake his reticence for indifference, or a steeliness against emotion, but he felt things more deeply than anybody she'd ever met.

She'd fought her attraction to him every step of the way, but last night she'd been helpless against it. She'd been overtaken by the look and feel of him, the desperation in his voice when he'd said, "Please don't answer."

Unlike anything she'd ever experienced, the groundswell of sexual sensation brought on by his caresses had completely undone her. The control had belonged to him, not to her, and that loss of herself had been terrifying.

But also thrilling. If the climb had been that incredible, what would the cresting have felt like? She couldn't help but wonder, and regret—

"Laurel?"

Nearly jumping out of her skin, she whipped around to find Irv standing behind her and dressed to go out. "You were a million miles away, girl. What were you thinking about?"

"Nothing."

"Huh. Didn't look like it to me." He watched her for a moment. "I threatened to shoot him. If you want me to, I will."

Ignoring that, she patted her pocket to make certain she had her pistol. "Are you ready?"

Laurel insisted on driving even though they were taking Irv's truck. He gave in way too easily, leaving Laurel to believe that even though the bullet wound had closed and healed well enough for him to leave his bed, his arm remained infirm.

He brought Ernie's map with him, although he claimed to know where his partner had likely relocated their stills. "He showed me the place once, bragged on it being nearly perfect like our other spot."

"Is it on your property?"

"Barely." When she shot him a doubtful glance, he added defensively, "Barely counts."

They drove for half an hour. When they saw a flicker of firelight in the distance, Laurel slowed down. "They may start shooting before they realize it's us."

"Honk the horn three times. That's the signal."

The new location had the natural attributes of the original. Ernie and Corrine had both stills reassembled, and both were cooking. Over cups of coffee they told Laurel and Irv about the harrowing night they had spent moving everything.

Ernie said, "Soon's we got the trap off that fella's arm and put him in the hole, I ran for my truck, brought it to the site, and started loading everything up. Even with a gimp arm, she did aw'right," he said, looking over at Corrine.

"I like to've wore myself out," she said. "But, in a way, it was good we had to take everything apart and put it back together here. I learned a lot. But I don't want to do it again anytime soon."

"We wasn't sure you'd get the map," Ernie said. "It was her idea to leave it."

Laurel told them about her seeing the convoy from the shack and racing over the hill to beat it. "Although, at the time, I didn't know it was lawmen. It could just as well have been rival moonshiners. Imagine my shock to see the place deserted and not knowing what had happened to you."

She finished telling the rest of it. "I can't explain what inspired me to get the primer. Irv figured out what the drawing meant."

Ernie tossed the dregs of his coffee into the dirt and watched as it was absorbed. "Was the thief I trapped a Johnson?"

Laurel nodded. "He and a younger cousin."

"He die in the hidey-hole?"

"Miraculously, no, but his arm was amputated."

He nodded solemnly. "Then he pro'bly won't be stealing no more."

"Probably. But that was a big price to pay for a few crates of moonshine."

"Yep, it was, Miss Laurel. But given the chance, he'd've killed us without blinkin'."

Thatcher had reasoned the same. She said, "It's believed that was his intention."

"What about the cousin who ran out on him?"

"Shot and killed last night," Laurel said. "They feel for sure by his own kin." She related the circumstances, but didn't refer to Thatcher by name, only as "a deputy" who was seeking information about Wally's murder.

As though reading her mind, Corrine asked, "You seen any more of Mr. Hutton?"

Irv harrumphed and kept his head down, poking at the logs in the cookfire with a stick. Laurel said, "He came by one evening to check on Irv's progress." Quickly changing the subject, she asked Ernie about their renewed production. "Can you step it up?"

"We brought six barrels of mash with us that were close to ready. The rest, we had to pour out. Luckily we had enough supplies to mix up more yesterday and today."

"We've got two crates you can take with you," Corrine said with pride. "I got 'em ready myself while Ernie was mixing the mash."

Two crates wouldn't have excited Laurel a few days ago, but now she was glad to know she had them. She didn't tell the others about the O'Connors buying from another moonshiner, knowing that they, particularly Irv, who mistrusted the twins, would disapprove. *She* disapproved.

They discussed more about the operation, then Laurel expressed her misgivings. "Tup and Elray Johnson found our stills. How well hidden are you here, Ernie?"

"Pretty good, I reckon, or I wouldn't've moved us here." He glanced around at the others. "But about them Johnsons finding us..."

"What?" Irv said.

"Just seems unlikely is all," Ernie said. Without looking directly at anyone, he added, "Unless they were keeping an eye on the shack."

"Why would they be doing that?" Laurel asked.

He shrugged his bony shoulders. "If somebody was to've tipped 'em off."

Laurel's ears began to roar as Thatcher's words came back to her in a surge. *Elray swore he was there when Gert told his great-uncle Hiram who the culprit was.* The culprit meaning the female moonshiner.

Gert knew Laurel was dealing in whiskey. She had been there when Laurel and Lefty had sealed their deal. She'd been livid to learn that Laurel had sheltered Corrine. Narrowed down, that would be in one of two dwellings: their house in town, or the shack.

If it had been discovered that Corrine was living in the shack, if she'd been seen going on foot over the hills, if she'd been followed to the still, Gert would have had the perfect setup for revenge against both Corrine and Laurel.

Good God. Everything that had happened in the last forty-eight hours was a consequence of Laurel's going to the roadhouse that day. Thatcher had said he was afraid they would wind up on opposite sides of a fight. He wasn't afraid of it at all. He already knew that she was moonshining, and last night he'd warned her that, thanks to the vengeful Gert, the Johnsons did, too.

"Corrine, things have become dangerous. You have to come back to town with Irv and me," she said. "You're too far from the shack to be going back and forth on foot."

"Ernie and me done talked about it," the girl said. "I'll stay here and help him do runs till we catch up."

"Ernie?" Irv asked. "What do you think of that plan?"

He shifted self-consciously. "When she ain't blabbing, she's handy."

Laurel came to her feet. "It doesn't matter what Ernie thinks. It matters what I think."

The three of them looked up at her like she'd lost her mind, and very possibly she had. She walked away from them, pressing her fingers against her temples where her pulse was beating fast and hard. There had to be a way out of this, not to save her own skin, but to protect these three and the twins.

The logical solution to all their problems would be to shut down completely. But then what?

She couldn't stop Ernie and Irv from carrying on as they had before her interference. Corrine, having shown an enthusiasm for making corn liquor, would likely join them.

The twins were young, daring, and resourceful. They obviously had other contacts in the illegal liquor trade. With their winning personalities, they would prosper.

She would bake and sell pies.

The dreariest part of that prospect would be that Gert would continue to thrive, turning victims of mistreatment and misfortune into prostitutes for her gain.

Laurel slowly came back around to three pairs of eyes looking at her expectantly. Corrine would actually be safer out here than she would be in town where she was much more likely to be seen by someone who would return her to Gert. But this was hardly a Garden of Eden.

"Corrine, are you sure you want to stay here?"

"Oh, I don't mind at'all. I'm enjoyin' bein' out in the open."

Irv and Laurel looked to Ernie for his opinion. "She's proved herself to be right smart," he said. "Nimble and quick, too."

"All right," Laurel said, but not without reluctance. "For the present, she stays. Please get the crates loaded into the truck."

Although Irv couldn't be of much help, he accompanied Ernie.

Laurel stayed behind with Corrine. "I'll be back the day after tomorrow." She glanced over at the tent. "By then, if you've changed your mind about your situation here, you can come back to town with me. You'll have a home with Irv and me."

"I know what you're askin' without coming right out with it. Ernie treats me regular, not like a whore."

"You were never a whore, Corrine. You were a victim of circumstance."

"Well, anyway, Ernie has his cranky moments, usually over my jabberin', but he's nice. Even without me asking, he dug a latrine for my private use."

Laurel tried to contain her smile. "That was thoughtful of him."

The men came back for the other crate. As soon as they were out of earshot again, Laurel said, "Corrine, the morning after Irv got shot, and you and I were having breakfast, you talked to me about Gert and how upset she'd been with Wally Johnson for the beating he gave you."

"Upset? I'll say. She carried on something fierce."

Laurel remembered what Corrine had told her that day, but she wanted to hear it from her again. "What made Gert so angry?"

"'Cause I looked like roadkill, and she wouldn't be making any money off me, and money is all she cares about.

"She was so mad at Wally, her face turned purple. She hollered cuss words, threatened him with a meat cleaver, and ordered him to get his ugly self out of her place."

Laurel patted the girl's shoulder. "Ernie needs help, and you seem content to be here. But I'm worried about your safety."

"You got no call to be."

"Yes, I do, Corrine. Believe me."

"Ernie's protective."

"I'm sure. But he may not always be around. You need to protect yourself."

"I will, Miss Laurel. I promise."

"Well, I want to make sure of that."

FORTY-SIX

———◆———

The landlady called Thatcher away from the supper buffet to the telephone in the hall. "Keep it short," she said as she handed him the earpiece. "There's others who use it, too, you know."

Thinking it might be Trey Hobson at long last, he leaned into the mouthpiece mounted on the wall. "This is Thatcher."

Bill Amos said, "Can you get over to Doc Perkins's office?"

"Right now?"

"Right now."

"Who's sick?"

"Just come. Don't say anything to anybody."

The sheriff disconnected. Thatcher hung up, stared at the telephone in puzzlement for several seconds, then, responding to Bill's urgency, ducked back into the dining room to take his hat from the rack.

The crabby Mrs. May said, "Are you eatin' or not?"

"Not." He was aware of Chester Landry's interest in his abrupt departure, but he didn't acknowledge the man as he rushed out. He feared the emergency pertained to Daisy Amos.

Having to walk several blocks, he was winded by the time he reached the professional building on Main Street where he'd been told the elderly doctor had a clinic that took up half the third floor. It was past quitting time for anyone else who had office space there, but the main entrance was unlocked. Thatcher went in and climbed the stairs two at a time.

A door with the doc's name printed on it opened into a waiting room where a woman was seated near a small table, smoking a cigarette. She was unkempt. There were blood smears on her dress. Her eyes were red-rimmed, her expression harsh. "Who are you?"

He took off his hat. "Thatcher Hutton."

"What are you doing here?"

Before he could reply, Bill Amos opened a door with "Examination Room" stenciled on it. "I called him," he said to the woman, then hitched his head, indicating for Thatcher to join him in a small room with glass-fronted supply cabinets on two walls. The center was dominated by the examination table.

"Through here," Bill said as he led Thatcher through yet another room into an operating room. He drew up short when he saw the table on which a female person lay.

A white sheet covered her from toes to chin. All that showed was a mass of thick, dark hair and her face, which looked like it had had a head-on collision with a locomotive.

Wearing a white lab coat, Doc Perkins was washing his hands at an industrial-size porcelain sink. Thatcher recognized the strong smell of antiseptic from his days in the army hospital.

Bill said, "That's Norma Blanchard."

Stunned, Thatcher remembered the pretty, shapely woman with the saucy walk whom he'd seen going into Gabe Driscoll's house late one night. "She dead?"

"As of when I called you. I wanted you to see her to get an idea of what we're dealing with here."

Thatcher wanted to object to the plural pronoun. In his mind, he'd taken a stand against the likes of the violent Johnsons, but he hadn't been sworn in as a deputy yet, and he wasn't wearing the badge. However, now wasn't the time to go into all that.

Thatcher said, "Who's the woman outside?"

"Miss Blanchard's sister. Patsy Kemp."

She was no doubt the woman who'd chauffeured Norma to Gabe Driscoll's house, but Thatcher hadn't gotten a good look at her face that night and wouldn't have recognized her.

Bill said, "I asked her to stay, so we could talk to her about the assault."

"Assault? This wasn't an accident?"

"No. Mrs. Kemp brought Norma to Dr. Perkins around four o'clock. She was barely alive. He evaluated her condition and called me right away. She never regained consciousness." To the doctor, he said, "Give him a run-down. No medical jargon, please. Plain talk."

The doctor unhooked the wire stems of his eyeglasses from behind his ears, removed them, and began polishing them with the towel he'd used to dry his hands.

"Her nose is broken. Pulverized, actually. Fractured cheekbone, broken jawbone, three loose teeth. A flap of scalp about an inch in diameter had been ripped away. I sewed it back, but that's the least of it."

He replaced his glasses and looked down at the draped figure. "The back of her torso appears to have been pummeled repeatedly, I suspect with fists. I also tweezed out several shards of mirror glass that had sliced through her garment." He pointed to a silky dressing gown wadded up in a chair.

"I detected three broken ribs. Others may have been cracked. She might have survived, in time, and under the care of physicians better trained and skilled at treating the more serious of her injuries."

"What were they?"

"She has a sizable bruise and swelling above her left kidney. It's so precisely placed, it appears the organ was targeted. Perhaps by the heel of a shoe. I suspect the blunt force caused internal hemorrhaging. She bled to death."

The doctor's eyes looked apologetic behind the round lenses of his glasses. "I did what I could, but I'm a country doctor, unqualified to deal with something like this. Perhaps Gabe Driscoll would have been a better choice."

Bill glanced at Thatcher, then turned to the doctor. "Tell him the rest."

The doctor bowed his head and addressed the floor. "She was raped. Barbarically. Considerable damage was done to tissue."

The men stood silent, looking neither at each other, nor at Norma Blanchard's still form. After a moment, the doctor covered her face.

In a quiet voice, Bill said, "Her injuries are of such a sensitive nature, I'd like to keep the details between us, doc."

"Of course."

"Do you mind if we use your waiting room to talk to Mrs. Kemp?"

"Not at all. I'll stay with Miss Blanchard until the ambulance arrives."

"Ambulance?" Thatcher asked.

"I want the autopsy done in Dallas," Bill said. "They have a lab, forensic specialists."

Thatcher took a last look at the sheet-draped figure then followed Bill from the surgery and back out into the waiting room. Patsy Kemp hadn't changed her position since Thatcher had come in.

Bill pulled a chair over closer to her and motioned for Thatcher to do the same. When they were seated, Bill said, "I'm awful sorry this terrible thing has happened, Mrs. Kemp."

She gave him a curt nod.

"This is Thatcher Hutton."

"So he said."

"He's new to my department. We'd like to ask you some questions, gain as much information as we can, in an effort to catch the person who assaulted your sister."

She sat stony-faced.

Bill asked softly, "Where's her baby?"

"I dropped him off with a lady I buy fresh eggs from. She has a baby close to Arthur's age. She'll wet-nurse him and look after him until I can pick him up."

"Good." Bill paused, then said, "You know the extent of what was done to your sister?"

"I found her, remember?"

"Do you know who attacked her?"

"No."

"At any point, was she conscious?"

"Conscious but out of her head."

"Did she say—"

"Did you see her mouth? She couldn't talk."

Bill eased away from her, as though sensing, as Thatcher did, that pressuring her wasn't the tack to take. "Tell us what happened today."

"Do we have to do this now?"

"Do you want us to catch the man responsible?"

Bill won the stare-off. She took a deep breath. "Today started out like any other. I did chores while Norma tended to Arthur."

"You told me earlier that the assault took place while you were away from the house."

She told them about receiving a telephone call from First State Bank. "I don't remember the man's name. He asked me to come in and take care of a matter. Something I needed to sign. Arthur was down for a nap. Norma was primping. It was easier to go without her than to wait for her to get ready. She was very particular about her appearance."

She glanced toward the examination room. Her eyes turned watery. "Norma wouldn't have wanted to live looking like that. Jesus God." She shook a cigarette from her pack. When she had difficulty striking the match, Thatcher struck it for her and held it to the tip of the cigarette.

She gave him a nod of thanks.

The men allowed her time to compose herself and take a few puffs before Bill asked, "What time did you leave the house?"

"One-thirty. I was trying to beat it to the bank before it closed. But when I got there, nobody knew anything about a phone call. There wasn't a problem with my account. I didn't know what to make of the mix-up, but rather than waste a trip to town, I stopped in Logan's for some groceries." Her voice trembled. "I'll never forgive myself for not going straight home."

Thatcher noticed that her hand was shaking when she flicked an ash into the ashtray she was holding on her knee.

"I could hear Arthur screaming the minute I pulled up to the house. Norma wouldn't let him whimper without picking him up, so I knew something was wrong. I ran into the house. Arthur was still in his bassinet, where he'd been when I'd left. He was wet and hungry, but otherwise okay.

"Norma…" She choked up and had to force the words out. "She was facedown on her bed. She wasn't moving. There was blood. I would have thought she was dead, except that she was making sounds like…like…I don't know…a wounded animal."

She took another drag off her cigarette. "I'm not sure she knew it was me who was handling her. She flailed her arms, trying to fight me off. I liked to have never gotten her into the car."

"No sign of who had been there?"

"Don't you think I would have told you by now?"

"Was anything missing that you noticed?"

"I didn't take the time to look, sheriff."

"I ask only because if the house had been ransacked, it could have been a vagrant."

"The house hadn't been ransacked."

"You sister's bedroom?"

"It was a mess, but it always is. The vanity stool was overturned, the mirror had been shattered. Glass was everywhere."

"When you left for your errand, had you locked the front door?"

"Yes."

"Was it locked when you returned?"

She had to think for a second, then said, "No."

"Was the lock damaged?"

"I think I would have noticed if it had been broken."

"Then it's possible that Miss Blanchard knew her attacker and let him into the house."

She bent her head down and massaged her forehead.

Bill cleared his throat. "Where is Mr. Kemp?"

"His name is Dennis. He's in Colorado."

"What's he do there?"

"Sets dynamite. He blasts through mountains for railroad and highway construction." She raised her head and gave Bill a baleful look. "Is this important?"

"When did you last hear from him?"

"Barking up that tree will be a waste of your time. Every two months I go to see him. He hasn't come home since Norma moved in with us."

"They didn't get along?"

"Couldn't stand each other. She called him a bore. He called her silly and conceited." In a mumble, she added, "Among other things."

"If there's so much animosity between them, why did she come to live with you?"

She hesitated, looking resentful of the question. Finally she said, "Because the man she had been living with in Austin kicked her out for cheating on him. She had no money, no job, nowhere else to go."

Bill asked her to write down the name of the company her husband worked for. She did. The sheriff tucked it into his breast pocket.

"What about the father of her son?"

She smoked, saying nothing.

Bill prompted. "Had Norma been asking him for money? Demanding that he marry her? Something like that?"

Having smoked her cigarette down, she ground it out. "I wouldn't know, Sheriff Amos, because I don't know who Arthur's father is."

She caught the skeptical look Thatcher and Bill exchanged. "You don't believe that? It's true. Swear to God, I don't know." She turned to Thatcher. "You're young and good-looking. Were you acquainted with my sister?"

"No, ma'am. But I saw her once."

"Did your eyes pop out of your head?"

He gave a shy smile, and she snuffled.

"Norma had that effect on men." Turning back to the sheriff, her momentary mirth disappeared. "She used her looks to her advantage. She had a lot of men. But to be dragging her name through the dirt while her body is still warm just doesn't sit right with me."

Before Bill could respond, Thatcher said, "It isn't right. But neither is a brutal, fatal assault. What Sheriff Amos is trying to do is find out who did it. The more information you give him, the better chance he has of catching the man and seeing him punished."

Patsy's chest caved in a little. Her hostility cooled. As she thought over what Thatcher had said, she picked at the loose stitching on the handbag in her lap. "Norma had been carrying on an affair with Dr. Gabe Driscoll."

She looked at Bill and Thatcher in turn. He wondered if she noted that neither was surprised to hear this.

Bill asked, "For how long?"

"Close to a year."

"Where did they rendezvous?"

"He always came to the house. Or did. He hasn't been there since the night his wife disappeared. Norma wasn't happy about not seeing him."

"Up until Mrs. Driscoll's disappearance, how often did they meet?"

"Two or three times a week. He would come by while he was out making rural calls. But he isn't Arthur's father. Norma was already pregnant when she met him. She only passed the baby off as his to reel him in. She set her sights and went after him."

Watching her closely, Bill tugged at the corner of his mustache. "Did they conspire to get rid of Mrs. Driscoll?"

"I don't think Norma had anything to do with it."

"Mrs. Kemp—"

"I'll tell you why," she said, cutting Bill off. "Norma didn't consider Gabe's missus competition. She had convinced herself that Gabe would ultimately choose her and Arthur over 'that fat German cow,' as she called her.

"She had big plans for Gabe to move her and Arthur into that large, pretty house. As his wife, she would become a society maven. I told her she was delusional. But I also saw how besotted Gabe was with her." She shrugged. "Maybe he gave in to her impatience."

"Gabe claims to have been at your house twice on the day his wife went missing. Once in the afternoon, once late that night."

"He was, but not to help with Arthur's breech birth, because Arthur was already a month old. Gabe came that afternoon. He held the baby for half an hour and spent another thirty minutes in the bedroom with Norma. They were lovey-dovey. She begged him to stay longer and was pouty when he left.

"When he came back that night, it was a different story. He was frantic. I mean berserk. Batshit crazy. I had to deal with him myself because Norma was out."

"Out where?"

Thatcher could tell she was reluctant to answer, but finally she did. "There was someone else. Before Gabe, and the whole time she was with him."

"The baby's father?"

"That would be my guess, but I don't know. It was a very secretive affair. She always went to him. She was with him that evening of Mrs. Driscoll's disappearance. When she got back home, Gabe was there, but he was too distraught even to ask where she'd been."

"What time did she get home?"

"Midnight or better. Honestly, I believe Gabe is rather thick. She smelled of sex. He's a doctor, right?" She snorted with derision. "Arthur was a hefty newborn. Any fool could see he was too big to be six weeks early, as Norma claimed. But Gabe never raised a question about his size or seemed to doubt that he was the father. In my opinion he's a loser."

Bill said, "But you covered his lie about the breech birth."

"I did, yes. Norma insisted that we back him up, for Arthur's sake, she said."

"Did Gabe kill his wife, Mrs. Kemp?"

"I swear to you I don't know."

"Did you ever question Norma about the convenient timing of Mrs. Driscoll's disappearance?"

"No," she replied in her wheezy smoker's voice, "I didn't want to know the answer."

Bill sighed. "When two people share a secret like that, it tends to erode the relationship, whether it's between siblings, husband and wife, illicit lovers. If it turns out that Gabe Driscoll assaulted your sister today—"

"Then all bets are off. I'll dance naked at his hanging. But..." She shook another cigarette from the pack. Thatcher lit it for her.

Bill said, "You were about to say, Mrs. Kemp?"

"I'm not sure Gabe has it in him to do that. I told you she was pouty when he left that afternoon. It was because he wouldn't make love to her. Our walls are thin. I could hear her trying to seduce him. He refused, saying it was too soon after the baby for them to have sex. So the way she was violated today just doesn't seem like him. Murder maybe, but not that."

"Not even if he'd found out the baby isn't his?" Bill asked. "Maybe he realized that he'd been duped, suckered into killing his wife and his own unborn child for another man's. That could have motivated him to fly into a blind rage."

She said, "Then they ought to hang the bastard twice."

———

Fifteen minutes later, the ambulance from Dallas arrived. Bill directed it to the back of the building, where Norma Blanchard's body was loaded. Patsy was going to follow in her car. She told Bill that her husband had family in Dallas, and that she had arranged to stay with them until her sister's body could be released for burial.

"Please remember that you're a material witness in two crimes," Bill said. "I'll need to reach you."

"I understand." She gave him her relative's telephone number and address.

As they watched her departure, Bill said to Thatcher, "She could also face charges of obstruction if Mila Driscoll suffered the fate I suspect. But I didn't want to tell her that."

They returned to the doctor's office so Dr. Perkins could sign off on departmental paperwork. Thatcher remained in the waiting room. He noticed that Patsy had left her last cigarette smoking in the ashtray. He went over and stubbed it out, then he and Bill left the office together and started downstairs.

Bill slipped a small stoppered bottle into the pocket of his jacket, and when he saw that Thatcher noticed, he said, "For Daisy."

"Is she all right?"

"For the past few days, she's had a stomachache. Doc said this would settle it."

Thinking of the picture gallery in the Amoses' foyer, Thatcher said, "I wonder if Mrs. Kemp has a picture of Norma."

"Lots. I saw them in the house when I went to interview them."

"That's good. When the boy gets older, he'll want to know what his mother looked like." Bill gave him an inquiring look, but he pretended not to see it and returned to the topic of the attack on Norma Blanchard. "I've been thinking about something."

"Don't hold back."

"A man in a blind rage would have killed her outright. Whoever attacked that woman wanted to punish her to death. There's a difference."

Bill took that in, then gave him a wry smile. "Don't talk yourself out of that badge, Thatcher. You were born for this." He continued on his way down the stairs. Thatcher followed.

As they exited the building Bill cursed under his breath. Bernie Croft was between them and the sheriff's car, waiting for his dog to finish peeing against a utility pole.

FORTY-SEVEN

———◦◦◦———

Hello, Bill. Hutton."

"Bernie," Bill said.

Thatcher didn't believe that the mayor's being here at this precise time was coincidental with his dog's bladder. He was right. When the dog lowered his leg and wandered off to sniff at a patch of weeds growing against the side of the building, Croft strolled along the boardwalk to join them.

He looked Thatcher over. "I heard you actively participated in the raid on Lefty's."

"Who'd you hear that from?"

"A mutual acquaintance of ours." Thatcher figured he referred to Chester Landry but didn't remark on it.

Croft turned to Bill. "This young man is practically your shadow these days."

"Thatcher is no one's shadow, Bernie. But if I can twist his arm, I'm going to sign him on as a deputy."

"That will raise eyebrows."

"It's certainly raised yours. Now, if you'll excuse us."

"I saw the arrival of an ambulance from my office window."

He looked across the street toward the second-story windows on the facade of city hall. Bill had told Thatcher that those office windows overlooking Main were to Bernie what the pope's balcony was to His Eminence.

He was saying, "If I read the insignia correctly, the ambulance came from Dallas. Who was it for?"

"Doctor-patient privilege, Bernie," Bill said. "You know I can't divulge the—"

"Was it someone I know? Why was he shuttled off in secrecy behind the building? Was it the Johnson boy? What was his name again?"

"Elray," Thatcher said.

Croft turned to him. "Elray, yes. I heard you tried to chase down his assassin. In fact, you seem to be Johnny-on-the-spot since you came to Foley. One can find you anywhere there's disorder."

Thatcher said, "That seems to make you nervous. I wonder how come."

Croft puffed up like an adder, but he faced Bill again. "You had just as well tell me who was in that ambulance. I'll wring it out of Dr. Perkins anyway. Save me the climb upstairs."

Bill relented. "A local woman was assaulted." Without going into detail, he told Croft what had happened.

"Jesus Christ," he said. "Who was she?"

"I'm keeping it quiet, Bernie, out of respect for the lady and her family's privacy."

"Very sensitive of you, Bill. But other ladies should be made aware that there's a rapist in our midst, don't you think?" He gave Thatcher a significant look.

Thatcher adjusted his stance to a more confrontational one. "Why don't you just come out and say it, Croft?"

"Say what?"

"Accuse me of preying on women."

"I already did."

"And it didn't stick."

"Gentlemen," Bill said quietly. "Let's not draw an audience, please."

The only audience they'd drawn that Thatcher could see was Hennessy, Croft's so-called chauffeur. Cap pulled low, he was leaning against the side of the mayor's car parked across the street, his posture a little too indolent to be genuine, his entire aspect one of menace.

Thatcher hadn't made out like he'd noticed him lurking there, but he was well aware.

Croft was adding to his list of complaints against the sheriff. "I just don't understand you. It's obvious to everyone except you, even to men in your department, that your judgment has become clouded of late. Mine hasn't. I'm responsible for the welfare of this town's citizenry, particularly those who can't defend themselves, our children, our female population."

"Oh, for godsake, Bernie," Bill snapped, "save the speech. The victim's name was Norma Blanchard."

The mayor reacted with a start.

"Obviously you knew her," Bill said.

"Not personally, but I knew of her. The pretty sister, correct?"

"She was pretty before today."

"Where was she attacked?"

"In her home."

Again he gave Thatcher a pointed glance. "Someone looking for a room to let?"

Thatcher moved in closer, wanting badly to knock this pompous hypocrite on his ass.

But Bill motioned for him to stay as he was, and for the sheriff's sake, Thatcher let the insult pass.

Bill said, "A vagrant is a possibility, of course. But initial indications are that she knew her assailant and let him inside the house. Her infant was asleep in the front room, so it was someone she trusted."

The mayor drew a frown and absently toyed with his watch chain.

"What is it, Bernie?"

He stopped fiddling with the chain, but his frown remained. "Something I wish I didn't know."

"About Miss Blanchard?"

"Yes, but I was told in the strictest confidence."

"If it's pertinent to the crime, then—"

"I'm not saying that," Croft said in a rush. "Not at all. It probably has no relevance whatsoever."

"Tell me and let me decide."

He sighed with seeming reluctance. "On the day following Mila Driscoll's disappearance, I spoke to Gabe by telephone. Mrs. Driscoll's relatives hadn't arrived yet, so while your deputy was using the bathroom, Gabe called me on the sly and confessed that he'd had a liaison with that Blanchard girl."

"Why would he have confessed that to you?"

"Because I had been his staunch proponent there in your office. I had promised to continue standing by him until his wife was found or her fate determined. Therefore, he felt I deserved to know that he harbored what he called 'a shameful secret.'

"I was thinking in terms of unsettled gambling debts, or blackmail, or fleecing hypochondriacs. Something like that. I never would have dreamed that Gabe Driscoll's dirty secret was a sexual fling. He's such a cold fish. I can't imagine him humping anybody, can you?"

Thatcher could tell that Bill was offended by Croft's terminology, but he pounced on the primary matter. "After that rousing sermon you just delivered about your civic responsibility, you tell me *this*? Why didn't you come to me with it before now? You didn't think an affair with another woman was pertinent to the sudden disappearance of the man's wife?"

"Calm down. It wasn't an *affair*. It was one afternoon of sexual congress that occurred the day after he and the Blanchard woman met."

"Only that one time?"

"That's what he told me. Tearfully. With contrition. Soon after this breach of his marriage vows, Mrs. Driscoll conceived. Gabe regarded her pregnancy as a sign of forgiveness from on high.

"Even though Mrs. Driscoll was blissfully unaware of his transgression, he atoned by lavishing attention on her. Pampered her with foot rubs. Picnics in her favorite spot near Pointer's Gap. Flowers and other romantic folderol. He never strayed again. I made him swear it on the Bible."

Mrs. Kemp had told Thatcher and Bill a completely different story, but it wasn't his place to cite that.

Bill said, "Although it's late in coming, thank you for this information, Bernie."

"I doubt it's relevant to what happened to the girl. If the rumor mill is credible, encounters such as the one she had with Gabe were not a rarity, but commonplace."

"Nevertheless, she suffered a brutal attack. I ask again for your discretion."

"Of course, Bill, of course. Good night." Croft tapped his thigh. The dog trotted up and rejoined his master, tongue lolling, tail wagging, ready to be off. As Croft came even with Thatcher, he said, "*Deputy* Hutton, don't think for a moment that badge on your chest makes me in any way nervous."

"I don't. But I don't wear it all the time. That's when you should be nervous."

Thatcher watched Hennessy hold open the backseat door of the town car for Croft and the bird dog. "Your mayor is the one who's got a shadow."

Bill looked over at the town car, then motioned Thatcher toward his own vehicle.

"I don't mind walking."

"I've got to go to the office anyway and finish the paperwork I started with Doc Perkins. But do you mind if I make a quick stop at home so I can give Daisy the stomach medication?"

"Not at all."

Once they were on their way, Bill said, "As bodyguards go, Bernie couldn't have hired a better one. Jimmy Hennessy—I doubt that's his real name—was in the IRA. Fought in the uprising in '17. Got a price put on his head for killing two British army officers. Outran his pursuers and made it to New York.

"Due to the large Irish population there, word got around, traitors talked, the city got too hot for him, he fled to Chicago. Same story there. Eventually he wound up here. All this is hearsay, you understand, probably embellished, but I believe the basics."

Bill made a corner, then said, "Only one afternoon of illicit romance? Do you believe that version?"

"No. Why would Mrs. Kemp exaggerate her sister's promiscuity in the wrong direction?"

"Exactly."

"And why did Driscoll do the opposite and swear on the Bible that he was with Norma Blanchard only once?"

"We'll ask him that tomorrow."

"Why not now?"

"I want to see what evidence the Kemp house yields. When we confront Gabe with this, I want to be as well-armed as possible."

When they arrived at the Amoses' house, Thatcher said he would wait in the car. "Take your time. I've got a lot to mull over."

Such as Laurel being a moonshiner, out of her league with big-time players like Landry and Croft, the Johnsons, and the unscrupulous couple at Lefty's.

Jesus.

Bill found Daisy in bed, listless and complaining of stomach cramps. He asked if she'd eaten anything, but she hadn't because she couldn't keep anything down. "Have you been drinking?"

"No, Bill." She reached for his hand and held it against her cheek. She was lying. He could smell whiskey on her breath, but he didn't want to start a row. She wasn't drunk, but she was obviously unwell.

He gave her half a dropper of the medicine. "Maybe it'll ease the cramping so you can sleep. I won't be long."

"I love you."

"I love you, too." He kissed her forehead. Her eyes drifted closed. It scared him how fragile she looked. Almost lifeless.

Shaking off that thought, he left the bedroom and had almost reached the front door when the telephone rang. He went back to answer it and could tell by the background noise coming through the earpiece that his long and strenuous day wasn't over yet.

Sixty seconds later, he strode to the car and climbed into the driver's seat. "Thatcher, do you have a gun belt?"

"At the boardinghouse."

"Then we'll stop there first."

"What's happened?"

"That moonshine war I knew was coming? Well, it's here."

FORTY-EIGHT

Thatcher was putting the frisky mare through her paces in the corral when he saw Laurel come around the corner of the stable. She stopped there.

The sight of her made his heart jump and everything below his waist go tight, which didn't improve his dark mood this morning. He wanted to strangle her for being the damnedest woman he'd ever met. He wanted to make love to her for the same reason.

The mare was being her uncooperative self, but he stuck with the training for five more minutes, then, with a subtle motion of his right knee, directed her to the paddock gate where he dismounted. He led her out and over to the water trough near the stable.

He said to Laurel, "You're out early."

"I need to talk to you and figured I would find you here."

Her hair was hanging down her back in a long braid beneath the straw hat he recognized, the one with the wide brim that cast a criss-crossing pattern of shadows over her cheeks, her pert nose, her plump lower lip.

To distract himself from thoughts of biting that lip, he ran his hand along the horse's neck as she drank from the trough.

Laurel said, "What's her name?"

"Serena."

"Pretty."

"Yeah, but it doesn't fit her personality. She's high-stepping and willful, doesn't pay attention to anybody."

He could tell by Laurel's peeved expression that she knew he wasn't referring strictly to the mare. In a crisp voice, she said, "I wouldn't have bothered you, except that I need to tell you something the sheriff ought to know."

"Then why don't you go see him?"

"Are you going to be civil and talk to me or not?"

"I'll be civil and talk to you, but I can tell you right now that you won't want to hear what I have to say."

"And what is that?"

"Stay and find out."

He made a nicking sound with his mouth and gave the reins a gentle tug. The mare fell into step behind him as he led her into the stable. Laurel trailed behind.

The shade was welcome, but the air inside the building was stuffy and hot and added to his overall grouchiness. Only after the mare was unsaddled, unbridled, and munching oats in her stall did he turn his attention to Laurel, who'd been standing in the center aisle, tapping her hat against her leg with annoyance for having been kept waiting.

"You don't like horses?" he asked.

"I don't mind them."

"Do you ride?"

"Not with any skill. On the family farm, we had plow horses and one mule. I could sit astride and hold on. What is it you wanted to say that I don't want to hear?"

"Have a seat." He motioned to a bale of hay. She backed up to it and sat down. He took off his hat and hung it on a nail as he wiped his forehead with his sleeve. "I've got a bucket of well water. Are you thirsty?"

"No thanks."

He went over to the bucket, ladled himself a tin cup full, and drank it down. She set her hat on her lap. When he came back to her, he propped himself against a post between stalls. "Ladies first."

"There's something worth Sheriff Amos's knowing, especially after what happened to Elray Johnson."

"Why don't you tell him directly?"

"Because you're privy to certain things that he isn't."

"Like what?"

"My visit to Lefty's. Have you mentioned that to him?"

"No."

"Or that I've taken Corrine under my wing?"

"No."

She wet her lips, pulled that enticing lower one through her teeth, making it difficult for him to concentrate on what she was saying.

"...so last night, I tested my memory of what Corrine had told me before. She described again how furious Gert was with Wally over the beating. Not because she had any sympathy or concern for Corrine, but because she was going to lose money while Corrine was out of commission." She paused to take a breath. "It occurred to me that Gert might have killed Wally over it."

"Huh."

"You sound skeptical. Don't you think she's capable of murder?"

He thought back on his single experience with the woman and the fury she'd unleashed during the raid. "I don't doubt it for a minute."

"But what?"

"A lot of people are capable of murder. Gert has her own suspect in mind. She thinks Wally was killed by the woman who has put a cog in the local moonshining machine. Remember that's what Elray told me seconds before he got shot."

"Of course I remember. But does this mystery woman even exist? Gert probably made that up to deflect—"

"Laurel, stop. Just stop." He walked over, grabbed her hand, and pulled her to her feet, sending her hat into the dirt and shocking her into silence. "Do you think I'm just a cowboy too dumb to know what you're into?"

"What do you mean?"

"Fucking hell," he ground out, not caring if she was scandalized by his language. "Finding that hair clip where the still had been clinched it, but I already knew that you and Irv weren't living off pies and his handyman business. I know the O'Connor twins wouldn't be delivering baked goods—baked goods, for crissake—to the oil fields if there wasn't more at stake."

"They—"

"Don't say anything. I don't want to hear anymore. I *can't* hear anymore. I'm official now."

"Just because you made that grand gesture of pinning on the badge?"

"Because Sheriff Amos swore me in as a reserve deputy last night."

"Oh. I see."

She pulled her hand free of his grip, but he wrapped his hands around her upper arms and held her in place. "Know why he needed another deputy? To try to keep moonshiners from killing each other."

"Killing each other?"

"The war Bill Amos saw coming was declared."

"What happened?"

"Three stills belonging to members of the Johnson family were destroyed by rivals."

"Who?"

"Don't know yet. But the outbreak of violence went on for most of the night. Stills were busted up. The hills ran with rivers of whiskey that had been poured out, sometimes by the sheriff's men, sometimes by competing sides, and it was hard to tell who was who. There were several shootouts, them against each other, them against us."

"You were in on these shootouts?"

"Because men were shooting at me. At Bill. At all of us. One of the other reserve deputies got winged. Best I know, nobody died, but it wasn't for lack of trying. Sheriff's department arrested over twenty men. Bill had them scattered to different jails, in this county and neighboring ones. He did that for their own safety. Those who name names don't live long. If Elray was here, he'd vouch for that."

She had stopped trying to get free. In fact, she was gazing up at him with apprehension. "Do you know the names of those who were put in jail?"

Her face had gone pale. He knew what she was desperate to know, but couldn't come right out and ask. "There were no familiar names on the lists I saw." Only when he said that did she begin to breathe again.

"I've warned you before, Laurel, and it hasn't done a damn bit of good. Maybe because I've beat around the bush. But I'm going to tell you straight out this time." He drew her closer. "If you don't stop what you're dealing in, and making enemies with folks like Chester Landry, Gert, the Johnsons, you could wind up hurt or even dead."

"I—"

"Listen to me, dammit. Retaliation seems to be the only way these people know how to settle a disagreement or even a grudge." Thinking back on Norma Blanchard, he added, "Being a woman won't protect you from violence or cruelty. Believe that."

He rubbed her arms up and down once, then released her. "You've made it plain enough that I have no say in how you choose to live your life, and you don't want me to have a say. But the fear of something bad happening to you keeps me churned up and makes me mad as hell at you. That's why I acted like a jackass when you got here."

She looked down. "I thought you were mad because I made you stop the other night."

"I wasn't happy about it."

"I know. I'm sorry I—"

"Don't apologize. It was my fault. I read you wrong."

She tilted her head up, looked at him directly, and said softly, "I'm only sorry that I didn't see it through. I'd like to know what I missed."

He waited to make sure he hadn't imagined that she'd said that, but her green eyes reflected sincerity, regret, and yearning. He slid his hand beneath her braid and curved it around the back of her neck. "I damn near died. I'm damn near dying now." He lowered his head. Their lips barely touched.

"Thatcher? You in there?"

He and Laurel sprang apart. Standing in the wide stable opening was Sheriff Amos, silhouetted by blinding sunlight.

"Yeah. Here."

The sheriff came forward a few steps, spotted Laurel, and took in the situation immediately. "Oh. Excuse me."

"Just as well you're here." Thatcher bent down and picked up Laurel's hat and handed it to her. "Mrs. Plummer actually came to ask me to give you a message. Now she can deliver it herself."

Laurel looked up at him with consternation, but she went along without protest when he motioned her forward. They met Bill halfway.

"How's your father-in-law, Mrs. Plummer?" he asked.

"Much better, thank you."

"Glad to hear it."

Thatcher said, "Bill, you remember the young woman Wally Johnson beat up?"

"Of course. Corrine something."

"Well." Thatcher took a breath and told the sheriff about taking Corrine from Lefty's following the raid. "The Plummers sort of inherited her that night. They've given her a home in exchange for her helping out."

"Really?" Bill looked at Laurel. "That was a very kind gesture, Mrs. Plummer."

"Corrine was in an awful situation. Not one of her choosing."

"Tell Bill what she told you about Gert."

"She went on a tirade over the Wally Johnson incident." Laurel talked without interruption for the next several minutes. She finished by saying, "Isn't it possible Gert was angry enough to kill him over it?"

Bill didn't dismiss the conjecture out of hand, but he did make a valid point. "Could this be Corrine's way of getting revenge on Gert for mistreating her?"

"Corrine's not conniving, she's candid. She isn't lying about this. I'm sure of it."

"I don't believe she is either, Bill," Thatcher said.

"No, me neither, really," Bill said. "I questioned her myself." He chuckled. "She was very outspoken about her feelings over Wally's demise. And I wouldn't put anything past Gert, including cold-blooded murder. Her greediness is legendary." He stroked his mustache. "Only thing I can't reconcile is why Corrine didn't tell me about Gert's tirade when I questioned her."

"Probably because she feared reprisal. She didn't feel free to tell about it until she had gotten away from there. Her intention wasn't to implicate Gert. That's my notion. But if Gert were to find out that Corrine had talked about it at all, she could still retaliate."

"I'll definitely follow up, but I'll leave the girl out of it. I promise. Thank you for bringing it to my attention."

"You're welcome." Laurel put on her hat. "If you gentlemen will excuse me, I need to get to work."

The three of them left the stable together. Bill said, "Thatcher, we need to get to work, too. I'll meet you at the car." He struck out in the direction of the auto garage.

Thatcher asked Laurel where she'd parked.

"I walked over. I didn't want it to look like—"

"Like you were coming to see me."

She shrugged guilty. "People talk."

"People can go to hell."

He ducked his head under her hat brim and gave her a lingering kiss. When he pulled away he said, "I'm making you a promise, Laurel."

She looked at him quizzically.

"If I ever get you in bed again, you can count on finding out what you missed."

Excited by Thatcher's final words to her, but also shaken by what he had told her about last night's unrest, the arrests, the shootouts, Laurel swiftly walked home. She planned to hastily gather supplies and then to drive out to the stills. She feared what she might find when she got there, and was equally afraid of finding nothing.

By the time she reached her house, she was winded, but when she saw Irv's truck there, she ran inside. He was standing at the cookstove cracking eggs into a skillet. She rushed over and hugged him from behind.

"Ouch! Mind my arm."

"Irv, I'm so relieved. My God! Last night—"

"Don't have to tell me about it. I lived through it." He flipped the frying eggs. "You want an over-easy?"

"No thank you. Are Corrine and Ernie all right?"

"They're fine. Pissed off because we couldn't do runs last night, just when we were rebuilding our inventory. By the way, I brought back crates packed with jars. I'll help you carry them down to the cellar once I've had a bite and a rest."

"Fine. Good. But what about last night?"

"We were all set to get both cookers going, but then we started hearing gunfire popping from every direction. Some of it might have been echoes, but there was enough of it, and close enough, to scare the bejesus out of us.

"We knew better than to light the fireboxes and become targets, so we scurried a distance away and took cover between rocks, huddled in the dark all night. Shootin' would break out every now and then. Didn't let up till almost dawn. We were glad to be alive to see the sunrise. Went back to the camp. Looked just like when we left it. They didn't find us."

He slid the eggs onto a plate, sprinkled both liberally with salt and pepper, and added a leftover biscuit. As he hobbled over to the table, he remarked, "Your color is hectic. What's the matter?"

"What's the matter?" She sat down across from him. "When you weren't here this morning, I thought you'd probably stayed at the stills all night because you were tired of being cooped up for so long. But when I heard about last night's ruckus—"

"Who'd you hear it from?" He mopped up egg yolk with half the biscuit and popped it into his mouth.

"Thatcher Hutton."

He gave a harrumph. "Figures."

"Why do you say that?"

"Did he come around to boast about all the men he killed?"

"He didn't kill anybody."

"Not what I heard. The boys at the filling station said—"

"The filling station?"

"Stopped there on my way into town. It's where you go to get a soda pop and the latest news. Word is that Hutton's the sheriff's new sharpshooter, said he dropped at least a dozen men last night. They say he's taken the sheriff's boy Tim's place in his daddy's affection. Said—"

"Nobody was killed."

"Then why'd he come over here if not to brag?" One of his eyebrows went up, the other down. "Or don't I know?"

She ignored the implication. "Actually, today I went looking for him to ask if he would pass along some information to the sheriff." She explained why she thought the blowout that Corrine had witnessed between Gert and Wally Johnson was important.

"Things were peaceful around here before that jug-eared runt was murdered," Irv said. "Now, look where we're at. Folks shootin' at each other." He crumbled the second half of the dry biscuit into the remaining egg yolk. "What about the O'Connors? Do you know how they fared last night?"

"They weren't around. They were making a delivery to Ranger."

"That was mighty convenient."

"Why are you still mistrustful of them?"

He waved his hand in dismissal. "They ain't at the top of my worry roster. Deputy Hutton holds that spot. Laurel, if you keep seeing him on a regular basis—"

"It's not on a regular basis."

"—he's going to find us out."

"He already has."

Irv wiped a napkin over his mouth, then held it there as she told him about Thatcher finding the barrette at the abandoned still site. "It was Corrine's, but it matched ones he'd seen me wear. A hair clip isn't conclusive evidence, of course, but even before he found it, he suspected."

"Has he come right out and accused you?"

"Not exactly."

"Not exactly?"

"We talk around it. For instance, he let me know that you and Corrine hadn't been arrested last night by saying he didn't recognize any names on the lists of arrests. He warns me to be careful."

"Of the likes of the O'Connors and that Chester Landry. But maybe he's the one you should be more careful of."

"He wears a badge now, but I truly believe he's looking out for us, Irv. He doesn't want us to get caught."

"For his sake as well as ours."

"How so?"

He thought over his answer. "Men like Hutton have this...fortitude. Honor. Whatever you want to call it. Unlike the most of us, it's hard to bend and damn near impossible to break. If he was put in a position of letting you off the hook, or enforcing the law he's now sworn to uphold, which do you figure he'd do?"

"I don't know, and neither do you."

"No, but I think *he* knows. That's why he doesn't want you to get caught."

FORTY-NINE

As Thatcher and Bill left Barker's garage, Bill told him they were headed for Gabe Driscoll's house.

"You're going to question him about the attack on Norma Blanchard."

"I am. But I should inform you that you're still Bernie's first choice suspect. He put in a call to me early this morning. He asked if I'd ascertained—his word—your whereabouts at the time Norma Blanchard was assaulted."

"Should I take that personally?"

Bill chuckled. "He's never going to like you, Thatcher."

"That doesn't hurt my feelings. I don't like him, either. We rubbed each other the wrong way from the start."

"Because you see through him. Also, he senses that you can't be corrupted or controlled." Bill gave him a sad look that said: *unlike me.*

"Gotta ask, Bill. Was he behind all that shit that happened last night?"

"I accused him."

"And?"

"What do you think?"

"He was walking his dog when it started." Thatcher swore. "We're his damn alibi."

"Hennessy's, too. Although Bernie wouldn't have wasted Hennessy on raiding other people's stills. But you can bet orders came from Bernie."

"What's he after?"

"The Johnsons' almost monopoly on the boom towns."

Thatcher said nothing for a time, thinking about the tightening web of danger being spun around Laurel. Then he asked Bill if Dr. Perkins's medicine had helped Mrs. Amos's stomach ailment.

Last night while Thatcher was retrieving his gun belt from his room, Bill had commandeered the boardinghouse telephone to call a woman in Daisy's bridge club, who had readily agreed to go sit with Mrs. Amos until Bill returned home, whenever that might be.

"The tincture seems to have helped. She hasn't thrown up again, but she was very weak this morning. I hope she can be persuaded to eat something. Her friend Alice Cantor said she would stay with her for however long she's needed."

"That's a huge relief."

"It is. My county was on fire last night, and probably will be again tonight. I've called in all my reserve deputies to help the regulars, but, hell, at least half of them make moonshine themselves or take graft from those who do. That mess, along with the Blanchard assault, it's like the damn sky is falling. Hated to pull you away from whatever you were doing at the stable."

Thatcher gave a half laugh. He didn't hate it near like Thatcher did. He'd have liked to have more time alone with Laurel.

Now, however, he needed to concentrate on the upcoming interview with Dr. Driscoll. Weeks ago, he'd realized that he would never be entirely cleared of suspicion in Mrs. Driscoll's disappearance until someone else was proved to be the culprit. Even though he'd joined the ranks on the side of the law last night, he still wasn't wholeheartedly accepted by the other men. The more Bill relied on him, consulted him on tactics and so forth, the more resentment Thatcher felt aimed his way.

This interrogation of Driscoll could turn that tide.

"I went out early to the Kemp house," Bill was saying. "Took a look around. It's as Mrs. Kemp described it. Norma's room looked like a tornado had hit it. There was blood on the bed. I left Scotty out there to try and lift fingerprints, but, if they do turn out to match Gabe Driscoll's, all that proves is that he's been there. Which we already know. Doesn't signify that he assaulted her."

"Where does that leave you?"

"Us. That's why I called you away from your work at the stable. You factor large in our approach."

"How?"

Bill took a sheet of folded paper from the breast pocket of his jacket and passed it to Thatcher, who unfolded the sheet and read the lines written in a spidery script. When he finished, he refolded the sheet and handed it back to Bill.

Thatcher said, "You're going to show this to Gabe Driscoll and gauge his reaction?"

"I'm going to show it to him," Bill said as he slowed his car in front of the Driscoll house. "*You're* going to gauge his reaction."

As they went up the walk, Thatcher noticed that without the kind-hearted lady of the house there to oversee its upkeep, the place was beginning to look neglected. Weeds were sprouting in the flower beds. The grass needed mowing.

The sign at the gate had indicated that the doctor was in, but there were no other autos there, and when Bill rang the doorbell, it echoed through empty rooms.

Thatcher hadn't seen Gabe Driscoll since the morning in the sheriff's office when the doctor had viciously accused him of abducting his wife. In the intervening weeks, his hairline had receded, he'd lost a considerable amount of weight, and his eyes were sunken into their sockets. He looked like a man who'd just crawled out of a hole or was about to crawl into one.

Upon seeing them, he clutched the doorjamb. "Mila?"

"No, Gabe, sorry," Bill said. "But we'd like to speak with you. Are you with a patient?"

He shook his head and, after a second's hesitation, stood aside and motioned them in. Bill removed his hat and used it to gesture toward Thatcher. "You remember Mr. Hutton?"

"I couldn't very well forget him." The doctor regarded him with hostility. "I thought you were on your way to the Panhandle."

"Change of plans."

Bill said, "I've made him a reserve deputy."

The doctor tilted his head as though the sheriff might be joking and would add a punch line. Realizing Bill was serious, he said, "If this isn't about Mila, why are you here?"

"We need your professional opinion on a matter."

Still looking puzzled and a bit uneasy, he said, "Let's talk in my office. The other rooms aren't... I haven't had anyone in to clean."

He led the way and pointed them into chairs facing his desk. The doctor went around and sat down behind it. They didn't make small talk. Bill leaned forward and passed Gabe the folded sheet of paper he'd shown Thatcher in the car.

He said, "Yesterday, a woman was brought to Dr. Perkins. She was unconscious, her condition life-threatening. She soon died. Since it was obvious that she had been the victim of a violent crime, at my request, Dr. Perkins compiled a comprehensive list of her more serious injuries."

As the doctor's eyes scanned down the sheet, his brow became increasingly furrowed. When he reached the final two notations, he murmured, "Good God."

Bill said, "I had her transported to Dallas for the autopsy."

"Why did you bring this to me?"

"Doc Perkins is earnest and hardworking, but he's the first to admit that he's not as knowledgeable in modern medicine as you are. I'd like to know if you agree with his hypothetical notes on how the victim's injuries were inflicted. I could wait on the autopsy report, but that may take days, if not weeks. I want to move on this. The perpetrator must be found."

"Without examining the woman myself—"

"I realize I'm placing you at a disadvantage. I'm asking for a general assessment only. Generally speaking, do you agree with Dr. Perkins's hypotheses?"

Looking dubious, Driscoll ran his finger down the page. "Well, yes. Based on his descriptions, I would say someone hit her in the face repeatedly and hard enough to break bones. Probably with his fist, but it could have been an instrument.

"And, if the infliction is violent enough, blunt force to an organ can cause it to bleed even if it doesn't rupture. Dr. Perkins's description of the bruise on her back above her kidney indicates to me that she was stomped on rather than kicked. In regards to the rape, I concur with him. It wasn't about sexual gratification. It was defilement and had to be sheer torture for the poor woman."

Bill said quietly, "It was Norma Blanchard, Gabe."

The doctor's face went as white as the sheet of paper that drifted out of his fingers as they went slack. He began breathing hard and fast through his mouth. He blinked rapidly. Thatcher thought he might be on the verge of passing out.

He tried to stand, but his knees buckled, and he dropped back into the seat of his chair. He planted his elbows on the surface of his desk and held his head between his hands.

"Gabe?" Bill said.

For the longest time, he didn't respond, then, "Who did it?"

"We don't know yet, but we intend to find out. We thought you might shed some light on that since you were well acquainted with Miss Blanchard."

Driscoll lowered his hands from his head and looked from Bill to Thatcher and then back to Bill. Their expressions must have been telling. His shoulders slumped. "You know."

"About your affair with her? Yes."

"Patsy told you?"

"We spoke with her before she left to accompany Miss Blanchard's body to Dallas."

His prominent Adam's apple bobbed. "What about the baby?"

"Mrs. Kemp arranged for a woman to look after him until further notice."

Looking dazed, the doctor listened as Bill gave him a summary of what Patsy Kemp had told them. "This morning, one of my deputies checked with the bank. The telephone call appears to have been a ruse to get Mrs. Kemp out of the house. This wasn't a crime of opportunity.

"Mrs. Kemp arrived home to find the door unlocked, Norma on her bed. The baby, thank God, was unharmed." Bill leaned forward in his chair and asked softly, "Is the child yours, Gabe?"

His voice was a croak, but his answer was swift, simple, and unequivocal. "Yes."

Bill let that settle, then asked, "Had you and Miss Blanchard planned to marry?"

He was about to speak, thought better of it, and finally said, "I'm married to Mila."

"But did Miss Blanchard have expectations of taking her place?"

"I told her that making our affair public would be regarded with scorn."

"Especially in light of Mrs. Driscoll's disappearance," Bill said. "You can understand why folks might jump to judgment."

He looked at each of them in turn as though pleading for absolution. "I'm not proud of committing adultery. I didn't go looking for it. I'm not like that."

"Like what?"

"A skirt chaser. A tomcat. I'd been faithful to Mila. But the moment I saw Norma, she took my breath."

"How soon before you became lovers?"

"The very next day." He gave an account that matched Patsy Kemp's.

"And you kept going back?"

He nodded morosely. "I couldn't stay away from her. She was like a drug. I couldn't get enough. She was so exotically beautiful and…" He looked down at the sheet of paper on his desk and made a choking sound. "Who would do that to her?"

"A rival for her affection?"

The doctor blinked several times. "What?"

"Meaning no disrespect to Miss Blanchard," Bill said. "And I hate to ask so bluntly, Gabe, but even after the two of you became involved, did she see other men?"

"No," he exclaimed. "No, we are—were—in love. She had a very passionate nature and expressed her affection for me without inhibition. There was no one else."

"Okay." Bill looked and sounded unconvinced. "When did you last see her?"

"About ten days ago. She showed up here unexpectedly. She brought Arthur with her. At first I was annoyed. It was the middle of the day."

"You were afraid of what people would think?"

"Yes. She laughed off my concern, said it would look like she was bringing the baby for treatment."

"How long did she stay?"

"About an hour. Maybe a little longer."

"Is that the first time you'd seen her since Mrs. Driscoll disappeared?"

The doctor's eyes darted furtively between Thatcher and Bill, then he confessed to the late-night visit Thatcher had witnessed. "She came uninvited then, too. I didn't want to let her in, but Norma could be persuasive. A little pushy, even."

"A little pushy." Bill assumed a thoughtful expression. "Did her pushiness ever lead to arguments? Did you part on good terms the last time you saw her?"

There was a noticeable hesitation, before he said, "Yes. I enjoyed having that time with my son." When Bill didn't continue, but only steadily watched him, he blurted, "But I told Norma that for appearance's sake, I would come to her from then on."

"Did you go to her yesterday afternoon, Gabe?"

Driscoll shot a look toward Thatcher, looking like a creature who'd just realized he'd been cornered.

Going back to Bill, he said, "You think *I* did that to Norma? That's what this is about?" He lurched to his feet and, with contempt, took a swipe at the sheet of paper on his desk and sent it flying. "I would never, could never, do that to her. I loved her."

"Sit down, Gabe."

"How can she be dead?" he said, his voice cracking. "I did not harm her."

"I'm glad to hear it. Sit down and tell me about yesterday. Where were you midafternoon, say between one-thirty and three-thirty?"

The doctor assumed a posture of righteous indignation. Bill waited him out. After half a minute, Driscoll lowered himself into his chair. "I haven't called on my rural patients since Mila's been missing. I resumed my route yesterday."

"Why yesterday? Any particular reason?"

"I felt it was time that I stopped dwelling on my…my personal tragedy and got back to work."

"Can you provide us with the names of the people you saw, and the route you took?"

"Of course." He took a fountain pen and paper from his lap drawer and began listing names. When he finished, Thatcher sat forward, took the paper from him and pocketed it.

"Thank you, Gabe," Bill said. "I've talked myself dry and could do with a glass of water. Mr. Hutton?"

"Sounds good."

Thatcher could tell that Driscoll saw through the ploy and didn't like leaving them, but his other choice was to appear overly nervous. "Of course." He got up and left the room. His footsteps echoed down the hallway toward the back of the house.

Bill leaned toward Thatcher, his eyebrows raised in an unspoken question.

"He believes the baby is his," Thatcher said quietly. "He's convinced that her love was true and that he was her only lover. He's lying about them parting on good terms, though. There was something there."

"I caught that, too. Maybe she was being pushy about marriage plans. He was afraid of public opinion. That would have given him a motive to shut her up, and yesterday's route gave him opportunity."

Thatcher stated flatly, "I don't think he did it."

Bill was taken aback. "Why not?"

"If he'd've inflicted those injuries, he'd've come apart while he was talking through them."

"He lied to Bernie about seeing Norma only one time. He gave a good performance of an hysterical husband the morning after Mila's disappearance."

"But he wasn't at the scene of the crime." Thatcher bent down and picked up Dr. Perkins's list from the floor. "This amounts to the scene of the crime. I don't believe he did these things."

"But?"

"But I think he got rid of Mrs. Driscoll."

"To be with Norma?"

"He admitted that he couldn't help himself, that she was a drug and he couldn't get enough. Guys in the trenches would say he was pussy whipped."

"What do you say?"

"That's my thinking, too."

Bill gave him a wry grin, but it was short-lived and turned into a frown. "We don't have a body, Thatcher. Not a solid clue as to what happened to Mila. As you know, the prosecutor won't indict on circumstantial evidence alone. A mistress, even an exotically beautiful, sexually uninhibited one, isn't evidence."

Thatcher said, "Well then, only one thing left to do."

"Let him get away with it?"

"Get him to confess."

Before Bill could comment, they heard Gabe returning. He walked into the room carrying a glass of water in each hand. He set one in front of Thatcher, the other in front of Bill, and returned to his chair behind the desk.

Then the three sat with nobody saying anything. Bill drank from his water glass, then smoothed his mustache as he did when muddling through a dilemma. This time, however, Thatcher believed it was more for effect.

Finally he said, "Gabe, the view from where I'm sitting doesn't look good. Within two months' time, your wife has gone missing, and your mistress died of injuries sustained during a brutal sexual assault."

Gabe swallowed audibly but didn't say anything.

Bill continued, "Now either the stars just really aren't lining up favorably for you, or an enemy is setting you up to do you in, or you're doing yourself in. Help me out here."

The doctor took several shallow breaths, like he was pumping up his courage. "I've owned up to having a passionate affair with Norma. Like all lovers, we had our spats. But I would never have done to her what was done."

"You were with her on two separate occasions the day Mrs. Driscoll disappeared."

Mention of that out of context momentarily flustered him. "I told you that myself."

"I remember." Bill looked down and seemed to study the pattern of the rug between his boots. When he raised his head, he said, "Do you want to change anything you've told me about your activities on that day and evening?"

"No."

Bill looked over at Thatcher, his expression pained. Going back to the doctor, he said, "What you told me about that day was that a patient, as of then unnamed, was going through a difficult breech birth. According to Mrs. Kemp, that's not true. She said Arthur was already a month old. Which one of you is lying?"

Gabe placed his elbow on his desk again and rubbed his forehead. "I thought it would make me look bad if you knew I'd been with my mistress that night."

"Well, you're right about that."

Thatcher cleared his throat. Bill said, "Mr. Hutton? Something on your mind?"

"Um-huh. I recall Mrs. Kemp's description of Dr. Driscoll when he went back to her house that second time late that night. She said he was frantic."

Bill said, "He's right, Gabe. She did say that. Why were you frantic?"

"Because Norma wasn't there, and I needed her."

"Needed her? For what?"

"I'd just come from that ratty roadhouse where I'd tended to that girl. I think her name was Corrine. It had been a long day. I was exhausted."

"You went seeking the womanly kind of comfort Miss Blanchard could give you?"

"You're putting words in my mouth."

"Then, in your words, why were you frantic?"

"Because Norma wasn't there."

"That's close, but not exactly what we were told," Thatcher said. "Mrs. Kemp's words were that when you got there, you were 'batshit crazy.' You didn't get upset after learning that Miss Blanchard wasn't there. You were unhinged when you arrived."

Softly, Bill said, "Why, Gabe?"

The crackup was gradual. It seemed to Thatcher that it started at his thinning hairline and worked its way down his long face. His brows drew together above the bridge of his nose. His eyes filled with tears. The tip of his nose turned red and dripped a bead of snot. Then his lower lip began to quiver and he blubbered, "I did something terrible."

FIFTY

———◆———

Somewhere between his blubbered "I did something terrible" and the sheriff's office, Gabriel Driscoll grew a pair.

That was the only explanation Thatcher had for the doctor's change of heart. By the time he and Bill escorted him into the building, he had gone from a shattered man facing ruin to a haughty, self-righteous jerk.

Scotty and Harold, who were sharing a desk piled high with paperwork, stopped sorting through it and looked on with interest as Driscoll proclaimed that an affair was the only thing he had confessed to, and that if the sheriff and his fledgling deputy thought otherwise, they had misunderstood.

As though addressing a jury, he took the opportunity to profess his innocence. "When I said I'd done a terrible thing, I was referring to my infidelity. Nothing more. I sinned against my wife. And since you and your inept staff here haven't uncovered a single clue as to what happened to her, she'll never know how deeply I cared for her."

Looking at Thatcher with malice, he said, "You still haven't definitively accounted for yourself the night Mila disappeared." Then he turned to Bill. "I'm not saying another word without a lawyer present."

"Do you have one?"

"Not on retainer."

"I'll arrange for one, then. In the meantime, you'll wait in a cell." He instructed Harold to lock him up. As the deputy escorted Driscoll into the cell block, Bill quietly said to Thatcher, "I'm in no rush to call the public defender. Let's give him a while to ruminate on his sins against his wife."

When asked, Scotty gave Bill an update on the investigations being conducted relating to last night's events. "We ran down two more 'shiners trying to disassemble their still for relocation. I think they were relieved it was us who found them and not the Johnsons."

"Remember that the Johnsons were the targets and suffered the greatest losses," Bill said.

"Which is why they'll be primed for revenge," Scotty said. "I think we can look forward to another active night. Meanwhile..." He passed Bill a slip of paper. "Somebody from the governor's office. He's called twice. Asked you to call him back."

"He say what for?"

"He said the governor wants to know what the fuck is going on out here and what in holy hell you're doing about it. Says moonshine wars make the state look bad."

"The governor didn't have the guts to call and tell me himself?"

"He was giving the invocation at a prayer breakfast."

They all had a chuckle.

Harold returned. Bill asked him to put through the long-distance call to the governor's office. He asked Scotty to call the coroner's office in Dallas and ask about the timing of Norma Blanchard's autopsy, while Bill himself placed a call to his house and spoke with Mrs. Cantor about Daisy's condition.

While they were occupied, Thatcher wandered over to the county map tacked to the wall and began to study it. He half-listened as Bill conversed with his wife's friend and then spoke to the governor's toady. To an outlandish extent, Bill downplayed the seriousness of the previous night's crimes, even referring to it as "mischief."

When Bill hung up from that call, Thatcher said, "Mind if I get back to work? I've got horses to exercise."

"Of course. I've got plenty to do here while Gabe wallows in remorse. If I need you, I'll come find you."

Thatcher left, knowing that he might be hard to find for the next few hours. Neither the sheriff nor anyone else would know where to look.

Laurel and Irv transferred the crates he'd brought from the stills to the cellar where they would be stored until the O'Connors came for them that evening. Irv apologized for being unable to do his share of the lifting, carrying, and moving.

"I'd rather you let your arm heal," Laurel told him as she put the last crate in its place.

She also loaded supplies for Corrine and Ernie into Irv's truck. As he climbed up into the driver's seat, he said, "We'll have to wait and see if hell breaks loose again before we decide whether or not to do runs tonight."

"Don't take any chances. If there's the least sign of trouble, lay low. Promise."

"I promise. Keep your pistol handy."

She patted her skirt pocket and waved him off.

The kitchen was hot, and only got hotter from the ovens as she baked and the afternoon wore on. She had just taken the last pies out of the oven and set them to cool when there was a knock on her front door.

It was too early for Davy and Mike, and they always came around to the back. Pushing wisps of damp hair off her heated face, she went through the living room to the front door. The windowpane in its upper half gave her clear sight of the callers. Her heart stuttered, but since she'd been seen, she had no choice except to open the door.

In the background, a recent model car was parked in the street, a large man standing beside it. Out of reflex, she patted her skirt pocket, but she smiled. "Hello."

"Mrs. Plummer. You may not remember meeting me. It was a cursory introduction in—"

"The sheriff's office."

Mayor Bernie Croft said, "Your baby daughter was very ill. I heard about her passing. My condolences are long overdue."

"Thank you." Her gaze shifted to his companion, who removed his bowler hat.

The mayor said, "Mr. Landry says you two have met?"

"Briefly. How do you do, Mr. Landry?"

"Mrs. Plummer." He gave her a courtly little bow and a smile that flashed gold.

"What can I do for you gentlemen? Sell you a pie?"

The mayor laughed. "As delicious as that sounds, we'd rather you sell us your corn liquor."

Laurel called upon every reserve of discipline she had not to react. "I beg your pardon?"

"May we come in?" Landry said.

With the speed of comets, several options whizzed through her mind. None were good. But the worst of them would be to refuse them entry. That would only arouse suspicion.

"Of course." She stepped aside. Croft and Landry came in. Before shutting the door, she cast a furtive glance toward the car and chauffeur.

Her guests looked around at the empty front room. She said, "As you see, I haven't furnished the parlor yet, so I can't offer you a seat."

"Personally, I think furnishings would detract from that handsome spandrel," Landry said and moved to stand under it. "Craftsmanship like this is rare these days."

"Let's get to business, shall we?" Croft turned to her. "Mrs. Plummer, are you acquainted with a man by the name of Thomas Johnson?"

"No."

"You might never have met him, but you know who he is. He goes by the nickname of Tup."

...we found Cousin Tup. In a hole in the ground with his arm mangled... Thatcher's words echoed, but she tried to remain impassive. "I'm sorry. I don't know him."

Croft smiled. "Well, he knows you. His arm was caught in a bear trap set by you. He lost the arm."

"How terrible for him. But I still have no idea what you're talking about."

"I visited him in the hospital yesterday."

"So he's a friend of yours?"

"No. I paid him a courtesy call as a public servant."

"It must have cheered him to be so honored."

"Not in the slightest. Mr. Johnson used gutter language to denounce me and my elected office. But then, he wasn't in the best of moods. The nub is festering. They may have to do additional cutting."

She looked over at Landry, who still had his head back, admiring the room divider. Not a hair out of place.

"Mr. Johnson was also elaborately cursing the individual responsible for his misfortune." He smiled. "You, Mrs. Plummer."

"I?"

"You may think I've come to censure you."

"Censure me for what, Mr. Croft? For setting a bear trap, which I would have no earthly idea how to do? It sounds difficult and dangerous."

He pulled his watch out of his vest pocket and checked the time. "I have a schedule, so let's cut to the chase. You were brought to the attention of the disreputable Johnson clan by one Gertrude Atkins.

"She went to Hiram—I'm sure you've heard of him, as his name is widely known in moonshiner circles. Gert alleged that it was you who killed Hiram's kinsman, Wally."

"Obviously this woman is deranged."

"She also informed Hiram that you are poaching on his family business in the boom towns, and even in many local establishments, including her own. Tup and a younger Johnson, Elray, were sent to your still to teach you a lesson. How did they know where it was, you ask? Gert tracked a runaway whore to the shack once occupied by you and your father-in-law. From there it was easy to find the location of your industry. Is the purpose of Mr. Landry's and my visit becoming clearer now?"

"No, but this fanciful narrative is entertaining. However, I also have a schedule, mayor. I'd like for you to leave."

He said, "Don't mistake my reason for being here. I assure you I didn't come on behalf of the wretched Johnsons. I wish them all in hell. You see, the Johnsons and I are archrivals." He smiled again. "You've gotten yourself on their fighting side. I've come to offer you my protection."

"You have me at a complete loss. Protection from what?"

"Capture, incarceration. If you're lucky, that is. If the Johnsons don't get to you before the law does."

"Don't you represent the law, Mr. Mayor?"

"I represent the business interests of the community."

"As well as your own."

"If I prosper, everyone does."

"Hmm."

"Here's how it works. You give me your contacts in the boom towns. Together, Mr. Landry and I can increase that trade double-fold, triple-fold. You'll supply us with all the whiskey you can produce, but we'll take over the distribution. This system greatly decreases the risk to you, your operation, and your associates. We provide this protection for a percentage of the net."

"I say again, I have no idea what you're talking about."

"I'm talking about a ten percent take. Which is a token, really. You obviously have a very good distiller because your product sells so well. You're savvy, and you have backbone. Admirable qualities to be sure, especially in a fair lady.

"But your foremost asset is your *friend*, Thatcher Hutton, who is now serving as a reserve deputy sheriff. A lot of information could be acquired by sharing a mattress with someone inside the sheriff's office."

Heat rushed to her head. She looked over at Chester Landry, who was watching her with a smarmy smile, as though waiting to see how she was going to worm out of this.

She turned back to the mayor. "You insult me, sir. You also insult Mr. Hutton. I have pies delivered to the boom towns. Is that what you want a slice of? I didn't think so. Get out of my house."

He grinned, but the smile didn't reach his eyes. "Mrs. Plummer, you're quite charming and glib, but pleading ignorance is a waste of time. Many of the moonshiners already under my protection buy from the same suppliers of goods as you. I know exactly how many fruit jars and pounds of sugar your father-in-law purchases for you on a routine basis. I know the gentleman in Weatherford who sold him copper recently. In turn you've insulted me, my intelligence, by pretending that you aren't distilling illegal whiskey."

"I don't even drink."

"I'm familiar with this house," he said, seemingly out of context. "It has a sizable cellar."

Landry suddenly became animated. "I understand that it backs into the limestone hill," he said. "Is that right?"

"Yes."

"What an engineering marvel."

"Hardly, Mr. Landry," she said. "It's a rather crude construction, actually."

"Nevertheless, I would love to see it."

Laurel's heart was in her throat, but she said, "Follow me."

She led them through the dining room, the kitchen, and out the back door. As she began moving aside offshoots of the honeysuckle, Landry asked, "Is the cellar accessible only through this door?"

"Yes. But the fragrance is so nice I can't bring myself to prune the vine."

"Not only is it lovely to smell, it's useful. It partially conceals the door."

She saw another flash of gold in Landry's jaw when he smiled. She pushed open the door. At the top of the stairs, she said, "Please be careful. These steps are steep and rickety."

"Why not turn on the light?" the mayor said.

"It doesn't work."

He reached up and yanked on the string. The recently installed electric light, which had been one of the projects on Irv's list, came on.

"Voilà!" Landry said.

Laurel tried to look surprised and pleased. "My father-in-law must have changed the bulb. I've been after him to do it."

She preceded the men down the stairs. When she reached the bottom, she turned to face them. "Mr. Landry, note the inexpert connection of the rock wall to the interior.

"And, Mayor Croft, you're quite right about the goods that Irv purchases for me. He's a fix-it man, you know. He's made me copper pots, which I use when stewing fruit for my pie fillings. The recipes call for pounds of sugar. I can barely keep up with my demand for pies, so, while fresh fruit is in season, I've made provision for the fall and winter months by canning." She raised her hands to her sides, inviting them to take a look.

The surrounding walls were lined with shelves laden with fruit jars of pie fillings.

FIFTY-ONE

H e would pick the hottest day of the year to do this, Thatcher thought as he guided his mount into a shallow creek, where he reined in the pinto gelding so he could drink. Thatcher uncapped the canteen of water he'd brought with him and drank from it. After draping its strap back over the pommel, he dismounted, took off his bandana, dipped it into the creek water, then wrung it out before tying it back around his neck. The coolness was a welcome relief from the blistering heat and scorching sun.

The pinto was one of Fred Barker's horses for rent. Thatcher had asked if he could take him out for a couple of hours. He also asked to borrow a rifle from Barker, telling him he wanted to get in some target practice. Barker hadn't hesitated to grant both requests, but had remarked that it was one hell of a hot day to be either shooting or taking a pleasure ride.

Thatcher wasn't going on this ride for the fun of it. He'd chosen this particular horse because of his stamina. He also needed a stolid horse, one not easily spooked. He didn't know anything about his destination, but he'd envisioned it being desolate, rugged terrain, and he'd been right.

He'd ridden cross-country out of town, but had kept the roads in sight, using them and landmarks he'd seen on the county map to guide him to a pass between two sizable hills. He'd found it right where it was supposed to be. Pointer's Gap.

The pinto finished drinking and raised his head. Thatcher patted him on his neck and swung up into the saddle. "Let's go take a look-see."

He adjusted his hat to block the late-afternoon sun from his eyes. As he came out the other side of the creek, he pushed the responsive horse into a gallop to cover the last quarter mile of level ground. Before daylight ran out, he wanted to explore as much of the gap as he could.

When he reached the twin inclines and the narrow pass cleaving them, he slowed the horse to a walk. He flushed a covey of quail from a grove of mesquite trees. He saw a jackrabbit in a losing race against a bobcat, a nanny goat and two kids that had likely discovered an opening in their owner's fence, and countless horned toads skittering across the crusty earth. A foot-long lizard dozing on a flat rock slid to the ground when he and the pinto clomped past.

The wildlife were at home in this inhospitable landscape. They belonged to it and in it. Thatcher was searching for something that didn't belong.

Just as the sun was setting, he spotted it.

Corrine hummed as she stirred the pot of beans suspended above the cookfire, which she'd let burn down to embers. The sun had set, but even though it wasn't full dark yet, flames would signal their location to anyone—lawmen or outlaws—who might be scouting the area.

Seated on side-by-side boulders several yards away from her, Irv and Ernie were watching Corrine, sharing a jar of moonshine, and discussing whether or not to risk distilling tonight.

"What do you think, Ernie?"

"Her beans are right tasty."

Irv growled with annoyance. "Not talking about her. What do you think about firing up the stills?"

Ernie took off his newsboy cap and fanned his face with it. "What's Laurel say?"

"She said to lay low at the first sign of trouble. Made me promise. But before that, she was expressing concern about our shortage caused by last night's shutdown."

"I hate to worry her about that."

"She'd hate to see us landed in jail or shot. So, tell me what you think?"

"I don't know, Irv. Might be imprudent."

"Where'd you get a word like imprudent?"

"My granddaddy used it whenever he got an itch on the back of his neck. Meant he sensed trouble. He'd say it might be imprudent to cook that night."

"Well, I wish he was here to tell us if his neck was itching. But since he ain't, what do you think?"

Ernie turned his gaze to Corrine. "If it was just you and me, I'd say to hell with it, let's take our chances. But it ain't just us two we've got to consider anymore."

Irv looked back and forth between Ernie and the girl, and clarity dawned. "Good God a'mighty. It's like that, is it?"

Ernie grinned. Rather stupidly, Irv thought. "She and me have took up."

"Hell, Ernie, you're old enough to be her—"

"Uncle. We figured it out."

"Have you figured out how you're going to support her?"

"She won't cost much. She don't take up hardly any room. She's little but carries her weight. Like an ant." He grabbed the jar of whiskey away from Irv, took a swig, and, keeping his eyes forward, said, "I know what's got your dander up. You're thinking how can I like her after she's been a whore."

"I don't judge the girl for that. You ought to know me better, Ernie. I just didn't see this coming. Took me by surprise, is all."

"You and me both," Ernie said, smiling in that stupid way again. "Me looking how I do, I never counted on having a woman. But

Corrine said she's no raving beauty, either. She looks fine to me, though. Appearances don't matter."

Irv shook his head and chuckled. "No, I guess they don't, or my Dorothy would never have taken to me."

"Beans are ready," Corrine called from across the clearing. "Are y'all gonna come eat or continue to talk about me like I ain't here?"

After gathering around the fire and filling their tin plates, Corrine said, "I got an opinion on whether or not we do a run." Snootily, she added, "If anybody's interested."

"Let's hear it," Irv said.

"How do you spell imprudent?" she asked Ernie.

As an aside to Irv, he said, "I'm helping her with her letters." Then to Corrine, "E-m-p-r-o-o-d-u-n-t. I think. It means—"

"I figured out what it means," she said. "And I think if your granddaddy was here, he'd say his neck was itching something fierce and we should lay low."

She tilted her head back and looked at the sky. "It was so hot today, the sky was almost white, hardly any blue. When it's this hot, people turn cranky, tempers get short. Things that've been simmering tend to boil over.

"If we don't cook tonight, Laurel will be disappointed we didn't make product. But if we got killed, she'd keel over herself. She's had enough people die on her. I don't want that lady to have more grief on account of me. That's my say."

"Irv?" Ernie said. "You get the last word."

He pondered it, then said, "I 'spect you're right, Corrine. After supper let's move to where we hid out last night. We'll be locked and loaded, prepared to defend ourselves, but let's hope we won't have to." He gazed off into the distance in the direction of town. "But I'm scared that no matter what we do, Laurel is going to come to grief."

"Jesus, Mary, and Joseph." Mike O'Connor's blasphemy echoed off the limestone wall of the cellar. "They came down here?"

"They invited themselves," Laurel said. "There was no graceful way to refuse. If we hadn't installed those false shelves, they would have caught me red-handed. All those evenings I spent stewing fruit and berries saved us."

It also had helped to have a father-in-law to whom nailing scrap lumber together to form shelving had been the work of only a few hours. The exertion had pained his wounded arm for days after, but he would be glad to hear that his effort had prevented a catastrophe.

"The mayor likes to push his weight around," Davy said. "He's a blowhard."

"Don't underestimate how sinister he is under all that bluster," Laurel said. "He frightened me, and so did Landry. At least with Croft you know where you stand. Landry lurked and listened, all the while smiling like a snake oil salesman."

Mike said, "Yeah, he's a sneaky one."

"How do you know Chester Landry?"

"We don't," Mike said, "but we've seen him around, usually at Lefty's. I know the smile you're talking about. Like he knows you're the one who farted."

Laurel said, "Thatcher warned me of him."

"When was this?"

"Oh, it's *Thatcher* now?"

Davy spoke over his brother, but Laurel addressed Mike's question. "That was Thatcher's purpose for coming here the night you saw him in the yard. He cautioned me about Landry. I didn't take him seriously. I should have. Croft made it clear that he and Landry are committed to squashing the Johnsons."

"Do they realize how many Johnsons there are?" Davy asked. "They're like cockroaches."

Musing aloud, Laurel said, "I wouldn't be surprised if Croft's and Landry's operation isn't just as large. They're more discreet, but ambitious and every bit as ruthless as any Johnson. I wouldn't be surprised to learn that they initiated all the trouble last night."

"Exactly what did Mr. Croft propose?"

"The upshot was that he and Landry have a pool of moonshiners producing for them, and they want me to become one of them. An 'or else' was implied."

"You're not thinking of joining them?"

"Absolutely not. I haven't worked this hard to pay middlemen ten percent. I suppose we should be flattered that they considered us enough of a threat to bother. Croft even admitted how good our liquor is and how well it sells."

"What happened after your grandstanding?"

"They complimented me on the pie business's expansion and left."

Mike frowned. "I don't like it. These men aren't fools, Laurel. They were too dignified to go tearing down shelving looking for your stockpile of 'shine. They backed off, but they're drawing up another plan of attack. Mark my words. Next time I doubt they'll be so polite."

"Then we've got to move our whiskey to another hiding place away from the house," Davy said. "Safer for the whiskey, safer for Laurel."

"That would require careful planning," she said. "First, we have to find a place, and we can't do that tonight. Not with the county already a powder keg. And forget delivering to Ranger tonight. It would be too risky."

"Don't worry about us," Davy said. "We know to be on the lookout."

"On the lookout for what?"

Mike smacked his twin on the side of his head. "You never could keep your friggin' mouth shut."

"On the lookout for *what*?"

Mike shot his brother a drop-dead look, then said to Laurel, "The other night, a truck loaded to the gills with whiskey was hijacked between here and Ranger. The poor bastard was dragged from his truck, blindfolded, manhandled into the woods, pushed to his knees, and told not to move or speak. He had a gun held to his head while all his whiskey was taken from his truck and put into the other vehicle.

"He never saw how many of them there were, but they made short work of it. When they were done, he thought he was dead for sure.

But he was threatened with the removal of body parts a man holds dear if he was seen on that road again. He was ordered to spread the warning to anyone whose ambition was to get rich selling 'shine in the boom towns. He was left there with a drained gas tank. But he lived to tell it."

Laurel said, "The Johnsons are hijacking now?"

Davy and Mike shared a look, then Davy said softly, "*He* was a Johnson."

"Lawmen don't terrorize," Mike said. "They would have identified themselves, confiscated the liquor, and placed him under arrest. Had to be a competitor who plans on taking over."

Laurel lowered herself into a chair at the kitchen table. Hearing of this on top of Thatcher's warnings this morning, and the visit from Croft and Landry this afternoon, left her rattled. She needed time to assimilate all this and plan her next course of action. But in the meantime, people for whom she was responsible were more vulnerable than she. "Lord, I hope our stills aren't cooking tonight. And you absolutely cannot make the trip to Ranger."

Mike said, "We're going."

"I forbid it."

"Our contact up there is waiting and watching for us," Davy said.

"He's not a patient man," Mike said.

Davy added, "Neither are his thirsty customers."

Laurel said, "Tonight they can get their whiskey from someone else."

"One of Croft's deliverymen would be waiting for just such an opportunity to wedge in. In which case, you'll be handing Croft exactly what he's after."

Davy nodded in agreement with Mike. "That would be bad for our business."

"So is being hijacked," she said.

Mike placed a hand on her shoulder. "We're making the delivery, as scheduled. Nothing to fret about. We've thought of a way to throw them off track."

Davy winked.

FIFTY-TWO

———◦◉◦———

Darkness had fallen by the time Thatcher returned to Barker's from Pointer's Gap. The auto garage was closed for the night. He needed to return Barker's borrowed rifle, but he was relieved that he wouldn't be delayed any longer than necessary.

He stabled the pinto and saw to it that he was well rewarded for his patience and endurance that afternoon. He stored the saddle and tack, went down the row of stalls to make sure that all the horses were content. Not all were. He calmed the restless ones with soft talk and stroking, then secured the stable with his own sixth sense of uneasiness.

Taking Barker's rifle with him, he walked across the bridge into town. Martin's Café was open, but there were few diners tonight. For the most part, downtown was closed and locked up, as though braced for a storm.

With reason. One was brewing. Distant lightning brightened the sky just above the horizon. Every surface, whether natural or manmade, radiated the heat it had absorbed during the day. The air felt charged by something more ominous than low atmospheric pressure.

Thatcher entered the boardinghouse and went upstairs unnoticed.

By a stroke of luck the third-floor bathroom was available. He made quick work of bathing and exchanging his dusty work clothes for his black suit. He buckled on his gun belt, pinned the deputy badge to the lapel of his coat, and took Barker's rifle with him.

In and out of the boardinghouse in under ten minutes, he set out on foot again. Only Bill's car was parked in front of the sheriff's department. Inside, he was alone but on the telephone.

Thatcher propped Barker's rifle against the wall beneath the gun rack, took off his fedora, and slumped tiredly in a chair. Bill completed his call with a "Thank you very much," and hung the earpiece in its cradle. "Dennis Kemp checks out," he said to Thatcher. "Hasn't missed a day of work since he began the job. He was there yesterday."

"Mrs. Kemp told you you'd be barking up the wrong tree." Thatcher looked toward the door that led into the cell block. "How is he?"

"Sullen when I took him his supper. The public defender hasn't made it in yet."

"Have you called him?"

"Considering all the arrests last night, I'm sure he had his hands full today with arraignment hearings. Driscoll can sulk till morning."

"How's Mrs. Amos doing?"

The sheriff's forehead wrinkled with concern. "Still ailing. If she's not better by tomorrow, I may take her to a doctor in Stephenville. Mrs. Cantor agreed to stay with her overnight if I can't get home."

"You're expecting more trouble?"

He waved his hand to indicate the empty office. "I've got every full-timer plus a dozen reserves like you patrolling in pairs. I want to keep a lid on things if we can. Vain hope, probably."

Thatcher drew his long legs in, leaned forward, and placed his elbows on his knees. "You've got plenty of trouble right in here, Bill."

He reached into his pocket and pulled out a strip of cotton fabric roughly six inches in length and three inches wide. One side was flat, the other gathered. The weave was unraveling at both ends. The cloth had been weather-beaten, but under its coating of dust, the scarlet color was vibrant.

Thatcher set the piece of cloth on the edge of the sheriff's desk. He spoke softly so not to be overheard by the man in the cell. "I went exploring this afternoon and found this. I recognized it right off. When I talked to Mrs. Driscoll, she was wearing an apron made out of material printed with red and yellow apples. It had a red ruffled border."

Through the window, Thatcher saw a lightning bolt, closer this time, but it took the thunder a count of seven to reach them. The storm was headed this way but wasn't right on top of them yet.

Bill seemed not to notice the weather. He was fixated on the fabric scrap. "Where'd you find it?"

"Pointer's Gap. Caught between some rocks, piled up, but not by God or Mother Nature. They'd been stacked."

"Pointer's Gap. Where Gabe took his missus picnicking."

Thatcher scoffed. "The nearest I came to finding a picnic spot was a stream off the north fork of the Paluxy. No deeper than a foot at its deepest. It had a ripple, but not what I'd call a current. A few scraggly trees along its banks. If he was trying to romance his wife with a picnic, a prettier spot would have been in his own shady backyard."

"When Bernie told us that Gabe had taken her there, I remember thinking that same thing."

"That stream is about a quarter mile from the gap, and between them is wasteland. If he took her out there, it definitely wasn't to picnic."

Bill acknowledged that with a frown. "How'd you get out there?"

"Horseback."

"That's six, eight miles each way."

"I'm used to it. Or was," he said, wincing as he shifted in his chair. "I may be a bit saddle sore tomorrow."

Both of them smiled, but they quickly became serious again. Bill asked, "Did you disturb the pile of rocks?"

"No, just tugged that piece of cloth from between them. It ripped when I pulled, so there's more of it under there."

"Could you find the place again?"

"With no problem."

Bill smoothed his hand over his mustache a few times. "Gabe doesn't have a horse that I know of. How would he have gotten her out there?"

"There's a road, more like a trail, that comes in from the southwest on the other side of the hill. I figure he took care of Corrine at Lefty's—"

"With Mrs. Driscoll dead in his car?"

Thatcher shrugged. "This is just my guess, Bill."

"Go on."

"When he finished up at Lefty's, he drove out, circled back to the gap on that lonely road, carried her body the rest of the way until he found a suitable spot. Maybe he stumbled upon a natural depression, maybe he dug one. But he buried her and stacked those rocks on top. It was dark, so he missed that." He pointed to the remnant of ruffle. "As hiding a body goes, he chose a good spot. If that cloth had been dull in color, I would've missed it."

"Good work, Thatcher."

"Knowing what you're likely to find under those rocks, it doesn't feel good. Not good at all."

Bill waited a beat before continuing to theorize. "On his way back into town, Gabe's conscience grabbed hold."

"Or terror of being caught."

"Either way, he realized the magnitude of what he'd done and headed to his mistress for solace. Then what, Thatcher? Did Miss Blanchard know he'd killed Mila, or not? Did she calm him down and coach him on what to do next, what to say and how to perform when questioned?"

"Mrs. Kemp doesn't think so."

"She could be lying. She may know all too well that Norma was complicit."

"Could be."

"But you don't think so?"

"If Norma had lived, maybe her sister would've lied to cover for her. But why would she lie for her now?"

"To protect baby nephew Arthur from disgrace? Hell, I don't know." Sighing, he covered his face with both hands and pressed his middle fingers into his eye sockets, his weariness evident. "I don't know anything anymore."

"Two things you know," Thatcher said.

Bill lowered his hands and looked across at him.

"One. Norma Blanchard can't be held accountable even if she masterminded the murder. Second thing, you've finally got a piece of evidence. It's not a decomposed body, but that apron trim might be enough to bring Driscoll to his knees."

"He's proven to be mule-headed."

"Won't hurt to try."

Bill took the strip of cloth with him as he entered the cell block. Thatcher followed him to the last cell, where Driscoll was reclined on the cot, eyes closed, pale hands clasped over his stomach. "Unless you have a defense lawyer with you, go away."

"You'll want to see this, Gabe."

Thatcher and Bill waited him out, and his curiosity got the better of him. He opened his eyes and levered himself up on his elbows.

Bill dangled the strip of red cloth. "Recognize this?"

"No."

"Thatcher did." Bill explained how Thatcher remembered seeing the ruffle on Mila's apron.

Driscoll shrugged. "She wore an apron every day of her life."

"In the kitchen while baking shortbread," Bill said. "Around the house as she was dusting the furniture. But why would she wear one to Pointer's Gap?"

Mention of the landmark sparked a stunned reaction. His gaze darted to Thatcher, then back to Bill. "What was he doing out there?"

Bill ignored the question. "He found this caught in a pile of rocks. What do you know about it, Gabe?"

"Nothing."

"Explain to me how a ruffle off Mrs. Driscoll's apron got stuck between two rocks all the way out there in no-man's-land."

"Why are you asking me? Why don't you ask *him*?" He came off the cot and charged the cell bars, shoving his hand through two of them and grabbing Thatcher by his necktie. "Do you really think he just wandered out there and accidentally found this? Where's your common sense, sheriff? He knew where to find it, because he buried Mila's body out there. It was him all along. Don't you see?"

A crack of thunder startled them all. Driscoll actually let go of Thatcher's tie and fell back a step away from the bars, as though they'd suddenly been electrified.

The first clap was followed by a second, then a third. And then a salvo. Simultaneously, Thatcher and Bill realized that it wasn't thunder.

It was gunfire.

FIFTY-THREE

———◦◉◦———

Chester Landry watched from the shadows as Laurel Plummer bade the O'Connor brothers goodbye. Even from this distance, he could tell she was anxious about sending them out tonight. She touched each of them on the arm, and clung for a moment, like a mother reluctant to wave her children off to school for the first time.

Final instructions were issued and goodbyes said, and the pair drove away in their truck. From the outside, it looked like a rattletrap held together with baling wire and crossed fingers.

But as it drove past Landry, he was close enough to feel the vibration of the new engine the twins recently had had installed. The swap-out had been done in a barn on a farm that had been foreclosed on years before. The mechanics, who'd helped themselves to the empty space, catered to moonshiners and bootleggers who were trying to outdo, or at least to equal, the horsepower had by lawmen, government agents, and each other.

He wondered if Mrs. Plummer was aware of the new oomph under the battered hood of the O'Connors' truck. He would guess she wasn't. The O'Connors were too cocksure of themselves by far. Brimming with piss and vinegar, they took needless chances, seemed to thrive on excitation, and routinely flirted with calamity.

But he couldn't fault them. He reveled in risk-taking.

Lights were on inside, affording him a view through the window into the kitchen. He watched Mrs. Plummer drink a glass of tap water at the sink. Then she moved about the room nervously, picking up this or that, setting it down, opening a cabinet door only to close it without putting anything in or taking anything out.

He saw her actually wring her hands. At one point, she lifted her pocketbook off a peg adjacent to the back door, as though she were about to leave, then changed her mind. She seemed troubled and restless, feeling compelled to do something, but unsure of what she should do.

His timing was perfect.

He emerged from the shadows and crossed the yard. The honeysuckle vine brushed his shoulder as he neared the back door. He knocked, but stood to one side, keeping himself concealed in the darkness until she appeared behind the screen.

He stepped into the light and tipped his bowler hat to her. "Mrs. Plummer."

Her lips tightened with dislike. "What are you doing here?"

Her hand moved to her side, where she no doubt secreted a firearm in the pocket of her skirt. Probably a Derringer. A whore's pistol. Small but lethal if fired at close range.

"May I come in?"

"No, you may not."

"You sound adamant."

"I am."

"Why?"

"It would be improper."

Amused by her hypocritical stance on propriety, he said, "Improper because your father-in-law isn't at home? He's away this evening?"

She realized that she'd trapped herself into admitting she was by herself, but rather than quail, she drew herself up taller. She looked above and beyond him at the lightning that streaked the sky.

"It's about to storm," she said over the boom of thunder that rattled the windows of her house. "You wouldn't want to get wet, so leave now and don't come back. You and Mr. Croft were fishing in the wrong pond today. In any case, I said everything I had to say. Now if you'll—"

"That's what I wanted to talk to you about. Our visit today." He gave her a look of rehearsed chagrin. "You have every right to be miffed."

"Don't talk down to me."

He held up his hand in a pacifying gesture. "Mr. Croft often gets carried away. His strident manner is a character flaw which I've pointed out to him on numerous occasions. Sadly, to no avail. His overbearing approach to you was tactless and clumsy. He came on like a buffalo when a swan would have been more effective. It's little wonder to me that you turned him down."

"Did he send you to make amends?"

"No, I came entirely on my own."

"I don't want your apology. I want you to leave."

"But I didn't come to apologize."

"To do what, then? Ask me to reconsider your deal?"

"No," he said smoothly, "I came to offer you a better one."

His statement startled her, but not as much as the gunshot that punctuated it.

Numerous blasts followed, the rapid popping sounding like the finale of a fireworks display.

Even before the barrage stopped, Laurel stunned him by shoving open the screen door. She shouldered him out of her way and began running in the direction from which the shots had come.

Landry went after her, shouting her name.

She didn't even slow down.

Bill locked the door between the office and the cell block while Thatcher retrieved Barker's rifle and took another from the rack for Bill. Moving swiftly and without a single word being spoken between them, they exited the building and got into Bill's car.

While Thatcher loaded and checked the weapons, the sheriff drove at top speed through downtown. Main Street was already filling up with curiosity-seekers streaming in the direction of the apparent shootout. Thatcher noticed that one man in the crowd still had his napkin from the café tucked into his collar.

Bill shouted at the onlookers and angrily waved them out of his way. He used his horn to bleat out warnings for them to move aside or get bowled over. Bill gave the car more gas as it trundled across the bridge.

On the far side of it, they rounded a bend to find the road blocked by a disabled truck. Both doors stood open. The radiator was spewing steam like a teakettle.

The truck had been riddled by bullets. The driver had made it out. He lay sprawled in the road. The passenger was still in his seat.

"Jesus." Bill used the handbrake to bring his car to a skidding stop. Thatcher, noticing movement in the underbrush to his right, was out of the car before inertia rocked it to rest. He leaped across the ditch in pursuit.

The woods were as dark as midnight. Bursts of lightning only served to momentarily blind him. But the brilliant flashes followed by complete darkness were reminiscent of nighttime battles, and he'd had plenty of experience with those. Conditioned reflexes took over. Rifle up, he ran on, dodging trees, ducking low branches, doing his best to avoid pitfalls in the undergrowth.

Ahead of him, men were shouting to each other. The words were indistinct, but their connotation was urgency. If they kept up the racket, they'd lead Thatcher straight to them. But then he heard the sound of an auto motor sputtering to life.

"Fuck, fuck." He pushed himself harder, but by the time he reached the road, all he saw of the retreating car was the wink of its taillights as it disappeared around a curve. Any attempt to run it down on foot would be futile.

He didn't even break stride as he reversed direction and ran back toward the site of an evident ambush. He cleared the woods and jumped the ditch again, then paused to catch his breath and take in the scene.

The crowd of onlookers had increased in number. Two more sheriff's department vehicles were parked on either side of Bill's car. Deputies had divided up. A few were grouped around the man lying face-up on the pavement. Others had formed a semicircle in the open passenger door.

Harold and another deputy Thatcher didn't know had the tailgate down and were shining flashlights into the back of the truck.

Thatcher lowered the rifle and made his way over to Bill, who was kneeling at the side of the man lying in the road. It was one of the O'Connor twins, although Thatcher couldn't have said which. He was bleeding from several wounds, but his lips were moving, and Bill was listening intently.

"His brother's dead." Thatcher turned. Harold elaborated without being asked to. "The twins came around the bend there, caught fire from the trees on both sides of the road. They didn't stand a chance. Somebody wanted to make a point."

"Whoever it was came through the woods from the road that parallels this one." Thatcher pointed. "I chased them, but they had too good of a head start. Didn't see how many, but all of them fit into one vehicle."

Harold nodded, then said, "Hell of it is, if this had to do with the illegal liquor trade, they got the wrong guys. All they were hauling was a bunch of pies and jars of fruit fillings."

"Get away from me!"

The voice was shrill but Thatcher recognized it instantly and spun around. Laurel was struggling to escape the grasping hands of Chester Landry. Thatcher was in motion before he even thought about it. He swung the rifle barrel to waist level and ran toward them, shouting, "Let her go!"

Laurel managed to wrestle herself free, but Landry reached for her again, catching hold of the back of her skirt and bringing her up short. She whirled around and slugged him in the face with her fist.

"Landry!" Thatcher yelled. "Let go of her!"

Seeing Thatcher bearing down on him, and recognizing the hellfire he represented, Landry immediately released Laurel and ran for his life, disappearing into the woods on the other side of the road.

Over his shoulder, Thatcher hollered to Harold, "Go after him." The deputy took off running.

Thatcher ran to close the remaining distance between him and Laurel, but she was on an undeterred path toward the truck, and she was in a crazed state.

Thatcher overcame her and grabbed hold of her arm with his free hand. She turned her head and looked up at him, wild-eyed and frantic. "That's the twins' truck. I heard the shooting."

She jerked free of his hold and continued on. Thatcher called her name, and, when he caught her again, they engaged in a tussle not unlike the one she'd been in with Landry.

"Laurel, stop it. Laurel!" He finally got her to stand still. "One is wounded but alive. The other is gone."

It took several seconds for the message to sink in, then she threw back her head and wailed, "Nooooo."

He tried to draw her to him, but she took in the badge, the gun belt around his hips, the rifle he still carried. When it all registered, she threw off his hands to free herself. "Damn you!" she yelled as she ran backward. "Stay away from me."

Realizing the conclusion she'd drawn, he said, "No, Laurel. It wasn't me. Wasn't us. This was—"

But he was talking to the empty space where she'd been standing. She knocked onlookers aside as she plowed through them to get to where Bill still knelt beside the wounded man. She gave another wail when she saw him and dropped to her knees.

Harold huffed up to Thatcher. "He was too fast. I lost him in the dark."

With cold determination, Thatcher said, "Don't worry. I'll find him."

———

Hiram Johnson sat in a filthy, upholstered armchair with his bare, bloated right foot propped on a stool. An open jar of moonshine was on the windowsill, along with a flyswatter, both within easy reach. A Bible lay open on his lap.

Mayor Bernard Croft had never seen such a disgusting sight in his life and doubted he ever would. The old man's rotting foot stank to high heaven. It was as though the walls of this house seeped the rancid odor of generations of Johnsons. The unmoving air smelled of dirty hair, dirty feet, decayed teeth, tobacco-laced expectorant, and baby shit.

The foulness of it all sickened Bernie. He could barely keep his dinner down.

Of course he'd known more or less what he was letting himself in for when he'd requested this meeting. He'd sent Hennessy to parley with Hiram, requesting an assemblage of the clan so that Bernie could address them collectively. Hennessy had been instructed to stress that Bernie would be assuming all the risks, because the meeting would take place on Hiram's turf.

Bernie would be walking into the lion's den, but the goal was to end the strife between his faction and the Johnsons. Give and take. Negotiation. Compromise. A fair division of territories. The goal being to end this silly and counterproductive war.

They had congregated. The house was overflowing with representatives of the myriad branches of the family. They had listened to Bernie's impassioned speech. It was time to make his final pitch and close the deal.

He stood before Hiram. "This feud would eventually play itself out, Mr. Johnson. You've lived long enough, been a businessman long enough, to know that ultimately things work themselves out and life returns to the way it was before.

"But in the meantime, this destructive bickering costs us both revenue. People get hurt. People die. It's a waste. If we stop fighting each other, we can devote ourselves to fighting our common enemy, which is this new goddamn federal law." He ended on a high note that elicited guffaws from many.

Not, however, from the old man, who spat into his coffee can. "You can have Ranger," Hiram said. "But I want Breckenridge and any other boom towns that spring up between here and the Red River. You can have anything south of here."

"There won't be any boom towns south of here because there's no oil south of here. Not for hundreds of miles. As you well know."

"West then," Hiram said. "Show him the map."

A man in greasy overalls stepped forward and passed Bernie a faded map. He studied the lines that had been drawn on it to demarcate territories. "This is attractive to me. They're already drilling out there west of Abilene, around Odessa."

"So more than fair, I think. Take it or leave it." He spat again.

"If I take it, it amounts to a cease-fire. Agreed?"

"Agreed."

"And it goes into effect immediately?"

Hiram nodded.

"Splendid." Bernie stepped forward, right hand extended. With an evil gleam in his eye, the rotting son of a bitch wiped tobacco spittle off his lip before clutching Bernie's hand. Despite his revulsion, Bernie gave him an enthusiastic handshake.

"I was so optimistic about the outcome of this meeting that I brought you a gift, Mr. Johnson." He signaled Hennessy, who'd been waiting out on the porch. "I've brought you a case of Kentucky bourbon, direct from my most trusted bootlegger in Dallas and Fort Worth."

Oohs and ahhs of appreciation rippled through the compacted gathering of bodies as the case was carried in and set on the floor in front of that putrid foot.

"Enjoy." Bernie's leave-taking was unceremonious. It was barely even noticed. Hiram was already swilling from a bottle of the whiskey. His relatives were greedily converging around the case.

Together Bernie and Hennessy walked toward the town car. Looking back over his shoulder at the party underway, Hennessy asked, "How long before the poison works?"

"I've decided it takes too long. Did you bring along some of your toys?"

"Always, boss."

Bernie grinned as he climbed into the driver's seat. "Give me ten minutes to get to the highway, then light her up."

FIFTY-FOUR

Bernie entered his house through the front door, and automatically locked it behind him.

He had driven himself from Hiram's house to the intersection with the highway, where he'd gotten to enjoy the fireball. When Hennessy caught up with him, the Irishman had taken his traditional place in the driver's seat while Bernie got into the back and savored his success during the trip into town. The Johnsons not blown to smithereens in the blast would have been cooked to well done in the fire.

Both he and Hennessy were confident that they hadn't been followed. Hennessy had waited to be certain that Bernie made it safely inside his front door, then struck out on foot. He lodged in a seedier part of town. He didn't fear that on his walk home anyone would be fool enough to accost him.

Through the side window on the front door, Bernie checked the street one last time. It was empty, nothing moving save for Hennessy, disappearing into the downpour.

Tomorrow, when Mayor Croft was told the shocking news of the conflagration, he would publicly attribute it to a lightning strike. The old Johnson place would have been a tinder box, he would say.

The poor souls inside, a great number of the legendary clan including the patriarch, had stood little chance of escaping the flames.

For the town's biweekly gazette, he would wax poetic about the tragedy. He would milk it for all it was worth. But now, as he collapsed his umbrella and hung his hat on the coat tree, he wanted to cackle with delight over his triumph. He stepped into the parlor and reached for the light switch.

"Leave it."

Bernie fell back against the doorjamb and clapped his hand over his heart. "Jesus, Chester."

"Why, Mr. Mayor. You jumped like someone with a guilty conscience."

The darkness was relieved only by light from a streetlamp shining through the front window curtains. Bernie's eyes adjusted. Landry was sitting with his typical indolence in an easy chair, legs crossed.

He said, "Where have you and Hennessy been off to tonight?"

Bernie went over to a cabinet and took out a bottle of bourbon and two glasses. "A better question would be what are you doing inside my house at this hour, sitting in the dark?" He poured an inch of bourbon into each glass and carried one over to Landry.

"Thank you." He clinked his glass against Bernie's but didn't drink from it.

Bernie settled himself on the divan facing Landry's chair. "Well?"

Landry propped his drinking glass on his knee and stared into it for a moment. "My welcome in your little burg has worn thin, Bernie."

"You're leaving?"

"Tonight."

Bernie's eyebrows shot up. "Tonight? How long do you plan to be away?"

"Forever. I'm severing our partnership. As of now."

This was an unexpected turn, but not at all disappointing to Bernie. Landry's welcome had been wearing thin with him, too. Initially, he'd needed a man like Landry to grease the skids into the bootlegging trade.

But Bernie's own contacts in the cities were well established by now. The value of Landry's usefulness had decreased. It certainly wasn't worth the percentage he demanded. If Landry wanted out, Bernie wasn't at all sorry to bid him farewell.

Nevertheless, he attempted to look bemused. "Why?"

"Bad business practices."

"Whose?"

"Yours."

It was an effort for Bernie to conceal his outrage. "I don't ask for or require the approval of a slick dandy like you, but I am curious. Can you give me an example of the business practices you oppose?"

"Gladly. For example, with a little courting, a little finessing, Laurel Plummer might have been won over. Instead, you bullied her. That tactic didn't flatter you. It didn't cast a favorable light on me, either, which I resent. It also failed. Colossally."

"She'll come around."

"Oh, I seriously doubt that. Not after you had her errand boys ambushed and shot all to hell."

Bernie snickered. "How did the duo fare? Did they survive?"

"I don't know. I was spotted near the scene. Although I'm not proud to admit it, I ran." He swirled the whiskey in his glass, the only sign of his simmering anger. "You took that action upon yourself, Bernie. You executed that ambush without consulting me."

"Because you would have wavered when action was called for."

"I would have acted with more discretion, as I did with Randy. The problem was solved, but it was neat. Nobody's curiosity was aroused."

"We needed to make a splash," Bernie said. "We needed to do something that would get the lovely widow's attention."

"Well, you succeeded at that. But this bloody display will also draw the attention of people who aren't so lovely. Bad for business, Bernie. Bad for business. Because now, you're going to be in the bull's-eye of a crackdown, beginning with a thorough investigation by local law."

"I've made Bill Amos a eunuch, and his department is a joke."

"His newly appointed deputy isn't what I'd call a jolly sort."

"Hutton? I'm not scared of him."

"Another example of your foolishness."

"How dare—"

"If Hutton doesn't give you pause, the Texas Rangers are even less jocular than he is. The governor is a colorful character, granted. But he's been known to send in troops to help curtail a lucrative bootleg trade. When they all come gunning for the ringleader in this area of the state, I want to be far removed from you."

He set his glass on a small table at his elbow, then stood. "I let myself in through the back door. I'll go out the same way."

Bernie came to his feet. "You smug prick. Do you expect me to believe that you're just walking away, leaving money on the table, retiring?"

Landry stopped and turned back. "Did I say that?" He flashed the sly grin that Bernie had come to detest. "I've never met a woman who didn't love shoes. And there are women everywhere, who have men in their lives who enjoy a drink." The grin widened to reveal his gold tooth. "I won't have any trouble drumming up business." Then he whispered, "Watch your back, Bernie."

Thatcher didn't see Chester Landry's car among those parked at the boardinghouse, but he didn't let that stop him from taking the front steps two at a time. The house was dark except for a few dim lights providing barely enough illumination for him to see his way up the staircase. He knew Landry occupied room number four on the second floor.

He knocked. Silence. He knocked again and put his ear to the door. He heard nothing.

Across the hall a door opened and a head popped out. He recognized the boarder, but didn't recall his name. He said, "He's not there. He left this afternoon."

"Did he say where he was going?"

"Nope. Just cleared out his stuff—"

"Cleared out? You mean he moved out?"

"Lock, stock, and barrel. Took all his shoe samples. Seemed to be on short notice."

Thatcher twisted the doorknob, but it was locked. He jerked on it harder. When it didn't give, he backed up a few steps.

"I don't believe Mrs. May would approve—"

Thatcher kicked in the door. The room was empty. The bed had already been stripped of sheets. Replacement bedding and a bath towel were folded and stacked, awaiting the next boarder.

Thatcher searched every drawer in the bureau, opened the closet, checked under the bed. He flipped back the mattress, but there was nothing beneath it except rusty bed springs.

"What the hell do you think you're doing?"

The landlady was standing in the open doorway, hands on her hips. She looked like a hag during daytime. The nighttime variant was worse.

Nevertheless, Thatcher moved in on her. "Did Landry say where he was going?"

"No, and I didn't ask," she said. "Ain't my business, is it?"

"He's moved out for good? He's not coming back?"

"Not your business, neither."

Thatcher tapped the badge on his lapel. "Sheriff Amos will disagree. Should I send him over to talk to you?"

She folded her housecoat closer around her and jutted out her pointy chin. "He said he was taking over a new sales territory and wouldn't be back. Paid me for a few extra days because he'd failed to give me notice. Packed up his automobile and headed out. That's all I know."

"What time did he leave?"

"I can't—"

"What *time*?"

"Four-thirty. Thereabouts. He interrupted me while I was busy setting up the sideboard." She sniffed. "Which I didn't appreciate one bit."

Thatcher stepped back into the hallway and addressed all the boarders who now were watching curiously from their open doorways, as they had the night he'd been taken into custody. Some shrank back. "Anybody know where Chester Landry was going? Did he ever say where he was from?"

"All I ever heard was Dallas," one said. That was followed with murmurs of agreement.

"He ever mention family?"

No one answered, but one asked, "Wha'd he do?"

Thatcher said, "If anyone hears anything from him, or about him, come get me. Sorry to have woken you up." He jogged down the stairs and out the front door.

Five minutes later, he stood dripping rainwater in the waiting room of Dr. Perkins's clinic, explaining to Bill what he'd learned. "Landry had prepared to run even before the ambush."

"Leading you to believe he may have been instrumental in that?"

"He might have planned it, but he didn't participate."

In unison Thatcher and the sheriff turned toward Laurel, who'd spoken from the chair that Patsy Kemp had occupied days before. Laurel looked small and defenseless, with shoulders hunched, hugging her elbows.

She said, "He was at my back door when the shooting started."

Bill walked over to her. "What was Chester Landry doing at your back door?"

She was about to answer, when Dr. Perkins came out of the interior room. His lab coat was bloodied. Laurel shot to her feet. He didn't keep them in suspense. "My nurse and I successfully removed two bullets. The third went through his lower left abdomen. I've done what I can. He's still with us."

"Is he out of danger?" Laurel asked.

"No, Mrs. Plummer. He survived the surgery, but he's not in the clear." Seeing her distress, he said, "But he's young and strong. His vitals are good. If he can stave off infection, he has a good chance of recovery. Men with far worse wounds have recovered."

Laurel covered her mouth and took a deep breath. "Does he know about Davy?"

"He demanded that I tell him," Bill said to her. "It was just before he lost consciousness, so it may not have sunk in."

"It did," Dr. Perkins said, looking bleak. "He came to and was most fretful over it before we sedated him."

Laurel gave a soft sob. "Can I see him?"

Dr. Perkins looked her over. Her dress, shoes, and stockings were spattered with mud and streaked with Mike's blood. "He's still out cold, Mrs. Plummer. He won't know you're there. And, uh, infection is a major concern. Tomorrow would be better."

Only then did she seem to realize how bedraggled she looked and the reason for the doctor's hesitancy to let her near his patient. But she stood proud and composed. "I'll be here first thing in the morning."

"I need to get back." Dr. Perkins retreated and shut the door.

The three of them filed out of the waiting area, Laurel leading the way. Bill and Thatcher had conferred briefly at the scene of the ambush before Thatcher had gone in search of Landry. At the time, the sheriff had dispatched men to comb the woods on both sides of the road in search of clues. They recovered dozens of shell casings from numerous weapons, but nothing else.

Bill had remarked then that he hoped the rain would hold off until daylight tomorrow when a more thorough search could be made of the woods and the road on which the getaway car had sped away.

Thatcher could tell how disheartened Bill was when they reached the exit of the office building to see that the lightning and thunder had moved east, but a hard rain was being driven sideways by a strong wind.

"So much for tire tracks and footprints," Bill said as he motioned Laurel and Thatcher toward his car. They dashed through the rain and piled in.

When they reached Laurel's house, it was in total darkness. "Thank you for the ride." She opened the backseat door herself, got out, and ran toward the house.

Thatcher watched her go inside, then turned his head and looked at Bill.

Bill gave him a knowing smile. "Busy day in store for tomorrow. Gabe Driscoll. Now this ambush with one man dead. You're only a reserve, Thatcher. I've got no claim on you. But I'd sure appreciate your help."

"I'll stop by the stable and see if Fred can spare Roger to tend to the horses tomorrow."

"Early then."

Thatcher nodded, got out, and ran through the torrent to Laurel's door.

FIFTY-FIVE

The electricity was out in Laurel's house. When Thatcher entered the kitchen through the back door, she was lighting a kerosene lamp. She blew out the match and situated the glass chimney.

She said, "You know what's funny?"

He propped Barker's rifle against the wall and hung his dripping hat on the wall peg. "I can't think of a thing."

"Davy would've been the first to laugh over being killed for a truckload of pies and fruit fillings. It was his and Mike's idea. They'd cooked it up even before I told them about Mayor Croft and Chester Landry visiting today. I was—"

"Hold on. The mayor and Landry came here?"

"To try to coerce me into joining their...I don't know the word. Syndicate? Did you know the mayor is a bootlegger? Anyway, they showed up at my front door this afternoon."

In a thready voice, she pieced together broken sentences to relate what the pair had proposed. Thatcher wasn't surprised by any of it except for Bernie Croft's brashness. "Who did the talking?" he asked.

"The mayor."

Up till now Croft had used his political office as cover. If he was stepping out from behind it, he must be feeling damned confident that he couldn't be touched. That was a troubling prospect.

"When they left," Laurel was saying, "I had the shakes. I knew I hadn't seen the last of them. But I didn't think their reprisal would come this soon or be so...deadly."

Tears filled her eyes. "When I told the twins about that visit and the reason behind it, they admitted that a truck had been hijacked just a few days ago." She described the incident to Thatcher.

"I suppose the only reason they let that Johnson man live was so he could put his family and the rest of us on notice. Nevertheless, the twins were keen on going tonight."

"But without whiskey."

She nodded. "They weren't selling just my whiskey. They had been dealing with another moonshiner, who's up closer to Ranger. They'd bought several crates from him and had hidden them someplace accessible, so the product would be on hand when they needed it.

"In view of this recent hijacking, they had counted on selling what was in that stockpile, but would continue to make the trip from here to there with pies only. In the event they were intercepted, the joke would be on whoever had stopped them.

"Their thinking was that after they were caught with only pies as cargo, they would be left alone. You see? Isn't that just like a prank the two of them would pull?"

She gave a dry, forced laugh, and she began to quiver like a shell-shocked trooper on the verge of cracking.

He spoke her name quietly, and when she'd blinked him into focus, he asked about Landry. "Tell me what happened with him."

"He must have been watching the house, because he came to the back door almost immediately after the twins left. He said Mayor Croft had been overbearing and tactless, and that he didn't blame me for turning them down. He said he had come, not at Croft's behest, but on his own, to make me a better offer. I don't know what he was going to propose, because that's when the shooting started. The instant I heard the gunfire, I had a premonition, a sick feeling."

She touched her stomach. "I took off running. Landry came after me, and caught up. From there, you know. You saw."

"The coward ran and got away."

"Mike was lying in the street, and Davy was dead. They made such easy targets as they came out of the curve in the road." She appeared to want to say more, but her throat seized up. She had difficulty swallowing.

"Laurel, it wasn't lawmen who ambushed them."

She looked down at the floor, but he didn't think it registered with her that the puddle around her muddy shoes had been formed by her dripping clothes.

"Sheriff Amos called it sabotage," she said. "Moonshiners mistaking the twins for rivals. And they were. They *were*. For me." She pressed her fist to her chest. "I let them go tonight, knowing the danger."

She covered her face with her hands and began to sob. "Irv kept telling me it wasn't a lark. You warned me. But, no, I was conceited and stubborn, and thought that I was above the fray, that I couldn't be touched. And because of that vanity, Davy died."

Sensing that she was about to collapse where she stood, Thatcher crossed over to her and enfolded her in his arms. "The O'Connors knew they were playing a dangerous game. They knew the risks."

"But it's my fault."

"No, Laurel. They loved the thrill. With or without you, they would have become part of this trade."

"I tried my best to talk them out of going tonight. Honestly, Thatcher, I did. But they were bent on it. If Mike lives, he will never get over losing his brother. Never." Her forehead dropped against his sternum and she began to sob harder. "I can't do this anymore. Even if I wanted to continue. I can't. I can't risk another life."

"You've got to stop risking your own." He scooped her up into his arms and headed for the staircase.

Feebly, she pushed against his chest. "Let me down."

"You're sopping wet. Your teeth are chattering, and you're about to drop."

He carried her into her bedroom, set her on her feet, and propped her against the wall. He went around the room pulling down the window shades and lit the lamp on her dresser, keeping the flame low. He folded back the bedcovers.

She hadn't moved from where he'd left her. For the longest time, they stood facing, staring into each other's eyes.

"You're fragile right now," he said. "I promised I would never take advantage of you, and I meant it. I'm putting you to bed. If you don't want me in there with you, say so now."

She didn't move or speak.

Keeping his eyes locked with hers, he reached down and untied the thong holding his holster against his thigh, then unbuckled the gun belt and set it in a chair. His coat was wet. It clung, but he worked himself out of it. He flipped his braces off his shoulders, opened several buttons of his shirt, then impatiently pulled it over his head. Shoes and socks went next. He unbuttoned his fly but stopped there.

He knelt in front of her and slipped off her shoes. Sliding his hands up her legs under her skirt, he found her garters, rolled down her stockings, and peeled them off her chilled feet.

When he stood up, he reached behind her head, pulled out what few pins remained in her hair, and dropped them to the floor. As her hair tumbled down her back, he combed his fingers through it.

"Thatcher, I—"

With abject misery, he moaned, "Please don't shy from me, Laurel."

"I'm not. It's just..." In a purely feminine, self-conscious gesture, she touched the tear tracks on her cheeks, then moved her hand down to her collar, which she drew closed over her throat. "I'm not very tidy."

His heart thumped with restored anticipation. Her voice was husky from weeping, and so seductive he wanted to trap it inside her mouth and taste it. "I don't need you tidy. I need you now."

He placed his hands flat against the wall on either side of her head, lowered his, and used his nose to nudge open the collar she'd closed. He pressed an open-mouth kiss on the side of her neck, nibbled up the slender column of it to her ear where he breathed, "I won't hold back."

"Please don't. Make me forget."

"What?"

"Everything."

That sighed consent unleashed a primal urge in him to claim, possess, mate. He came up against her and covered her face with kisses, then slanted his mouth over hers. He ate from it, unable to draw as much from it as he was yearning for, greedy for. He went back and back and back for more. He slid his hands from the wall to her breasts. There was no corset to prevent him from massaging and reshaping them. She leaned into the caresses in unshy offering.

Somehow he managed to keep their mouths fused as he pulled her blouse free of her waistband and unbuttoned it. The buttons were small and round and devils to work free of the wet material, but at last he got them undone, and her blouse was off.

He skimmed his hands over her front, feeling the warmth of her skin through her chemise. He compressed the tips of her breasts between his fingers and heard her breath flutter around his name as she sighed it.

After two failed attempts, he found the fastening of her skirt and undid it. The skirt, weighted with rainwater, crumpled to the floor. Laurel stepped out of it, leaving her in only her chemise and underpants.

He took her hands and tugged her forward as he backed up to the bed and sat down on the side of it, then wrapped her in his arms and pressed his face into the giving softness of her middle. Hands splayed over her back, he held her there and breathed her in.

Then he drew her down onto the bed, turned her to lie on her back, and, following her down, half covered her body as he kissed her. She clasped his head, digging her fingers into his hair.

His hands moved over her, charting the dips and swells of her body until he reached the hem of her chemise. He bunched it to her waist, pushed it up over her breasts, and pulled it over her head. She lifted her hair free of it, tossed it over the side of the bed, and lay back, drawing him back down to her.

He kissed her breasts, suckled them in turn as he stroked the plain of her stomach with the backs of his fingers, moving a little lower with each brush of skin over skin until he encountered the row of tiny buttons on her underpants. He toyed with them, plucked at them, then popped them free. He worked the garment over her hips, down her thighs, past her knees, and off.

The hair in the vee of her thighs was soft against his palm as he cupped her. Sliding his fingers deeper, he dipped into her and caressed, then rolled onto his hip, opened his fly, and made the head of his cock slick with the moisture his fingertips had collected.

He levered himself above her. Her thighs hugged his hips. His first probe found her tight, but yielding. He pressed inside, barely breaching but snugly securing himself in silky heat. He forced himself to hold there. But Laurel was looking up at him with lambent eyes, puffing soft and rapid breaths through her lips. Her fingers linked behind his neck. So he rocked into her incrementally, inch by intoxicating inch, until he was gloved by her.

His breath soughed loudly in the otherwise silent room. He bracketed her upper body with his forearms, leaving his hands free to touch her eyebrows, cheeks, lips. He kissed her gently. At least it started out that way, but her tongue tangled with his, and he resumed the hungry kisses of before.

She angled herself up against him, rubbing belly to belly, restlessly grazing her nipples against his chest. Her hands coasted down his spine to the small of his back, then into his loose trousers and onto his butt. For hands so small, they squeezed him with surprising strength, insistent on pulling him closer, deeper.

He heard the primal growl that came from his own throat as he began to move. Slow, penetrating glides. Near withdrawals before sinking deep, deeper. Shallow, rapid strokes that appealed to his carnal instinct to come. To come *now*.

He didn't. But he tilted his hips just enough to change the point of friction, to enable a prolonged grind against that elusive little bead that he had acquainted her with. Her first climax had alarmed her. She had resisted and rejected it. Now she was arching up in want of another.

He'd had wet dreams about just this, about Laurel's desperate reaching for the abandon he could give her.

His control slipping, he groaned her name in a plea, a prayer.

Her breath turned choppy, then stopped altogether as her body bowed and went taut. She gave a soft, startled cry, then began milking him with such perfection, he almost waited too late to pull out.

Really not since Derby had come home from Europe had Laurel felt completely at rest. This must be the way it felt when a beguiling narcotic channeled through one's veins, replacing distress, anger, grief, all things horrid with a honeyed peace. The languor was lovely. She had no wish to move.

Not until Thatcher did. And then she opened her eyes to watch as he walked over to the dresser and took off his pants. His tall frame was spared lankiness by wide shoulders, defined muscles and tendons, and a perfectly formed, firm backside.

"You mind me getting naked?"

She sought his eyes in the mirror above the dresser from which he'd obviously been watching her watch him.

A worry line appeared between his eyebrows. "Are you embarrassed now by what we did?"

"No. Only embarrassed that you caught me admiring the view."

The line faded and he grinned as he poured water onto a cloth and washed himself, then filled the bowl from the pitcher, got a fresh cloth off the towel rack, wet it, and brought it back to the bed. She couldn't keep herself from admiring the front view, too. He was generously apportioned.

He sat down on the side of the bed and washed her stomach

with the cloth, then passed it to her. Reaching beneath the sheet, she cleaned herself between her thighs.

"I'll get some Sheiks," he said. "But, except for the flu, I didn't catch anything over there."

Derby had explained to her why servicemen had been encouraged to use prophylactics. He'd assured her that he had.

Thatcher got back in the bed and stretched out beside her on his side, his elbow on the mattress, his fist supporting his cheek. He pulled back the sheet that she had draped over her hips and surveyed her with frank interest. His absorbed gaze made her turn rosier than she already was.

"You are embarrassed," he said.

"Bashful." She lowered her eyes and addressed his chin. "I've only been with Derby. I don't know how to act with you."

"Don't *act* at all. Just be you."

"Can I tell you something?"

"Something good, I hope."

"An admission." She reached out and placed her hand on the meaty part of his chest. Her fingers lightly stroked the dusting of hair. "I wanted to see you without your undershirt."

"What?"

"The night you brought Irv home. You'd used your shirt to stanch the wound and were wearing only a Henley. It fit so tight that I got some idea of what you must look like under it. I couldn't stop looking, imagining, and wishing I could see your bare chest."

He gave her a lopsided grin. "I was wishing I could see yours, too." He palmed her breast and ran his thumb across the nipple. "More than just see." He bent his head and caressed her nipple with his tongue then sucked each into his mouth before leaning away from her. "I've daydreamed for hours about doing that."

"You have?"

"Since I saw you wrestling with that sheet. Even that saggy dress you had on couldn't keep me from wondering what was underneath. Every time the wind kicked up, I got a fairly good idea."

"You gave no sign."

"I thought you were married."

"Have you ever been?"

"Married? Naw. There weren't any girls on the ranch except for one hand's mother, who cooked for Mr. Hobson. The girls in town were just, you know. Us cowboys made that house a stop on our alternating Saturday nights off."

She folded one arm beneath her head. "You never had a special girl, Thatcher? One who either got away, or who you left behind?"

"No."

She just looked at him.

"No," he repeated.

"You've never been in love?"

"No." He lifted a strand of her hair off the pillow and began winding it round and round his index finger. "There was a woman in France. Not one of the 'French girls' you referred to," he said wryly. "She was a nurse in the hospital. She was from Scotland. When she talked it sounded like bells jingling."

"Was she pretty?"

"In her way. Every soldier in the ward liked her. They'd flirt with her. She'd flirt back. All in fun. Whenever one would die, she took it hard, because she'd lost her fiancé during the first year of fighting. That's why she volunteered." He pulled his finger from the curl of hair he'd formed, laid it back on the pillow, then began to trace the shape of her eyebrow.

"She was crazy about horses, found out that I was a cowboy, wanted to know all about my life on the ranch in the wild, wild West. Sometimes after her shift, she'd come sit with me and we'd talk."

When he didn't continue, Laurel whispered, "There's more to this story, I think."

He gave a small shrug. "When I was discharged from the hospital, I was given a three-day leave before I had to report for duty. She invited me to stay with her. She had a small place. Only one room and a toilet, but she'd made it cozy."

"How often did you stay with her?"

"Just that once. After that three days, we said our goodbyes."

"Did you write to each other?"

"No."

"Did you see her after the war?"

"No."

"Did you try?"

"No. It wasn't like that, Laurel. She was a caring person. For all the cheer she gave her patients, she was sad. Still in love with her fiancé. We were a comfort to each other, that's all. Two people trying to take some pleasure where there was damn little to be found. Those three days were just a time-out from the hell going on around us."

"Like this is now?"

He quit concentrating on her eyebrow and met her gaze directly. Placing his arm around her waist, he spread his hand wide over her bottom and pulled her against him. "Nothing like this. Nothing's ever been like this."

His deep kiss became a long, continual one that caused renewed arousal to spiral inside her sex. Gradually, the kiss changed character, taking on heat that melted any lingering inhibitions. Up till now the word "erotic" had hinted at dark and mysterious things of which she had no experience or knowledge. Now, she felt steeped in the essence of the word's definition.

Thatcher ended the kiss only to whisper against her lips, "I have to have you again."

Her desire for him had also risen to the level of need. "Yes."

He murmured indistinctly as he moved to lie between her legs. "I'm going to kiss you."

But he didn't do as he was wont to and cradle her face in his hands. Instead he clasped her hips between them and blazed a trail of wet kisses down the center of her body.

His hands assumed mastery over her movements, but their guidance was gentle and unrushed. He repositioned her legs to accommodate his shoulders, cupped her behind the knees and raised them, stroked the backs of her thighs, then slid his hands under her bottom. It was a delicious shock to feel the prickliness of whiskers against her navel, in the valleys under her hipbones, and on the insides of her thighs.

She couldn't hear everything he whispered directly against her, but she felt the words as they formed on his lips, felt the warm breath that wafted over her sensitive flesh as he spoke them.

She never would have imagined that his mouth could be both softly persuasive and aggressive at the same time, but it was. His tongue was simply wicked. It shattered her, and she surrendered to it utterly.

She was still in the throes of her orgasm when he braced himself above her. In a possessive push, he sheathed himself. He gave only a few more rapid thrusts before his body tensed and she felt his pulsing deep inside her. She closed around him as tightly as she could, and they held that way, until they both went listless.

Long moments later, he placed his hands at each side of her head and sank his fingers into her hair, tangling the strands around them as though he wanted to be ensnared.

He remained heavy and full inside her, filling her. His face was feverish against her neck. His breath, which had been gusting, eventually slowed. He inhaled deeply once and exhaled slowly.

Before he slept, he spoke a single word. "Laurel." Only that.

It was enough.

FIFTY-SIX

Thatcher's clothes were still damp, but he had no choice except to put them back on. He was moving quietly so not to waken Laurel, who was a damn tempting sight, hair streaming over her pillow, face relaxed in sleep. Her bare shoulder had escaped the covers. He thought of leaning down and kissing it but was afraid she would wake up. She needed her sleep.

Last night, after napping for a while, they'd gone downstairs to the bathroom and bathed together by the glow of a kerosene lamp. She had overcome some of her shyness and had asked delicate questions. His candid answers had made her blush. But not to be outdone by "French tarts," she'd asked him to coach her on how to please him. It was he who'd wound up in thrall of her ardor. And talent.

They'd fallen asleep, spooning, but he'd awakened an hour later, hard with wanting her again. She purred in permissive response to his hopeful nudges, but when she tried to turn, he reached across her and spread his hand over her middle, holding her in place.

"Ever since that damn rooster attacked, and your bottom bumped up against me..."

Just thinking about that slow, drowsy sex made him want to be coupled with her again. But each of them was facing a challenging day. She would be grieving Davy O'Connor and consoling his brother. Sheriff Amos was expecting him.

He gave her one last, longing look, then slipped out of the bedroom unheard.

Fred Barker was already in his shop when Thatcher arrived to return his rifle. "Why don't you keep it?" Barker said. "After what happened last night, I reckon you might need it."

"You heard about the ambush?"

"Heard the ambush as it happened. Wife and me thought fire-crackers were going off. This morning, learned different from the milkman. That O'Connor boy was a hell-raiser. I'd've locked my daughter up was he to've come anywhere near her. But being gunned down like that..."

Barker shook his head in sorrow. "Somethin's gotta give around here, Thatcher. Hang on to that Springfield. It's not like it's the only rifle I have."

"Thanks. I'll take good care of it." He asked Fred if he could spare Roger to do the stable chores. "Sheriff wanted me to be on hand today."

Fred spat into the dirt. "He's gonna need all the men he can get. Do you believe a lightning strike caused that fire?"

"Fire?"

"Jesus, Thatcher. You ain't heard about that?"

The sheriff's office was more crowded than it had been since the morning the search for Mila Driscoll was organized. Then, Thatcher had only heard the commotion from his jail cell.

This morning, as he entered the building, he had to wedge himself between the interior wall and the throng of men surrounding Bill, who was standing in the center of the large room, fielding dozens of questions even as he issued assignments.

"We don't know how many confirmed dead yet," he was saying. "I'm afraid to calculate. Relatives we've talked to said that Hiram had called a clan conference. The only acceptable excuses for not attending were that you were being born or dying.

"There could have been dozens inside that house, including women and children. So far, we haven't come across any survivors. Which leaves us knowing squat about what happened during that meeting."

Thatcher listened as did everyone else as Bill shared what little he had learned. Hiram's nearest neighbor, with whom he wasn't on the best of terms, had heard a "loud bang" the night before.

"He took it for a lightning strike, rolled over and went back to sleep. This morning when he noticed several thin trails of smoke coming from the direction of Hiram's place, he thought he ought to go check."

When not a single Johnson appeared on their private road to challenge him for trespassing, the neighbor had become even more apprehensive of what he would find at the dead end.

"He said the house had been incinerated," Bill told those gathered around him. "Despite the rainstorm last night, parts of it were still smoldering. He drove to the nearest telephone and called me." Bill stared down at his boots for a moment. "All I can say is, it must've been a hell of a blaze. It's a scene out of hell."

Bill had left a team of deputies there to keep curiosity seekers away. Even those few Johnsons who hadn't attended the meeting, but had immediate family members who had, weren't allowed beyond a certain point.

"I've requested a team of state investigators specially trained in arson to come up from Austin. May be tomorrow before they can gather all their gear and make the drive. In the meantime, the rest of you continue investigating the ambush on the O'Connors. You have your duties. Get to them."

Many shuffled out. Others got on telephones. Bill came over to Thatcher, who said, "Sorry I wasn't here earlier."

"Be glad you missed it."

"The Johnson place?"

"Thatcher, if that fire wasn't an act of God, it was the work of Satan himself. There were kids in that house. Babies."

Thatcher had seen charred bodies of soldiers on the battlefield and of civilians in bombed-out villages. He had hoped never to see such a grotesque sight again. Neither he nor Bill said anything for a moment, then Thatcher asked if Mike O'Connor was still alive.

"Last word I got, he was holding on, but they're keeping him sedated. Doc Perkins said he'd let me know as soon as he's stable enough to be questioned."

Thatcher nodded absently, then asked about Gabe Driscoll's present frame of mind.

Bill said, "I haven't been in to see him this morning. Someone else took him breakfast."

Thatcher took a look around the room. It hadn't escaped others' notice that he and Bill were conferring privately, a privilege that Bill didn't afford everyone. Scotty and Harold tolerated Thatcher, but only to an extent. Most of the veterans of the department still regarded him with suspicion and hostility. He was sure that some held to the belief that he was guilty of doing something to Mila Driscoll. That continued to plague him. Whether or not they ever welcomed him into the fold, he had to lay that misconception to rest.

Which is why he wanted to speak to Bill alone. "Let's go take a look at that road where the getaway car was waiting for the shooters."

"I doubt we'll find any clues."

"I doubt we will, too, but I'm afraid these walls have ears."

Bill gave him a sharp look, then announced to the room at large that he would be back shortly.

Laurel woke up later than usual, with a fully risen sun lighting the bedroom through the shades Thatcher had lowered last night.

Thatcher. At the mere thought of him, warm happiness suffused her. She was a bit disappointed that he hadn't stayed until she woke up, but she knew the hard day he had in store.

At the same time, she was almost glad he wasn't facing her across the pillow just now. She blushed at the thought of ever looking him in the eye again. The things he'd taught her!

Derby had regarded himself as quite a Casanova. His lovemaking had been vigorous, and he'd strutted that as a sign of his virility. He'd always taken for granted that she was satisfied, when the gratification had been his alone. The sex had been for him, not her. To be fair, she didn't believe he'd been selfish. He simply hadn't known any better.

If not for Thatcher, neither would she.

He had awakened her to levels of sensuality she'd never known were available or would have dreamed possible. In response to her apprehension over what he expected, over what she could expect from him, he'd been patient and persuasive. His touch, knowing smile, and whispered words had been temptation made manifest. His tenderness, passion sanctified. Throughout the night, he'd given her rapturous pleasure and had taken his.

But in addition to the fervent lovemaking, he had also attended to her wracked emotions. Without words, he'd held her close against him. Just that. His quietude had assuaged her grief over Davy's murder, her anxiety over Mike's condition, her distress over the unknown future.

That thought prickled something at the back of her mind, some revelatory thought. But it had been fleeting, as elusive as the glimmer of a single firefly in a dark wood.

Once, when she was a young girl, she'd chased a lightning bug through the woods that bordered her daddy's cotton field. It had flickered only one time, but she'd been certain she'd seen it, not imagined it. She'd plunged after it in the hope of catching it to put in a jar near her bed. She'd darted through the trees and underbrush, had run in circles, until she had exhausted herself and had given up the chase in defeat.

She felt as frustrated and downcast now not to have netted that flash of clarity. It had been meaningful enough to give her instant pause, to raise goose bumps on her arms.

She closed her eyes, lay perfectly still, and strained to recapture it. But try as she might, she couldn't. It had retreated into the recesses of her subconscious. Maybe it would show itself at another time, probably in a moment when she wasn't searching for it.

Having been lazy long enough, she forced herself to get up. She washed and dressed, and was pinning up her hair when she heard the back door open and the scrape of footsteps in the kitchen.

Her heart swelled. Maybe Thatcher had come back for a good morning kiss after all.

More probably, though, it was Irv, returning from the stills. She dreaded having to tell him, Corrine, and Ernie about the O'Connors, but she also hoped that they hadn't heard the dreadful news from someone else first.

She pushed the last pin into her hair, and then started downstairs, calling as she went, "Irv?"

Once in Bill's car and on their way, Thatcher asked after Mrs. Amos.

"Not doing good, I hate to say. I'm worried, Thatcher. No ordinary bellyache lasts this long. With all these crises going on, if I can't take time off to get her to a doctor, I'm going to ask her friend to take her."

"What about Dr. Perkins?"

"He'd just give her more drops. She needs to be examined by somebody born *after* the Civil War. Have you heard of that sanitarium in Temple?"

Thatcher shook his head.

"Couple of doctors down there—names are Scott and White—

are building quite a reputation. I may look into getting her in down there."

They drove along the road where Thatcher had last seen the getaway car's taillights disappearing around a bend. Bill drove beyond that point, then pulled his car to the side of the road.

"This is pointless. What's on your mind?"

Thatcher said, "Have you sent anybody out to Pointer's Gap yet?"

"It was on my list of things to do today, but with the ambush, the fire, I haven't had the men to spare, and you'd have to go with them to show the way. So, no."

"Have you arranged for a lawyer for Driscoll?"

"It's not a priority."

Bill's expectant expression prompted Thatcher to get on with it. "This is going to sound like I'm beating around the bush but bear with me."

The sheriff checked his pocket watch. "It's a busy day. Five minutes, Thatcher."

"Last night when you dropped Laurel and me at her house, she was on the brink of a breakdown."

"Over Davy O'Connor."

"Sure. But also, yesterday afternoon she had an upsetting visit from Bernie Croft and Chester Landry."

"Let me guess. They wanted her to merge her business with theirs."

Thatcher said nothing. Bill waited a few seconds then sighed with exasperation. "They're bootleggers, Thatcher. They wouldn't have been interested in Mrs. Plummer's pie business."

"I'm not saying anything about her."

"You don't have to. I've known for years that old Irv dabbled. He didn't cause anybody trouble, so I looked the other way. Other moonshiners did, too, because he didn't put too deep a dent in their market. But the lady has gotten everybody riled."

"Croft and Landry for sure."

"She turned them down?" Again, Thatcher remained silent, but Bill nodded as though Thatcher had replied. "In return, they shot up her delivery boys."

"At the scene of the ambush, Harold said to me that somebody had wanted to make a point. I think he was right. I think it was Croft."

"What about Landry?"

"He was with Laurel when the shooting started, remember?"

"Now I do. I had asked her about it, but we got off on Mike O'Connor's condition, so I never received an answer. Was he a decoy, sent to keep her occupied while the O'Connors were being ambushed?"

"That's possible, I guess. But what Landry told Laurel was that he'd returned to make her a better offer."

"Behind Bernie's back? A double-cross?"

"Landry is weaselly enough."

"Oh, I agree. But are you suggesting that while he was negotiating with Mrs. Plummer, Bernie acted alone?"

"I don't think Landry is above removing somebody, but he wouldn't go about it like that. He wouldn't have made a spectacle."

"Like the ambush."

"And like a 'hell of a blaze.'"

Bill looked at him with raised brows. "Hiram's place?"

"Hennessy was in the IRA. They're famous for blowing things up. They make explosive devices out of tin cans. That fire at the Johnsons' place might not have been sparked by lightning."

"Christ, Thatcher. Do you have any idea of the shit you're wading into here? Bernie Croft isn't a man you trifle with."

"No, Bill, you can't *trifle*. You gotta hit him with more than a slap on the hand. You gotta kick him in the balls and then cut them off."

Bill lapsed into thought, tugging at the corner of his mustache. "We'd have a hell of a time proving that Bernie ordered that ambush or the fire. He's got loyal toadies. They would never give him up."

"They'd hang first?"

"I would."

Thatcher looked at him, stunned.

"You think I'm a coward? I guess I am," he said ruefully. "But it's not my skin I'm concerned about. Daisy's life is the bargaining chip Bernie holds over me. That's why I don't buck him, Thatcher. He doesn't even have to carry out his veiled threats. It's the fear that he will that keeps me—everybody—from crossing him beyond a certain point."

Thatcher turned his head forward and stared through the grimy windshield. "Maybe he carries out more threats than you know of. I told you this would sound like beating around the bush—"

"And time's winding down."

"Who told us about Pointer's Gap?"

"What's that got to do with—"

"Who, Bill?" The answer being obvious, Thatcher continued without pause. "Why did Croft drop that out-of-the-way place into the conversation? Like he just happened to think of it while explaining Driscoll's lust for Norma Blanchard?"

"Which we already knew about."

"Yes, but Croft didn't know we knew. He made certain we did."

"Bernie has been Gabe's advocate. Why would he plant in our minds the notion that Gabe could have assaulted Norma?"

"He did more than that," Thatcher said. "He beat us over the head with it. Makes me wonder why."

FIFTY-SEVEN

When Thatcher and Bill returned to the sheriff's department, it was still a beehive of activity. As soon as Bill came through the door, a dozen written messages were handed to him. He scanned the notes, then delegated various tasks to his deputies and staff.

Scotty approached and said under his breath, "The governor himself called this time."

"If he calls back, put him off. Tell him—"

"And the Texas Rangers are here."

Bill snorted. "Well, that was to be expected. Actually, I'm glad to have them. How many?"

"Two."

"Where are they?"

"Having a meal over at the café. Said they'd be back in thirty minutes."

"How long ago was that?"

Scotty checked the wall clock. "Twenty-seven minutes ago."

Bill turned to Thatcher. "Do you want to wait to confront Driscoll until we have more time?"

"Do you?"

By way of an answer, Bill said to Scotty, "When the Rangers come back, tell them we're trying to squeeze a confession out of a prisoner, and ask them to cool their heels a while longer."

"The governor?"

"Suggest he have a drink." Bill pushed open the door leading into the cell block. Thatcher followed him and closed the door behind them.

Driscoll was fit to be tied. "Where is my lawyer? What the hell is going on out there? It sounds like a carnival. I've been yelling for someone to get in here, but I've been ignored." Glaring at Thatcher, his voice went shrill. "And why is he still wearing a badge when he should be in here instead of me?"

In contrasting calmness, Bill said, "Because he's not a murder suspect, Gabe."

"I did not attack Norma. I would never have done that."

"No, we don't think you did. The patients on your rural route vouched for your whereabouts during the time frame when she was assaulted."

"Then why am I still locked up?"

"Because you killed Mila. Didn't you?"

"No." He gave an obstinate shake of his head.

"Did you plan it with Norma, or did you act alone?"

"I did *not kill my wife.*"

Disregarding the denial, Bill said, "I think Mrs. Driscoll's body was in the car with you when you went to Lefty's. Eleanor Wise just missed you loading it because you had parked around back."

Up till then, Thatcher had let Bill do all the talking. Now, he said, "I can't figure the murder weapon."

"Good point," Gabe said tightly. "Sheriff, are you listening? What did you use, Hutton?"

Unfazed, Thatcher said, "No obvious weapon was found inside the house. Either you used something commonplace that wouldn't be considered a weapon, or you took the weapon with you and tossed it somewhere along the way to Lefty's, or you buried it with Mrs. Driscoll's body at Pointer's Gap."

"I didn't—"

"And why Pointer's Gap?" Thatcher continued. "It's rugged country."

"You would know, wouldn't you?" Driscoll sneered. "You took Mila from our house that night and took her out there—"

"In what, Gabe?"

His head swiveled back to Bill. "What?"

"Thatcher was on foot. How would he have gotten her out there?"

Before the doctor could respond, Thatcher picked back up. "Why did you choose Pointer's Gap?"

"I didn't! I've never even been there."

"What about the picnics with your wife?"

Driscoll looked at Bill. "What is he talking about?"

"The picnics," Thatcher said, bringing Driscoll's attention back to him. "The ones you and Mrs. Driscoll went on at Pointer's Gap."

"That's absurd. First of all, I hate picnics. Where did you even get a crazy idea like that?"

Thatcher waited a beat, then said quietly, "From Bernie Croft."

The doctor looked like he'd been struck with a two-by-four right between the eyes. He gaped at Thatcher for a ten count, then took several short, shallow breaths. "Bernie told you that?"

Closely monitoring Driscoll's every reaction, Thatcher left it to Bill to explain how they'd come to hear about Pointer's Gap, when and where their seemingly casual conversation with the mayor had taken place. "To aid us in our investigation into the assault on Miss Blanchard, Bernie felt compelled to mention your affair with her, and then your earnest attempt to atone for it by paying more attention to your wife."

Gabe was swallowing convulsively.

Bill went on. "His offhanded mention of Pointer's Gap—"

"It wasn't offhanded," Driscoll blurted. He slumped forward against the bars, clutching two of them to help himself remain upright. "It was his idea."

"What was his idea?"

He remained silent and gave a mournful shake of his head.

"It was Bernie's idea to do what, Gabe? Say it."

"I can't. He'll kill me."

Thatcher leaned in and whispered to him, "If you betray Croft, he may very well kill you. But if you don't come clean, you have me to be scared of."

Gabe looked at him with fright. Thatcher gazed back, unblinking. The doctor was quick to yield. He turned to Bill and stammered, "B...Bernie took care of the body for me. He had men meet me at Lefty's. They took Mila."

"Was she dead, Gabe?"

He nodded.

"You killed her?"

"Yes." He lowered his head and began to cry.

Thatcher backed away from the bars separating them. He exchanged a glance with Bill. They'd gotten the confession they'd been after, but having Mila Driscoll's fate confirmed was a dismal triumph.

"How'd you kill her, Gabe?" Bill asked softly.

Just then Scotty came barging through the door at the end of the corridor. "Sheriff?"

"Not now," Bill said.

"It's—"

"Not now!"

"It's Mrs. Amos."

Bill spun around to his deputy. Scotty spoke so hastily, he tripped over his words. "Her friend Mrs. Cantor called, says Mrs. Amos is in pain something awful. Her stomach. Said it might've been, uh...whiskey. Said she caught her with a bottle of bourbon half empty."

"Jesus." Bill looked at Thatcher. "I have to go."

"And the Rangers are back," Scotty added.

"Screw them. Stay with Driscoll," Bill said to Thatcher. "Get it all on paper. Have him sign—"

"Wait! Your wife has severe stomach pains after drinking bourbon?" Gabe had stopped crying, but had turned whey-faced and his lips were rubbery. "He said it was for the Johnsons."

In a matter of seconds, Bill had the cell door unlocked, had grabbed Driscoll by the throat, and had backed him against the wall. "Who said? Bernie?"

Driscoll gave a wobbly nod.

"Said what was for the Johnsons?" Bill shook him, thumping him hard against the wall. "*What?*"

"Arsenic. In the bourbon."

With the regard one would give a rag doll, Bill dragged the doctor from the cell and pushed him down the hallway with the unstoppable propulsion of a cowcatcher.

———

Scotty had come along. He was with Bill as he burst through the front door of his house, shouting his wife's name. By the time Thatcher had towed Driscoll from the car, up the walk and into the house, Bill was on the landing, barging past a middle-aged woman who was wringing her hands with anxiety and saying repeatedly, "I don't know what to do for her."

Scotty hung back to explain the circumstances. "It'll be all right, Mrs. Cantor. We've brought Dr. Driscoll."

Thatcher, with a grip on the back of Driscoll's collar, pushed him up the stairs and into the bedroom. Bill was seated on the side of the bed, bending over his wife, who was writhing in apparent agony.

She reached out and clutched Bill's hand. "I think I'm dying."

"You're not going to die." He raised her hand and kissed the back of it, hard. "*You are not going to die.* I'm going to fix it."

He left the bed, walked over to Driscoll, drew his pistol, and pressed the barrel of it against the doctor's forehead. "If she doesn't survive this, I am killing you first, then Bernie Croft."

"Gastric lavage," Driscoll said.

"What?"

"Pump her stomach. I need to pump her stomach with salt water. I'll need my equipment."

"Describe it."

Thatcher was amazed by how suddenly Driscoll slipped into professional mode. In seemingly perfect control, he gave Scotty a description of the tubing device he required and told him in which cabinet it was stored in his office. "But the house is locked."

"Kick the damn door in. Shoot out the lock," Bill said to his deputy. Scotty rushed out and thumped down the stairs.

Daisy groaned pitiably and extended her hand toward Bill, who holstered his pistol, but shouted to Driscoll, "Do something now!"

The doctor shrugged off his coat. "We need to induce vomiting."

"She's been vomiting for days."

"But she hadn't ingested half a bottle all at once. This is acute. We need to induce vomiting." He rolled up his shirtsleeves. "Where can I wash?"

"Across the hall."

Thatcher followed him as far as the door to the bathroom and watched as he lathered up and rinsed his hands. As he was drying them, his gaze met Thatcher's in the mirror above the sink. "Are you expecting an apology for my false accusations, Mr. Hutton?"

"I don't give a fuck in hell about an apology from you. But you owe your wife one. How'd you do it?"

"I hit her on the back of the head with an iron skillet. The skillet in which she baked the shortbread you enjoyed so much." He folded the hand towel and hung it just so on the metal bar, then went past Thatcher and returned to the bedroom.

Daisy was lying on her side, knees pulled to her chest, moaning and gripping her midsection. Bill was leaning over her, stroking her face and talking softly.

Thatcher noticed a half-full bottle of name-brand bourbon sitting on the bureau. He went over and got it, knowing it would be valuable evidence against both Driscoll and Croft.

As he left the bedroom unnoticed, Bill was holding back his beloved's hair as she retched into a basin held by the man who had poisoned her...at the direction of Bernie Croft.

Bernie said, "Hello, Gert."

"Ain't you heard? We're shut down. Good as anyway."

"I'd like to talk to you."

"We'll talk when you get the law off my back."

"In due time."

"Due time," she said scornfully. "No more graft, you hear me?"

"I'll get you back to normal soon."

"You been sayin' that, but in the meanwhile, Bill Amos is having our road patrolled nightly. All that attention is keepin' away customers too scared of being caught in another raid.

"Much longer, and we won't have any hooch to sell, 'cause Lefty's drinkin' it all up. Stays drunk, ain't no use to me. No pussy to sell, neither, 'cause all them twats upstairs has sneaked off one by one. Took their inspiration from that Corrine, I guess. I'm losing money by the hour, and you're doin' nothin' but takin' up space, Mr. Mayor."

He smiled. "I'm here to make it up to you, Gert."

She honked a laugh. "Ain't likely. Everybody knows you look after your ownself."

"This benefits us both."

She squinted at him through an exhalation of cigarette smoke. "Whut does?"

"I've brought you a present."

He turned. Hennessy was standing at the side of the town car. At a signal from Bernie, he opened the back door and pulled a bound and gagged woman from the car.

Croft said to Gert, "I believe you're acquainted with Mrs. Plummer."

Laurel had gone into the kitchen, expecting to find her father-in-law rummaging for the makings of breakfast.

Instead, Bernie Croft had been rifling through her recipe box.

Fanning one of the cards at her, he'd greeted her pleasantly. "Good morning, Mrs. Plummer. This lemon chess pie sounds delicious."

And then from behind her, a heavy hand had been clamped over her mouth at the same time an arm as strong as an iron band had encircled her waist.

She'd raked her nails across the hand over her mouth and knew by the profanities grunted near her ear that she'd drawn blood, or at least had caused pain. She'd struggled and kicked, but she'd been held fast while Croft had tied her hands behind her with a thin but sturdy cord that dug into her flesh. The hand over her mouth had been removed and replaced by a handkerchief, which had caused her to gag.

She'd been carried to the long, black car she'd seen parked in front of her house the day before. She'd been thrust into the backseat, no doubt by the burly chauffeur. Croft had climbed in beside her. They could have been out for a Sunday drive for all the attention she paid him until they'd made the turnoff to Lefty's.

She'd looked at him then, and his chuckle had been villainous. Or perhaps it had only sounded that way to her because she knew him to be a villain.

When they'd reached the roadhouse, Croft and Hennessy had gotten out. Croft had gone to the door, which had been answered by Gert. After a brief conversation, Croft had signaled Hennessy to get her from the car and bring her forward.

Now, upon seeing her, Gert stepped out onto the porch. She flicked her cigarette into the dirt and clapped her hands together. "Well, I be damned. You really did bring me a present, Bernie. It ain't even my birthday."

Laurel dug her heels in, kicked against the chauffeur's shins, twisted and turned her body, did anything she could think of to make his job more difficult. She didn't delude herself into thinking she could escape someone of his size, but she refused to meekly cooperate.

When they reached the porch steps, Croft instructed "Hennessy" to pat down her skirt pockets.

"Already did there in her kitchen."

He had, but with a sinking heart, Laurel had known he would come up empty, and he had. Irv would never let her hear the last of it. If she lived through this.

"Search again," Croft said now. "Right pocket. Yesterday, I saw her patting at it. Giveaway habit."

Hennessy did as told, even shoving his hands into her pockets and digging deep. "Nothing, boss."

Gert snickered. "Try her garters."

Laurel looked defiantly at Croft as he motioned for his muscle man to do as suggested. Hennessy knelt in front of her and ran his hands up and down both legs, higher than her garters. Being groped by him was a desecration of Thatcher's caresses. She wanted to scream.

As Hennessy came to his feet, he grinned at her. "Nothing but smooth skin."

She forced herself not to react either to his molestation or disgusting leer.

Croft then hitched his chin at Hennessy, who pushed her lower spine hard enough to knock her off balance. She fell forward onto the lowest porch step. Without her hands free to catch herself, she landed on her elbow. Pain sizzled up her arm and into her shoulder. She couldn't cry out for the handkerchief in her mouth. Even had she been able to, she wouldn't have given this trio of degenerates the satisfaction.

"No call for rough stuff, Hennessy," Croft said. "Yet."

He reached down and helped Laurel to her feet and guided her up the steps. But once they reached the porch, she yanked her arm free of his deceptively solicitous grip.

He took the white linen handkerchief from her mouth. It was monogrammed with his initials. Feeling her saliva on it, he frowned with distaste. She would have liked to spit in his eye, but reasoned that, at this point, her best defense was to show as little reaction as possible. But while her features remained composed and indifferent, she was quaking on the inside. No one knew where she was. Not Irv, Thatcher, no one.

Croft raised a hand to shade his eyes. "Gert, let's take her inside, get her and her delicate skin out of this sun. We wouldn't want her to burn."

Gert gave a phlegmy laugh as she pulled open the squeaky screened door. "Of course not, wouldn't want that to happen."

Hennessy stayed outside.

The room was as Laurel remembered: cavernous, dim, and hazy with cigarette smoke. There was no sign of Lefty. Only an ominous silence came from upstairs. The shotgun lay on the bar. Gert walked over to it, sat down on a stool, and lit a fresh cigarette as though settling in for the floor show.

Laurel realized she was it.

Croft pushed her into a chair, then dragged one over, stationed it directly in front of her, and sat down.

"Mrs. Plummer—can I call you Laurel?—where is Chester Landry?"

Of all the things he could have said, that question was the least expected.

Gert must have thought the same. She came off her stool with a thud. "Chester Landry, *my ass*. Ask her where my girl's at. Soon's I find that scheming little bitch, I'm gonna wring her neck, and let Miss High Horse here watch while I do it."

Croft acted as though he hadn't heard her and remained focused on Laurel. "Where was Landry headed when he slunk off last night?"

Laurel laughed. "You could have asked me that without going to all this elaborate trouble."

"Then tell me where he is."

"I have no earthly idea."

He sighed. Then, with shocking alacrity and force, he backhanded her across the face.

FIFTY-EIGHT

Following the stomach pumping procedure, Daisy Amos was resting more comfortably. Thatcher knew Bill hated leaving her side and resuming his duties, but he was hard pressed to do so on this of all days, when three major investigations demanded attention and action.

He asked Thatcher to escort the doctor downstairs to the parlor where he would soon join them. "Put these on him." He produced a pair of handcuffs.

Bill remained in the foyer with Scotty, who had been communicating with headquarters by telephone. He reported that the two Texas Rangers had divided up. One was getting information from the deputies who'd investigated the scene of the ambush. The other had gone to the Johnson homestead to assess the devastation there in advance of the arrival of the arson specialists.

Thatcher overheard Bill ask Scotty to locate Bernie Croft. "Don't approach him. Don't indicate that you're looking for him. Just let me know where he is. Me and me only."

"Yes, sir." The deputy left.

When Bill entered the parlor, Driscoll said, "I hope you can trust Mrs. Amos's friend to make her drink the water I prepared." He'd added honey to a large pitcher of water and had left it on the bed-side table.

"Even if she continues to throw up for a time, she needs the water. It will help flush the arsenic from her system naturally through urination. I've heard that the honey helps. Chemically, somehow. Also eggs. She should be fed eggs. The sulfur in them—"

Bill interrupted him. "You told Alice all that. I'm confident she'll follow your instructions to the letter."

Driscoll held up his cuffed hands. "Are these necessary?"

"They were for Thatcher when he was suspected of the crime you've confessed to. They stay on. You poisoned my wife."

"Bernie brought two cases of liquor to my office and left them to be spiked with a slow-working poison, so it wouldn't be immediately noticed. He told me those bottles were to be 'gifts' for members of the Johnson family. I had no way of knowing that Mrs. Amos would be allotted some, too."

Bill had admitted to Thatcher during his tell-all on the porch that Croft was Daisy's supplier of bootleg whiskey. That he'd given her bottles spiked with arsenic was indicative of the malice he felt toward Bill as well as Daisy for choosing Bill over him.

"Is she still in danger?" Bill was asking Driscoll. "And you had better not bullshit me."

"The arsenic will remain in her system, but for how long depends on a number of factors. That's why I emphasize flushing it out and neutralizing it as much as possible."

"Could she still die of it?"

"It can cause complications, organ damage and so forth, that can eventually prove fatal. It's a toxin, after all. Had I not acted so swiftly and given her the lavage, more than likely she would have succumbed."

To Thatcher, Driscoll was a complete mystery. He was like the doctor in that book. Two men with opposing personalities living inside the same body. One minute Driscoll was bawling like a child caught misbehaving, the next he was calm, detached, even defiant.

Within an hour the man had admitted to poisoning bottles of liquor he knew would be consumed by human beings and had confessed to murdering his wife and unborn baby. Thatcher rather agreed with Patsy Kemp, who'd said with bitterness: They ought to hang the bastard twice.

Bill was now asking Driscoll why he had agreed to poison the bourbon.

"Bernie had me over a barrel." He poured out the whole sordid story about Croft trying to recruit him to transport booze on his rural route. "I was offended. I'm a physician, not a bootlegger."

He looked down at his linked fingers. "But then, the night Mila...When I needed Bernie to see me through that crisis, he did so. He and that old bag at Lefty's quickly set up the incident with the prostitute so I would have a cover story for leaving the house at that hour of the night."

"Did Gert know about Mila?" Bill asked.

"I don't believe so. Bernie said she was a whore at heart and wouldn't ask questions so long as she was paid." He sighed deeply. "Anyway, after that night, he owned me body and soul. I was subjected to a lot of humiliation from him. I tolerated it, believing I had no other choice. But when I found out that he'd told Norma about Pointer's Gap, I—"

"What?" Bill held up his hand. "Run that past us again."

"Norma knew about Mila. She sprang it on me the afternoon she brought Arthur to the house. I was floored, flabbergasted. Bernie was the only person who could have told her, except for the men who actually buried the body, and they were all Mexicans who didn't even speak English.

"I had trusted Bernie to keep the secret. We'd made a pact. When I learned that he'd told Norma, I accosted him on the street." He described a volatile encounter in an alleyway. "I was livid."

Thatcher sat forward and placed his forearms on his thighs. "You were livid. What about Croft?"

"Smug. He said I was naïve to think that he wouldn't have held some collateral for doing me such a huge favor. I told him that Norma was using it to pressure me into marriage. He agreed that people would become suspicious if she and I married too soon, and that Norma should be made to understand that. He offered to speak to her on my behalf, but I told him I would handle it. I...I hadn't gotten around to it."

Thatcher looked over at Bill, who, like him, appeared to have realized the significance of Bernie Croft's offer to impress understanding upon Norma Blanchard.

Bill stood and pulled Driscoll out of his chair. "Just so we understand one another, Gabe. If Daisy gets well, you'll stand trial and be judged by a jury of your peers. If she *succumbs*, you won't live to see trial."

Driscoll jerked his arm free. "There's gratitude for you. I saved your wife's life, and you repay me by issuing threats? First him," he said, looking at Thatcher with scorn, "now you. Isn't it against the law to threaten a suspect in your custody? Doesn't that violate a lawman's code of ethics?"

"I don't give a damn." Bill hauled off and slammed his fist into Gabe's face. He fell backward and landed on the floor, out cold.

There was one knock on the front door before Scotty pushed it open and walked in. He looked down at Driscoll. "What happened?"

"He was trying to escape," Bill said. "When you get him back to the jail, put him in shackles, too. What about our mayor?"

"That's what I came to tell you. I know where he's at."

———◆———

"What I think? We ought to go into town and check on her."

"We heard you the first dozen times you said that."

Corrine gave Irv a malevolent squint. "Well, apparently you ain't listening, old man. Miss Laurel said if she didn't come tomorrow, which was yesterday, she'd come the next day, which is today."

"Day ain't over, is it?"

Ernie looked up at the sun. "Noon or better. But she has a point, Irv."

"Aw, you're just horny. You'd agree with anything she said," Irv grumbled, shooting a glower toward Corrine.

"You said yourself you was scared Miss Laurel would come to grief," she said. "Didn't he say that, Ernie?"

Ernie tugged on his long earlobe. "Seems I do recollect—"

"I remember sayin' it," Irv snapped. "And I still hold to it. But you," he said to Corrine, "agreed that we should lay low till we got the all clear. Laurel wouldn't want us to show ourselves till it was safe. We've got no idea what all went on last night. I doubt much did on account of that storm. But still..."

Corrine stood and dusted off her seat. "Well, you can sit here till you become a fossil like in them rocks over yonder. I'm going." She marched off toward Irv's truck, which they'd camouflaged with cedar boughs.

"How are you going to get there?" he called after her. "You can't drive."

She started pulling the cedar branches off the truck and slinging them aside. "I can drive good enough. Ernie's been teaching me."

Irv turned an accusatory look on his friend. Ernie guiltily raised his bony shoulders. "In my spare time."

"Hell's bells." Irv started after Corrine. "I'll drive us." Over his shoulder, he said to Ernie, "You stay and guard the place. Don't do no cooking till we get back and keep those firearms within your reach."

"Y'all be careful."

Bill instructed Scotty to return Driscoll to the jail, leave a man there to guard him, then to bring a carload of deputies to Lefty's.

He also ordered Scotty not to leave town without obtaining an arrest warrant for Mayor Bernard Croft. Looking dubious, Scotty asked how the sheriff planned on arranging that. "I'm calling the judge now."

Scotty left with Driscoll, who had regained consciousness. His shouted protests over being treated inhumanely were ignored.

Bill placed a call. Thatcher overheard him threatening a judge to expose both his bribe-taking and the mistress he kept in Stephenville if he didn't have the warrant ready by the time Scotty got to the courthouse to pick it up.

After completing the call, Bill went upstairs to check on Mrs. Amos. He didn't stay long. "She's better. Sleeping," he told Thatcher as they left the house.

Less than five minutes after Scotty's announcement that Bernie Croft had been seen heading for Lefty's, the sheriff and Thatcher were speeding toward it, having no idea if their quarry was still there.

Croft's notable town car, with Hennessy behind the wheel, had been spotted taking the turnoff to Lefty's by a deputy who'd come off guard duty at the Johnsons' property and was on his way back into town.

Bill took the turnoff now but didn't go far off the highway before stopping. As he checked his pistol to make sure it was loaded, he said, "I'm waiting for that warrant."

"I'll reconnoiter." Having checked his own Colt, Thatcher clicked the cylinder back into place and opened the passenger door. "Just in case I don't come back, that poisoned bottle of bourbon is in your kitchen cabinet behind a box of oatmeal."

"Only you would think of that right now."

"Could make the difference in a verdict." He hooked Barker's rifle onto his shoulder by the strap.

"Take these, too." Bill passed Thatcher a pair of binoculars. Thatcher recognized them as army issue and looked at Bill, who said, "They were among Tim's effects."

Thatcher left the car door ajar and jogged over to the trees that bordered the road. They were sparse, providing only marginal cover as he moved among them. The sun was high and hot. Last night's rain steamed up from the spongy ground. Thatcher was breathing heavily by the time the roof of the roadhouse came into view.

He proceeded in a crouch. Still about a hundred yards away

from the building, he spotted Croft's auto parked in front. A boulder provided him an advantageous spot from which to take a closer look. Situating himself behind the outcropping, he propped his elbows on it and looked through the binoculars.

He wasn't surprised to see Hennessy leaning against the front fender of Croft's car, smoking a cigarette. He whisked a fly off his face. He took a handkerchief from his pants pocket and wiped the back of his neck with it. He turned once and looked behind him down the road. Seeing nothing, he faced the building again.

Thatcher focused the binoculars on the screened entrance, and then on each of the front windows, but could see nothing through any of them. He watched for a couple more minutes. Nothing happened. He was about to turn away and return to report to Bill, when the screened door was pushed open and Gert appeared.

She called out something to Hennessy. Thatcher didn't catch her words, but the former IRA fighter responded immediately by tossing away his cigarette and climbing the steps to go inside.

———✦———

Laurel had lost track of time under the barrage of Croft's questions, few of which she knew the answers to. He didn't believe that, so he continued relentlessly.

He hadn't hit her again, but the threat of his doing so filled her with dread. Her ears were still ringing. The side of her face throbbed. She could feel it swelling.

The blow had also fueled her contempt. She took pride in knowing that the only way the Honorable Mayor Croft had managed to subdue her was to strike her while her hands were bound. Some big man he was.

He never raised his voice. He ignored Gert's snorts of derision over his "going too easy on her." At her suggestion that she take a whack at Laurel, Croft had said, "I don't want her dead."

"I ain't gonna kill her till she tells me where she's hid that girl. She ain't reappeared at the shack."

"You see, Laurel?" Croft spoke with the dulcet tone and phony smile of a public official making a campaign promise. "If you'll just tell us what we want to know, we can end this unpleasantness."

What you'll end is me.

She feared she wouldn't live out this day, but she didn't know the answers to Croft's questions about Chester Landry. Why would he think she would? And she would never give Corrine over to Gert.

Croft asked her the same questions repeatedly, her answers never varied, but she began replying with mounting hostility. With her hands bound behind her, and Gert's evident affection for her shotgun, Laurel didn't have any means of fighting back except to show her loathing and defiance of both of them.

"Let's try one more time, Laurel," Croft said. "Landry went behind my back and offered to form a partnership with you, didn't he?"

"No."

"You've admitted that he returned to your house last night."

"Yes, but our conversation was interrupted by gunshots. We ran to the scene of the ambush. From there he disappeared. I've told you this a dozen times." Brazenly, she asked, "Did you have Davy O'Connor killed?"

Ignoring that, he said, "You never saw Landry again?"

"No."

"He just ran away."

"Yes."

"He didn't say where he was off to?"

"No. If you ordered my friend's execution, may God damn you," she yelled.

"Landry didn't lure you into a business arrangement that excluded me?"

"He couldn't have lured me into anything. He was slimy. I wanted nothing to do with either of you. If you want to know his whereabouts, go in search of him and stop wasting your time with me. I can't tell you something that *I don't know.*"

Croft sighed theatrically and looked over at Gert. "Get Hennessy."

Those two words caused Laurel's stomach to lurch, but she kept her expression impassive as the man came inside and took up a position to the left of and slightly behind Croft.

Laurel didn't acknowledge that he was there, didn't dare to look at him, not wanting to see on his ugly face either a fearsome threat or a taunting smile that would remind her of his groping hands.

Croft gave Hennessy a sidelong glance, then, when he came back around, slapped Laurel hard enough to knock her chair backward. Her head hit the floor with a crack. Hennessy stepped around, jerked her to her feet, righted the chair, firmly planted it in front of Croft, and pushed her down into it.

Croft's arrogant face swam into her vision through tears of pain and fury.

"One last time," he said softly. "Where is Chester Landry?"

"Go. To. Hell."

He heaved another sigh and gave her the look of a disappointed parent. "Since you're resistant to my rough handling, perhaps you'll be more receptive to Mr. Hennessy's sweet talk." He waited a beat before smiling and adding, "Upstairs."

Thatcher made his way back to where Bill was waiting. He got there just as a car bearing the sheriff's office insignia pulled off the highway and rolled to a stop behind Bill's car. Scotty, Harold, and three others got out. All were heavily armed with shotguns, rifles, and handguns.

Bill motioned for them to gather around Thatcher so he could brief them on what he'd observed. "I only saw Gert and Hennessy, but Croft is bound to be in there."

"No indication of what was going on inside?" Bill asked.

"No. I couldn't get close enough to hear anything without being seen. It was quiet, though. No ruckus."

Bill asked Scotty for the warrant and placed it in his breast pocket.

He addressed Harold and one of the other deputies. "You two set up a roadblock. Don't let anyone get past you, either going in or coming out." They nodded understanding.

"Scotty, and you other two, approach the house on foot. Flank it, cover the back. Stay in the trees and out of sight unless hell breaks loose. Thatcher and I will approach from the front in my car."

As Bill continued giving instructions, Thatcher took off his suit coat, rolled it up, and placed it on the floorboard of Bill's car. He didn't want anything between him and his holster, which he tied to his thigh.

Those in the group noticed and exchanged looks among themselves. Thatcher ignored the suspicion and resentment still directed at him, but Bill must've sensed it. He said, "Gabe Driscoll has confessed to killing his wife. He alleges that Bernie Croft arranged to have her buried out at Pointer's Gap. Thatcher was wronged."

To a man they shifted their gazes to him, but he gave a small shrug and kept his attention on Bill.

"Okay then," the sheriff said, as though a weighty matter had been settled. "We'll try to peacefully serve the warrant," he said, "but I don't expect Bernie to surrender without a fight. Thatcher, anything to add to what you've already told us of the situation?"

"Yeah. Croft's man Hennessy is no amateur. Given the chance, he'll kill you. If you get into it with him, don't hesitate. Put him down."

They acknowledged the advice with grim nods.

Bill said, "All right. Let's go."

"Who's that?" one of the deputies said.

They all turned. Irv Plummer's truck was rattling like a peddler's wagon up the road. It came to a stop behind the second department vehicle.

Bill swore. "Get him out of here."

But before anyone could act, Corrine hopped down from the passenger seat and came running toward Thatcher. "Mr. Hutton? What's going on?"

"We're serving an arrest warrant."

"For Gert?" She turned to Bill. "I hope it's for Gert."

"Not today."

"Fair warning, y'all. She keeps a loaded shotgun on the bar within reach."

Looking past Corrine, Bill said, "Mr. Plummer, you can't be here."

"It's a public road."

"Not now, it's not."

"Irv, you need to get going," Thatcher said.

"Oh, you think that badge gives you the right to order me around?"

"Take it up with me later, Irv. For right now, get Corrine and clear out."

Irv looked around at the group of solemn men, and the firepower they carried, and seemed to grasp the seriousness of the situation. He said to Thatcher, "The girl saw the marked cars, insisted on turning in and finding out if Gert was finally gonna get her comeuppance. But I see y'all got business, so we'll be on our way. Come on, girl." He put his hand in the crook of Corrine's elbow.

She shook him off, saying, "What the hell's *he* doing?"

They all followed her line of sight. Lefty was staggering out from a grove of mesquite trees. Seeing them, he stopped. Swaying on his feet, he slowly and unsteadily raised his hands in surrender. "I had no part in it. Didn't want no part in it."

The two deputies closest to him took him by his skinny arms, and half-dragged, half-carried him over to the group. "Swear to God, it was none of my doing." His protruding Adam's apple slid up and down. "I sneaked out the back while's they were occupied." His knees gave out, and he would have gone to the ground if the deputies hadn't been supporting him. "I'm kinda drunk."

Bill said sternly, "Well, you've got one second to sober up. What's going on back there? What don't you want any part of?"

"I'm scared 'fore it's over they're gonna kill her."

"Who?"

He rolled his eyes and finally blinked Irv into focus. "His daughter-in-law. Ain't that why all y'all are here?"

FIFTY-NINE

Thatcher waited for no one. He tossed the rifle into the back of Bill's car, got behind the wheel, and, thanks to the electric starter, was already accelerating by the time Bill had caught hold of the open passenger door. He stood on the running board until he could clamber into the seat.

Scotty shouted, "All hell has broken loose." He and the other two deputies sprinted after the car, grasped whatever handhold they could get, and hopped onto the running boards.

Thatcher was merciless on the motor. He didn't spare the tires, either, making no attempt to dodge rain-filled potholes. When the roadhouse came into sight, he aimed the hood of Bill's car at the rear end of Croft's town car. As he braked behind it, mere inches away from colliding with it, the deputies leaped off and divided up as Bill had instructed them to. Scotty took off toward the left side of the building, the other two went right.

Thatcher pulled his pistol and hurdled the front steps, then flattened himself to one side of the screened door. "Laurel!"

No answer.

Bill made it to the porch and stationed himself on the other side of the door. "Bernie, we know you have Mrs. Plummer. Send her out unharmed."

Nothing.

"I have a warrant for your arrest, Bernie."

From within, Croft laughed. "That's hilarious."

Bill said, "You're right. Let's skip the official stuff, save taxpayers the money of trying you for the murder of Davy O'Connor and the arson murder of the Johnsons. I'll simply kill you for poisoning Daisy."

There was no response, and Thatcher was done fucking around. He signaled to Bill that he would open the screened door, since it opened out toward them, and he was on the left side. Bill nodded.

Thatcher reached for the handle and flung open the door toward Bill. Thatcher hit the ground and rolled across the threshold. He was greeted by two shotgun blasts. Gert must have fired both barrels. Thatcher registered that she would need time to reload. Bill must've had the same thought as he came through the opening with his pistol blazing.

He drew fire from two positions: behind the bar and from above. Thatcher looked up. Hennessy was on the landing at the top of the stairs, holding Laurel in front of him, one hand clamped over her mouth, his other aiming a pistol at Thatcher.

Don't hesitate. Put him down.

Sooner than Thatcher could think it, he fired at the bridge of Hennessy's nose. The man showed an instant of surprise, then fell back, dead before he hit the floor. But when he released Laurel, she went somersaulting down the stairs. Thatcher realized her hands were bound.

He shouted her name, but got no answer.

A bullet struck the floor within an inch of his face, sending up splintered wood. A chunk hit him on the cheekbone, barely missing his eye. He rolled away from where he was, came up in a crouch, and took cover behind a table.

"Bill, you okay?"

"I want these sons o' bitches."

"Hennessy's not a worry."

"Dead?"

"Yep."

"Hear that, Bernie?" Bill taunted. "Your hired gun is in hell."

Their repartee had given Thatcher time to scan the room. He couldn't see Gert, but figured she was behind the bar, reloading. It had to have been Croft's shot that had struck the floor near him, which gave him an idea of the mayor's accuracy. He wasn't a bad shot.

He waited, crazy to know where Laurel was. Was her neck broken, her back? Had she hit her head and was lying unconscious and defenseless?

Croft showed his head above the bar. Both Thatcher and Bill fired a volley. Soda pop bottles shattered against the back of the bar, but Thatcher got no indication that Croft had been hit.

Where was Gert and that goddamn shotgun?

Bill was off to Thatcher's left. When Croft raised his head again, Bill fired two shots. Thatcher used the cover to take up another position. He still couldn't see Laurel. He couldn't place Gert, either, and that bothered him. He would have expected another blast from the shotgun by now. Unless one of their shots had struck her and she was down.

Couldn't count on that. Too much to hope for.

He had to know where Laurel was and if she was hurt. From his present vantage point, he couldn't see the bottom of the staircase where he featured her crumpled, broken, bleeding.

Croft was keeping him and Bill pinned down.

A shadow fell across the screened door. Croft fired at it. The shadow disappeared.

Thatcher, who was nearest the door, whispered, "Who's that?"

"Scotty."

"Hennessy's dead. Croft's behind the bar. Have you seen Gert?"

"No. Mrs. Plummer?"

"Alive when we got here. Now..." Thatcher couldn't bring himself to venture a guess.

"What do you want me to do, Thatcher?"

"Stay put, but be ready."

While carrying on the whispered conversation with the deputy through the screen, Thatcher had reloaded. Bill, who'd been exchanging potshots with Croft, also had to pause to reload. Thatcher waited until he was done, then motioned to Bill that he was going to intentionally draw Croft's fire, giving Bill a chance at him.

Bill acknowledged.

Thatcher took a breath, then surged to his feet and ran toward the staircase, banging into tables, overturning chairs, reaching across his torso to fire back toward the bar.

Croft took the bait. As soon as he showed himself, he and Bill exchanged a barrage. From beneath his left arm, Thatcher turned and fired three rounds at Croft before diving beneath a table. He rolled onto his back and fired toward Croft again, but he had disappeared behind the bar.

Thatcher flipped the table onto its side and hunkered behind it so he could reload. "Bill?"

"Bernie's hit. Wounded, at least."

"Are you okay?"

"Yeah."

Thatcher knew that wasn't true. He was breathing like a man who'd been hit. But where? How bad? He couldn't ask without also giving Croft the advantage of knowing.

"Bill, can you cover me?"

There was a grunt, then, "Ready."

Thatcher sprang up and sprinted over to the staircase.

There was no sign of Laurel. Not below, midway, or above.

She tumbled. On her way down, one body part or another struck every tread of the steep staircase. She landed hard. The wind was knocked out of her.

"Laurel!"

The first time Thatcher had called out to her, Hennessy's hand had been over her mouth. She couldn't respond this time, either, because she hadn't regained her breath. And Gert had been waiting for her at the bottom of the staircase.

She crammed a sour dishcloth into Laurel's mouth and lifted her off the floor. The madam was more solidly built even than Hennessy and seemed twice as strong. She was certainly as mean and merciless.

Laurel struggled, but without the use of her arms, and with every inch of her body pulsing in pain, she was virtually defenseless. But she'd be damned before she gave up.

In an attempt to get Thatcher's attention, she banged her heels against the hardwood floor. But, as she did, gunfire exploded, seeming to come from all directions at once and drowning out the sound.

Gert hit her on the temple with the barrel of the shotgun, dazing her. She had the will but not the coordination to resist when she was dragged past the bar, into a narrow passage, and through a door. The area into which Gert shoved her was darker, cooler, and smelled of booze.

Head still reeling, she realized that she was in Lefty's infamous back room.

In the front room, Thatcher was in a gunfight. Thatcher could die.

That prospect was more terrifying to her than the actuality of Gert, who was standing over her, loading shells into her shotgun. When she snapped it closed, she crammed the barrels beneath Laurel's chin.

And Laurel's last thought: *I love Thatcher.*

Thatcher stared at the emptiness at the bottom of the staircase.

Laurel was unhurt. She'd gotten herself to safety.

No. If she'd been able to respond to his shouts, she would have. Unless she hadn't wanted to give away her position to ... *Gert.*

Gert hadn't been behind the bar reloading. She'd abandoned

Bernie to fight it out with Bill while she was settling her grudge against Laurel.

But if Gert had fired the shotgun, he would have heard it. Laurel would be dead at the bottom of the stairs. Gert had a reason for keeping Laurel alive.

Hostage.

Okay, so where had Gert taken her?

The back room. Had to be.

Thatcher processed all this within a millisecond. By the time he'd completed the last thought, he was already moving in the direction of the back room. But as he reached the open space at the end of the bar, he was met with a hail of bullets.

He fell back and ducked under the counter. He waited, breathing hard but as quietly as possible. He would be no help to Laurel dead.

His mind tapered down to the single purpose of killing Bernie Croft. Now.

Gun hand extended, he stood up and moved into the space at the end of the bar, intentionally making himself an easy target. Croft was lying on his back in a pool of soda pop and his own blood. He must've spent all his bullets in that last barrage, because the pistol lay on the floor at his side.

Thatcher drew a bead on him.

Croft's eyes showed stark fear, but he couldn't speak for the blood bubbling from his mouth. He was frantically clawing with both hands at the multiple bullet wounds in his torso. His bloody watch fob kept getting in the way of his futile attempts to stanch the gushers of blood.

It would be a mercy kill. To hell with that. Thatcher lowered his gun. "Scotty!"

Scotty and the two other deputies rushed in, weapons drawn.

Already on the move, Thatcher said, "See to Bill. Croft's gut-shot."

"Dead?"

"Yeah. He just hasn't stopped breathing yet. Two of you follow me."

Thatcher ran into the dark, narrow passage behind the bar that led to the back room. "Laurel!" He tried the door. It was locked. "Laurel!"

He put his shoulder to the door. It burst open just as two gunshots were fired.

———◆———

"You're my ticket out of here, princess." Gert yanked Laurel to her feet and began hauling her across the room toward a rear door.

Having taken several blows to the head, the sudden movement sickened her. Bile filled the back of her throat, but she knew that with that disgusting rag in her mouth, she would choke to death if she retched. She forced down the fiery bile.

The shooting in the front room had stopped. She heard scuffling footsteps and shouting, but the only distinct word she heard was her name.

Hearing Thatcher's voice coming nearer spurred her, imbued her with energy she would have thought unattainable. More than that, it filled her with die-hard determination not to let this ogress defeat her.

She jammed her feet against the floor, trying to halt or slow Gert's progress.

"Move! I'll shoot you!"

Laurel didn't believe she would. She was Gert's bargaining chip, but only for as long as she stayed alive.

A thumping noise came from beyond the door behind them. "Laurel!"

"Shit!" Gert muttered.

Try as she might, Laurel couldn't match Gert's strength, and they reached the back entrance. She still held the shotgun beneath Laurel's chin, but Laurel thought that if she could hold out for just a moment longer—

Gert reached around her and pulled open the door.

Corrine was standing within two feet of the threshold.

Taking advantage of Gert's surprise, Laurel lunged sideways.

Corrine stretched out her arm and fired two rounds point-blank into Gert's throat.

───◆───

Thatcher crashed through the door in time to see Gert drop the shotgun. She clutched her throat with both hands and staggered backward as blood spurted from between her thick, tobacco-stained fingers. She landed on the floor like a felled redwood, her eyes wild.

Even before they went unseeing, Thatcher was kneeling beside Laurel and yanking a rancid dishcloth out of her mouth. In seconds, he had her hands untied. He ran his hands over her to reassure himself that she was intact.

She placed her hands on his chest, saying in a rush of breath, "She caught me at the foot of the stairs and stuffed that cloth in my mouth. I couldn't call out to you."

He pulled her to him and placed his chin on the crown of her head. He looked at Corrine. "How'd you get here?"

"Irv and them deputies setting up the roadblock got into an argument over who was moving what vehicle first. It got to be a real pissin' contest. Ain't that just like men? I run off while they weren't looking."

She grinned and extended her hand, palm up, on which lay the small Derringer. "I come to give Miss Laurel her pistol back."

SIXTY

The J.P. was summoned to declare Bernard Croft, Jimmy Hennessy, and Gertrude Atkins dead. Lefty, who seemed relieved rather than upset to learn that Gert had departed this life, was taken in for questioning and to sleep off his bender. He would keep Gabe Driscoll company in the cell block that night.

Bill had taken a bullet in the thigh. It had missed major blood vessels, but was buried in the muscle and would need to be surgically removed. Irv offered to transport him to town in the back of his truck. Deputies carried him over and placed him in it.

Laurel insisted she would be fine when her head cleared, but everyone else, especially Thatcher, was just as insistent that Dr. Perkins should check her over. He personally tucked her into the backseat of Bill's car, drove her to the clinic himself, and hand-delivered her to the doctor and a nurse.

They gowned her and left her lying on the table in the examination room, where Thatcher was granted a private moment with her while they assembled what they would need to treat her mild injuries.

She scooted over, creating a spot for Thatcher to sit. He clasped hands with her and looked her over. "Do you hurt anywhere?"

"A little bit everywhere. Bumps and bruises, mostly."

"Your head?" He wasn't sure she was aware of the large bruise on her temple.

"The nurse already gave me aspirin powder. What happened there?" Tenderly she touched the cut beneath his eye made by the wood splinter.

"Nothing."

She kissed her fingertip and barely touched it to the scrape. "I have some good news. Mike O'Connor is in a room down the hall. He's holding his own, Dr. Perkins said. He predicts a full recovery. But he also told me that, in a lucid moment, Mike vowed on his Saint Christopher medal to get revenge for Davy."

"Maybe he'll have a change of heart."

"I doubt it," she said wistfully.

So did Thatcher, actually.

To get her off that subject, he said, "You and Corrine will have to give your statements about what happened with Gert. It'll be a formality."

"Of course."

"But I have one question. Why did Corrine have your pistol?"

"When all the trouble started happening in the hills, I was afraid for her safety. Even though Ernie—"

"Who's Ernie?"

She smiled. "I'll tell you about him sometime."

He fingered a strand of her hair. "I think we both have a lot to tell each other."

"Give me a hint."

He softly kissed her lips.

As he eased away from her, she whispered, "I can't wait to hear the rest."

From the other side of the door, Dr. Perkins cleared his throat. "Mr. Hutton, they need your help with Sheriff Amos downstairs."

"Be right there." He stood and bent over Laurel. "I'll see you later."

"Yes. However late it is."

As he backed toward the door, they stretched out their arms, keeping their fingers touching for as long as possible before they fell away.

———•———

Thatcher exited through a door in the rear of the building, where Irv's truck was parked. As he approached it, he overheard Corrine saying to Irv, "Miss Laurel said you'd have a hissy fit if you knew she'd given me her little gun. But good thing she did. I can't wait to tell Ernie about Gert. He'll be so proud o' me."

Deputies were grouped around the tailgate, talking quietly among themselves. Thatcher felt a kick of apprehension. "What's the matter?"

"He won't come out," Scotty said.

"What do you mean? He can't walk. Lift him out and carry him."

"We tried. He threatened to fire all of us. He said he wouldn't go under the knife till he had talked to you."

"Thatcher," Bill called. "Get in here."

The others shuffled aside as Thatcher made his way to the raised tailgate and looked over it into the bed of the truck. Bill was lying on his back, sweating profusely and in obvious pain.

"What the hell, Bill? Doc's got everything ready for you upstairs."

"I need to talk to you. Get in. You others," he said, raising his voice, "make yourselves scarce."

Thatcher lowered the tailgate and stepped up onto it, saying over his shoulder, "Give us a few minutes."

"Uh, Thatcher?"

He paused and looked back. Harold was threading the brim of his hat through his fingers. It seemed he'd been appointed the spokesperson. "We, uh. You did okay out there today. I mean, damn good." The others nodded. "We'd all take you out for a beer, except, well, you know. This danged Prohibition."

The awkward invitation was their way of apologizing for the slights. Thatcher bobbed his chin. "A beer would go down real good. Some other time."

They all breathed a collective sigh. Scotty said, "We'll wait over here." They moved away as a group, giving Bill the privacy he'd asked for.

Thatcher hunkered down beside him. "What's this bullshit about?"

"Leg's hurting like a bastard."

"Then let us get you in there so the doc can fix you up."

"I'm scared of ether."

"You'll sleep it off."

"I sent one of the men to tell Daisy. Hated to. Alice Cantor sent back word that she's doing a lot better. Got some scrambled eggs down her. She'll bring her to see me tomorrow."

"That's good news. Let's go."

Bill caught Thatcher by the sleeve.

"Something else." He settled his head on the floor of the truck and stared at the tarpaulin stretched overhead. "Soon as I'm able, I'll be turning myself in. I took Bernie's bribes. Let Hiram...others...get away with murder. Like killing that boy Elray. He'll be on my conscience for a long time."

Thatcher wanted to say *Mine, too*, but Bill didn't give him a chance.

"Being lax kept things peaceful. But I'm a crook, same as the rest. Past time I owned up to it." He blinked sweat from his eyes and grimaced with pain.

"This confession can wait, Bill."

"No, it can't." He returned his gaze to Thatcher. "If I were to die on that table, you'd never know unless I tell you now. And that would be a tragedy."

"You're not in your right head, Bill. You're talking nonsense."

He clutched Thatcher's sleeve tighter.

"From the start, I saw in you..." He made a dismissive gesture. "I already told you why I wanted you to work with me. Tim. All that. I wanted it bad enough, I lied to keep you here."

His face contorted, and it wasn't sweat in his eyes, Thatcher now realized. It was tears.

He choked on his next words. "I told you that your Mr. Hobson had died."

SIXTY-ONE

The house was two-story, with a white clapboard exterior trimmed in sky blue. Thatcher was relieved to see that it was as nice a house as the growing city of Amarillo afforded.

He went through the gate of the iron picket fence and up to the front door. His knock was answered by a gray-haired gentleman with a benign smile and gentle brown eyes behind wire-rimmed eyeglasses. Thatcher had been told that he was a prosperous accountant.

"You must be Mr. Hutton." He extended his right hand and shook. "I'm George Maxwell. We received your telegram yesterday afternoon. Ever since, he's been watching the clock like a hawk."

Thatcher was led through the main rooms of a house that smelled like lemon oil and homemade bread. The bedroom he was ushered into was bright with sunlight filtered through gauzy curtains.

A woman who was bent over the bed adjusting the covers straightened up and turned as she heard Thatcher enter. "Welcome, Mr. Hutton. My name is Irma."

"Ma'am."

"Would you care for something to drink?"

"Thank you, but I'm okay for now."

She gave him an understanding smile. "Then I'll leave you to your reunion." As she passed him on her way out of the room, she said, "Bless you for coming." She and her husband withdrew and closed the door behind them.

Thatcher almost wouldn't have recognized the person on the bed. His memory was of an average-size man, but one who had seemed larger than life, a man robust enough to fit into the seemingly endless landscape that he'd lived on, worked on, and loved.

Propped against a stack of fluffy pillows, he looked diminished. The stroke had paralyzed his left side and distorted that half of his face. The eye was permanently closed, his mouth drawn downward.

No, Thatcher might not have recognized Mr. Henry Hobson Jr.

But Mr. Hobson recognized him.

His right eye was lit up with joy. He raised his right hand and reached out toward Thatcher. Although his countenance and reduced form were unfamiliar, Thatcher would have known that calloused, crusty hand anywhere. It had taught him how to rope and shoot and brand, how to pack a saddle bag, start a campfire and put it out safely, how to hold a poker hand, tie a necktie, and how to use his table manners. It had patted his shoulder in congratulations for achievements, and had squeezed it with encouragement following failures.

Just about anything worth knowing he had learned from Mr. Hobson, the principal lesson being that a man was only as good as his word. He crossed over to the bed and took Mr. Hobson's hand in his. "I promised you I'd be back."

———◦———

In his mind, Thatcher had replayed the telephone conversation with Trey Hobson's secretary, and realized how the condolences he'd extended had been misconstrued as a reference to Mr. Hobson's debilitating stroke, not to his demise.

The Maxwells told him that following the major stroke, Mr. Hobson had suffered several minor ones, and that his doctor predicted a cerebral "event" from which he wouldn't recover.

"Irma has nursing experience," Mr. Maxwell explained. "Several years ago we began making our spare room available to patients in Mr. Hobson's condition. When he was dismissed from the hospital, we had a vacancy and invited him to move in. His son agreed that being with us was preferable to a nursing home."

And the kind couple were far preferable to Trey, Thatcher thought.

The Maxwells gave him a bedroom on the second floor and treated him like an honored guest, but largely he was left free to pass the time with Mr. Hobson.

His visit stretched into weeks.

He and his mentor spent hours together in the homey bedroom. For the most part, Mr. Hobson stayed in bed, but occasionally Thatcher would move him into a chair where he had a better view out the window. He couldn't converse, but he was an attentive listener and expressed himself eloquently by using his right hand to gesture and his right eye to blink twice for yes, once for no.

Thatcher read to him daily, either from the newspaper or from the dime novels he loved about the wild West, cattle drives, and shoot-'em'-ups. Thatcher shared war stories, some funny, some harrowing.

He told Mr. Hobson about his jump from the freight train and the unpredictable turn his life had taken since. He described in detail all the people with whom he'd become involved to one degree or another.

As he talked about them, Thatcher realized that even those with whom he'd barely crossed paths and would never see again had been woven tightly into his memory and would stay there forever.

He got angry all over again when he told Mr. Hobson about Bill's deception, the selfishness behind it, the betrayal of a man he'd come to respect. Mr. Hobson didn't immediately respond, and then he moved his right hand laterally, parallel to the ground, as though saying *Let it pass*.

And of course, Thatcher talked about Laurel. He described her physically but was frustrated by the inadequacy of his words. He groused about her stubborn streak but admitted to Mr. Hobson that he'd lost his heart to her sassiness. He could have sworn the old man chuckled.

Often Thatcher just sat with him, saying nothing, hoping that Mr. Hobson was as content simply being in his presence as much as Thatcher was simply being in his. It was during those quiet times that Thatcher reflected on his experience of the past several months, and began to realize that there might have been a purpose behind everything that had happened, a governing why for that he hadn't perceived while he was living it.

He wondered if Mr. Hobson, somehow, even in his limited capacity, had influenced that insight.

⁂

One morning, Thatcher asked Mr. Maxwell if he could borrow his car. "I'd like to drive out to the ranch."

Having spotted the car's wake of dust from a mile away, Jesse was waiting for it outside the bunkhouse, holding a shotgun across his chest. The dog, who was part wolf, sat growling at his side.

When Thatcher stepped out of the car, Jesse dropped the shotgun, called off the animal, and, although he was well past seventy, ran out to embrace him, thumping him on the back and laughing.

They opened a contraband bottle of mescal and spent the day sharing it and recollections. They laughed with hilarity over some. Others made them pensive or downright sad.

Thatcher was reunited with his saddle. It was on a stand inside the bunkhouse. Thatcher ran his hand over the smooth leather. "It's never looked better, Jesse. Thank you for keeping it in good condition."

When the old ranch hand asked about his former boss, Thatcher told him he'd considered packing Mr. Hobson into the car and bringing him along.

"But I think he's too frail to have made the drive out here." Thatcher gazed off into the distance, past the empty corrals and cattle pens where the dust had settled for good, and the whoops and hollers of rowdy cowboys would never be heard again. The magnificent span of the Panhandle's horizon was now interrupted by the silhouettes of drilling rigs. Thatcher added, "And it would have broken his heart."

When it came time for Thatcher to leave, his double-handed hand-shake with Jesse held for a long time in an unspoken acknowledgment that this was goodbye.

One afternoon Irma Maxwell knocked softly on the bedroom door then came in carrying a plate with a sandwich on it. "Since you didn't come to the table for lunch..." She halted midway across the room.

Thatcher's chair was pulled up close to the bed. His hand was wrapped around Mr. Hobson's. "He passed." He cleared his husky throat. "About ten minutes ago. No event. It was dignified and peaceful."

He spent that night with the Maxwells, but in the morning he came down-stairs carrying his duffel bag already packed. He wanted to make a clean break before Trey arrived. Yesterday when notified of his father's death, he'd told Mr. Maxwell that he "couldn't get away" until this morning.

Thatcher didn't think he could be civil to the self-centered bastard, and it would be disrespectful to Mr. Hobson to create tension or cause a scene. Besides, attending a stuffy funeral, Mr. Hobson in a casket, him in a pew, didn't seem a fitting end to these meaningful weeks they had spent in each other's company.

He declined the Maxwells' offer of breakfast before he left. "Thank you, but there's a train at nine-forty. I'd like to make it."

"Before you go." Mr. Maxwell went over to a chest and took a shoe box from one of the drawers. "When Mr. Hobson was moved in here with us, this was among his things."

He handed the box to Thatcher. His name was written on top in Mr. Hobson's bold scrawl. Before he raised the lid, Thatcher heard the familiar jingle and knew what he would find inside: Mr. Hobson's spurs, still dirt-encrusted from his last ride.

SIXTY-TWO

Not entrusting his saddle to the baggage car, Thatcher boarded the train with it on his shoulder. He set it in the seat in front of him where he could keep an eye on it. He took the seat next to the window.

To discourage interaction with other passengers, he pulled his cowboy hat over his eyes, slumped in his seat, and pretended to be asleep. The train chuffed out of the station.

He must have dozed, because he was roused by someone asking, "Is this seat taken?"

Damn. Thatcher shook his head. "No."

"Aw, good. The cars are crowded."

The passenger settled into the seat. "Where are you headed?"

So much for discouraging conversation. Thatcher took off his hat and placed it on his knee. He put his thumb and middle finger into his eye sockets and rubbed them. "Abilene. Then east from there."

"Back to Foley?"

Surprised by that response, Thatcher glanced at his seat partner, did a double take, then his right hand automatically went for his pistol.

"You're not wearing your gun belt. I checked as you boarded. I didn't want you to shoot me before I could explain myself."

The smile he flashed was not that of a pimp. In place of the gold tooth was a normal white molar. "You thought you'd seen the last of Chester Landry, didn't you? Well, you have. And, God, what a jerk he was. I'm glad to be shed of him."

He had medium brown hair that was wavy and loose, not slicked back with pounds of pomade. He was dressed in a conservative dark suit, with a pinstripe vest and unremarkable necktie.

Thatcher looked around to see if they were being observed, possibly to reassure himself that he wasn't dreaming. No one was paying him any attention except the man seated next to him. Thatcher said, "Who the hell are you?"

"Lewis Mahoney, detective, Dallas PD. I'll show you my badge if you insist, but that can be awkward, because I'm presently on loan to another agency, working undercover."

"What agency?"

"I can't tell."

"That's convenient."

"Actually it's a nuisance. Because I would like for you to believe me, Mr. Hutton. I'm sure you have questions. I'll answer those I can."

"What happened to Randy?"

"He was drawing too much attention to himself. I was afraid that Croft was going to have him killed, so I had to get him out of there. I lured him to Dallas by promising him a position in my fictitious bootlegging operation. I took him to a speakeasy to celebrate his new employment. It was raided, as planned. Dallas police arrested him, as planned. I escaped arrest, as planned."

"Like at Lefty's."

He made a wry face. "No, that wasn't planned. I just got lucky that night. Anyway. Randy. Arresting officers promised him clemency in exchange for names. That of Chester Landry topped his list, of course. Not the most loyal of acquaintances, a young man of meager charac- ter, and negligible morals, but not deserving of having his throat cut by Jimmy Hennessy." He looked at Thatcher shrewdly. "By the way, congratulations on that outstanding display of marksmanship. You're already a legend. I'll bet Wyatt Earp is pea green."

Thatcher ignored that. "You know, some suspected me of being a secret agent."

"Croft was convinced. You bedeviled him, Mr. Hutton."

"I'm glad to hear it. But I'm talking about friends who figured me for a spy. I'd hate doing what you do, Mr. Mahoney."

"Yes, you would. The integrity thing."

"Doesn't it ever bother you to rat out people who've befriended you?"

"It would if I didn't stay focused on the big picture."

"Which is what?"

"First and foremost, I'm an officer of the law. I despise this Prohibition act, because it is already making lawbreakers out of law-abiding people, and turning petty criminals into villainous racketeers. Croft, for example."

"My understanding is that he was always corrupt."

"Yes, but he hadn't gone so far as to murder anyone. Greed rid him of restraint. Even in the short time I knew him, I saw it happening, and it was frightening. Mark my words, Hutton, the next war this country fights is going to be against violent crime syndicates that give no quarter."

"Like Davy O'Connor's assassination. Firing the Johnsons' house."

"Exactly like that. Jesus," he said, shaking his head. "For months I'd been coordinating a countywide raid. Several agencies, working together, we were going to nail Hiram Johnson and Bernie Croft." He made a helpless gesture.

"Croft moved first. Hard and fast and without my knowledge. Incidentally, we've identified the men who ambushed the O'Connors. All were on Croft's payroll. They've got prices on their heads. Somebody will turn. We'll get them."

"You went to Laurel Plummer that night and told her you wanted to make her an offer."

"I was going to reveal myself for who I am and ask her to become an informant for me. In exchange, I would see to it that she and her associates would be granted clemency for moonshining." He chuckled. "Looking back on it, it was a bad idea."

"For putting her in danger like that, I would have killed you."

"As I said, a bad idea." Again, he laughed softly. "I don't advise getting on her fighting side. She has a wicked right hook." He worked his jaw laterally.

When Thatcher didn't react, he said, "I can see that you're not amused." He paused as though seeking a better way to express himself. "Let me assure you that I'm often bothered about the betrayal aspect of my job. But I don't go after the small-timers like your Mrs. Plummer. I'm after the bad guys, the ones who would have ultimately gotten rid of her for no other reason than that she was becoming a pest."

"Croft."

"Or someone like a Chester Landry, but the real article."

"I was afraid that was exactly what was going to happen."

"I figured. Your *protectiveness* was apparent."

Thatcher didn't comment on that. "How'd you know I'd be on this train?"

"I knew you were in Amarillo, and the reason for your being here. I'm sorry about your friend."

"Thanks. But why were you keeping tabs on me?"

He smiled, a genuine, unaffected smile. "First because you're damned interesting. Then because the more I saw of you, the more I came to believe that you had missed your calling."

He withdrew a business card from the pocket of his vest and handed it to Thatcher. "There's a good man, a sheriff, in Bynum. Know it?"

"No."

"East Texas. Pretty country. Piney woods. Lakes full of fish. Bynum's a sleepy little town where not much happens. Except that, on the county line, there's a horse racetrack." He punched Thatcher in the arm as he said that. "Racetracks draw sinners like moths to flame. But now that there's no legal drinking or gambling, the sinners are restless, and the sheriff has more than he can handle. Think about it."

He scooted out of the seat. "My stop is coming up. It's been a pleasure chatting with you. I trust in your integrity to keep this meeting to yourself. And should we ever meet somewhere—"

"I wouldn't give you away."

"I know that." He extended his hand. Thatcher shook it. Looking directly into Thatcher's eyes, he said, "I've enjoyed making your acquaintance, Hutton. Take care."

Then he turned and walked to the end of the car, opened the door, and stepped through to the next car.

SIXTY-THREE

One morning Laurel woke up with a grasp on that missed flicker of illumination she'd had after her night of lovemaking with Thatcher. She couldn't let it go or even leave it to languish. It was so long overdue, she was compelled to share it without delay.

She dressed and went downstairs. Irv was finishing up his breakfast. "I left a pan of biscuits warming in the oven. Sit down, I'll pour you some coffee."

"Let's go for a ride."

He turned to her, a puzzled look on his face. "Now? Where to?"

"Just come, please."

She lifted her straw hat off the peg and put it on, took down her purse, and went out through the back door. Mumbling something about "nutty female notions," Irv followed.

Ten minutes later, Laurel sat down on the narrow strip of grass between Pearl's and Derby's graves. She motioned for Irv to join her on the ground.

"I won't be able to get back up."

"Yes, you will. I'll help you."

He lowered himself to the ground on the other side of his son's grave. "What's going on, Laurel? What's the matter? Are you sad over him?"

She knew he wasn't speaking of Derby. Thatcher had left without a word and hadn't come back. No one knew if he would. She cried herself to sleep most nights. She was in dire need of comforting. Yet, the person who could ease her misery was the source of it.

She was furious at him for that. But her yearning for him was like a sickness. "This isn't about him."

"Told you not to trust him."

"You did," she said softly. Idly, she began pulling up the dandelions that had begun sprouting on Pearl's grave. "Something's come to me recently."

"A package?"

"No," she said, smiling. "Nothing tangible, although I do consider it a gift of sorts."

"I think when Gert clouted you on the head, she knocked something loose."

She laughed softly. "You might be right. In which case, I have her to thank for this." He opened his mouth to say more, but she held up her hand. "It's enlightenment. It's been trying to worm its way into my consciousness. I think subconsciously I wanted it to stay put. I've resisted facing it. But I woke up this morning with it firmly seated in my mind. And please stop looking at me like I belong in a loony bin."

"Well, how am I supposed to be looking at you? You ain't making a lick of sense."

"Then I'll make it plainer." She dusted loose dirt off her hands. "Irv, you know how bitter I felt toward Derby for abandoning me."

"You had a right to be."

"Not really. Because I also abandoned him."

"What are you talking about?"

"I've never told you about our start. We met at a dance. Which was forbidden to me, of course. I sneaked out and went with a girl-friend. Derby was handsome and fun, someone I knew my parents would disapprove. I'll admit that was a large part of the attraction. Our whirlwind romance and hasty marriage was my deliverance. Just six weeks later, he left for Europe. I was a bride. Then the war ended, and he came home. To a wife.

"If he had returned with a shattered leg, I wouldn't have expected him to run sprints, would I? But in my selfishness and...and immaturity, I guess...I expected him to pick right back up where he'd left off. Giddy in love. Lighthearted, optimistic, oozing charm.

"But it soon became apparent that Derby was no longer that romantic hero. What's become clear to me is that I, unintentionally, applied pressure on top of the pressure he was already feeling. I didn't support him the way I should have."

"Laurel—"

"No, please. Let me get this out."

He dry-scrubbed his face with his hand and motioned for her to continue.

"I cleaned and cooked and slept with him like a dutiful wife. I begged him to talk to me about the things that were haunting him. I pushed him to try this, to do that, to get help. I swear to you that I did all of this out of love. I hated that he was suffering and seemingly unreachable.

"But I've come to realize that what I considered encouragement must have sounded like harping to him. He even said so just before he shot himself. 'I'm sick of you nagging me about every goddamn thing.'

"God knows I wanted to rescue him. But what he might have needed most was for me to stop flapping around him dispensing advice, and just to *be*. Be there. To hold him tight without saying anything. That's what I didn't do. I didn't allow him to face his fears within the cradle of my arms."

Irv frowned down at the turf over Derby's grave. There was still a slight mound that had yet to flatten out. "You're being too hard on yourself, Laurel. I told you Derby always had that darkness in him."

"I don't know that I could have fixed him, Irv. It's vain of me to think that I could have prevented him from taking his life if he was determined to do so. We'll never know. But, given how damaged he obviously was, I didn't give him credit for struggling through each day as well as he could.

"I laid all the blame on him for what he did. That was unfair." She reached across the grave and took Irv's hand. "You fault yourself for having to leave him when he was a boy. In your circumstances, you did the best you could. It was important for me to tell you that I could have done better by Derby."

He sat for a moment without saying anything, then squeezed her hand. "I couldn't have chosen a better daughter-in-law if I was to have picked you myself."

She had to clamp her lip between her teeth to keep it from quivering.

He cleared his throat noisily and said, "Now that's done, come hoist me up."

SIXTY-FOUR

Thatcher walked from the train station straight to her back door, which stood open. He watched her through the screened door as she placed a circle of rolled-out dough into a pie tin and began working the edges with her fingers.

"Fluting."

She started at the sound of his voice. For a span of ten seconds, she held his gaze, then went back to what she was doing. "Go away."

"Didn't you get my telegram?"

With one flour-covered hand, she gestured toward the drainboard, where the torn-up pieces of a telegram lay scattered. "'I'm coming for you.' You have your nerve. Get away from my house. I'm busy."

"I had to go, Laurel."

She stopped fiddling with the dough, but kept her head down, looking at her handiwork rather than at him. "Sheriff Amos told me about Mr. Hobson."

"How'd that come about?"

"Well, after days of hearing nothing from you and not knowing where you were, if you were alive or dead, I went to see the one person who might know what had happened to you. He was still recovering from the surgery." Finished with the pie crust, she reached for a dishcloth and wiped her hands. "He told me about his lie."

She set down the cloth and looked at him sorrowfully. "That was an awful thing for him to do, Thatcher. Did you make it to Amarillo in time?"

He opened the screened door and went inside. "He passed last Wednesday."

"You got to see him?"

"Yeah." He searched her eyes. "Laurel, I know it must've looked like I had run out on you, but I had to go, and I had to go right then before anyone could try to talk me out of it, or delay it, or whatever.

"And I don't regret that decision. I loved the man, and I wouldn't give anything for the time we had together before he died. I don't blame you for being mad. Just please try to understand."

She had softened considerably. "Of course I understand, Thatcher. I was more afraid for your safety than mad." She covered a laugh with her hand. "No, I was furious."

He smiled. "You had reason."

She glanced at the telegram she'd ripped up. "Where have you been since last Wednesday?"

"I made a side trip to Bynum."

"In East Texas? That's more than a side trip."

"We can talk about it later. Is Irv here?"

"No."

"Are you expecting him?"

"He's staying out with Ernie and Corrine tonight."

Thatcher still didn't know who Ernie was. "Turn off the oven."

She placed her hands on her hips. "I'm in the middle of baking pies."

He went to her, put his hands at her waist, and drew her to him. "Turn off the oven."

Not long afterward, they lay naked and entwined, her hair as tangled around them as the bedsheet. He lay on his back with one knee raised, she with her head on his chest, which she lightly strummed with her fingertips. "I gave in way too easily."

"Easy, hell." He cupped her bottom and scooted her hip up against his. "It took me twenty whole seconds to get you up the stairs."

She laughed, then took his hand and nestled it between her breasts. "No teasing, I truly am sorry that you lost Mr. Hobson."

"I didn't lose him. He'll always be there."

"Will you tell me stories about him?"

He tilted his head down and tipped hers up so he could look into her face. He ran his thumb across her lips, but, being too moved to speak, only nodded.

She returned her cheek to his chest. After time, she asked, "What was in Bynum?"

"A job."

He felt her go still. "It's not a horse training job, is it?"

"No." He lifted her off his chest and turned onto his side to face her. He laid it all out and was more worried than he wanted to admit when she didn't immediately embrace the idea.

"It seems so random," she said. "Where'd you hear about it?"

He gave her a half smile. "I met a man on the train out of Amarillo. He told me about it."

"It sounds good, Thatcher, but you could have the same job here."

"It would be hard for me to work for Bill again."

"I get that, but—"

"And I can't wear a badge and be married to a local moonshiner."

"You haven't even asked me to marry you."

"Will you marry me?"

"No."

He laughed and nuzzled her neck. Sliding his hand into the vee of her thighs, he whispered, "You don't have to give me your answer right away."

He kept her occupied for the next half hour, rearranging her limbs to allow him access to enchanting spots, turning her this way and that to explore and entice, lazily mapping her sweet body with his hands and lips and tongue. He tormented her with his dalliances until she gasped *now*.

He pushed into her, and the fever pitch that he'd aroused in both of them combusted. He emptied all the sadness and disappointment, uncertainty and longing that he'd experienced in the past few weeks into her.

He was now convinced that everything that had happened since his leap from that freight car had been predestined. He'd been making his way home. But not to a place. To a person. He would only ever be home with this woman.

Still breathing hotly, he rested his forehead against hers and pushed his fingers up into her hair. "I love you, Laurel."

"I believe you do."

"And you love me."

"I'm thinking it over."

"Naw, you love me, and you're gonna marry me."

"You don't know that."

"Yeah, I do. I have a knack." He melded their mouths, and by the time he ended the kiss, he'd convinced her.

The next morning, over breakfast, he said, "On our way to Bynum, I thought we'd stop over in Dallas, and get married there. Spend a couple of nights in a hotel. In a hotel *bed*."

At the stove, she sent him a smile over her shoulder. "I've never been in a hotel. And I've only seen the skyline of Dallas from a distance. Tell me about Bynum."

"It's pretty. Green. Lots of trees. I looked at a house that has a barn."

"You could keep horses."

"I could teach you to ride."

She carried over a plate of hotcakes and set it in front of him. Lips smiling against his ear, she whispered, "You already did."

He pulled her onto his lap. "You took to it good, too." He lowered his head and snarled against her breast.

She pushed him away. "Stop that. Irv could come in. What's the kitchen in this house like?"

"Large and airy. You could bake to your heart's content. I'll bet you could sell slices of pie at the racetrack."

"There's a racetrack?"

"Um-huh." His hand had ventured inside her housecoat and was toying with her nipple through her nightgown. "It causes some excitement. But otherwise, it's a sleepy little town where nothing much happens."

His mouth replaced his plucking fingers. She leaned her head back and gave him access. Faintly, she said, "Your hotcakes…"

They got cold.

———————

Thatcher went to the boardinghouse. Mrs. May greeted him with her characteristic geniality. "Don't think you're crawling back, 'cause I done rented your room." She'd packed everything in his trunk and put it in her root cellar. He retrieved his belongings and happily left the place for the last time.

He went from there to Fred Barker, literally with hat in hand, and profusely apologized for having left without notifying him. "I didn't even return the rifle you loaned me."

"No never mind," Barker said. "Sheriff sent a deputy over with the rifle and a note, explaining. 'Fraid some of the owners of the horses you were training came to get them."

"I don't blame them a bit."

That week, he worked at the stable several hours a day, exercising the horses belonging to Barker. On his last day, as he was about to leave, he said, "I'll always be in your debt for hiring me that first day."

"I ain't ever been sorry for it. Never saw a horseman good as you. I'm gonna miss havin' you around. Roger's plumb heartbroke." They shook hands. "Good luck to you, Thatcher."

Thatcher tipped his hat and walked away. Barker called after him. "I like them spurs."

Thatcher smiled back at him. "I'm gonna try to earn them."

———◦———

Bill was sitting in one of the rockers on his front porch when Thatcher drove up in Laurel's car. He got out and walked to the porch. As he sat down in the second chair, he motioned toward the cane propped against Bill's. "How's the leg?"

"Okay. Just aches. Some days worse than others."

For a time, neither said anything, then Thatcher asked after Mrs. Amos.

"I'm taking her to Temple. They've got a three-month program, but she hasn't had a drop since the arsenic thing. She wants to get well. We've been talking a lot about Tim. I think she's finally come to terms. The other day, we even laughed over something he'd done when he was a boy."

"That's good, Bill. That's real good. She'll be all right. I'm sure of it."

Bill waited a moment, then said, "Mila Driscoll's body was recovered."

"No trouble locating it?"

"Not after I passed along your description of that rock pile. Her uncle took her remains to New Braunfels for burial."

"Driscoll?"

"The sorry son of a bitch has fired two defense lawyers already, and they were glad of it. The judge granted a change of venue, so at least he's off our hands. If the state doesn't hang him, he'll spend the rest of his life behind bars." He looked over at Thatcher. "You'll probably be subpoenaed to testify when he comes up for trial."

"I'll be there."

"Patsy Kemp took Norma's baby boy and moved to Colorado to join her husband. They never could have kids, so they're happy to have him. I told her we suspected that Bernie Croft had fathered the boy, and that in all probability he'd been the one to assault Norma. She was shocked. She'd never met Bernie, only knew him to be the mayor."

"Miss Blanchard took that secret to her grave. I wish she'd kept the one that got her killed."

Bill gave a solemn nod, then said, "Still looking for Chester Landry. He's nowhere to be found. That one is slippery as owl shit."

"Yeah."

They rocked in silence until Bill said, "They charged me with misdemeanors only. Gave me one year and probated that."

"You're not a crook, Bill. You just got caught up and couldn't get out."

"Naturally, first thing I did was tender my resignation. But there's a group of county officials already urging me to run for reelection when the probation is up. Can you believe that?"

"Yeah, and I'd bet on you winning."

"How sure are you?"

"Royal flush sure. This is Texas."

The two laughed lightly, then Bill's smile gradually faded, until his mustache drooped. "I heard you're leaving."

"Tomorrow."

"Bynum? I've met the man you're going to be working with."

"He mentioned it. At a sheriff's association meeting?"

"In Austin. A while back. Before the war. He's a good man." He stared into the near distance. After a time he said, "You could stay here, Thatcher, take over while I'm on probation."

"No, that should be Scotty."

"You'd be leaving anyway, though, wouldn't you?" He hung his head. "For what I did, I apologize, Thatcher."

Thatcher made the gesture that Mr. Hobson had, a silent grant of forgiveness. "That's not the reason I'm going." Before continuing, he waited until Bill had raised his head and was looking straight at him. "This is your place, Bill. You found it, or it found you, but it's where you were meant. I need to make my own place."

"With Laurel Plummer? I trust she's going with you?"

"If I have to strap her to the back of the car."

"How will you two reconcile your job with her moonshining?"

"Davy O'Connor getting killed shook her to her core. When she started out, she underestimated the danger. But seeing firsthand all the blood spilt, she's sworn off. From now on, she wants to stick to pie-baking."

"Well, I wish you all the luck."

"Thanks. You, too." Thatcher stood.

Bill used his cane and pushed himself to his feet. They shook hands. Bill said, "I'm not proud of lying to you, Thatcher. But, God help me, I can't regret that I did."

Smiling at Bill from beneath the brim of his hat, Thatcher said, "Me neither."

Laurel returned home after running errands to find Irv and Mike O'Connor in conversation beside Irv's truck.

She had visited with him several times during his recovery. He was still paler and thinner than he'd been before he'd been shot. The twinkle in his eyes had dimmed, and it would probably be a while before they regained their full wattage, if they ever did.

But when she alighted from her car and walked toward them, the familiar dimple appeared in his cheek. "Ah, here's the lovely Laurel. I've been waiting on you."

Irv made his excuses and went into the house.

When they were alone, Mike said, "I understand that tomorrow's the big day. I thought I ought to come say my goodbyes to you now in private, while your sullen cowboy wasn't lurking about."

"You and I have nothing to hide from Thatcher."

"More's the pity." He slapped his hand over his heart like a wounded, rejected suitor, and she could have sworn he was Davy. "If that lucky bastard ever treats you bad, promise you'll come find me. I'll rub him out."

She laughed lightly. "I promise."

He reached into his pants pocket. "I have a going-away present for you." He took her hand and dropped a Saint Christopher medal and chain into her palm.

"Mike." Taken aback, she stared down at the gold necklace, then looked up at him, so touched her eyes turned misty. "Is it—?"

"Yes."

"I can't accept it. You should keep it."

"I have a matching one, and Davy would love knowing it was dangling around your pretty neck. He and Saint Chris are now your guardian angels." He lifted the necklace out of her hand and slipped it over her head. She pressed the medal against her chest.

They looked at each other, both unable to speak, so they hugged. When he released her, he said gruffly, "Be happy, Laurel." He tipped his cap and walked away.

───◆───

Everything they were taking was piled up in the empty living room. Thatcher's saddle sat atop his trunk. Laurel had packed her clothing in the same suitcase she'd had with her the night she'd arrived at the shack with Derby. She was taking Pearl's baby clothes and all the recipes in her mother's handwriting. Most everything else she was leaving behind, because it would be needed. Corrine and Ernie had decided to move into the house.

"I love the idea," Laurel said to Corrine. "You couldn't stay out there during the winter months."

"Ernie and me could live in the shack and be just fine."

"But why would you when there's a whole upstairs here that would be going to waste. Stop trying to talk yourself out of it. The decision has been made. Besides, I'll feel better knowing that someone is here looking after Irv."

Corrine watched as Thatcher and Ernie—who had finally been introduced—began to load Laurel's car. "It's not going to be the same without you here, though," the girl said wistfully.

"No. But you have the post office box key. I'll be writing to you at least once a week, so don't forget to check it."

"If it weren't for you, I couldn't read them letters you'll send."

Laurel reached out and pulled the girl to her. "I'm going to miss you."

"Me too, Miss Laurel." Lowering her voice, she said, "I wouldn't trust you to nobody but him," she said, casting a glance at Thatcher as he swung his saddle onto his shoulder. "He's quality."

"Yes, he is."

As they broke their hug, Corrine dashed a tear from her eye, then said, "Oh hell, Ernie, you're gonna bust open that suitcase carrying it like that." She went over to instruct and assist him.

Laurel went in search of Irv and found him in his room. He was sitting on his barrel seat, staring at the floor.

"What are you doing in here?" she asked.

"The girl told me I was gettin' in the way more than helping. And she's right. Arm still hurts if I move it a certain way, and this damn bum hip." He muttered the rest, but she knew that his crankiness wasn't due to his ailments or Corrine's criticism.

She sat down on the end of his bed, facing him, and said softly, "I'm going to miss you, too. Terribly."

Frowning, he said, "It ain't too late to change your mind. I've worked the rails over there in East Texas. It ain't like here. It's humid. They got mosquitoes as big as turkeys. Alligators."

"I don't think there are any alligators in Bynum."

He harrumphed. She reached for his hands and held them. "Be careful with your new enterprise."

His bushy eyebrows shot up. "Enterprise?"

She gave him a look. "The first giveaway was catching you in a tête-à-tête with Mike O'Connor yesterday. I thought you didn't trust his dimples."

"Who said I do?"

She continued, "Another giveaway is all that busywork you and Ernie have been doing down in the cellar. Did you really think I would believe that you two are opening a machine shop?"

"Why not?"

"A machine shop with a mirror along one wall?"

He gave up the pretense. "With Gert dead, Lefty abandoned the roadhouse. Nobody knows where he ran off to. The county's condemned the building. The girl remembered that long mirror, so we helped ourselves to it and the gramophone. They'll give the place some class."

"I suppose you'll serve Ernie's moonshine. Is Mike supplying the bootlegged liquor?"

"He's got some good connections."

"I'm sure."

"The girl will make snacks to serve."

"When do you open?"

"Soon as you and Hutton clear town."

"Does this speakeasy have a name?"

"Blind Tiger."

She laughed. "Isn't that rather obvious?"

"The girl likes the way it sounds." He tipped his head toward the kitchen where Thatcher could be heard responding to Corrine's chatter. "Will you tell him?"

"He's going to be my husband."

"He's going to be a lawman."

"But he hasn't been sworn in yet. One thing, though. Will there be girls?"

"Hell no. I'm too old, Ernie's too much in love, and the girl would never hear of it."

"What about your fix-it business?"

"I'll keep it up for show."

"Just promise me that you'll be careful, Irv. Keep it exclusive. Locals only. People you know. No roughnecks."

"Like I said, classy. Discreet like. Hush-hush."

"Don't let Mike take unnecessary risks."

"None of us wants to get shot at again."

"If things get hot—"

"We'll head for the hills. Don't you worry none."

"I will."

"I know."

She patted him on the knee, then stood and placed her hands on either side of his face, tipped his head down, and kissed his bald pate. "You've become very dear to me, Irv. Thank you. For taking care of Pearl and me. For everything."

His eyes filled. He wiped his nose with the back of his hand and came off his barrel seat. "I'd better go see if I'm good for something."

Another round of goodbyes was said outside.

As they pulled away, Thatcher reached across the seat and placed his hand on Laurel's knee, giving it a squeeze. "Are you sad?"

"Melancholy." She looked back to see the three of them still there, waving. Then, as one, they turned and filed back into the house. "But they're a family. I had become the odd man out."

As they drove past the cemetery, Thatcher switched the Model T into low gear. "Do you want to stop for one last visit?"

"No. Irv and I were here only a few days ago. He's promised to keep the graves well tended." She didn't share the conversation she'd had with Irv about Derby, but she said, "When I think about Pearl, I don't think of her being in the ground. I think of her sweet face looking up at me as she nursed. I'm not leaving her here. I'm taking her with me."

Thatcher pulled her closer, and she rested her head on his shoulder. "It was thoughtful of you to ask. Thank you."

They continued on their way. But she felt pressed to be candid with him. "Thatcher, we've joked about my accepting your proposal, but marrying you is a bigger step for me than you realize."

He pulled the car off the road onto the shoulder and gave her his undivided attention. "I've known that. But your past with Derby is your private business. I didn't want to dig into it until you invited me to."

"Which I appreciate, but you should know this."

"Okay."

"After he did what he did, I vowed that I would never again surrender control of my life to someone else."

"I don't want *control* over you, Laurel. I want *you*. If you're scared of marriage, we don't have to do it. A piece of paper isn't going to make me any more bound to you than I am."

"You'd be willing to do that?"

"Not overjoyed about it, but willing. I'd like it if you used my name, though. Not because I care what you call yourself, but because I wouldn't want people thinking bad of you, or our children."

She touched his face. "You really do love me."

He took her hand and kissed her palm. "I really do. But I can be stubborn, too. I'll never stop asking you to be my wife."

"I accept, Thatcher. I'll marry you today, because you're incredibly wonderful, and I love you with all my heart. But don't ever stop proposing. Ask me every day to marry you."

He grinned. "If you swear always to say yes."

"I will."

ACKNOWLEDGMENTS

Doing the research for *Blind Tiger* was some of the most fun I've had during my writing career.

Mired in the muck of 2020, I went back one hundred years, looking for something interesting to write about. *Prohibition.* It became law in January of 1920.

I soon became fascinated by the anecdotal personal histories of moonshiners, bootleggers, and the lawmen who doggedly chased them. No doubt many of these stories were embroidered for dramatic effect or the aggrandizement of the storyteller. But I got the feeling that, whether comic or tragic, they were too far-fetched *not* to be based on truth.

One fact is indisputable: for the thirteen years that Prohibition was in effect, alcohol and blood flowed in comparable quantities.

I want to give special thanks to former Garland Police Department detective Martin Brown, whose nonfiction book *The Glen Rose Moonshine Raid* (The History Press) acquainted me with a sliver of Texas history that I never knew, although I'm a native and have lived most of my life within an hour's drive of this small town that inspired my fictitious town of Foley.

Glen Rose earned the reputation of being the Moonshine Capital of Texas. In 1923, Texas Rangers, in conjunction with informers and local law enforcement, busted up one of the most profitable illegal liquor syndicates in the state—and that was saying something!

In this novel, I tried to capture the spirit of those wild times, and I hope you enjoy reading *Blind Tiger* as much as I enjoyed writing it.

Sandra Brown
May 2021

ABOUT THE AUTHOR

Sandra Brown is the author of seventy-three *New York Times* best-sellers. There are more than eighty million copies of her books in print worldwide, and her work has been translated into thirty-four languages. In 2008, the International Thriller Writers named Brown its Thriller Master, the organization's highest honor. She has served as president of Mystery Writers of America and holds an honorary doctorate of humane letters from Texas Christian University. She lives in Texas.

For more information you can visit:
SandraBrown.net
Facebook.com/AuthorSandraBrown
@Sandra_BrownNYT

YOUR BOOK CLUB RESOURCE

READING GROUP GUIDE

DISCUSSION QUESTIONS

1. At the beginning of the novel, Derby tells Laurel that he's moving their young family from Sherman to Foley, Texas. Laurel is shocked and understandably anxious about what she feels is an impetuous decision. In your own life, have you ever had to make an abrupt change, one that required you to adapt very quickly to new circumstances? How did you cope with the transition?

2. Thatcher observes that Dr. Driscoll's wife, Mila—like many Germans before, during, and even after the war—was subjected to resentment and suspicion from her American peers. After experiencing Mrs. Driscoll's kindness toward Thatcher, how did this revelation make you feel? While the events of *Blind Tiger* take place more than a hundred years in the past, similar events are reported in present-day news. In your opinion, what steps can people take today to ensure this kind of discrimination doesn't happen in the future?

3. Under President Woodrow Wilson, in an attempt to create a more "temperate" American society, the Eighteenth Amendment—the legal prevention of the manufacture, sale, and transportation of alcohol in the United States from 1919 to 1933—went into effect. Instead of bringing about Wilson's admirable goal, Prohibition resulted in a rise of organized

crime and bootlegging became major business. Why do you think the institution of Prohibition failed?

4. In your view, were the men and women who distilled and sold alcohol throughout Prohibition doing what they could to feed their families? Or do you feel they were taking advantage of a difficult situation?

5. How did you feel when Thatcher was accused of abducting Mrs. Driscoll? The only evidence the sheriff had against him was the word of the Driscolls' neighbor, who distrusted Thatcher because he was a stranger. How did the neighbor's reaction mirror conflicts taking place today?

6. One of Thatcher's many talents is that he has a "knack" for reading people. Do you have a similar ability of your own, something that has helped you get a leg up or get out of trouble in your own life?

7. Thatcher believes "dumb fate" brought him to Foley. Do you believe in fate, predestination, or divine will? Or do you believe coincidence threw Thatcher and Laurel together?

8. Laurel experiences two very personal losses over the course of the novel. Initially, she feels her grief will break her, but she learns to love again, first with her stand-in father, Irv, then with her friendship with Corrine, and later with Thatcher. How did the characters support one another throughout the novel, especially when it came to grief and trauma?

9. The story is set in a dangerous, unpredictable time in Texas. Law enforcement was looking for bootleggers, bootleggers were competing for market share, and undercover agents

were active on both sides. How much did you know about Prohibition before reading *Blind Tiger*? Were you familiar with organizations like the Anti-Saloon League?

10. After Thatcher helps Laurel take care of Irv's arm, Laurel makes this observation on boundaries: "Once a boundary [is] breached, it [is] difficult, if not impossible, to reestablish." Have you ever had to reestablish a boundary with someone? How did you go about repairing the relationship?

11. After Norma is found badly injured, Bill, Thatcher, and Norma's sister, Patsy, discuss Norma's romantic relationships. Over the course of their conversation, Bill observes that big secrets tend to "erode" relationships, whether those relationships fall between siblings, married couples, or lovers. Do you share Bill's opinion? Or do you think some secrets are worth keeping—and may, perhaps, even preserve relationships?

12. In a time of great difficulty and poverty, Laurel, Gert, Corinne, and Norma worked, in their own ways, to achieve financial independence and stability. Discuss the industriousness of the women in the novel and the personality traits that helped them survive—and even thrive—in such an unforgiving time.

13. Discuss Sheriff Bill Amos's character. Given his actions throughout the novel—his motives for hiring Thatcher, the way he cared for his wife, the way he kept the peace in Foley as sheriff—would you consider him to be a good man or a bad one? Why?

14. At the end of the novel, Laurel sits down with Irv and apologizes to him, telling him she shouldn't have pushed Derby to

get over his inertia, but instead should have "[held] him tight without saying anything . . . allow[ed] him to face his fears within the cradle of [her] arms." Do you agree or disagree with the statement? Have you ever found yourself unsure of what to do in the face of a loved one's struggles?

15. After Derby's death, Laurel declares that she will "never again surrender control of [her] life to someone else." Did this declaration resonate or conflict with your personal views on marriage? Why or why not?